Praise for
To Cook a Bear

"Sumptuous." —*Publishers Weekly*

"There is much more to this wonderfully idiosyncratic novel from Sweden; it is not only a riveting, psychologically astute mystery but also a work of history, natural history (the pastor is a gifted botanist), and religion. Superb." —*Booklist* (starred review)

"Multifaceted, mysterious, and engaging . . . A book quivering with commitment and compassion, but also with foolishness and unconstrained brutality." —*Verldens Gang* (Norway)

"Niemi is a born storyteller. *To Cook a Bear* is a beguiling and seductive read." —*Crime Time* (UK)

"Divine." —*Dagbladet* (Sweden)

"Niemi succeeds in constructing a story that works as a murder mystery and as a compelling study of a dangerously inward-looking community." —*Sunday Times* (UK)

"Niemi's writing—that of a narrator and a poet, a dreamer and a storyteller—brushes the highest peaks of the most delicate lyricism, rising strongly out of the abyss of the darkest mystery." —*Corriere della Sera* (Italy)

"A masterpiece of narrative." —*La Vanguardia* (Spain)

PENGUIN BOOKS

TO COOK A BEAR

MIKAEL NIEMI was born in 1959 and grew up in Pajala, in the northern-most part of Sweden near the Finnish border, where he still lives. He is the author of *Popular Music From Vittula*, which has sold more than one million copies. It won the Swedish August Prize and has been trans-lated into more than thirty languages.

DEBORAH BRAGAN-TURNER is a former bookseller and academic librar-ian, now a translator of Swedish literature, including works by Per Olov Enquist, Anna Swärd, and Sara Stridsberg.

To Cook
a Bear

MIKAEL NIEMI

Translated from the Swedish by
Deborah Bragan-Turner

PENGUIN BOOKS

PENGUIN BOOKS
An imprint of Penguin Random House LLC
penguinrandomhouse.com

Originally published in Great Britain by MacLehose Press, an imprint of Quercus, 2020
Published in Penguin Books 2021

First published in Swedish as *Koka björn* by Piratförlaget, Stockholm.

LIBRARY OF CONGRESS CATALOGING-IN-PUBLICATION DATA
Names: Niemi, Mikael, 1959– author. | Bragan-Turner, Deborah, translator.
Title: To cook a bear / Mikael Niemi ; translated from the
Swedish by Deborah Bragan-Turner.
Other titles: Koka björn. English
Description: [New York] : Penguin Books, [2021] |
First published in Swedish as Koka björn by Piratförlaget, Stockholm.
Identifiers: LCCN 2020002632 (print) | LCCN 2020002633 (ebook) |
ISBN 9780143133902 (paperback) | ISBN 9780525505693 (ebook)
Subjects: LCSH: Laestadius, L. L. (Lars Levi), 1800–1861—Fiction. |
Sami (European people)—Fiction.
Classification: LCC PT9876.24.I29 K6513 2021 (print) |
LCC PT9876.24.I29 (ebook) | DDC 839.73/74—dc23
LC record available at https://lccn.loc.gov/2020002632
LC ebook record available at https://lccn.loc.gov/2020002633

Printed in the United States of America
1   3   5   7   9   10   8   6   4   2

Set in Bembo Book MT Std
Designed by Sabrina Bowers

To Cook
a Bear

KENGIS, NORTHERN SWEDEN,
close to the Finnish border, 1852

PART ONE

❖

Out in the forest
Writing a line
My faithful damsel
Singing so fine
My deepest wish
Invading your heart
The pain of love
To thee will impart

1.

I WAKE TO A COMPLETE ABSENCE OF SOUND IN A WORLD BIDING ITS time before coming to life. Enclosed by darkness and sky, I lie with my eyes directed like conduits toward the great expanse, but there is nothing there, not even air. In the midst of the vast silence my chest begins to tremble and shake. The waves intensify; something growing inside threatens to force its way out. My ribs are pried apart like the bars of a cage. There is nothing I can do except submit to this formidable force, like a child groveling on the floor at the feet of an enraged father, never knowing when the next blow will strike. I am that child. I am that father.

Before the world is fully formed, I rush out into the dawn with my knapsack on my back and the hand-forged ax in my fist. A short distance from the low barn I stop and shelter at the edge of the forest, pretending to busy myself with my clothing in case someone should see me and start to wonder; I wind a shoelace round and round, empty my cap of invisible lice, pretending to shake them onto the swarming anthill at my feet. All the while I watch the farmyard out of the corner of my eye. The first smoke of the morning rises from the cabin stove, signaling that the household is astir.

And then she emerges. Empty pails swing from her hands. Her headscarf stands out, white like a winter ptarmigan; her face is a circle of light, her eyes bright, her brows dark. I imagine the smoothness of her cheeks and her small rosy lips singing softly, shaping tender little words. The cows, their udders taut, low in response and expectation when she opens the heavy barn door and slips inside. It all happens at such speed, far too fast, and I try to keep my senses sharp, to hold this picture so that I can summon it again and again. And yet it is not enough. I have to see her tomorrow as well. Her swinging hips under the apron, the gentle round of her bosom, the hand that grips the latch on the barn door. I steal closer, almost breaking into a run across the farmyard as if I were a thief, and at the door I stop. I let my hand close round the handle. My rough, sinewy hand on the place where hers, so small and soft, has just been. Inside, her fingers squeezing the cow's large teats, squirting white jets into the pail. For a split second I pull on the handle as if to enter, but I promptly turn and hurry away, afraid someone will have seen me. But I keep it in my hand for the rest of the day. The warmth from her skin.

2.

AT MEALTIMES I ALWAYS WAIT UNTIL LAST. I HOLD BACK IN THE corner while the pastor's wife places the heavy cauldron of oatmeal on the table. It is smoking and black as death on the outside, as though fetched straight from the devil's inferno. But inside, the porridge is light and golden, slightly grainy, creamy where it sticks to the wooden ladle. Brita Kajsa stirs with the broad wooden spatula, digging down to the bottom and then up again, breaking the skin that has formed on top and filling every corner of the cabin with the aroma of hay and pollen. The children and hired hands sit waiting; I see their pale faces, a silent wall of hunger. Her expression stern, she takes the bowls and gives large scoops to the older and smaller dollops to the younger ones; she serves the workers and the visitors who have dropped in. When they all have received their share, heads are lowered and fingers intertwined across the table. The pastor waits until there is quiet, then he too bows his head and gives heartfelt thanks for everyone's daily bread. They eat in silence, apart from the sound of chewing and the licking of wooden spoons. The older want more, and more is given. The breaking of bread, the eating of cold boiled pike with deft fingers, bones piling up on the table like shiny pins. When everyone has almost finished, the mistress will chance to cast an eye toward the corner where I sit.

"Come and eat too."

"It doesn't matter."

"But come and sit down. Make room for Jussi, children."

"I can wait."

I see the master turn as well. His eyes are glazed; I detect the pain in them and how he struggles to conceal it. A brief nod from him brings me to the table. I hold out my *guksi*, the wooden cup I crafted myself up in Karesuando, the one that has accompanied me on my life's journey. At first it was white as the skin of a suckling babe; over time it has darkened with sun and salt and a thousand washings. I feel the weight when the mistress empties her ladle and I watch her scrape the sides to gather more, but I am already back in my corner, cross-legged on the floor. The sticky, barley-tasting porridge I devour has cooled by now to the same temperature as my mouth. I feel it slip down my throat, then enclosed by my stomach's muscles. There it grows into the strength and warmth that will help keep me alive. I eat like a dog, ravenous and watchful.

"Come and have some more," the mistress urges.

But she knows I will not come. I eat only once. I take my allotted portion, never more.

The cup is empty. I wipe my thumb like a swab round the curved surface and pass my tongue over it; I lick and suck until it is all clean. It slides gently into my pocket. The cup is what provides me with food, drawing to it the edible things that happenstance delivers. Many times, weak with hunger, I have been close to collapse. But whenever I took out my cup, it was filled with a fish's head. Or a reindeer's blood. Or with frozen berries from a mountain slope. Just like that. And I have eaten and regained my strength. Enough to withstand the day. This is all I hope for and this is how I have survived. This is why I sit down on the floor, for never would I assert myself or make demands, never snatch like a raven or snarl like a wolverine. I would rather turn aside. If no one sees me, I stay in the shadows. But the mistress, she sees me. I ask for nothing, but she provides nonetheless. Her brusque kindness, the same concern for all beings, for cows, for dogs. All living things need to survive. That is about the size of it.

I MIGHT LEAVE AT ANY moment. As a wanderer does. I am here now, and the next thing you know I am somewhere else. I get to my feet, grab my knapsack, and walk. That is all. When you are poor, you can live like this. Everything I own, I carry with me. Clothes on my back, knife in my belt, fire striker and cup, horn spoon, pouch of salt. Their combined weight is almost nothing. I am agile and fleet of foot, in the next river valley before anyone misses me. There is hardly a trace of me left behind, no more than an animal's. My feet tread on grass and moss that spring back up. When I build a fire I use old firepits, and the ash I make settles, invisible, on the ash others have made. I answer the call of nature in the forest, lifting up a clod of earth and replacing it afterward. The next traveler can place his foot right on top without noticing a thing; only the fox can detect a faint human scent. In winter my ski tracks fly across the pillowy skies of snow several cubits above the ground; and on spring's arrival all the pockmarks left by my sticks will melt away. It is possible for humans to live this way, without damaging, without disturbing, without really existing: being like the forest, like a host of summer leaves and autumn detritus, like midwinter snow and myriad buds opened by the sun in spring. When it is finally time to leave, it is as though you have never been here.

3.

M Y MASTER IS WROUGHT WITH ANGUISH. I SEE HIS LIPS CONTORT, smack, and pucker around words that will not form. His enemies are drawing ever nearer; not a day goes by without more attacks and more contempt. And the only thing he has in his defense is a pen. Against their swords and cudgels he lifts his quill, but the words will not flow. At each attempt I want to beat myself, pinch myself hard to relieve him of his burden. Anything that will let the light into his mind. He could have been my father. That is how I think of him, but when I hinted at it once it made him angry, and I saw the color rise in his averted cheek. I sink down onto the rug and like a loyal dog I wait, nose resting on paw, hour after hour, ready to follow him at any moment.

His brow is furrowed by years of thinking. It is dirty, marked by tobacco juice perhaps, or soot from the lamp wick. His hair is long and hangs in greasy strands that he brushes aside from time to time, like dangling branchlets. Alone he treads a path through shadows and overgrown marshes, in places where no one has ventured before him. He is, however, not entirely on his own. I follow him in silence, padding behind him with my nose on his trail: the tarred leather of his curled-toe shoes, the rustle of their straw lining, the damp wool of his trouser legs. He pushes farther on into the unknown, but I am always there. My stomach is empty, but I don't complain.

ON ONE OF OUR treks we sat down by a natural spring. As we slaked our thirst, he gave me a thoughtful sideways look.

"What makes a good person?" he asked eventually.

I had no answer.

"What makes us good, Jussi?" he persisted. "What does it mean, to be a good person?"

"I don't know," I muttered.

The master continued to stare at me, radiating a strong light, a warmth.

"But look at the two of us, Jussi. Look at you and me. Which one of us is good, would you say?"

"It's my master."

"Don't call me master when we're in the forest."

"I mean . . . the pastor."

"And why?"

"Because the pastor is a priest. You give us God's words. You can give us the Lord's forgiveness."

"That's my job. Can a job alone make a person good? Are there no evil priests?"

"No, none at all. I can't imagine that's the case!"

"Priests who drink, who fornicate, who beat their wives half to death. Truly, I have encountered them."

I didn't answer, but fixed my gaze on the smoldering polypore we had lit to ward off the swarms of gnats.

"Look at yourself, Jussi. You're no glutton, no drunkard."

"But that's because I'm poor."

"You don't brag. When something is offered, you're the last to step forward. If someone pays you a compliment, you deflect it."

"I don't, Pastor. It's just . . ."

"Often I don't even notice you're there. I have to turn and look at you to be sure. If you're so quiet that you disappear, how could you be evil?"

"But the pastor does so many good things."

"Does that come from God, Jussi? Think about it, think about it. Could it just be the devil of ambition whispering in my ear? Luring me with worldly ostentation and applause? When I die, I hope people will remember me as one of the greats. Whilst you, Jussi, will be wiped out like a phantom that never existed."

"I'm happy with my lot."

"Is that really true?"

"Mm."

"That's what makes you good. You're the kindest, finest person I have ever met."

"No, Pastor."

"Indeed you are, Jussi. But wait. Listen. Does that make you a good person?"

"I don't think so."

"No. Maybe all you can do is follow your nature. Fundamentally you and I have very different ways. And that's why I compare the two of us so often. Which of us walks the right path? How should we live, essentially? My accomplishments are significant, it's true, but so too is the hurt I inflict. I make enemies, I wound my opponents and trample upon them. Whilst you turn the other cheek."

He could see that I wanted to protest and he raised his hand.

"Wait, Jussi. Is that what makes you good? Is that what the Creator meant?"

For several moments I gazed at a horsefly traveling up and down his trouser leg, its shimmering green eyes shining brightly as it tried in vain to bite through the cloth.

"I taught you to read, Jussi. You borrow my books, you're improving yourself. I can see that you think, but what do you do with your thoughts? If someone picks a fight with you, you turn aside, you simply pick up your knapsack and walk away. You flee to the north, to the mountains. Is that how we should confront the world's foolishness? Think about it, Jussi. Are you right never to fight back?"

"Wretched worm and wanderer that I am."

The pastor couldn't help but smile when I recited from his favorite hymn.

"You're an observer, Jussi. I've noticed it. You study the world around you, don't you?"

"Yes, but . . ."

"You want to understand what the world and human beings are made of. But are you putting your pound to work, Jussi, as the parable teaches? That's my question to you, Jussi. What are you doing to combat the world's evil?"

There was nothing I could say. My throat tightened. I felt wrongfully accused and I wanted to run away and leave him there; I am so quick that I would be out of reach in the blink of an eye. He saw my anguish, leaned forward, and laid his hand upon my arm. That was how he held on to me: he fastened a string to my wing, as though I were a sparrow, frantically flapping.

IT WAS THE PASTOR who taught me to see. To learn that the world around you can be transformed entirely through your gaze. All my childhood I wandered through mountain valleys and birch forests, crossed pine moorlands, and splashed over swaying bogs. This countryside was mine. I knew it inside out, this barren northern land of stony riversides and twisting animal trails.

And yet I had seen almost nothing at all.

I remember when the pastor took me on one of his "excursions." My birch-bark haversack was filled with food and drawing materials and sheaves of thick gray paper, and we covered a considerable distance. As evening approached we made camp in a *lehto*, a grove of trees surrounded by a waterlogged mosaic of marshland. We were both tired. I built a fire and started to prepare our camp for the night. He broke up loaves of bread and cut dried meat into thin strips, as we settled down on the spruce twigs to regain our strength. The air was full of buzzing, biting mosquitoes. The pastor offered me some tar, but instead I pulled a handful of needles off a stalk beside me, crushed them, and rubbed them on my wrists. The pungent smell they exuded repelled the mosquitoes.

"Wild rosemary," he said.

"What?"

"The plant you rubbed on your skin. *Ledum palustre*."

"*Ledum . . . ?*" I mumbled.

With an eager look on his face, he leaped to his feet.

"Follow me!"

We left our knapsacks at the camp. The pine moorland sloped down and soon the dry ground gave way to wet, undulating bog. I could sense his enthusiasm as he quickened his pace, his head bent, his eyes searching in all directions.

"I've wanted to visit this garden of herbs for so long," he said. "And at last I'm here, standing before these riches."

I looked. It was a bog. It was wide and it was wet.

"What do you see, Jussi?"

"Nothing."

He half turned and smiled.

"Nothing? What about all this?"

"Grass."

"No, Jussi. It's not grass. It's sedge."

"Oh yes, sedge. I see sedge."

He took a deep breath and turned toward the marshland. I realized that out there was our destination. It was the beginning of July, and the water was still high. We were wearing clothes that covered us completely and had scarves wrapped round our necks as a shield against the clouds of flesh-eating insects hatching in every pool.

"From this point I can see more than ten species, Jussi. And I'm only talking about the sedges. And then there's the osier, that mysterious genus. Have you noticed how many different kinds there are here? Can you make them out?"

"No."

"And look over there! We'll examine them more closely tomorrow. See how bright they are!"

"Does the pastor mean the flowers?"

"Orchids, Jussi. Orchids in our barren northland. Look! Right in front of you!"

I looked down and saw, protruding by my foot, the tiny stalk I had almost trodden on.

"Look carefully, Jussi. Bend down. An orchis. The flower is irregular, with six tepals and a labellum."

The stem was covered with deep-pink blossoms. He held the stalk gently, and I had to kneel down in the wet to take a proper look.

"Closer, Jussi, closer. And then sniff."

With my nostrils right up to it, I breathed in. The hint of a faint, almost imperceptible sweetness, and then it was gone.

"Did you smell anything? Did you?"

"Yes . . ."

"I say to myself, that is what God smells like."

WHERE PREVIOUSLY I HAD seen merely trees, grass, and moss, now I faced a cornucopia of treasures. Wherever I turned my gaze, new discoveries lay in wait. And everything could be identified and allotted its own page in God's mighty lexicon. It was a marvel to observe how diverse all the little plants could be. To discover in a magnifying glass that the stem was covered in small, silvery hairs, that a leaf edge could be serrated or wavy or notched, and that these characteristics were not accidental, but each and every one pertaining to its own species.

The pastor explained how all plants were classified into genus and family. How monocots had parallel leaf veins, in the same way as grasses and lilies, while dicots had a midrib from which smaller veins branched off, as in birch leaves. Why some plants were showy with flamboyant flower heads, such as the crown of the water lily or the tall, spiky flowers of the fireweed, in order to be fertilized by insects. Whereas others, such as the gray-greenish elder or grass flowers, were barely visible, scattering clouds of pollen in the wind. The flowers with four petals were named *Cruciferae*, the ones like brushes were called *Umbelliferae*; there were blooms shaped like cups, there were legumes with blossoms resembling a butterfly. The pastor could stand in reverence at the sight of a richly flowering marsh and with a sigh lament that life was too short, far too brief to embrace all of this. Then he would drop to his knees and hold his magnifying glass to the stem he had just discovered down there, scarcely the height of a finger.

It was the pastor who taught me the secret of memory. Knowledge was best retained when acquired through the eyes. When you happened upon a plant you had never seen before, this is what you should do: first walk around it and observe it from all angles; next bend down and inspect every tiny detail of the leaves, their point of growth, the shape of the stem, the sepals, the color of the pollen. Absolutely everything had to be appraised. In this way a mental image would be preserved. And the next time you came across it, albeit ten years later, the joy of recognition would be awakened. It was more difficult with names—all that Latin; there I had to resort to tedious repetition. When I heard that the frothy white meadow-sweet was called *Filipendula ulmaria*, though I tried to repeat it twenty times, a hundred times even, it had deserted me an hour or two later.

After numerous excursions with the pastor, my way of seeing altered. Shrubs and trees assumed the form of friends, of individuals I came to know as living beings. "Well, there you are, soaking up the sun. And with your brother and sister too." When summer arrived I experienced the pleasure of reunion. I looked forward to seeing every plant and worked out when it would bloom. The very fact that the plants became familiar meant that I had a keen eye for any anomaly. Deep in a waterlogged forest of spruce I might encounter something new and unknown. In the past I would have trampled on it without another thought. But now I stopped to point it out. The pastor smiled with glee.

"*Corallorhiza trifida*," he said. "Coralroot. Not entirely common here in the north. Well done, Jussi. Well done."

His encouragement brought color to my cheeks and I hurriedly bent down. I recognized the typical orchid shape, the six tepals, and the labellum's distinctive appearance, and I began to recite: *Corallorhiza trifida, Corallorhiza trifida* . . .

Soon she too would be my friend.

4.

ONE EVENING THE PASTOR AND I WERE IN HIS STUDY, PRESSING our latest finds. We had discovered them in a marsh not far from Kengis. Some insignificant stalks of sedge in particular had caused the pastor to quiver like a gun dog. With great care I carried the specimens home in his vasculum, the roots gently laid bare and wrapped in a soft cloth, and now I was helping him exchange the damp gray paper for dry, in order to best preserve the plants. Together we tightened the plant press, pulling the cord until it creaked and then securing it with the wooden pins.

We were interrupted by the sound of the front door opening and a stranger's voice asking for the pastor. This was immediately followed by a knock and the pastor's daughter Selma peeping in through the crack in the door.

"Father?"

The pastor wiped his hands on a rag and gathered up the wad of tobacco I had just cut for him from the twist.

"I'm coming."

At the same moment the study door was thrown wide open and a rawboned youth barged in. There was something disturbing about him, a preoccupied look in his eye, something uneasy. The man was afraid.

"Reverend," he stammered in Finnish, "the reverend must come."

The pastor looked calmly at the visitor. His expression betrayed no displeasure at being disturbed. Yet I knew that he jealously guarded his time in this writing chamber. The man was standing there with sweat dripping from the end of his nose, his shirt soaked as if he had been running for hours. His arms were flailing in an effort to stress the urgency, as though he were striking at something.

"What's happened?"

"She's . . . we don't know . . . she was in the woods with the cows."

"Who are you talking about?"

"Our maid, Hilda . . . Hilda Fredriksdotter Alatalo."

I looked up when I heard the name. I knew the woman. She had been hired on one of the farms nearby, and I had often seen her in church with the rest of the servants. She was a pale, chubby girl with an upturned nose, a little slow in her movements. She always held a handkerchief in her hand, in the manner of an old lady. Whenever her spirit was moved, she used it to dry her eyes and nose.

"Yes?"

"The girl's . . . gone. Reverend must come at once."

The pastor gave me a look. The hour was already late and we were both tired after a long day's trekking. But it was summer, and some light would remain throughout the night. The youth detected our hesitation and stamped his feet, giving the impression that he wanted to grab hold of the pastor and forcibly drag him away.

"We're coming," the pastor said. "Jussi, will you give him something to drink?"

I hurried out into the cabin and handed a ladle of water to our sweat-drenched visitor, who drank it like a horse.

IT WAS THE EARLY hours when we reached their farm. The man who had come to fetch us was called Albin and was the eldest son of the house. All the way there, he ran thirty meters ahead of us, stopped to wait for us to catch up, then ran on again. The pastor and I kept an even, steady pace, accustomed as we were to journeying on foot. Everyone inside the farmhouse must have been watching through the window, for as we drew near they rushed out to meet us. There was the master, his wife, and behind them a swarm of sleepy children with tousled hair. The master and his son didn't pause to offer us anything, but started at once down a path into the forest, where we followed. The sun was nearing the horizon in the north, as we struggled through the tangled undergrowth. The master was called Heikki Alalehto, and in confused and incoherent bursts he told us how the maid Hilda had gone out into the woods with the cows as normal that morning, but hadn't returned for evening milking. Most of the herd had plodded back to the farmyard by themselves, but there was no sign of the maid.

"Perhaps the girl has gone looking for a missing cow?" the pastor suggested.

Heikki agreed that it was a possibility. But she had never been away so long before.

Every now and then they shouted her name. The echo of their voices rebounded off a distant ridge. The pastor and I walked in silence; I saw his eye rest on a *Gramineae* that appeared to be unfamiliar to him and I noticed how he hastily picked the sample and placed it in his knapsack.

Deep into the forest, we came across a place where someone had set up a modest camp. A few sticks remained in a burned-out fire.

"She usually takes a rest here."

Heikki was just about to trample down the campfire when the pastor took hold of his arm. For several moments he stood without speaking, studying the scene. His gaze moved from the firepit to the broken spruce twigs she had been sitting on. A small milk pail lay overturned; its lid had come off and milk had splashed onto the moss, so white it seemed luminescent. The pastor inclined his head to mine.

"What do you see, Jussi?" he said in a low voice.

"Well, that . . . Hilda had been sitting here, having a rest. She made a fire. And then she knocked over the milk canister."

"Do you know it was Hilda who knocked it over?"

"No-o-o . . . I don't."

"Use your eyes. Tell me what happened, Jussi."

He spoke in an undertone, but his voice was filled with intensity. With an impatient hand he brushed away the hank of hair constantly falling in front of his eyes. I made an effort to register every detail, trying hard to summon up the girl's image.

"Hilda was sitting by the fire having a rest. It would have been in the middle of the day, when the sun was at its highest. That's when a person usually feels hungry. But all of a sudden something happens that makes her run away. Although . . . for all I know she doesn't run, but she does, I think. That's what it seems like. And then maybe . . . maybe she gets lost. Can't find her way back. That's what might have happened. At least, I think so."

"Proceed only on the basis of what you can see," the master said, pinching his lower lip with his thumb and index finger. "Stick to the facts. What do we have before us?"

I realized he was disappointed in me. I spent several moments struggling to deduce more from the scene.

"Her headscarf is still hanging on a bush. So she didn't have time to take it when she ran away. And therefore she must have been in a hurry."

"Good, Jussi."

Heikki was shifting impatiently from one foot to the other, noticeably on edge. He wanted us to stop talking and start searching, but the pastor was determined we should wait. He half closed his eyes, squinting in a strange kind of way.

"Her headscarf is hanging on the bush to dry," he said. "In which case it must have been midday and warm enough to make her perspire. Despite the temperature, she lit a fire so the smoke would disperse the mosquitoes. The fire was still burning when she ran off, but it's out now. We can see that the wood in the middle has burned down and a dusting of ash has blown in an easterly direction over the lingonberry twigs. There isn't a breath of air at the moment, but it was blowing in an easterly direction this afternoon. Hence it must be several hours since she disappeared. Was she alone?"

"Er . . . I think she was. Or rather, I'm sure she was."

"How so?"

"If there had been someone with her, she would have been wearing her headscarf, as befitting the respectable girl she was."

"That's possible. At any rate, she was sitting here eating a piece of bread when something happened. The milk canister was tipped over and she dropped the bread on the moss."

"Dropped . . . But there's no bread here, is there?"

The pastor pointed to the snag of a pine tree standing right next to us.

"Do you see what's on the branch? Thin white flakes. It's milk that's dried. Some little birds must have been hopping around in the milk and kept returning to the branch. Something edible, probably a piece of bread, must have ended up in the spilled milk."

"Of course!" I exclaimed, impressed.

"So the girl rushes away. You can see footprints in the moss. Strides the length of someone who's running."

Only now did I notice the scarcely visible indentations he was indicating.

"But there are . . . there are bigger tracks as well?"

"Good, Jussi. From someone larger than her. And heavier. You can see the prints are pressed deeper."

Heikki, who had been standing there listening to us, suddenly let out a groan. Before the pastor could stop him he ran over to the trunk of a pine tree and pointed. There was evidence of fresh damage to the bark. Heikki ran his fingers over the deep gouges.

"*Karhu!*" he said, a look of horror on his face.

"Bear!" I echoed, aghast.

The pastor examined the claw marks with care.

"We have to muster people for a search party," he said. "Somebody needs to tell Sheriff Brahe. I'm afraid something's happened to the poor girl."

Heikki nodded, plainly scared and glancing around nervously in the summer night. He began running back down the path toward the farm, while the pastor remained where he was. I saw the master carefully lift the milk pail and inspect it from all angles. He put his finger in the spilled milk, swirled it gently round and spread it out, and then picked up something long and almost invisible. I realized it was a hair. He cleaned it, wrapped it in a piece of cloth, and put it in his pocket. With the same care, he investigated her knapsack, which was still laced up, propped against a tussock. Without comment he studied the claw marks on the tree one more time. We began to follow the footprints, our eyes peeled. I saw the pastor bend to pick something up before we continued. The impressions were visible for about fifty steps, until the ground rose and became harder. There the tracks were more difficult to follow, and we soon lost them completely.

With mounting concern, we started back toward Heikki's farm. I shouted Hilda's name and looked around uneasily. The thick mass of willow branches suddenly seemed threatening. Anything large could hide in there and at any moment it might charge out and sink its jaws into the tendons of my neck. His lips moving, the pastor appeared to be talking to himself, or perhaps to higher powers. For my part, I gathered up a heavy branch to swing in the air. At regular intervals I smashed it against the tree trunks as we passed and heard the dull thuds recede into the misty veils of the summer night.

5.

I T WAS SUNDAY AND THE CHURCHGOERS WERE GATHERING OUTSIDE Kengis Church. I stood among the congregation keeping a furtive eye out for my beloved. She was usually in the company of some of the other maids, a posy of summer blossoms in which she was the prettiest of all. I used to follow the girls into the church, walking a few steps behind, close enough to smell her fragrance. Sometimes there was a throng at the church door, people pushing from the back, and then I might find myself so close to her that I could touch the cloth of her dress. Only the fine warp and weft between me and her warm nakedness. Every Sunday I hoped that it would happen.

The owner of the foundry was not yet present, it being the gentry's wont to be among the last to arrive and undoubtedly meant as a slight upon the pastor. Sohlberg had voted against the appointment of the controversial prophet from Lappmark and afterward contested the decision; he would rather have had the mild-mannered curate Sjöding. The pastor, on the other hand, had established from the start where the battle lines would be drawn:

"Finns and Swedes genuflect before the brandy barrel, they crawl on all fours when brandy takes the strength from their legs, they blubber to God with their heads full of brandy."

He had achieved success in Karesuando, where the parish had been made almost entirely dry and the one who held on tightest to the bottle was the sexton. Even the innkeepers had emptied out their liquor barrels and redeemed themselves. But it was a different situation in the parish of Pajala.

"A third are innkeepers, a third old sots, and a third miserable wretches who can't live without subsidy," the pastor had declared.

Now the judgmental burghers of Pajala were huddled in murmuring groups. There was Forsström the merchant and Hackzell the bailiff, surrounded by their families and lackeys. The gentlemen had reported the reverend to the cathedral chapter for the deplorable tone of his church services. People shrieked, men danced with women in the aisle, and the pastor himself employed an exceedingly coarse and offensive mode of speech inappropriate for church. When the bishop was made aware of the shenanigans, the pastor would indeed be in hot water.

Many were of the opinion that the pastor was quite simply insane. Rumors about his rampage in Karesuando had spread far across the north country. But if some were fearful, there were more who were curious. Who wouldn't want to listen to a crazy priest? And so church folk traveled from miles around to enjoy the show.

The corpulent sheriff Brahe arrived now from the village road wearing his uniform, driven in a horse-drawn carriage from Pajala. He alighted, wiped the perspiration from his neck with a checked handkerchief, and swayed slightly from side to side with a hefty gait suggestive of an ox. He casually greeted people left and right, conscious of his importance. For several days he had led the search for the missing maid Hilda Fredriksdotter and inquisitive onlookers now flocked around him to hear what had happened. Constable Michelsson, a head shorter and of considerably slighter build, climbed down from the coachman's seat. In his hand he clasped his modest cap, his thin lips intermittently drawn together in a shape resembling a snout. Michelsson was ginger, but despite his young age his hair had already thinned and only a sparse ring remained round his chalky pate.

I edged nearer, to hear Sheriff Brahe warn the churchgoers about the killer bear that was prowling around out there. During the search they had discovered traces of the monster: moose calves had been found slaughtered, their remains scattered over the ground, and anthills had been torn up by the force of mighty paws. But the poor girl hadn't yet been found. The beast must have devoured every last bit of her. Brahe cautioned people not to go into the forest alone, and if they must, to take a sturdy wood ax for self-defense.

From the direction of the parsonage women's voices could now be heard.

"*Pappi, Pappi . . .*"

Hands were raised and people pushed forward. I realized the pastor was on his way. He was so short that he had to clear a path through the crowd by swinging his arms in what were practically swimming movements. A young maid threw herself at him, flung her arms around his neck, and broke into convulsive sobs. The pastor mumbled something in her ear, but she wouldn't let go and the people closest had to help shield him. The gentry could be seen exchanging knowing looks. All the pastor's women. Ahem! You could guess what went on behind the closed doors of pastoral visits.

Now another horse-drawn carriage arrived, from which the foundry owner Karl Johan and his young son emerged. Sohlberg was wearing a dark suit with a shirt and waistcoat. He was an enterprising gent who had come here from the Karlskoga area as a works inspector and had gradually acquired all stakes in the foundry. People bowed and curtsied and doffed their caps as he strolled up to the assembled burghers. He and his son nodded briefly to the pastor, who was standing some distance away; the coolness between them was noticeable. Sheriff Brahe saluted the foundry owner and made a suggestion to him that I couldn't hear. But then I saw Sohlberg take out his large purse and extract a few notes.

"Reward offered to anyone who deals the death blow to the killer bear!" he said loudly.

His mid-Swedish dialect was unusual in these parts, and several people looked blank.

"*Kyllä se hyvän rahan saapi joka karhun tappaa*," Sheriff Brahe translated.

He put the money in his livery hat and looked around, clearly delighted to be the center of attention. Forsström and Hackzell hurriedly produced their wallets. Brahe left it to Michelsson to take charge of the collection among the crowd, and soon the clink could be heard of copper coins from the less well off landing in the cap.

"Would the reverend like to contribute?"

Michelsson watched him with his moist blue eyes.

"I have no money on me."

"None at all?"

Michelsson couldn't disguise the sarcasm in his voice. He was stingy, the new parson, it was common knowledge. After all, huge sums were pouring in from new believers, but wasn't most of it ending up in the parson's pocket? Or so gossip had it.

When the pastor turned and entered the church, the troop of converted souls crowded in after him. I heard him caution those nearest to him against idolatry, they must remember he was merely an instrument of the Lord. But religious revival was like a fire. Not even he could control it. And when it came to preaching, he pulled no punches.

"Until now the clergy have preached the gospel to the rich. To whores who have shown no remorse, to thieves who have carried on stealing. They have heard such a sweet gospel promised that the milk of harlots has gushed and traders in liquor have shed snake tears. Whereas I preach to the poor, the grieving, doubting, burdened, weeping, for all those who have lost hope. How does it help an innkeeper to tell him that he is decent and good? It helps him on his way to hell. Instead the priest should say to the fornicators: 'Your father is the devil. You are fighting the Holy Spirit. If you do not repent there is no one who can pluck you out of hell.'"

The pastor's voice was melodic and composed. His simple, unpretentious Finnish steadily permeated the congregation. It was not long before the first wailing could be heard. A swaying arm was raised in the air. Now one of the old women stood up, closely followed by another. A rocking motion spread along the pews, the crush intensified, people stepped out into the aisle to have more room to move. It was terrifying to see their faces, their eyes were fixed, jaws clenched and grinding, incomprehensible words mingled with cries and consternation. I felt the pastor's gaze, bent my body forward, and moved back and forth in time with my neighbors on the bench, hiding my face as I glanced furtively across to the women's side. There she was. My beloved. Her chest heaving as she breathed, her eyes half closed, her lips forming murmurs. Filled with despair, I felt the intensity of my desire for her. My face creased with tears, and following the others' example I held it up to the light and showed the pastor my unsightly wet cheeks.

The mill owner shuffled uneasily, his jaw muscles tightening. Hackzell took out a piece of writing paper and made a note. There they sat, surrounded by their own shrieking workfolk, the maidservants, farmhands, and crofters of Kengis and Pajala, who raised their clenched fists to the heavens. The force of this crowd was alarming. Surely no good could come of it?

But the pastor ruthlessly continued his tirade, driving the pack further and further until they were teetering on the edge of hell's abyss and beheld the flames and the lakes of brimstone with their own eyes and smelled the fetid stench from the underworld. Only then, when all seemed lost, did he take a deep breath. And with that he let the light in. At first a mere ray, and then a sword, and finally a blaze of light, whereupon the Savior himself appeared to float above the altar in his crown of thorns, blood trickling from the side. The Son of God himself held out his hand. And the workers' clenched fists opened up like flowers, their fingers transformed into white petals reaching for salvation, tremulous with hope. And, having superhuman strength, the Savior took hold of the congregation and pulled them out of the burning house, lifted them up, and held them in his arms like baby birds. And they pecked up the dripping honey of the gospel and like frightened children found safe shelter in their heavenly parent.

And all around, husbands and wives, brothers and sisters, even neighbors and enemies, could be seen embracing one another and asking for forgiveness, while the flesh and blood for Communion was laid out by the altar rail. With perspiring maids and crofters, I knelt and received it on my tongue. That which was called Jesus.

AT THE END OF the Mass the pastor announced the promise of a reward for slaying the local killer bear. He also requested that anyone who knew anything about the disappearance of the maid Hilda Fredriksdotter Alatalo should inform Sheriff Brahe.

After the service many of the worshippers pressed forward to thank the pastor, to touch him, assure themselves he was real. He followed the mob out onto the parvis and soon found himself besieged. There were awakened souls, there were those who repented their sins, and there were others who were mostly intrigued. Everyone wanted a little piece of the pastor. I hung back in the nave, and when no one was looking I sat down on the women's side. The pew had cooled down, but this was where she had been sitting. I hastily dropped to my knees. Rested my nose against the wood and breathed in her scent.

The next moment I heard a cough. I leaped to my feet and looked around in terror, belatedly realizing someone was lying down on one of the pews. It was a woman dressed in black, breathing strangely, viscid phlegm slavering from the corners of her mouth.

"*Haluaisin . . . haluaisin puhua* . . . I would like to speak to the pastor . . . Bid the pastor give me his blessing. . . ."

A foul smell emanated from her rotten teeth when she reached for me. She was struggling to sit up, but only managed to move a fraction before she slipped off the pew. I heard the dull thud of her head hitting the floor. Everything happened too fast for me to intervene. Nervously, I attempted to help her to her feet; her nose was pouring with blood and there were even bubbles of red between her lips. I swiftly placed my arms under her neck and behind her knees and lifted her limp body. Her clothes stank of urine. She was heavier than I had imagined, but with a huge effort I managed to stagger out into the bright light. I stood on the church steps. The old woman coughed and I felt something wet splatter over my face. When I saw the appalled gaze of the onlookers I realized it was blood. All I could do was stand there with the black bundle in my arms. Stand there holding this dying body while the congregation stared at me.

"What's the little *noaidi* doing now?" I heard them cry.

I promptly laid down my burden on the church steps and hurried back into the shadows of the church.

6.

MY MOTHER USED TO SAY I WAS EVIL. IT WAS A DIFFICULT THING for a child to hear. She said I did evil things, that I stole bread or hit my sister. I did many evil things. I knew while I was doing them that they were wrong, but I did them all the same. But it's one thing to be disobedient and feel a stinging slap against your cheek. It is far worse for a child to hear that he has been created evil, that his intrinsic, true nature comes from the devil. If you hear it time and again from an early age, if it is repeated often enough, it becomes a wound that will heal only to tear apart, heal again and tear apart, weeping and oozing and then hardening to a thick scab. I often think of it as a shabby leather glove, so old the reindeer hairs have long since worn off, wrinkled by long, hard toil, soaked and dried and cracked by sweat and pus many times over until it looks like a worn-out shriveled lung. That is what my soul looks like, my sorrow.

When I encounter other people I think how easily they glide through life. They greet one another with warmth, they can chat about simple things and laugh at petty troubles instead of being vexed. A fellow can say to a woman that her steps are so light, perhaps she has a sweetheart? Just like that. And the woman doesn't seem to take offense and she might reply that slow girls never fill a berry pail. And then they can stand and exchange pleasantries, and as they do, something unseen happens between them. Something that makes them both happy, something warming and still present after they have gone their separate ways. Or it may be in the shop where you want to buy some trifle, a pouch of rock salt or tobacco. And the merchant prattles on. About the weather and how the plants are growing and people who have come and gone, and you can only throw in a yes or a no. There is something in my nature that puts people off. Perhaps it is because of my shameful soul, because of the damage my mother inflicted upon me. Or maybe I would have been like this regardless.

I am not lovable. No one looking at me breaks into a smile or feels the easy joy I have seen in others. No woman meets my eye with a grin, but instead she will tense and turn away. When I state my errand the girl in the shop gives a curt response. It makes my life a lonely one, but I understand that it has to be like this. Whenever I have tried to appear cheerful or jocular, it has all gone wrong and only made me look odd.

"Tobacco," I say. "Please may I have some royal tobacco?"

But there is no smile from the girl behind the counter. No mischievous twinkle, no jaunty comment about how this, one of Sweden's least regal parts, unfortunately won't receive its delivery of royal tobacco until next week, when the court purveyor passes in his four-horse landau. I am met with only an averted gaze at the shelves.

"I'll have a twist of ordinary tobacco, then," I mumble, fiddling with my purse as I take it out. I spill some coins, they roll over the floor like eyes, and I crawl around on all fours like a sow. Gathering up the hard copper rounds. Dropping them onto the shop counter.

WHEN THE SILENCE FEELS too great, I walk down to the river. Preferably in the evening when the day's chores are done, when man and beast are both at rest. I stand on stones visible now that the water level has dropped after the spring floods. The river is flowing right in front of me. It is like glass, I always think, like the parsonage windowpanes. An everlasting glass floor sliding along, smashed in the rapids into smithereens and spume. Lacerations splitting open the water's tender skin and letting its entrails well up from the deep. A waterfall's alarming noise, warning of danger. A glimpse of black stone skulls in the swirl, boat hulls careering past with a hair's breadth to spare. But then it all flattens out again, the river spreads its arms into a vast pool. The agitated voice stills, the foaming surface heals and levels. While underneath it all remains.

The river washes away all the ugliness. I balance on the stones and let anxiety drain out of me. I give myself up, let my innermost thoughts be carried away and disappear. Perhaps the river is the most perfect representation of life. The soul that has no beginning and no end, it simply is. The river thinks for me. It helps me endure. I might feel pinned down, but it tells me that everything is in motion, nothing lasts. If I look at the river for long enough, I am turned into water. It is a powerful experience. When I am the river, I am the one who is becalmed, whereas the banks begin to move. I lie outstretched to my full length while on either side the land sails by, the primordial forests and marshland bogs. I let it all be and embrace my summer sky.

This is the image I try to conjure up in the evenings when anxiety takes hold of me. While I close my eyes and keep very still, blurry clouds pass overhead. The good sleep of the river, restorative and healing, its gentle purl drowning out the buzz of the mosquitoes.

I often reflect that i have the pastor to thank for my life. It was he who created me, once and for all. He fixed me in time, and thus I became a person. From then on I was in the book, I was registered.

Now my name can never be forgotten. Because surely the worst thing to befall you is to be forgotten while you are still alive. To go through life without ever being legitimized in letters. Letters of the alphabet are like metal spikes forged with the skill of Walloons, hot at first and pulled straight out of molten iron, gradually cooling and turning red, and in the fullness of time becoming black and strong. I think of them as plants: the contorted trunks of tortured trees, twisted peatland pines or crooked birches found on mountain slopes. That is where the letters are. Sometimes I stop and find a K, a squiggly A, or perhaps an R; the outlines of black branches are writing on the air's gray paper. You can read them. If you take the time, remarkable tales can be deciphered in them.

The summer I was registered in the book, I was crouching by the cart path, sore, beaten, my stomach empty. Sometimes I might receive a crumb from passing wayfarers, a sliver of rancid fat from the shank they were slicing, a little wad of spat-out tobacco you could suck to forget the hunger. I saw his figure from afar and instantly felt fear. There was something harsh about him, an urgency in his pace. He was clothed in coarse woolen wadmal, his hair was long and unkempt; he could have been taken for a tramp. But his eyes were watchful. He peered around the whole time, switched his gaze from one side to the other, sometimes up to the crowns of the trees and the next moment down to the tips of his toes, whereupon he would suddenly bend down and pick up a tiny straw. With mounting alarm, I tried to squeeze myself into the grass at the side of the track, to make myself invisible. But naturally he noticed me. Poised to run, I said nothing. But then I tried stretching out a suppliant hand.

"*Onkos sulla nälkä*?" the stranger asked in Finnish. When I didn't reply, he changed to Sami.

"*Lea go nealgon*? Are you hungry?"

I understood both languages, but I was afraid of being beaten.

My dirty, childish hand shook, but I forced myself to keep it there. He rummaged in his knapsack for a moment before bringing out a darkened bentwood box. He dipped his hand in and scooped something up. When he drew it out I could see his thumb was yellow. He held it out to me, a grown man's large, protruding thumb topped with a sticky hat. He nodded solemnly. I tried to take hold of it with my own hand, but he waved it away. He quietly placed his thumb against my tightly shut lips and dabbed them. I could feel the stickiness and licked it automatically. Something inside me ignited. The roof of my mouth started to sing. He waited until I opened my mouth again. This time I sucked the blob in. Rapturous warmth filled my mouth. I smacked my lips and I felt the globule melt and fill my palate with the color of sunshine. And now nothing could stop me. I was like a calf, licking and sucking until his thumb was clean.

"Was it good?" he asked.

"Good" was the wrong word. I had never tasted anything like it. I hadn't even known that the world could contain something so exquisite.

"It's called butter," he said. "*Voita.*"

"More," I whispered in Finnish.

He looked at me in his intense, critical way.

"What's your name?"

"Jussi."

"What's your father's name? *Mikäs sinun isän nimi on?*"

I stared at the ground.

"How old are you? You must be nine? Or ten?"

"I don't know."

"You don't know?"

He bent down closer and I thought he was going to hit me. Instinctively I squeezed my eyes shut and hunched my shoulders. But the hard blow never came. Instead I felt his fingers in my hair, over my little ear.

"Do you know who the blessed are? Do you know who the kingdom of heaven belongs to?" I shook my head again.

"It is the children."

I had never heard anyone say anything like this. When I cautiously looked up, his face was close to mine. He observed me silently. His eyes were pale blue with flecks of Sami green. Like the streams. And the mountains.

THAT NIGHT I SLEPT in a proper house for the first time. I had spent the night in barns, in forest huts and *goahtis*, in all manner of burrows and gullies, or simply under the drooping branches of a fir tree. But never before had I slept in a log cabin. At first I was reluctant, and I tried to sneak out into the cowshed to make a nest for myself in the hay, but he promptly brought me back. I balked at lying in a bed; I kicked and tossed until he accepted that he had to make my bed on the floor. The house was occupied by an elderly couple, friends of the pastor's, who sat talking to him for a long time after supper. Their calm voices were filled with the commonplace, and with love. I rolled myself up in the scratchy blanket they had given me and felt the food warm me from within like a lamp. The pastor had spent the whole evening trying to make me tell him about my parents and my family, but I just kept repeating that I was on the move. He knew I came from the north. From my clothes he judged I was a Lapp, but he couldn't be sure. The name Jussi was Finnish and I could speak both languages.

Imperceptibly, I drifted off. I was so unaccustomed to falling asleep like this, without being cold or hearing my stomach roar, without the need to protect my face from biting insects. Not even my stick was at the ready, the one I had in case a wild dog should approach. I imagined I was lying in a boat on a large stretch of still water. My hands were clasped behind my head, my eyes turned to the sky. The clouds on high were traveling just as I was, steering like ships toward the horizon. Someone—it must have been an angel—rowed the boat with effortless strokes. I dared to sleep on my back, although that position held the greatest risk, for it exposed the stomach, the softest part of a person, the belly, the easiest to penetrate with knives or teeth. But I was far from the treacherous shores and their beasts of prey, no ill could befall me here, everything was safe. And the helmsman, the figure of light, would guide me safely through the foaming rapids.

I quietly fell asleep like the child I was, slipping into the unfamiliar river landscape to the gentle stroke of the oars. I don't know how much time elapsed. Everything was blank and blurred, until suddenly my eyes opened wide and I was seized with indescribable terror. Without moving a muscle, I could sense the heinous threat of imminent danger. There in the semidarkness of the cabin; the ceiling, the walls, the towering furniture. And a wild animal, a lion, its black jaws wide open, its paw raised to strike at my head.

"*Rauhotu*," came the whisper.

A hand brushed my cheek, its warmth and life almost surreal. I felt the fingers, the gentle brush of the fingertips.

"Shhhh, shh . . ."

The pastor moved his face closer until it was right next to mine. He had lain down beside me and I felt the warmth of his body. Hesitantly, he placed his arm around me and held me.

"You were screaming," he said softly. "You were writhing around, screaming."

"A-a-h-h," I gasped.

"But I'm here now. I'm here, they can't get you."

"It was . . . nothing."

"Did you see a bear? Were you afraid?"

I was shuddering. I wanted to flee, force my burning limbs to let me bolt and rush out of the cabin, tear through the forests and marshlands until my heart burst. But his strong arms restrained me.

"There, there, my child."

His breath smelled of tobacco and herring. Like a recumbent ox, he made himself comfortable beside me. I was going nowhere.

In the morning, when the housekeeper started clattering the firewood and preparing the porridge, I was on my own. I sat up and could see from her bemused look that I must have caused a commotion during the night and kept them awake. The farm dog came in and sniffed at the corners of my mouth and then at my private parts and down to my kneecaps, at which point I hurried out into the yard. At that moment the pastor was coming out of the privy, buttoning up his trousers.

"Come with me," he said brusquely.

I didn't reply.

"We'll eat first and then you're coming home with me."

It was a long walk to the parsonage in Karesuando and when we arrived he led me into a small room inside the log cabin. I had never seen anything like it. Along the walls were shelves filled with flat leather-bound objects. For the first time, I beheld books. He reached for one of them, opened the cover and leafed through the closely written pages.

"How old can you be? And is your name really Jussi? Maybe you were baptized Johan or Johannes? Surely you've been baptized?"

The pages were gleaming white and I just wanted to stroke the surface of the paper with the tips of my fingers. Black curlicues in long columns could be seen on page after page. The pastor thumbed back and forth, frowning. He exchanged the book for another, searching everywhere.

"What are your parents called? Your father and mother? Surely you know their first names, at least?"

I shook my head.

"And where did you grow up? Who looked after you?"

"A witch," I said.

Pausing, he raised his eyes from the book's pages and regarded me quizzically.

"A witch?"

"Yes."

"But what was she called? Even witches have names."

"Sie . . . Sieppi . . ."

"Sieppi? Is she a Lapp?"

I began to shiver as a chill swept through me.

"They're not people," I said.

Clearing his throat, the pastor fiddled with his tobacco knife and then his writing implements before returning to the book.

"You look ten or eleven years old. But I can't find you anywhere. We can't have this."

There was no answer to that and I sat in silence.

"Your name shall be Johan. We can call you Jussi, but you'll be baptized Johan Sieppi."

"Not Sieppi!"

"Very well, Sieppinen, then. Johan Sieppinen."

The pastor was smiling now. He opened the inkpot and dipped the pen into it. Then he seized a jug of water and poured some into a glass bowl.

"Do you want to enter the Christian faith?"

"But . . ."

"That's a yes."

"Yes."

"Then I baptize thee, Johan Sieppinen, in the name of the Father . . . and of the Son . . . and of the Holy Ghost."

The water ran in a cold trickle down my forehead and under my collar. He dried me with the sleeve of his jacket, and looked at me with such compassion that it warmed my heart.

"And when would you like to have been born, Jussi? There aren't many people who can choose their own birthday. Shall we say yesterday's date, the twenty-ninth of June? That's the day we met. And what about the year of your birth? Shall we say you turned eleven yesterday? Does that feel like a good age?"

Without waiting for an answer, he turned to the back of the book, where there were a few blank pages.

"I'll record you as of no fixed abode, temporarily residing in the parish. So . . . Johan Sieppinen . . . born the twenty-ninth of June . . . 1831."

He held the book up and pointed to a wavy line, moist with fresh ink.

"There you are, Jussi. Now you exist."

7.

MY BELOVED. I CAN SEE HER FROM AFAR, COMING TO MEET ME along the cart track. I am out of breath after running all the way over the meadows to intercept her, but I do my utmost to appear relaxed and let a smile play on my lips. My idea is to address her casually so that she might stop or at least slow her pace. Maybe to meet her gaze briefly, look into her clear blue eyes, and coax a dimple onto her otherwise smooth cheeks. As she approaches I see she is weighed down; in one hand she is carrying a lidded pail and the narrow handle is cutting into her fingers. She keeps changing hands and bends her body over in the opposite direction to balance the weight. I try to think of something to say that will sound as natural as possible, but my heart is pounding so hard I feel sick. The nearer she comes, the worse my condition. My vision clouds and I feel my throat constrict, which makes it hard to breathe; I normally only come this close to her in the church aisle when we are all pushing our way out after the service. I want to flee, but at the same time this is where I want to be more than anywhere else, on this village road with the woman I love. She is very close now, at any moment we'll pass one another. She has noticed me but turns her face toward the ditch, and that might be the reason she doesn't catch my croaky greeting. Once again she switches hands and I see my opportunity. I will help her carry and thus afford myself the right to accompany her part of the way. I reach out to take hold of the sharp-edged handle.

"Allow me . . ." I manage to mutter.

But she gives a shrill scream and tries to snatch the pail back. When I, at long last, meet her gaze, it is entirely black. Her face muscles are twisted and her soft pink lips are now as sharp as a pocketknife. Bewildered, I loosen my grip, but then she loses her balance and stumbles. The pail overturns and fish come spilling out onto the grass; shiny, newly cleaned fish bodies, pike and perch and here and there a grayling, slithering like silver between our feet. I feel my face burn with shame and hastily kneel down to scoop them back into the bucket. As I do so she gives me a hefty kick, which strikes me in the chest and sends me staggering backward.

"Hello! What are you doing?" comes a gruff voice.

"He's pestering me!" she cries, pointing at me squatting there with a huge pike in my hands.

"Clear off!" yells a man, and as he approaches he removes his belt and swings it menacingly in front of him.

I drop the pike into the pail. I recognize the man as Roope, one of Sohlberg's workers, a broad-shouldered youth with a ginger mustache, who is taller than me by a head. I spring to my feet like a cat and adopt a crouching position. Roope is feared for his viciousness and yet I don't hesitate. It all happens so quickly, I have no time to think. I only know that now I have to flatten him. With all my weight I have to topple him and hammer my fists into his face until it is soaked in blood. My entire soul, all my sorrow and shame, turn to uncontrollable hatred. He senses it, I see him waver, he swings the belt with such force that the metal clasp whistles through the air. And maybe he will manage to deliver a punch, but after that he'll be done for.

"He's just standing there, keeping his mouth shut!" Roope screams.

How I wish I had a bold retort, something caustic, wounding. But I can't think of anything. Inside me there is just a calmness, a motionless void, and as my beloved raises the fish-reeking pail like a shield before her, I am of two minds. Still I say nothing. And then I turn and walk away. When I look over my shoulder they are walking in the other direction, side by side, as though they belong together. Roope is carrying the heavy bucket for her. I see them chatting. Laughing heartily, he turns and gives me a scornful look, and she does too. I feel the sticky slime from the pike on my hand. My chest aches where she kicked me. She struck me right over my heart. There is a pain in my ribs. As I lift my hand the strong smell of fish hits me. With great care I place my lips against the edge of my little finger, on the skin by the third knuckle, the place where our two bodies met. Where my skin brushed against hers when I grabbed the handle. Where I touched her sheer sweetness.

8.

T HE FIRST THING I NOTICED WAS THE SMELL OF SMOKE. IT WAS SO alien, so different from the aromas that surrounded me every day. But in all the gray and brown there was a burgeoning hue. It seemed to be emanating from the parsonage. Tjalmo the dog was standing on the step to the porch, pawing restlessly, her head down, as if she had been given a telling-off. My first thought was that someone had started a fire over at the foundry, it smelled like ignited juniper needles, with a sprinkling of tar and maybe a dash of gunpowder. I kept my eye on the parsonage door. There was still time for me to turn back, just walk away, as the elk does when it detects a strange scent, vanishing like a gray silence over the marshes. But I am like the fox, attracted to the unfamiliar, hovering between fear and curiosity. My eager little nose sticks out at the front of my body. I hesitated for barely a second, and then I opened the door and slipped in.

Inside, the smell was overwhelming. Now I worked out that it was tobacco. It didn't come from the pastor's pipe, as I had expected, but from a tan-colored stem with a glowing diamond at the end. It was the first time I had seen a smoking implement like this. Strikingly long fingers closed round the brown tube; they were wide and jointed in more places than the fingers of a common countryman. They led, via a thick wrist, into an indigo-dyed coat sleeve, passing into a reclining body that was almost puffy, at once both muscular and fat. The stomach formed a natural center to this sizable personage. He had been given the best seat, the armchair, the one nobody but the pastor usually sat in. Now he was semi-recumbent in it, evidently at ease, making use of all the chair had to offer by way of comfort: the gently beveled backrest, the elbow pads, the foot support on which his heavy round heel was resting. He held the smoking instrument in his left hand, while with his right he made elegant sweeping gestures as if he were winding wool. The most prominent feature was his mouth. It could have been a girl's. The lips were blood-red, without being painted, the top one curving high like Cupid's bow, sucker-like, the lower one wet and glistening, dark as a freshly removed liver. And the whole time these lips were moving. Through the smoke, through the unfamiliar fragrance filling the entire cabin, there rose the melodious, almost angelic sound of a man's voice.

Seldom have I heard such a beautiful timbre. The voices of the village men were quite different, for the most part harsh and unrefined. They were used chiefly in two contrasting situations: either deafeningly shrill—for commanding horses and reprimanding children—or wearily subdued—at evening mealtime after a hard day's work. Their voices almost never adopted the modulation this man was using now. I had never heard the like. At first I thought he was singing; the sound was of a meandering melody. But then I noticed that he wasn't rhyming. This was no hymn, nor was it a *joik*, the language being neither Finnish nor Lapp. This man was speaking the language of the king and the bishop, the language you could hear at the marketplace in Kengis or coming out of a horse-drawn carriage arriving from afar. It was that weaving, bobbing language called Swedish.

Most of the time the pastor sat quietly listening. Now and again he interjected with a short comment, posed a question, or raised an objection. A short pause would ensue, a sharp intake of breath, and then the voice resumed at a slightly quickened tempo, marginally faster, but still so elegantly melodic.

Women's voices are beautiful when low and mellow, I find. Whereas girls who are vain have shrill voices; at a glance from a boy they squawk and squeak like sparrows. The opposite is true of men: the deepest voices are the dullest. A dense forest through which the sun can barely penetrate. But this man's voice opened a glade; or rather, presented a magnificent view as if from a mountaintop, boldly launching itself like a bird of prey and sailing forth through the light. Buzzards and eagles came to mind, the surprisingly high-pitched calls of the bird world's dukes and kings. While the humble villager sounded like the mountain finch, the noise he emits suggestive of spitting tobacco.

While the man was limbering up his vocal cords, a column of gray ash was accumulating at the end of his glowing stick of tobacco. Longer and longer it grew, until it suddenly collapsed in a shower of silver onto the cabin floor. As the man spoke, he directed his gaze to the ceiling as if it were from there his strength derived. The pastor's daughter Selma sat entirely motionless before this apparition; she, like me, had never encountered anything like it before. Even the pastor's wife, Brita Kajsa, seemed impressed, sitting by the fireplace, half turned away. Unlike me, the rest of the household could understand the man's Swedish tongue, they could follow all the finer nuances he drew, pick up all the little drollities that made them laugh.

The armchair creaked and his ample bulk swayed as he changed position and balanced his remarkable smoking contraption on the edge of the best china plate, now cleared of food. He reached for his luggage, which was no humble knapsack or haversack, but a square brown trunk. He positioned it across his thighs and unfastened the lock, every judiciously elegant gesture raising our expectations. He lifted up the lid as though it were so very heavy and cautiously pushed it back until it was lying on the table. Whereupon he pulled out an elongated bundle tied with a bright red ribbon. His nimble fingers loosened the knot and he held up the scroll, slowly letting it unroll. As he did so, whatever it was transformed into something shiny: a lustrous surface of intense colors, a shimmering expanse against a darker background, and, finally, a pair of eyes looking into mine.

Startled, I realized that it was a face. No, it was more than a face: the hair was arranged in a large chignon fastened with a precious jewel, the skin of the neck so pale that it appeared almost white, a woman's neck, slipping down inside a dress. And what a dress. The fabric was deep red, gathered around the woman's body in the most exquisite folds and drapes and caressing the arms, which held a cumbersome stringed instrument. I didn't know what it was called, but it consisted of a brown, lacquered body in the shape of a human torso, which she was stroking with a bow. And as for her eyes, they were veiled as in a dream but leveled straight at the beholder. She was entranced by the music. And through her eyes I could hear and experience what she was feeling in her other world.

The man explained that he had painted the woman down in Härnösand. That much I understood with my meager Swedish. The woman had been sitting and playing in front of him and looked just like this. She had been holding this instrument, called a *shello*. I committed the word to memory, to keep it forever; *shello, shello, shello*.

With an involuntary sigh I acknowledged that the man before us was a genius. His visit, this conversation, his work of art, they had affected us all mightily. The man was showing us a world I could hardly believe existed, but which his skill had manifested for all, including me. I could even hear the rustling of the dress.

Eventually the man's purpose became clear. On the sturdy table, on the solid plank of Finnish pine, he placed a bottle of something transparent and yellow. When he pulled out the cork and let the children smell it, they laughed or backed away. The sharp, woody aroma reached even me. Next to it he put a bowl, together with some slender brushes and a thin wooden board that bore the traces of dried paint. After that he lined up pot after pot, each bearing a little label. Last of all he brought out another roll. But when he unfurled this one, it was white and bare. With a broad sweep he applied the dry brush to the surface. His fingers and the handle seemed organically joined and the brush became a sixth finger, growing directly from his flesh. And in my mind I saw the picture take shape. He was painting with air. He filled the space with a face, a gentleman in a formal, dignified pose, one hand on a . . . hunting rifle? No, something smaller, a hymnbook, perhaps, a postil? Yes, now that I could see it all in front of me, I knew that the painting would be quite perfect, that it would capture the pastor in all his glory. The pastor would obviously be portrayed at work on his herbarium, and in his other hand he would be holding not a weapon, not a pen . . . but something small, something ostensibly trivial, and yet more important than anything else. It was a newly discovered *Carex*, one of the most insignificant plants in this wild region, one that had been named after him, *Carex laestadii*.

The pastor was clearly impressed. I saw that he too had been captivated by the artist's charm. The portrait in all its splendor was actually already painted. All it wanted was immortalizing as a work of art. For a certain fee, of course. An appropriate sum for this humble craftsman in the illustrious halls of painting. A sum that was not exactly small; a sum that was, in fact, when he finally named it, quite large. A great deal larger than many people in the parish could have afforded.

But even as he said it, I was thinking, What is the price of perpetuity? What is worth more to the pastor than existing for the rest of time?

With graceful movements he placed the painting equipment back in the chest. His hands were so unlike anything I had seen, the large fingers could mold and shape, finish at a precise point, follow the curve of a single hair, capture the flash in an eye the same second it occurred.

Amid much mutual paying of respects, the pastor prepared to take his leave of the artist, who asked to be called Nils Gustaf (they were already behaving like close friends). I gathered that the pastor had been given some time to think about it before completing the transaction. Nils Gustaf stressed that the opportunity would soon pass, and that after a visit to the Kengis foundry he would be leaving these parts, possibly never to return. As always in this life, it was a matter of seizing the day.

As Nils Gustaf walked past me, I stopped him. I showed him what I wanted to know, holding my hand as if there were something in it and slowly moving it toward my mouth.

"What . . . is . . . one of those called?"

At first he didn't appear to understand. But then it dawned on him and he burst into a short laugh, with a sound as beautiful as his speaking voice. And he told me.

Now I had two words. The first was *shello*. What the woman was playing was called a *shello*. And the second, the thing he was holding between his lips and sucking on. The thing that was long and brown.

It was called a *siggar*.

9.

THE PASTOR WAS ILL AT EASE. I SAT ON THE FLOOR IN THE CORNER and watched him read the letter that had arrived that morning. He rose to his feet, sucking on his large pipe, and frowned when he discovered it had gone out. He stood there poking and tapping it, his craving for nicotine intensifying like a fever all the while. Several times he held the paper up to the light at the window, to be able to see better. Lately he had been complaining that his eyesight seemed to be getting worse and worse. I hurried across to cut off some tobacco from the twist on the table and watched him greedily fill the bowl of his pipe with the flakes.

"So now Bishop Juell's in on it too! Do you know of him, Jussi?"

"No."

"Bishop on the Norwegian side. The revival is spreading over there as well, but not to everyone's pleasing."

"Really?"

"People are giving up drink, Jussi! And when the taverns can no longer rake in cash from liquor sales they're going to lose substantial revenue. A number of priests side with the innkeepers, as does this Andreas Qvale they're writing about."

"I don't know him."

"An enemy of the revival. A priest who only does it for the money. Before the revival movement men like him could rule the roost, but not anymore. When he held a service in Skjervøy Church, newly awakened souls from Kautokeino came to protest. During the service there were calls for him to repent, for the priest himself to start living like a Christian. But instead of listening to their words, he had them thrown out for disturbing the peace. From what I hear it was Aslak Haetta, Ole Somby, Rasmus Spein, Ellen Skum, and one or two others. Do you know them?"

"Those are the family names of some of the reindeer herders up there."

"Well, the following day Qvale was supposed to be giving Holy Communion. But the Sami had gathered at the church door and were exhorting everyone who came not to celebrate Communion there."

"Because of the priest?"

"Of course. So Qvale had the Sami locked in one of the church cabins for the duration of the service. And afterward he reported them all to the bailiff."

Puffing energetically on his pipe, the pastor sat down at the desk and began writing Sunday's sermon. He muttered under his breath, moving his lips, rewriting, crossing out. I saw him fashioning the words, honing them; it was obvious that in his mind he was already standing in the pulpit. The smoke swirled as the words filled the sheet of paper, until he paused and read it out to me.

"Virtuous harlots, honorable thieves, sober drinkers, and up-standing innkeepers. Ye who are gathered before the cross after sup-ping whore's piss on the way to church, do you think that God doesn't see? Do you feel the snakes writhing inside your guts, shiny and black with forked tongues . . . ?"

I could only nod in agreement. The pastor's words were like iron skewers. For him they were not mere language: as well as tools and implements, bolts that could build steps up to heaven's door, they were also knives that made sinners quake and sweat. With my own eyes I had seen the drunkard stagger out of the pew, full of remorse, to throw up in a snowdrift. Such was the power of the master's oratory that his words could rend the hardest rock or reduce silent heathens to tears.

The page was soon full. He turned it over, but there was already something written on the other side. He hastily searched through his desk and found an invoice of some kind, turned it sideways, and proceeded to fill the empty spaces in the margins. The pastor often ran out of paper; deliveries out here were slow and unreliable and the cost was high. If I could have gifted our master anything, it would have been paper. I would have placed it next to his inkpot, a large pile of well-cut white sheets, ready to be filled with his thoughts. His writing ink was unsatisfactory as well; he often made it himself out of soot or rust that he scraped up, sometimes even from blueberries. Surely the king could send him a preparation from Stockholm? But the pastor, without complaining, took out his knife and pared the top of the quill to prevent the worst blobs.

Once again he stood up and gazed at the meadowlands outside the window. Then he turned abruptly, cheek muscles taut, and left the writing chamber without a word. There was always something preying on his mind. Often it was concern about his parishioners' circumstances. The perennial problem of prostitution in the Pajala region. The desperation of the poor. Sunday after Sunday he took his place in the pulpit and sowed his seed on rocky ground. Perhaps he was bored with preaching to the same congregation, with the same grousing old crones reaching a state of ecstasy, their *liikutuksia*, begging for forgiveness in a shower of tears, even though they must be among the whitest sheep in the congregation. The revival seemed to have begun to wane, the flames he kindled in Karesuando to be dying down, the devotion to be cooling.

Without speaking he put on his curled-toe shoes. I didn't know whether he wanted me to go with him, but I was always ready. I saw him grab the knapsack and the vasculum in which he always stored the plants he collected for the herbarium. Brita Kajsa asked how long he would be away, but he just gave a dismissive wave of the hand. This irritated her; it was the height of summer and there were many things around the place that needed doing, but he left her rebuke unanswered. His gaze was fixed on the far distance, he was no longer here, and when he snatched the rambling stick, I knew it was going to be a long day.

As we hurried through the village, people going about their business paused and gave a hasty bow when the pastor passed. He uttered a forced greeting in return, his entire demeanor indicating to me that he had no desire for conversation. The moment we were out on the cart track and the buildings were behind us, he relaxed. He stopped a couple of times to examine some examples of *Salix*, ran his fingers over the edges of the willow's leaves and studied the hairs on them through his magnifying glass. But he had something else in his sights. Our rests were only long enough to allow us to drink something and apply another coat of tar against the interminable mosquitoes. I knew better than to offer, but during one break I managed to take his knapsack and shoulder its not-inconsiderable weight. Thereafter his pace increased as we abandoned the cart tracks and made our way into the woodland.

With mounting unease, I realized where he was heading. We were on the same path Hilda Fredriksdotter had followed before the bear took her. When we reached the firepit where we had found her headscarf, the pastor halted. He wiped his brow and his eyes, as though in an effort to clear his vision. The tracks were difficult to distinguish now, the grass was standing up again, and the girl's possessions had long since been removed. The only interruption to the greenery was the sooty circle where the fire had been.

The pastor bent down and pressed his palm on the earth as if he could still feel the warmth of her body. The furrow in his brow deepened and his eyes scanned the forest, sweeping round in a full circle. I thought he was uncertain about where the hunting party had been searching, but after a while he lifted his gaze from the ground.

"*Maa vettää* . . . the earth draws," he muttered. "I think everyone who's walked in these forests has experienced this remarkable phenomenon. You believe you're wandering around quite aimlessly. Your feet can take whatever direction they wish, do you understand?"

"Yes."

"You amble along without purpose, thinking of nothing in particular. But suddenly, when you look down, you see you've ended up on a reindeer's trail. How can that be?"

"*Maa vettää*," I said.

"Exactly. The earth draws. It's like magnetism. You're drawn to where the terrain wants you to be. Reindeer and cows and elk and people and every other moving thing, we're all steered along the same paths without realizing."

Like the needle on a compass he slowly made a quarter turn. He raised his arm and pointed in an entirely different direction from that taken by the hunt.

"What's over there? That way?"

"Marsh," I said. "Undergrowth and bog."

He took a few hesitant steps. Cattle had been here, their hooves had sunk into the berry twigs, and the bushes' leaves showed evidence of livestock having grazed on them. Bent over, he traced the hoof marks, his eye peeled the whole time. He instructed me to accompany him ten paces to his left in such a way as to cover a larger area. But I had no more idea now what we were searching for than I had before.

The ground grew more and more waterlogged and soon the

spruce forest thinned out and turned into sedge swamp. There were clear signs that the grass had recently been scythed; the stalks were chopped off where the blade had struck. Out on a little island in the swamp stood a decaying hay barn. The pastor splashed out into the wet and I followed. Without marsh skis, we sank up to our knees and felt the undulating flarks roll uncomfortably beneath our feet, as if at any moment they would part and swallow us. The pastor followed a ridge, known as a string, where it was marginally less wet, until we made it to the barn and could catch our breath. We saw evidence of where the hay makers had stopped for a meal break and lit a fire. Twigs of spruce remained where they had sat, and the needles had started to drop. The hayrack posts were propped against the gable end of the barn in readiness for next summer. The barn was barricaded; instead of a door there were broad planks slotted into a rabbet. Together we lifted them out to get through the opening and then stood inside, hunched under the low roof, our feet on the hand-cut logs forming the floor. The barn was timbered but had large gaps to allow for ventilation, and the dry sedge hay was piled high. It had a warm, sweet aroma, a delightful summeriness that would be transported back by sleigh in late winter, the bounty that could be a cow's salvation.

I was about to go back outside when the pastor touched my arm. He pointed to a dip where the hay had been pressed down.

"Someone has been sitting there," I said.

"Or lying."

He viewed the hollow from various angles.

"Lie down over there, please," he said, indicating a different pile.

I did as he requested and enjoyed a few moments' rest in the soft hay that reached nearly to the roof. Then I had to get up so that he could consider the indentation I had made.

"Look!" he said enthusiastically.

I leaned forward.

"The first hollow is deeper than mine," I said.

"And why might that be?"

"The person lying there was heavier than I am."

"Lie down where you did before," he said.

Once again I stretched out in the hay. Just as I was making myself comfortable he flung himself on top of me. He was heavier than I thought and I could hardly breathe. Instinctively I tried to push him away, but he caught my wrists and held me down. I caught the sour smell of his sweat, the tar, the grease on his scalp, and I could feel the rough stubble of his beard. And then suddenly, with no word of explanation, he let go.

"What are you doing, Pastor?"

"Look at that, Jussi."

I was hot and angry and bits of straw were scratching my back, but he didn't appear to notice. He leaned forward calmly and measured the dip with his hands.

"You see, Jussi?"

"No."

"The hollows are the same depth now! Deduction: there were two people lying in the hay!"

I couldn't understand his excitement. Two people who had gone to lie down during a break in the harvest. Admittedly, it might suggest fornication, an unmarried farmhand philandering with a maidservant. We both knew that sins of that nature were not unusual. Eagerly the pastor knelt down to inspect the compressed hay more closely. He dug up handfuls of sedge and examined the stalks in the filtered daylight. Before long something caught his attention. When I leaned over, I saw that a number of the blades of grass were discolored by something dark. The pastor spat on it, and gradually dissolved the dried-up stain by rubbing the saliva in with his thumb.

He tasted it cautiously with the tip of his tongue. Then he held out his thumb to me. I remembered the butter on the earlier occasion. Without a word I tasted whatever was there.

"Do you recognize it?" he whispered.

I nodded. There was no doubt.

"Blood."

He hummed as he put the tuft of straw into his pocket. With both hands he continued his meticulous search through the hay. He pensively held something up between his thumb and forefinger. It was invisible to me, as though he were clutching air. But when he let it hang in the shaft of sunlight coming through the gaps in the wall, it glimmered like gold. It was a lock of hair, wavy and blond, as long as his forearm. It was scarcely credible that he had managed to distinguish it from the hay.

"Hilda Fredriksdotter Alatalo was fair-haired, was she not? Long, fair hair?"

"Yes."

"I found a strand of hair like this in the spilled milk at her resting place."

At once I recalled the invisible thing he had picked up and wrapped in a cloth.

"Do you think Hilda has been here, Pastor?"

"There are several hairs together. What does that tell you?"

"Maybe she . . . I don't really know."

"When do you lose several strands of hair at the same time, Jussi? When someone pulls it. When someone tears them out by force."

I had a sudden memory from a different time. Of the witch towering over me, yanking my hair, making me feel sick with the pain. I shut my eyes tight and cleared my throat until the nausea eventually subsided. The pastor seemed not to have noticed; with his magnifying glass raised, he was examining the strands.

"Hilda has a visitor at her resting place. Perhaps they've arranged the meeting in advance. Fired by temptations of the flesh, they hasten to the barn, where they can hide from the eyes of the world. Hilda lies down first, the man throws himself on top. In their aroused embrace, he tugs out some strands of her hair. Are we to believe that this is what happened?"

I couldn't help blushing. The scene was all too vivid in the bestial sweat and agitation of my mind.

"You'll recall that I looked at the milk pail, the one left at the resting place? I found marks on the rim where someone had drunk from it. Marks from not one mouth, but two, two different mouths. That was when I realized that Hilda had a visitor."

"But—but what about the bear?"

The pastor didn't answer. Instead, with remarkable patience, he carried on his search of the hay, laboriously changing position when his back began to ache. All of a sudden he swooped down and picked up something very small.

"How odd."

It was a tiny stem, hardly a finger joint in length, and dried up.

"What does the pastor mean?"

"*Cassiope tetragona*. It's unmistakable. Look at the leaves."

I looked more closely. They didn't have the appearance of leaves to me, more like small buds lying tightly one on top of the other along the stem.

"Arctic heather," he explained. "*Tetragona* means having four corners. The leaves are patterned in rows of four."

"Ah, I see."

With great care the pastor placed the plant in his vasculum and made a note in pencil.

"And what's so odd about it?"

"Use your brain, Jussi. Look around you."

I noticed how the pastor appeared to revel in his knowledge.

"The Arctic heather is a relatively common plant," he went on. "It's a widespread low-growing genus. Look around you. Do you see it here?"

"It was in the hay."

"Yes, among the sedge. But Arctic heather and sedge grow in different habitats. Arctic heather grows on the upland moors in the far north. Now, explain that if you can."

"Maybe it's growing nearby?"

"On all my excursions I have never come across it in the region around Kengis. It must have come here with the man she met. Perhaps it had fastened onto his clothing while he was up there? Or it might have been on his shoes or in a pocket? And it came off here, while they were locked in their ardent embrace."

"What about the blood?"

"Perhaps he hit her? Or else it shows that Hilda was a virgin and in their intimacy she lost her maidenhead."

The pastor made no further comment, but I could still taste the blood in my mouth. When I thought about where it might have come from, I was obliged to steady my shaking legs by leaning against the log wall.

"What does all this tell us?" the pastor went on, apparently unmoved.

"The scent of blood!" I exclaimed. "The bear must have picked up the scent of Hilda's blood. The creature was lying in wait for her when she left here."

The pastor struggled to his feet and walked over to the opening, where he peered out at the bog pools.

"I wonder whether . . ." he said.

Without further explanation he bent down and began searching along the edge of the bog. He had the air of someone looking for plants, or a berry picker hunting for cloudberries. He asked me to help him search for anything out of keeping with the surroundings. Somewhat reluctantly I squelched out into the swaying swamp water and moved in wider and wider circles, trying to find the tracks of a bear's paws.

But it was the pastor who made the discovery. Some distance out into the sagging swamp he let out an ear-piercing whistle, of the kind he had learned as a child in Kvikkjokk. I immediately hurried in his direction, water sloshing and splashing up to my thighs. As I drew nearer I could see the pastor bending over, his head dangling and his hands supported against his knees, as though struck by a sudden attack of vertigo. He was pointing down into one of the pools. The water was pitch-black, and the gray tip of something that might have been a wetland spruce poked out above the surface. But as I looked closer I could see it was a piece of the hayrack timber from the barn. The post was pushed so far down into the mud that it was barely noticeable.

The pastor took hold of the post and rocked it back and forth. Something pale waved about in the dark sludge, something that looked like hay.

Then, to my unspeakable horror, I realized that it was hair.

10.

I WAS AN ANIMAL. I LIVED LIKE AN ANIMAL, CONSTANTLY TRYING to find something to eat. The woman who called herself my mother could see my hunger, see how I licked the handle of her sheath knife for the lingering taste of fish oil on it. But she just sneered at me, as she lay there on the deerskin, her eyes watery, the brandy keg clasped to her breast like a suckling child. I particularly remember one incident: she laughed at me when I sucked on some gnawed bones that were so dry and smooth they could have been stones, not even any marrow left inside, just sharp splinters squeaking against my milk teeth. She laughed at my despair and then she brought out her tit. She pushed up her bodice, pulled out her tit, and asked me if I wanted some. It was large and flabby, she held it like a damp mitten and waved the wrinkled brown nipple.

"Here's something tasty," she slurred. "Tasty, tasty . . ."

I saw her black teeth, the claggy white saliva. She coughed up some spittle onto her palm and rubbed it into the nipple to make it smooth and heavy.

"Tasty, tasty . . ." she tempted me.

And I was so very hungry. I was desperate for anything at all, for soil, or ash, or mud. So I got down next to her sour-smelling body, lay down beside her. Her hand closed round my neck like a claw and she squeezed me so hard I could scarcely breathe. And I put her limp tit in my mouth and sucked, and at first I thought something was coming out, a little fat. But then I realized it was only sweat and dirt. She laughed until she choked and the tit bobbed up and down, and although I had stopped sucking she wouldn't let me go, she just squeezed me harder and harder as if she were trying to push me back inside her stomach, into her womb. And all I wanted was to recoil from this world and escape. In the end I bit her, bit hard with my milk teeth, and the witch let go then and punched me in the head, so I rolled away, a red blackness behind my eyes. An empty, red cavern.

WHEN THE PASTOR FOUND me by the side of the road, I hadn't yet become a person. But he registered me in the book. He created me, he joined me to a parish with his little squiggly lines. I existed after that. He patiently placed one of the schoolchildren's writing boxes in front of me, a simple wooden tray containing fine-grained sand. With a stick he scratched a curved shape. With a similar stick, I had to reproduce the shape as closely as possible. It was difficult to make the hook at the bottom, to make it curl evenly without wobbles and spikes.

"*J*," the pastor said. "It's called a *J*."

"*J*," I said.

"*J* is a good letter. Like the *J* in 'Jesus.'"

I didn't understand, but I pronounced it after him. The next letter was *U*, its half circle awkward as well. Not to mention the *S*, twice, the winding snake that had to coil there in the sand without biting or sliding away. Last came the *I*, a relief, just a straight line. If it had been up to me, all the letters would have looked like that.

Time after time the pastor flattened the sand, and even that never ceased to fascinate me. First all the effort, all the curves and twists in the sand. And then with a gentle sweep of the arm it was brushed away and was gone. I was there just now, the pastor explained. It said "JUSSI" in there just now. And the next minute it was empty.

Smooth, clean sand in which you could try again. The pastor wrote "JESUS." "JESUS" had an *E*, another good letter, and I could already do *J* and *S* and *U*. "Jesus" was the second word I learned. The pastor wanted to carry on, and now it was my turn to choose a word. But I couldn't think of one.

"What about 'MOTHER'?" he wondered.

I shook my head vehemently. Not "MOTHER."

"I know what. We'll do "MARIA." She was Jesus's mother. Can you imagine? Even our Savior, Our Lord Most High, had a mother."

So we did "MARIA." Yes, it was a good word. All straight letters, more or less.

11.

THERE WAS GREAT CONSTERNATION WHEN IT WAS REVEALED that the farm girl Hilda Fredriksdotter had been found dead. The pastor and I summoned the people living nearby, and along with a handful of curious hangers-on we dug the corpse out of the slime. The girl was laid on a stretcher made of poles and carried back to Heikki Alalehto's farm in a macabre procession down the trails. I saw the silt drip from her sludge-soaked hair. Her head rocked from side to side and seemed almost alive, as if she were shouting, "No, no!" at us all. No one spoke during the short pauses we took to catch our breath and change bearers and everyone avoided looking at the body. It was with enormous relief that we finally reached the farm. I felt dirty somehow, sullied, and I noticed that all those who had touched the body rinsed their hands thoroughly at the well. For the time being the body would lie in the sauna. The neighbor Elli-Kaarina was called, a thin old woman who looked after the dead. She had the girl moved to the bier and heated water to begin the job of washing off the mud. As she was making her preparations, I felt the pastor give me a discreet nudge. Together we entered the sauna and stopped her.

"We have to wait for the sheriff first," he said.

The woman looked at him quizzically but didn't object. There was really no hurry. She disappeared inside the cabin for a bite to eat while the pastor and I remained.

It was a gruesome scene. And yet the dead woman was still attractive. Her mouth was open, her eyes, wet with marsh water, stared up at the roof, and her complexion had an unearthly violet tinge, her arms spangled with purple patches.

But her hair was like an angel's. It fell in waves across the bier. I reached out my hand and touched it lightly with my fingertips. A woman's hair. The same as my beloved's, just a little fairer. So this was what it felt like. I tried to save the memory of the softness, the silkiness, for my dreams. The pastor moved my hand away. He took a step back and viewed the body from all angles, especially her hands and fingers and then her dirty feet and the thick skin on her soles. It was obvious that she was a cow-girl: there were scratches and scabs on her ankles where her bare legs had forced their way through the tangle of willow shoots. Her face was sunburned and there was a paler stripe at the top of her forehead where she usually wore her headscarf.

The pastor took several deep breaths. Then he removed his coat and rolled his shirtsleeves up over his elbows. He took some writing paper and a pencil out of his bag and made several quick notes before handing them over to me.

"You write it down, Jussi."

I stared at him. But he was serious; his eyes were sharp, his upper lip tight. I hastily wiped my hands on my thighs until they felt clean and dry enough to carefully receive the white sheet of paper. It felt so light, almost like chicken down. If I let go it would stay in the air, floating free. The pencil was made of wood and had a gray lead core. With a trembling hand I lowered the point toward the paper, but I didn't have the courage to let them touch. Holding the pencil felt like directing the blade of a knife at exposed skin.

"And we won't say anything about this, Jussi. Is that completely clear?"

I nodded and swallowed, though my mouth was dry. It was only the muscles in my throat convulsing, pounding like my heart.

The pastor quietly closed the sauna door through which the daylight had been streaming, and fastened it with the handle of a broom so that nobody could open it. He found a tallow candle, which he lit and placed on the sauna bench next to the girl's head. Then he cleared his throat and sank to his knees. At first I thought he was praying. But then I saw him start to stroke the top of her head. He parted the hair down to the roots and scrutinized every section from the temples backward, turning the skull to get to the back of the neck and continuing in this manner all the way round.

"Here." He pointed.

I saw a tiny mark where the scalp was damaged.

"This is where her hair was pulled out. Write: damage to left cranium, two inches above right ear."

Would I really be capable of writing this? I broke out in a sweat and wiped a drop from the end of my nose before it could fall. Then I put the piece of paper down on the bench. I cautiously pressed the point against the white fibers and watched the black appear, watched the first little dot extend into a shaky, crooked line. It felt like dirt, as if I were soiling a bleached bedsheet. I made my handwriting as small as possible, but all the same the letters seemed to widen out, becoming large and ungainly. Now the letters were standing there like elk grazing on long, straggly legs. No! I'd made a mistake as well! Streaks of black like pieces of straw shot across my vision as I struggled to correct it.

The pastor folded back the girl's collar. Her neck was an awful purplish black where the bear had gone for her throat. He brought the candle flame nearer and studied the wounds, then he took hold of her shoulders and lifted. He felt the dress, the hooks and eyes at the neck.

"They've been ripped off. What does that suggest?"

"Shall I . . . shall I write that down?"

"Note everything I say, Jussi. The girl was probably trying to defend herself. She must have been fighting for her life. You don't need to look now."

He took hold of the hem of her skirt between his thumb and forefinger and lifted it up over her thigh. I closed my eyes tight. But still, I wanted to see.

At first her thighs appeared to be white all over. But when he examined the backs of them we saw the signs of livor mortis. A large blue discoloration ran down the side of her left thigh. The pastor was shaken and pale and his voice wasn't entirely steady when he asked me to note the bruise.

Gently, he exposed her genitals. I couldn't understand how he could bring himself to do that. The pubic hair wasn't black like mine, but dark blond, almost the color of bronze.

"Write down that she bled. In her . . . that her virginity was taken. Something like that."

Virginity. I struggled to spell this, to transcribe the sound, with the pencil slipping in my sweaty grasp.

Next he gripped the pelvis and turned the body on its side. Her back displayed the reddish-violet marks of lividity. The pastor searched her dress and found a couple of yellowed stems of sedge.

"Dried sedge. *Carex nigra*. Spelled with an initial *C*. They must have got caught when she was lying in there in the barn."

It was an effort to keep up. Carecks with a *C*.

"Can you help me now? Hold her up like this."

He levered the body up into a sitting position. I pressed my hands against her shoulder blades. She was ice-cold. Her skin felt slippery and it made me think of fish, the belly of a pike. Her head fell heavily against her chest.

"What's this, then?"

High up on her right arm, behind her shoulder, were some black craters. Round, bloody puncture marks from something sharp. The pastor checked her blouse and discovered that it had corresponding holes. Small bloodstains showed where the skin had been pierced. The pastor took out his ruler and measured the marks precisely, and their distance one from another. Lower down on her back three parallel cuts were also visible. The pastor measured and I wrote the figures down.

"The bear's claws," I whispered in horror.

"Mm."

"It bit her and scratched her!"

He regarded me without a word. Then he did something that made me gasp. He quietly laid his hands round the girl's neck with his thumbs on her throat, slowly twisting round so that he could look at the bruises from different angles.

"Look carefully, Jussi. Can you see that the bruises tally with human hands?"

"But—but what about the claw marks?"

"Done with the blade of a knife. And the bite marks on the shoulder were made with its point. You can see from the clothes that the skin bled very little. In other words, the injuries were inflicted when she was already dead."

"So you mean . . . ?"

"Somebody wanted us to believe it was a killer bear."

I leaned closer to her neck. And now I saw that the pastor was right: there was no way the ugly bruises could have come from a bear's jaws. Silently we buttoned up her dress and laid the body out straight again.

The pastor glanced though my notes and put them in his jacket pocket. We stood in silence, trying to regain our composure. I felt ashamed, and I could see the pastor felt the same. We had crossed over a line. He carefully blew out the candle by her head.

At that moment we heard someone rattling the door, and I hurried over to remove the broom handle. The old woman stomped back in and was about to shout out but changed her mind when she caught sight of the pastor. He was kneeling on the sauna floor beside the dead woman. His hands were clasped together and in a low voice he was praying for her poor soul, that it should be at peace. His face gave no hint of what we had been doing, and when he raised his eyes his voice was as strong and clear as in the pulpit.

"We wished to be left alone!"

"I know, Reverend, I know. But the sheriff has arrived."

The woman scrambled to the side as the bulky form of Brahe squeezed into the sauna room. He was a head taller than the pastor, a head that was wide and fleshy and would have looked good on a sire bull. His eyes were small and beady under pale bushy eyebrows. His uniform jacket was undone and he, obviously suffering from the summer heat, had stuck two fingers under his collar. The backs of his hands were covered with coarse black hairs, not unlike insects' legs, and after he had wiped the perspiration from his forehead and his bulging cheeks, his face still glistened.

"And what is going on here?" he bawled in Swedish.

His voice was loud, but it was also hoarse, years of military bellowing having wrought their effect. With self-assured authority he stopped in the middle of the room like a boulder in a stream. Everything around him fell into line. Even the pastor pattered around until he'd adopted a suitable position.

"It was Jussi and I who found the girl," he announced.

For some reason this annoyed the sheriff. Waving his arms like a swimmer, he shooed us aside and pushed his way to the bier.

"Oh, bloody hell," he said. "Bloody hell . . ."

The old lady flinched at the curses and glanced over at the pastor to see his reaction. But we stood waiting while Brahe poked at the body with evident distaste.

"Yes, she's definitely damn well dead," he said.

He leaned forward with his hand over his large-pored nose to shield himself from the stench of death. But the smell that met him was of acid water and damp peat. He looked hurriedly around, found the sauna ladle, and pushed the woman's chin up.

"She's been bitten around her neck. Poor lass."

"It's most unlikely they're bite marks," said the pastor, but the sheriff stopped him with a toss of his hand.

"Anyone thinking of interfering with my examination can leave!"

His voice sounded thick with snot under his palm; he blew his nose directly into his hand and wiped it on the sauna bench.

"Turn her!" he ordered the old lady.

She tiptoed up, visibly shaking in the presence of these two important officials. As quickly as she could, she eased the cloth away from the top half of the body and revealed the back. With the handle of the ladle the sheriff tapped the wounds on the shoulder.

"Bear teeth," he said. "The brute bit her in the shoulder and then dragged his prey down into the bog pool. To eat later."

"She was . . . There was a broken hayrack post there as well."

"It must've been there since the harvest."

"It looked as though it had been used to push the body down."

The sheriff took a deep breath and glared at the pastor. Who was considerably smaller in stature and nearly twenty years older. But despite the physical disadvantage, I could see the pastor's anger was beginning to mount. He tilted his head back and stared at his opponent. Brahe took no notice of him but raised his voice even more.

"So it was the pastor who found the girl?"

"That's correct."

"The pastor. And that young Lapp boy over there."

The sheriff made a sweeping gesture in my direction.

"Jussi accompanied me. We examined the barn first and noticed at once that the hay had been compressed, as if someone had been lying on it. We found a mountain plant in the hay and some strands of hair we believe came from Hilda Fredriksdotter."

"How the hell do you know that? All women have hair."

"Sheriff Brahe may care to examine the girl's scalp."

"You attend to your job and I'll attend to mine."

The pastor looked as though he had a venomous retort to deliver, but made a visible effort to keep his lips closed. Instead he did an about-turn and walked briskly out of the sauna.

"And you too!" the sheriff said to me. "Unless you want to hear it in Lappish as well?"

He took aim with the ladle and I bolted after the pastor. Behind me I could hear the old woman clattering with the buckets and spooning out hot water.

12.

GLOOM AND FEAR SPREAD THROUGH THE DISTRICT. A YOUNG person had lost her life and at the end of each day people hurried home, anxiously keeping an eye on the undergrowth at the sides of the roads and paths. The collection for a reward for anyone who could slay the killer bear continued, with generous contributions arriving from near and far. Bait and traps were laid in the forests.

One daybreak the calm was shattered by a tortured bellowing. Bleary-eyed men with axes and iron bars rushed out into the woods, where it proved to be the sound of a handsome dairy cow from the nearby farm who had gotten caught in an iron trap. Its leg was broken and the poor creature had to be killed, so the farmer's wife had no choice but to stand in the farmyard whisking its blood, her tears trickling into the pail.

Sheriff Brahe relished the limelight as he paraded around the farms with Constable Michelsson in tow. This was a far cry from reports of theft and false accusations and covert boundary changes, the sort of thing that would usually occupy the majority of his time. He was served regular meals and brandy in the evenings, while the constable jotted down everything that needed to be sent to the powers that be. Hunting plans were drawn up, battues moved noisily from village to village, and bear sightings by cow-girls and villagers were monitored.

EARLY ONE MORNING WHEN the pastor was still in bed asleep, a visitor came to see him. It was a boy from one of the tenant farms; he must have been about ten and was so nervous he was trembling slightly as he drank from a birch-bark ladle. With the pastor's children flocking around him, he gulped it down and was given a refill. Selma tried to worm out of him why he had come, but the boy sensed his own momentary importance and waited patiently for the pastor. Brita Kajsa asked the parsonage housemaid to give him a piece of bread. He seized on it eagerly but didn't eat it, putting it instead into his trouser pocket. Then he sat down on the kitchen step and let his gaze wander around the parsonage, wanting to imprint every detail on his mind so he could recount it to his brothers and sisters. He marveled in particular at the metal pans, the shining copper dishes from Norway embossed with an animal pattern of deer and sheep among stylized trees. And in the middle of the flock of cloven-hoofed animals lay a terrifying lion with its teeth bared. It was right beside its prey; the next meal was chewing the cud by the side of the lion's claws. The whole scene radiated unearthly peace. It represented Paradise, the pastor had explained. The world before the fall of man. And, indeed, on the other dish a man and woman were sitting sharing a piece of fruit with a snake hanging from the branch of a tree. You wanted to grab hold of them and shake them, scream a warning before it was too late. But the young couple divided their fruit and the sweet taste flooded their palates with pleasure. And very soon the idyll surrounding them would all be gone.

The pastor finally emerged wearing a carelessly buttoned shirt and running his hand through his hair. The boy instantly rose to his feet, obviously scared in the presence of this great public figure. He pressed his slender back against the doorpost and bowed deeply.

"I bring a message to the reverend that the beast has been captured."

It sounded as though he'd been rehearsing the sentence. An adult had clearly given him instruction.

"What beast?" the pastor asked.

"The beast has been captured," he repeated.

"You mean . . . ?"

"The beast that ate up the girl. It was caught in the night. They want the pastor to come and verify it."

It was clear the boy was loath to use the word "bear." The pastor nodded hurriedly and asked the boy to wait for him to get ready. I had been prepared for departure for some time.

"Was it big?" I asked. "Did you see it with your own eyes?"

The boy kept his lips tightly sealed. Then he nodded smugly and scratched his dirty, mosquito-bitten ankles.

THE HUNT FOR THE killer bear had been going on ever since the reward was announced. A number of enterprising farmers had acquired an enormous iron trap with crudely serrated jaws. This grim instrument was buried and carefully camouflaged. The bait was laid next to it, a rancid pile of entrails retained after the slaughter of a pig, the stench of which carried far and wide and attracted foxes and crows. But soon the killer bear found the scent too and came closer, swiftly dispersing the smaller animals. When the creature lumbered up, followed by her two cubs, she stepped straight into the trap. Her paw sank into the iron jaws of the concealed snare and they slammed shut in a vise-like grip.

In the middle of the night the people on the nearest farm heard what sounded like someone shrieking out in the forest and their dogs began to show signs of agitation. They waited until dawn, summoned their neighbors and other villagers, and armed themselves with whatever was at hand. In trepidation they then made their way to the site. After stealthy inspection they were able to ascertain that the beast was trapped. One shot was fired from a rifle and, after a lengthy reloading procedure, a second, with the sole effect of making the beast even more ferocious. Moving close enough to strike it with an ax would have been suicidal, and no one had a spear. In the end they cut down some of the smaller fir trees. The branches were lopped off and the trunks used as clubs to rain down a storm of blows on the hairy skull. Blood gushed into its eyes, almost blinding the creature, with the result that some of the boldest men were able to go right up to it and hack at the bear's front legs with their axes. After several attempts they managed to sever the sinews in the hind legs too. Now that the animal no longer had the means to stand upright, the others could get close enough to rain blows until it breathed its last.

THE BEAR LAY IN a shaggy heap on the moss. The strong odor from the pig entrails was now mixed with the iron smell of blood. The animal had been severely mutilated, and the head was misshapen from all the ax blows. The eyeballs had been pushed out like boiled eggs, one of them dangling on a whitish stalk. Everyone was agreed, it was the right animal. The two cubs, who of course were also tainted by human flesh, were dispatched with well-aimed buckshot. Like hairy fruit, they tried to cling to the snag of a pine tree, before they came thudding down to share their mother's fate.

The farmers and workers closest to the scene danced around, intoxicated with pride. Smoke from a smoldering fire drove away the mosquitoes and blowflies, not to mention the swarms of horseflies attracted by the smell of blood. The pastor riffled through his pockets for a piece of paper and a pencil stump. He slowly walked round the animal, viewing it from every angle as he made notes. Because his expression was closed and introspective, it was impossible to discern what he was thinking. He asked the men to turn the animal onto its back. They took hold of the beast reticently, as though it might still make a lunge. With their combined force they managed to tip the body over into a supine position, its limbs akimbo. Now they could see the size of it, as long as the tallest of men and impressively broad across the chest. The body bore an uncomfortable resemblance to a human being, with its arms and legs stretched out, and its naked genitals. Its jaw was half open, the massive canines shining like dagger blades, shaped for slaughter and destruction. Hanging in the fur were the teats the cubs had licked and tugged. The pastor bent down and examined the bear's mouth. He sniffed at it like a dog. With both hands he prized the jaws apart and took various measurements with a small folding ruler he found in his inside pocket. He wrote down the figures on the piece of paper and pondered as he filled his clay pipe.

"Open her up," he said.

The men looked at one another askance. Not one of them had any experience of slaughtering bears. Somewhat reluctantly, one of them took out his knife and poked it into the belly. With difficulty he cut through the tough pelt from the rib cage down to the crotch. This exposed the innards, the convoluted coils of violet and gray. The pastor passed the writing implements to me, took off his jacket, and sank to his knees. He rolled up his shirtsleeves and at that point seemed to hesitate, but then he plunged his arms in up to the elbows and began to pull out the bear's long guts. The men helped by folding back the skin so that it was easier for the pastor to empty the abdomen. Still with his pipe in his mouth, the pastor gripped his pocketknife and cut through the membranous stomach wall. A grayish sludge spilled out onto the ground. Everyone recoiled at the putrid stench and someone could be heard retching. The pastor vigorously puffed smoke from his pipe and bent forward, the better to study the half-digested contents. He stirred them with his knife and turned to me.

"Plant components, write that down. Roots, leaves, stalks. This bear's diet appears to have consisted entirely of vegetables."

"But it was attracted by the bait," one of the farmers protested.

The pastor looked skeptical. He took out another ruler from his inside pocket, measured the bear's claws, and made a note. Then he straightened his back and wiped his hands, while simultaneously drawing deeply on his pipe. The smoke streamed from his nostrils as he looked around.

"We'll hear what the sheriff's opinion is," he said, gesturing into the distance.

The men turned to see the heavy, thickset shape of the sheriff making its way through the undergrowth. Constable Michelsson followed in his wake, and several paces behind them both, with a sizable pack on his back, came the artist Nils Gustaf. The village folk fell silent and respectfully moved aside. When the sheriff caught sight of the pastor, he greeted him guardedly, before walking with a wide-legged gait up to the she-bear and prodding her with his toe cap.

"Who's responsible?" he asked peremptorily. Like many people in authority he took pleasure in intimidation and assuming command. Cap in hand, the men said nothing.

"Evil be to him who evil does," the sheriff continued tersely, wiping the perspiration from his face.

The constable plucked at the cubs' fur and grinned.

"Two little man-eaters into the bargain, hee-hee," he sniggered.

"Well, I assume you'll be claiming the reward," the sheriff said to the men. "In which case you can stand your hand to a celebratory nip."

The men eyed each other and then the pastor. They attempted to laugh, if only to dispel the fear that had just crept into them. A bottle was ferreted out and tossed to the sheriff, who took several deep swigs. It was offered to the constable and Nils Gustaf as well, while the pastor looked on in disgust. Coughing and clearing his throat, the sheriff took out his thick purse and walloped it against his thigh, before ceremoniously counting out several large banknotes and silver coins. Michelsson was given the task of writing up each reward on expensive watermarked paper and the villagers were instructed to wash the blood off before they nervously gripped the quill to sign the receipt. The constable helped them direct the nib to the right place and then blotted it with some fine sand from a little jar.

"What are we going to do with the skin?" someone ventured to ask.

"That's the Crown's booty," the sheriff said. "The skin belongs to the king."

He grabbed the brandy bottle again and took one last draft.

"Though under the circumstances . . . of course you can bloody well have the skin!"

"And . . . do we have a right to the rest as well?" asked a man with crossed eyes.

"What do you mean by 'the rest'?"

The sheriff gazed round imperiously.

"You don't mean you're going to eat the bloody thing? You're going to tuck into a man-eater!"

"Only the cubs," the cross-eyed man argued. "We've never tasted bear before and people say it has a strong flavor."

"The meat's supposed to be stringy, but it has medicinal properties," said another.

"Yes, stringy," the cross-eyed man echoed. "We're hungry and we thought we could cook the bears."

He glanced hopefully at the man in uniform. The brandy had begun to take its effect and now Brahe couldn't stop himself. He broke into a belly laugh and the constable sniggered too.

"Well, I'm not one to split hairs! They say bear meat tastes like a cross between pork and grouse. And the only suitable drink to accompany it is brandy, the stronger the better!"

"'A cross between pork and grouse,' hee-hee," the constable said with a chuckle.

While the men had been drinking, the pastor's face had grown redder and redder. Now he took a step forward.

"I would like to keep the bear's cranium," he muttered. "For research purposes."

"The cubs' as well?"

"No, just the she-bear's. The actual skull."

"Take the damn thing. But we need a receipt. Michelsson, can you arrange that?"

The pastor put on his spectacles and signed the chit. Meanwhile, I drew my knife and prepared to skin the bear's head.

"Stop there!" came a sonorous voice.

It was Nils Gustaf. While all this had been going on he had rigged up his stand, taken out his sketch paper and pencils, and was now stepping round us in search of suitable angles.

"This heroic deed must be immortalized for posterity. Would you all please position yourselves as though the bear were still alive? As though it were about to attack you."

The artist's words were translated into Finnish. With a degree of commotion, the she-bear was turned back onto her stomach and arranged into as threatening a pose as it was possible to achieve.

"And I'd like the sheriff to stand close to the beast."

The aforesaid had nothing against being painted. He adjusted his cap and dressed his mustache with a little brush.

"Does the sheriff not have his saber?" asked Nils Gustaf. "To smite the attacking bear?"

Nils Gustaf could already see the painting in his mind's eye. The drawn saber would be angled so that it reflected the light, and become an almost metaphysical symbol, a lightning flash. But since the sheriff only carried his saber on high days and holidays, the blade of a scythe removed from its snead handle had to suffice. The men were placed in various poses and the sheriff was invited to suggest which one he himself preferred, as the artist sketched with his charcoal pencil. Swift sweeps of color were created by oil crayons, mainly green and brown, and dramatic emphasis was added with the bear's red blood. The size of the bear's mouth was exaggerated, as was the length of its teeth, and he allowed the villagers to take up various heroic poses with their axes and cudgels. All were instructed to remain perfectly still while the artist reproduced this dreadful battle between man and bear.

When the sketches were finished the slaughter began. Evidently satisfied with the day's proceedings, the sheriff took off his boots and sat with Nils Gustaf in the smoke from the fire. In a high Swedish that few of those present could understand they started to entertain one another with anecdotes of their travels. Stories of chasing reindeer-stealers and set-tos with local villains, dallying with loose women in urban settings. Constable Michelsson feigned preoccupation with the accounts but listened, all agog. I turned my attention to the bear's skull. With great care I extricated it from the precious skin. The skull itself was difficult to cut away from the neck vertebrae, but eventually I had the grisly, flesh-covered cranium in my arms. It was surprisingly heavy. I tied some sticks together so that I could carry it over my shoulder and then followed the pastor, who was already on his way to the parsonage.

13.

BEFORE LONG THE ENTIRE PARISH KNEW WHAT HAD HAPPENED. Here in the villages and hamlets of the north where major incidents seldom occurred, the bear hunt had been a long-awaited event. Everyone was relieved the killer bear had been captured and slain. The villagers who had done the deed became the region's heroes and they had to replay, again and again, the nighttime drama in which they had risked their lives. The foundry owner Sohlberg purchased the bearskins from the men and had them sent to the tannery as a trophy of the feat, to be hung on the wall in the manor house.

The pastor asked me to boil the bear's skull. The cranium looked gruesome with its shreds of flesh and maked, staring eyeballs, one dangling from its socket. I hauled the large pan out of the barn into a corner of the yard and poured several buckets of water into it. From the woodshed I brought the pastor's ax, the one forged at the Kengis foundry and bearing his initials etched on the ax-head. With rapid blows I cut the kindling and ripped off some birch bark. The flames soon rose beneath the black pot and after a while the first bubbles could be seen breaking the surface.

In the heat, the sour stench of slaughter disappeared. Instead, the steam rising from the simmering fat and meat smelled like a potful of Brita Kajsa's reindeer stew. The surface turned white with scum at first and subsequently gray with rolling brown bubbles. I skimmed off the foam with my *guksi* and threw it onto the grass. Tjalmo the dog was there in a flash to lick it up. The pot was boiling so fiercely that it splashed over the rim and made the fire sputter. I spread the firewood out a little when the meat appeared to have stopped frothing and the water cleared, revealing the white parietal lobe. The skull was not smooth as mine was, but striated with distinct grooves and ridges. With a birch stick I turned the skull so that it cooked evenly and didn't burn and stick to the bottom. It didn't take long for the scalp to come loose and shrivel up. I tried to scrape off the softened flesh with pieces of wood; the pastor had asked me to be careful and not damage the cranium. When they had cooled, I tossed the scraps to Tjalmo, who pounced eagerly on the tasty morsels. It was fascinating to see how the skull was constructed. There was a good deal of meat in the powerful jaw muscles where the lower jaw was attached. I hesitated at first, but then I drew my knife and cut a piece off. I looked around furtively, but there was no one around to see. The meat was dark, the color of liver, with a strong but not unpleasant smell. I quickly put it in my mouth. The man-killer. The meat was not completely cooked and I had to chew it well and for some time before I managed to swallow it. It wasn't exactly tasty. But now I had done it. I had the creature inside me.

The lower jaw soon loosened from the vigorous boiling, and I was able to start scraping off the gums to uncover the full length of the white canines. As I was doing this, I saw the pastor approaching. He shooed Tjalmo away, and the dog lowered her tail and backed off. With the aid of the birch stick, I lifted the cranium out of the bubbling broth so that he could inspect it.

"Good." He nodded. "Very good."

I carefully placed the hot bear skull on the grass, where it lay steaming as if on fire. The pastor took out a piece of paper covered in notations and studied them in silence. I recognized my handwriting. They were the notes relating to Hilda Fredriksdotter's dead body.

"Give me the lower jaw as well."

I gave it to him. With a ruler he measured the exact distance between the eyeteeth, both in the separated lower jaw and in the cranium itself. He then compared them with our measurements.

"The measurements don't correspond," he said.

"So it wasn't the bear?"

The pastor was stony-faced.

"I just wanted to be sure. I think the puncture wounds on the girl were made with the point of a knife after her death."

"But why?"

"So we would think it was the bear. You saw the cuts on the girl's back. If they had been made by a bear's claws, the marks would have been parallel. But you could tell the cuts had been made one after the other and, in addition, that the cloth of her dress moved position after every cut."

The pastor pulled Tjalmo toward him and tickled her under the chin. She licked his broth-scented fingers greedily.

"If the bear had wanted meat, it would have taken one of the cows," he went on. "I had my doubts about the bear story from the beginning."

"What about the claw marks on the tree? Didn't the bear scratch the tree trunk where the girl stopped to rest?"

"They were done with a knife too."

"How can the pastor be so sure?"

He held up the little pocket ruler.

"I measured the claw marks on the tree and they didn't match the measurements of the bear's paws at all. No, the killer bear we feared is walking about in human form."

"How did the pastor know that Hilda was hidden in the bog?"

"I didn't know."

"Does the pastor mean the perpetrator is still at large?"

The pastor nodded slowly.

"Imagine, Jussi. A man sees a girl on her own and is seized with carnal lust. Somehow, he lures her to the hay barn. There, he pulls her in. She resists. He strangles her. Immediately he realizes what he's done. To cover up his deed, he lays the blame on the bear. He simulates the slashes of a bear's claws and teeth before pushing her into the bog. And on the way back, he scores claw marks into the tree."

"But . . . can any man be so calculating?"

"It would seem so."

"We have to tell the sheriff!"

"Sheriff Brahe's report is already written. I've seen it myself. Hilda Fredriksdotter Alatalo's body exhibits evidence of a bear's teeth marks together with injuries sustained from a bear's paw. Bears are known to trample their quarry into the bog and this demonstrates the prowess of the seasoned brute that had to be dealt with. The creature wanted to tenderize the flesh and at the same time hide it from other beasts of prey."

"Does he even believe it himself?"

"You and I know the truth, Jussi. A man of violence roams free out there. A killer bear in human form. And when a bear has developed a taste for human flesh, what happens then?"

"It wants to have more?"

The pastor didn't respond. Instead he borrowed my knife and bent over the cranium. The skull had been crushed by the violent blows of the hunters' bludgeons and he carefully broke off the loose splinters and laid them out on the grass. I turned the skull upside down as he painstakingly prodded around the membranes with the point of the knife, and with a slurping noise the brain came away and slid onto the grass like a soft-boiled egg. It was squishy and wobbly, surprisingly small for an animal of such prodigious size. He leaned forward and studied the brain more closely, gently stroking the tip of his finger along the twisting corrugations.

"Do you think it's in here? Can you identify it, Jussi?"

I didn't understand what he meant.

"The soul," he said. "The bear's soul?"

He closed his hands around the brain. It had cooled sufficiently for him not to be scalded. He cautiously lifted it up as if it were a quivering egg and started to carry it toward the parsonage.

I didn't know what he intended to do with it. Draw it, perhaps? Or show it to his daughters? He was in a hurry, full of eagerness, and didn't notice Tjalmo fawning at his feet. The pastor stumbled over her and with a loud cry let go of the brain as he tried to regain his balance. The moment the bear's brain hit the ground, the tyke darted forward and in one swift gulp half of it had disappeared. The pastor was left frowning at the remnants in his hands. He looked at them from different angles, picking at them gently, before shaking off the slimy residue with an ill-tempered flick of his wrists.

14.

The funeral service for Hilda Fredriksdotter Alatalo was held on a Saturday. The church was full, curiosity intense. The coffin lid was open, and muffled sobs came from the pews. The girl's parents approached the bier, their backs bowed by sorrow. The father was old and thin, his face ashen, as if drained of blood. He laid his trembling hand over the clasped hands of his lifeless daughter and patted them clumsily before plucking at them as if he were trying to make her rise up out of the coffin. The mother dabbed at her eyes incessantly, her weeping utterly silent, but her tears soaked the funeral handkerchief she used to wipe her cheeks. Beside them stood the girl's only brother, a tall, strange boy. It was obvious he was a half-wit; he kept buttoning and unbuttoning his black coat, which was far too short in the sleeves. Perhaps because he had never worn anything with such fine buttons before. His lips were shining with spittle and he kept swallowing, but to no avail; it might have been his way of weeping. Now he was the only one his parents had left; God had not blessed them with more children.

The congregation was excited at the prospect of the pastor's sermon. Sheriff Brahe sat at the front in his uniform. He acknowledged the churchgoers' thanks with a curt nod to each one, an action that caused his blubbery cheeks to wobble, while he endeavored to maintain an air of solemnity and concern. When the pastor began to speak, they exchanged glances like arrows through the air. Then the sheriff turned his gaze to the altarpiece, puffing his cheeks out in a conspicuous fashion. Did he have something trapped in his teeth that made him so obviously distracted at the prospect of the litany? Constable Michelsson sat beside him, fingering the hymnbook.

The pastor spoke of summer's brief flowering. The prettiest summer blossoms felled by the scythe, seemingly to no purpose. But at another time, under winter's heavens, this dried hay would give life. In due course the victim would be a blessing sent by God and have her purpose.

I tried to listen but my mind drifted away. She had taken her place on the opposite side of the aisle. My beloved. She hadn't looked at me once; to her I was less than air. But that didn't matter to me, I delighted in just seeing her. In the manner of fingertips stroking a pebble polished by waves, its curves so soft that they feel like music, I held the edge of my little finger against my cheek, where she had touched it. My skin remembered.

And in the midst of all of this I seemed to have slipped into a dream. We were still in church, but now I was the one in the coffin. I lay there dead, my hands clasped, in the middle of the church, in full view of the congregation. The pastor was looking at me and so was the sheriff. Everyone in the pews was watching me. My beloved likewise; even her gaze was resting on me, and now it was filled with sorrow. Something bad had befallen me. I had done something, carried out some daring and admirable deed that no one had expected of me. And now they were all thinking: Who was he really? Why did I never get to know him? If only I'd known what was going on in his heart. . . . But now it was all too late. My body would be lowered into the darkness of the grave, and they would say to one another:

"Have you ever wondered how such a quiet person, someone so unassuming . . . could achieve something so great?"

I was roused from my dream by a dry rustling, the sound of the pastor pouring three scoops of sand onto the coffin lid. A feeling of shame rose up in me; I had let myself be moved by a thirst for glory. And yet, despite the sinfulness of my thoughts, they left a sweet taste that gave me a faint thrill.

I would show them. Somehow I would make them see me. I just didn't yet know how.

15.

THE PASTOR DEEMED IT TIMELY TO ASSESS THE TEACHING HE HAD instituted for a few weeks of summer in Kangosfors. We took up our positions in the narrow canoe belonging to the parsonage—I gripped the pole while the pastor rowed—and with arduous effort we made our way upstream to the confluence with the Lainio River. The water level was still quite high and the rapids caused us some trouble, but the flat-bottomed boat always slid over the stones into a new stretch of smooth water. Along the most difficult stretches we received help from local people, far more skilled at poling than I was, people who were glad to help their priest. The Lainio was narrower and shallower than the Torne and in several places the pastor wanted to go ashore to investigate the mountain plants that had taken root along the banks, washed here from distant uplands.

The summer lessons in Kangosfors were held in a simple timber structure that, judging by the smell, was normally used to house animals. We were met by Herr Mattsson, a serious gentleman, with a crooked neck caused by a fall that had rendered him unsuited to heavy manual labor. He had been appointed by the pastor to teach the youngest children, despite having significant problems reading himself. The previous incumbent had been Juhani Raattamaa, who was now teaching up in Lainio Village. It was said of Juhani that he surpassed even the pastor as a teacher, and that his oratory was so great that it provoked a religious revival among the pupils. Visitors came from far and wide to see the "crazy" students who might be lying on the floor writhing in remorse or grown so feeble they could no longer stand, or even leaping around in their wild blessedness. If one of the pupils behaved badly, Juhani simply took him in his arms and spoke calmly and gently, and it wasn't long before he made the child cry. He never needed to use the cane, as so many other catechists did.

Mattsson didn't possess Raattamaa's talent for inspiring children, but on the other hand, he was equipped with a blistering memory. He could rattle off almost verbatim many of the texts and sermons he had heard the pastor deliver.

"How is the work going in our young vineyard?" the pastor greeted him heartily.

Mattsson bowed as deeply as his stiff neck allowed and showed us into the schoolroom. I counted twelve boys, but only two girls.

"The Waara sisters are sick and bedridden," he explained.

"Is it bad?"

"It could be tuberculosis. I've requested that they stay at home to prevent it from spreading."

The children sat in twos, each with a slate onto which they were laboriously trying to copy the words Mattsson had written earlier on his own. When they saw us coming in, they stood up and bowed. Most of the boys were barefoot, now that it was summer. As they gripped the chalk and drew shaky lines, their hands looked rough. The pastor wasn't always able to interpret their writing, but he made encouraging noises. On Mattsson's board were the words: KEEP THE SABATH DAY HOLLY.

"We're going through the Ten Commandments," he explained a mite nervously.

The pastor rubbed out the second *L*.

"It's 'holy' with one *l*. And 'Sabbath' has two *b*'s."

"Sorry, Pastor."

"It's not easy."

Not one of the pupils dared to laugh. In silence they spat on their thumbs and corrected the spelling mistakes on their slates. They were peasant youngsters and Finnish-speaking like Mattsson, and the only books in their homes were the Bible and Martin Luther's *Small Catechism*. During the annual catechistical examinations, the pastor met their parents, many of whom could barely write their name. When the pastor asked them to read from a hymn, they pretended to follow the lines with their finger, while reciting the words from memory. It was clear they had memorized them before the pastor's visit. The Ten Commandments, Luther's explanations, the confession, and Our Father. Perhaps some of it had stuck from confirmation classes, perhaps a snippet or two from the pastor's sermons as well. But seldom anything that might be akin to theology. *Ordo salutis*, the order of salvation, was really known only to the awakened. And conversion meant nothing more than calling yourself a Christian. You might easily form the impression that the farm maid or the reindeer herder lacked the disposition for academic study. But even though they didn't read books, they knew the changes in the movement of animals at every moment in the year. They knew hundreds of reindeer marks by heart, and managed to find old pasture grounds, berry patches, and fishing lakes all the way from the high mountains to the coastline. They could give the details of all their kin to the third or fourth degree, build a house with only an ax, and sew the warmest clothes with threads of sinew. There was nothing wrong with their memory. In many matters, local people had a deeper understanding than all of Uppsala's professors.

But a new age was dawning, the pastor said. Why couldn't children from Tornedalen tenant farms become priests or teachers? The pastor and his brothers Carl-Erik and Petrus had achieved it, despite poverty and a childhood spent at the foot of the mountains. With knowledge, the people of the north could look forward to a brighter future. The peasant farmers could learn new and better methods of cultivation, gain awareness of new crops, animal husbandry, and processing and storage of food. Diseases could be tackled in a scientific way, medicines developed, infant mortality reduced. And with more education, the drinking would diminish, the pastor was convinced. A literate populace would rather buy books than brandy. And it all started with the children, with their crooked lines on the slates.

"The chalk has nearly run out," Mattsson whispered.

"Already?"

"Maybe the children are pressing too hard."

"Well, I've been promised a donation from someone's estate. I'll remind the bereaved relatives. And your salary will be paid very soon. I apologize for the delay."

"Thank you, Pastor."

"Thank our Lord."

We stopped beside one of the boys. He was blond and slight, mouse-like. He raised his shoulders and tensed himself as if anticipating a cuff on the ear.

"What is your name, my child?"

"Feeto," he whispered.

"But you were baptized Fredrik, weren't you? What do you think you'll be when you're big, Fredrik?"

He didn't answer. The other pupils stared at him inquisitively, expecting a punishment, perhaps.

"When you're grown up?" the pastor tried again. "Have you ever thought you might like to be a priest yourself?"

Several of his classmates began to giggle. The boy lifted his face, his eyebrows so fair you could hardly see them. His eyes were azure.

"I was a boy too once," the pastor went on. "A little boy who couldn't read. And today I know both Greek and Latin. Say '*Ordo salutis*.'"

"*Ordo sa . . . lutis . . .*"

"It's Latin and it means 'the order of salvation.' The order of salvation is like a staircase in front of us, extremely high and extremely steep. And Jesus Christ is at the very top. Can you imagine him? The light is almost too bright to look, but Jesus Christ is standing there with his arms wide open, waiting for us all. And, step by step, we can make our way there."

"Is there any food there?" somebody muttered.

"Yes, lots of food for everyone who's hungry."

"Butter as well?"

Mattsson was about to hit the boy, one of the older lads, whose lank, greasy hair hung over his forehead.

"Mountains of butter," said the pastor. "And there are reindeer steaks and pike, salmon and huge capercaillies. And freshly baked bread and enormous golden cheeses."

I could almost see the children's mouths watering. The pastor pretended to sniff at the smell of food as if it were coming from the roof.

"And we can all enter," he said.

"Yes," Mattsson concurred.

"He who opens his heart to God the Father will be seated at his right hand."

Mattsson closed his eyes as if in prayer.

"Is it only priests who can enter?" asked the lank-haired lad.

"No, everyone," the priest said. "All of you sitting here."

"But first you have to die," someone was heard saying.

The pastor looked at the white-haired boy, who stared back, but with no trace of insolence or facetiousness. Only earnest gravity.

The child had the look of an angel, seeming to see the truth so much more clearly than the others. The pastor was eager to take this boy into his charge, sit down with him at a table with a stack of books. Show him everything of beauty and grandeur in the world. The plants and the soil, the climate, psychology, philosophy, and not least the art of oratory that gives us a way into people's hearts. The young needed to be educated so that they could take over, when one day the old hung up their boots. The region needed pioneers who, with wisdom and tenacity, could lead the flock forward.

"Before we die, we have to live," the pastor responded. "And in order to live rich and responsible lives, we have to acquire knowledge. Did you know, for example, that you can propel boats with boiling water? It happens in America, and even in the south of Sweden. You introduce water into an engine. Then the engine starts to work and it produces enough power to propel an entire ship."

"What's an engine?"

"Something that can move by itself."

"So are people engines too?" the lad asked.

"No, we're not."

"Why not?"

Mattsson reached for the stick hanging on the wall. It was enough to silence the boy. With a sweep of his hand the pastor gestured toward the world outside the school window.

"An engine cannot feel anything. It has no conscience. A person, on the other hand, can choose to do good, to help others. It is you, my dear children, who can raise our lands out of poverty. Our diet will improve, and our homes too. Cows are going to give twice as much milk. Disease and drunkenness will be resisted. It is you who will lead us into a better age."

"Amen," Mattsson rounded off.

The children hastily put their hands together and said, "Amen," as well. The pastor appeared to be searching inwardly for an appropriate phrase from the Bible, but none came. Instead he let his gaze travel across the troop of children, their naked feet, their small, strong hands, their high cheekbones and scurvy scalps. They could have been helping with the animals at home, but they were sitting here at school. The region's future. This was what it looked like.

DURING OUR JOURNEY BACK downstream, the pastor talked about the future. He was of the opinion that the world had to change fundamentally. For many nations, the French Revolution of 1789 had led to struggle and travail; godlessness and depravity had caused violence and oppression. Man without Christianity was worse than a tiger; no one was spared.

"Following the initial delirium of freedom there is tyranny and barbarism. I fear there are more great revolutions to come. And even though old, outdated governments fall, there is always some ambitious new blackguard with his sights on power. And that is why we will never suffer from a lack of tyrants."

"But what about religious revival?" I asked. "Isn't that a revolution too?"

"Yes, certainly. But it is an inner revolution. Instead of overthrowing those in power, the battle is with inner tyrants. With self-righteousness, arrogance, pride, with desire for ostentation and carnal pleasures. Only when inner demons are brought down and slain can society undergo a lasting change. You heard the schoolchildren, Jussi, you heard their dreams. They talked about food. And of course we need food, that's true, but man needs spiritual sustenance too. On top of your stomach sits a soul, Jussi. And when the soul is hungry, it's not enough to bend your stiff neck and bow your head in the church pew and pray for forgiveness of your sins in accordance with the service book. It's like going to the shop and buying barley sugar and bringing the sweets home in a paper cone. You can eat them, but they won't sate your hunger."

The pastor continued to speak about the school, how in the future all the crofters and Sami would send their children to school and the poorest of families would be able to produce a master of philosophy, or even a professor. I kept the boat in the current, murmuring an answer now and then, but my thoughts turned in a different direction. In my head I could see my beloved. Her soft red lips against mine. Hunger.

16.

IN THE SUMMER, SAP RISES IN THE TREES. EGGS BECOME BIRDS THAT fill the sky; great clouds of insects hatch. The antlers on the bull elk's head grow longer; the salmon in the river splash and climb. Light flows continuously through every hour, making the summer one extended day, perpetual light that lasts for months. This is a good time to be living in the north.

The pastor was kneeling in the moss. He was studying a *Carex* and jotting down notes on a crumpled piece of paper. Suddenly a bee landed on his pencil. Perhaps the movement of the pencil was the attraction, perhaps there were traces of salt on his fingers. With a smooth swipe he caught the bee in his hand. I waited for the grimace of pain when it stung him, but the pastor only grinned. He let the downy little chap crawl out, holding it between his thumb and forefinger as he handed me the magnifying glass. I leaned forward and could see that its legs were covered with tiny hairs carrying golden orbs.

"Pollen," said the pastor. "From hundreds of flowers."

I returned the magnifying glass. He wanted to give me the bee, but I shook my head.

"It'll sting."

"No," the pastor said. "Not this one. It's a male."

I was suspicious, thinking it was a trick. Nevertheless, I cautiously took hold of the bee in my fingers. He was strong, thrashing to get free, his wings glimmering in the sunshine. And the pastor was right, he didn't sting me.

"The males are lighter. It's only the females that have a sting. It's her tube-like ovipositor that is converted into a syringe of poison, as I learned in Uppsala."

Warily, I loosened my fingers. For a second the bee sat perfectly still, as if taken by surprise. Then his flashing wings whirred into action and he toppled back into the greenery.

For a while we sat undisturbed, while the pastor lit his pipe. The sweet scent of the smoke smelled good and dispersed the horseflies drawn to our bare necks.

"I always have my son in mind when I see the bees," he said. "My little Levi. You should have seen him running about. He was the sort of toddler who would stand up under the kitchen table and when he hit his head on the tabletop and collapsed in tears, he would immediately stand up again. He was so full of force, the same appetite for life as the bees."

"What happened to Levi?"

"He and his twin sister Lisa contracted measles. It was dreadful. Their beautiful faces swelled up, their little bodies felt like red-hot pokers in my arms. Levi was affected the worst. The fever made him throw up every spoonful of water we tried to give him. In the end he just lay still, shading his eyes from the light with his chubby arm. I covered him up with a cloth. His breathing was so fast and he was coughing; it sounded like liquid in there, as though his chest were full of water. Brita Kajsa brought in a bowlful of snow and we stroked his skin with it to cool his burning body."

The pastor's eyes glistened at the memory. He gave a muffled cough and the long hank of hair fell forward over his face.

"Lisa got better, thank heaven, but Levi lay exhausted in the bed between Brita Kajsa and me. On the last night he seemed to grow a little livelier and he started moving slightly. He flung his arms out wide, twisting them back and forth, and his feet kicked at the sheet.

It was bitterly cold outside, a January night at its darkest. The stars were obscured by a black mist. And his little arms went round and round. Like this . . . like the wings of a bee . . . but his eyes were directed upward, as if he could see the angels. Perhaps he wanted to fly there. He was already on his way to them, upward, out into the black profundity. I tried to pull him back, to hold on to him, but I knew he was on his way. His movements grew weaker. Mucus came out of his mouth and nose. We kept wiping it, keeping his mouth open so that he could breathe. In the morning I wrapped his body in the sheet. Brita Kajsa wanted to take him from me, but I couldn't let go. We fought over the boy, it was horrible . . . But the Lord took him. He took from me the one I loved best, struck where it hurt most. . . ."

The pastor fell silent. I had a strange feeling of shame. Was that why he had taken me under his wing that time by the side of the road? Because I reminded him of Levi, so that I should take the place of the one he missed?

He leaned back into the foliage, lying down among the buzzing bees. I did the same. We lay there, side by side, looking up at the summer clouds sailing by.

"We ought to learn from the bees," he said suddenly.

I glanced at him, not really understanding.

"I've taught you the alphabet, Jussi. Now you can both read and write. But is there anything finer than the beautiful humming of the bees? Just listen."

He sucked noisily on his pipe, as if seeking comfort.

"Written words are vital, but what happens when you put them in your mouth? You have to bite them into pieces like fragments of pottery. Chew them until they are soft clay and then form them with your vocal cords and lips. Only then do they have real power!"

He flung out his arm.

"Like the apostles. They were Jesus's bees. Out they flew with pollen grains in their bee-fur, out across the earth toward the pistils' stigmas in every yearning human heart. And in the mountains and deserts the most beautiful flowers could suddenly rise up."

I gave a cautious nod.

"I write my sermons, of course I do, Jussi. But they only come to life in the pulpit, when the letters pass my throat and tongue. It's your mouth, Jussi, that will save the world. Your mouth and the living word!"

Well, yes, I thought. Yes, well . . .

"And there's another thing about the spoken word, Jussi."

The pastor knocked the ash out of his pipe.

"How are you going to find a wife if you never speak?"

I blushed. Naturally he had noticed my longing glances, my pitiful peeking across the church aisle. I angrily flattened a horsefly, so abruptly that its guts splattered over my shirt.

17.

ONE AFTERNOON, MILD-MANNERED ERKKI ANTTI FROM Juhonpieti paid a visit. In his usual respectful way he addressed everyone in the cabin; both servants and children were greeted with the same heartfelt peace of God. He wiped the blind eye that tended to run ever since he injured it in an accident in his youth. From his bag he took a piece of cloth that he proceeded to unfold. Inside was something hard and white. With the aid of a sheath knife he cut a piece off and handed it to me. I chewed and instantly experienced the taste of mountains and fjords.

"Dried fish." Erkki Antti smiled. "Straight from Norway. I was given a piece by some fellow believers."

The pastor chewed it and pulled a face.

"You need young teeth to gnaw at dried fish," he said.

"But it gives you all the strength you need for long days journeying on foot."

"Yes. Now tell us, dear Erkki Antti, how goes the work in the Norwegian vineyards?"

As they sat talking, a sweet, uncommonly spicy scent rose from the pot Brita Kajsa was warming over the hot stove. Applying force, she ground the contents and then added them to a pan of water and let it boil. After that, she served it in the china cups brought out only for the most cherished guests. Even I received a drop in my wooden cup.

"I've tasted the brew," she said, unable to suppress an excited smile. "Sometimes it comes to the shop with the deliveries, and then I seize the opportunity to buy some."

The beverage was black, almost oily. The taste made me think of the pine stump used for tar, heavy and burned, and the smell reminded me of wild rosemary.

"Coffee," Erkki Antti said, sighing with pleasure. "Praise the Lord!"

Brita Kajsa cast a glance at her husband and smiled.

"The pastor doesn't seem as fond of the drink as we are," she said. "But he for his part has his tobacco, and the women have to have their little vice too."

While we sipped the coffee in the growing conviviality, Erkki Antti reported on the progress of the religious revival on the Norwegian side of the border. Unfortunately, he had troubling news from Kautokeino.

"The awakened members of the Sami community there are still spreading unrest," he said. "A number of them disrupted the service Andreas Qvale was holding in Skjervøy."

The pastor nodded. "Yes, I've received a letter about it."

"Bishop Juell has sent a new reverend, one who has a command of Lappish, Nils Stockfleth."

"Quite right," the pastor said. "If the priest speaks Lappish, he'll get much closer to the people."

"Regrettably, it doesn't seem to have helped in this instance," Erkki Antti said. "Haetta, Somby, Spein, and a few of the others went to the parsonage to question the new reverend. They wanted him to say he shared their faith in the revival. But Stockfleth refused. Then the Sami yelled at him, saying that he belonged to the devil."

"This happened at the parsonage?"

"Yes, in the reverend's home. The Sami kept shouting curses at him and he was obliged to call for the new sheriff, Lars Johan Bucht. Together they managed to force the visitors out."

"And these Sami claim to be members of the revival movement?"

"Yes, the same movement Pastor and I belong to. Later, Stock-fleth was shouted at during a service by a number of awakened women. As a result, he refused to give them Communion because he thought they were renouncing Christ. In response, people started yelling and making a racket in church, both men and women. They shouted down the vicar's sermonizing, so he couldn't be heard."

The pastor silently gave this some thought. Brita Kajsa sipped her hot coffee and shook her head.

"How can the revival movement go so wrong?" she asked.

"It's not the revival," the pastor said.

"No, of course not. But where does all this stem from? The commotion and uproar and disorder?"

Even Erkki Antti looked down at the table uneasily.

"And what do the people up there say?" Brita Kajsa went on. "What are people's views on the revival?"

"I don't know if I . . ."

"Yes, tell us," she urged him. "Tell us exactly what you've heard."

Erkki Antti wiped his blind eye again, as if it had begun to weep by itself.

"Many of them accuse us of heresy," he said with embarrassment. "They think we run the devil's errands. That we are false prophets whose purpose is to destroy the church."

"Nonsense like that comes from our enemies," the pastor exclaimed.

"I know, I know . . ."

"We have nothing to fear," he said.

"But if the enemy is in our midst?" Brita Kajsa said. "If the devil sits down among us? How can we defend ourselves then?"

ERKKI ANTTI LEFT FOR his long walk home to Juhonpieti, as modestly as he had arrived. That night Brita Kajsa became aware of the pastor anxiously tossing and turning. She rested her hand on his chest and felt his heartbeat, faint and irregular.

"I should go to Kautokeino," he said.

"When winter comes, everything will calm down," she whispered back.

"The whole world seems to be against the revival."

"But there are thousands of friends by your side."

"It doesn't feel like that. In my mind, I'm fighting the dragon alone."

"And even so, we will win."

"Do you think so?"

"Don't you?"

The pastor drew a deep breath, expanding his chest. But inside he was empty and desolate. He felt like a house with broken windows and dry leaves swirling on the floor.

"Everything will get better," Brita Kajsa said. "Now even poor people can have hope and confidence."

"But in what?"

"Just look at Jussi. He already reads and writes better than the rich countrymen of Pajala."

"We lit the fire," the pastor replied. "And our intention was that it would give warmth and do good. But fire can bring destruction as well."

"Sleep now, dear husband."

He took her hand, more earnestly than he had done since they were sweethearts, and squeezed it long into the night.

PART TWO

❧

The sun is setting
The dogs start to howl
Alone I am waiting
For nighttime to fall
Before she speaks out
Her mouth will I seal
And she the poor sinner
A-hanging will feel

18.

A WIFE, THE PASTOR HAD SAID. I HAD ALREADY FOUND HER. FROM the first moment I saw her, I knew she was the one. But how could I get close to her, melt the frostiness she displayed toward me?

From the farmhands' conversations in the marketplace I learned that a dance was being organized. It was only for servants and simple folk, far away from the eyes of the powers that be. It would be held at a *kenttä*, a forest glade, in an isolated summer shed where no one would interfere. After the Saturday chores were done, people took a sauna, changed their clothes, and made their way there.

I didn't want to go. And yet I did want to. The young people of the district would be meeting there, but beside them I felt old. Or maybe it was fear. I didn't know, I was bewildered and my clothes were dirty and smelled of forest fire.

"Jussi?"

The pastor entered the sauna. He could move as quietly as a cat. I had just washed and was drying myself with a rag. I shyly turned away to hide my private parts and tried to flatten the hair on the top of my head.

"I hear there's going to be a dance this evening."

"I don't know anything about that."

"So you're not intending to go?"

I blushed, for he could see right through me. He had detected my very first lie.

"Dancing is to the devil as carrion is to the blowfly," I muttered.

The pastor looked away discreetly while I dried my crotch and hurriedly pulled on my trousers.

"The girl was murdered," he said grimly. "And only you and I will acknowledge the truth. A monster is prowling about out there."

"He could be far from here by now."

"I fear that he is not. If it's someone we think we know, someone in our midst—then he'll be at the dance this evening."

"But, the pastor . . . the pastor could have the event stopped."

"I could. Doubtless I could. . . . But I was thinking, what if you were to go?"

"I won't do that, Pastor."

"But if you did. You could keep a lookout for the killer. In all likelihood he is big and strong. The hands that strangled her are bigger than mine. He has been in the mountains—you remember the Arctic heather we found. He has a great lust for women."

I stared at the pastor. He laid his hand on my bare shoulder and I felt the warmth.

"Maybe I'll go after all," I mumbled.

"Be careful, Jussi. In the name of God."

At the door to the sauna he turned.

"And if anyone asks, I didn't know anything about this event. The dance, I mean. I was completely unaware that it was going to be held."

Low voices could be heard along the forest path to Kenttä. Crofters and servants came from near and far, full of impatient excitement. Farmhands and maids usually under close supervision looked over their shoulder, fearful lest the master call them back for some evening task. Around the shed the pine forest thinned out and opened to the grasslands, so the summer light could stream down unimpeded from the evening sky. Faint smoke floated over the meadows from a pine-tar fire, which would hardly have been lit for warmth, but for the agreeable atmosphere it would foster. Farmhands and maids stood in small groups here and there. Lowing was heard from the barn into which the cows had been taken for the night. But it was the shed on which everyone had their eye. From inside soft thuds could be heard, just like the sound of threshing. Every now and then someone raised a cry, let out a laugh. I felt a keen embarrassment when girls cast me a glance to see if they knew me, a sensation like needles pricking my skin. One girl pointed at me scornfully, whispering something that provoked hilarity. I wanted to turn and dart back into the forest, but I forced myself to stay. When a couple of fellows who had just arrived started walking toward the shed, I joined them as they trod a path through the tittle-tattle. I could smell brandy and saw one of them lift up his jacket and dig out a bottle from his waistband. Both of them took a substantial gulp and I froze when I recognized the larger of the two. It was Roope, the ginger-haired foundry worker who had shouted at me on the village road and threatened to hit me with his belt. He was glassy-eyed when he turned to look at me.

"What the deuce? If it isn't the pastor's little *noaidi*! Is it true he found you under a stone? You were lying under a stone, a troll who couldn't even speak."

His friend was impatient and opened the ramshackle gray door to the shed. I avoided Roope's fumbling grasp, bent down through the low doorway, and elbowed my way in.

Inside, in the twirling semidarkness, the air was thick and damp and considerably warmer. There was an acrid smell of sweat—and something else, something dangerous, something that came from deep inside the young bodies. When my eyes grew accustomed to the dark, I saw people moving side by side in a long chain, or, to be more precise, a circle; it was a ring dance. The women were on the inside, moving in one direction, and the men were on the outside, moving in the opposite direction, so that each man would face a new woman, then another, and so on. I found the closeness so threatening that I felt sick. I took cover by one of the walls and noticed several others standing there, shy youths who also didn't dare to enter the sweaty circle. The singer was standing in the corner, on a potato bin. He was a fine-boned youngster with a boyish face, strikingly short in stature, and his voice was very high, between a man's and a woman's. His singing was quite remarkable and unlike anything I had ever heard. He seemed to be laughing, it was hard to find a likeness to anything else. His voice went up, it trilled, and then dipped into a long descent down a steep staircase. You scarcely noticed him breathe, before the voice went up again and filled the room with a steady beat. "La-di-li-di, la-di-li-di, dum-dadi dum-da," he sang, his tongue seeming to go faster than humanly possible. There were no instruments here; I knew no one in the region who could afford a fiddle. I had heard cow-girls playing home-made flutes in the forest, the sound keeping them company and frightening off beasts of prey. But your own voice is still the best instrument; you have it with you all the time. The delicately formed singer held the whole gathering captive, warbling out round after round, as all the while the rocking motion brought the dancers closer and closer together.

And then the singer stopped. It happened so abruptly that people felt awkward. They found themselves standing far too close to one another and the silence was unnerving. The girls looked down at the floor, at their curled-toe shoes or their own wrists. One or two whispered to one another and there was a little jostling. The singer ceremoniously cleared his throat, getting rid of the spittle and phlegm, and took a gulp from a bottle. I watched him with utter fascination, this insignificant, puny man, to whom no one would have paid attention on the village road. But here he undeniably was the focal point. The people on the dance floor looked at him pleadingly, impatiently, everyone wanting to be back in the beating, warming heart of the music. The man gave a rather bashful smile as he searched through his musical treasures, shimmering there like hundreds of colors, until he caught the end of a new melody and tested it with his voice. Now came the words. It was a Finnish waltz, one of the mournful variety, about loneliness beneath a starry sky when your beloved has left you for another. A handful of couples formed and began to turn in the crowded room. But most withdrew sheepishly to the walls and just listened. Two girls happened to stand beside me and one of them accidentally knocked me with her hip. Noticing it, she stepped back, but for me there was a measure of secret happiness. She was so close that if I pretended to stumble, I could lean on her shoulder. Here in the hot shed, it was as though we were in a different world. No servants ruling the roost, no old folk sitting in the corner with watchful eyes. For some, there was a freedom here that working people never experienced anywhere else. The muggy air smelled sweet. It made you want to have more. Drink yourself as heavy and giddy as a bee.

And then, without any warning, a bottle was being poked at my mouth. It was Roope, his teeth looking sharp under his ginger mustache.

"Now the little *noaidi* is going to have some brandy. . . ."

I took the bottle without a word. It was sticky from his sweaty hand and his saliva and I thought about cracking it hard against his temple and making him drop to the floor. The scene unrolled so clearly before me. There was trampling and scuffling and screaming and blood. It was so satisfying to hit him, to let him have it, to give it to him until he caved in. But I stopped myself a second before his eyes widened with fear. And instead of hitting him, I drank. I put the top of the bottle to my lips and let the snake poison pour in. I took two big gulps, or was it three, and then I handed the bottle back. Roope's grin got broader and he walloped my shoulder as if we had instantly become friends. He leaned toward me unsteadily and wanted to talk—leaned far too close, as drunks are wont to do, something I usually found so uncomfortable. But suddenly I didn't mind. I watched Roope in the half dark, his shining forehead and wet lips, the stiff ginger hairs in his mustache that shook whenever he coughed as though about to vomit. Then he grabbed the nearest girl and went spinning around the room.

Never before had alcohol passed my lips. It was like swallowing fire, but only for a moment. The sensation was replaced by an aching egg in my stomach. It lay there swelling into a poisonous heart, beating and lashing. And then the egg broke, and the black shell burst, and out pushed taloned feet with scaly skin, and savage jaws, tearing and biting. The dragon was loose. I, myself, became a dragon.

I left Roope's friend, who tried to hang at my side but remained there swaying as I made my way along the wall. Quick glances came in my direction, but they were no longer spiteful, and now people averted their gaze. The woman who had mocked me earlier was tense now; she saw me approach and turned her back, raised her shoulders like a bulwark. My chest stretched and grew new ribs, my neck lengthened with two more vertebrae. My blood grew hotter, it started to roar and churn and seemed to course outside my body now, rather than inside; it was a thoroughly peculiar experience. Above all, I wasn't afraid. I didn't know I had been afraid, but now I was aware how much easier my movements were, as if my shell had fallen off. I walked once around the whole room, and then again. After that I went outside. And then in again. I didn't need to ask permission. The world had opened up to me. The old Jussi was left in a corner, just a phantom. He watched what was happening and thought, Jussi is drunk now, Jussi has tasted alcohol now. He spied around like a bird, but I didn't listen to his carping anymore. I stood right next to the singer, raised my eyes, and gazed at the dancers without fear. I knew many of them from the village, most I knew by name, but some were completely unknown to me. Perhaps they came from Finland, or the mountains or the sea. There was an urgency in the air, as if everything had to happen this evening. In a few hours the fair celebrations would be over and it would be Sunday. And the daily struggle would commence. Everything had to happen now, in a fever.

I knew it was the dragon. This was how he lured people. He walked about among us and blew darkness into our eyes, lovely, warm darkness. He was everywhere, in the fumbling hand, in the knowing look, in the stretch of the ankle, in the collar that opened to reveal the skin. I could feel the threat. Something bad was going to happen, a danger was approaching. I turned to the door and saw it open. I screwed up my eyes against the bright evening light outside.

And there she was. My beloved. My Maria.

She had removed her headscarf, uncovering her hair; she must have been warm after the walk, of course. With the evening light behind her, it looked as though there were a golden haze around her head, like in an altarpiece. A halo. She stopped in the doorway and looked searchingly into the dancing throng. She hastily exchanged words with the girl beside her. And then she entered. She still hadn't noticed me. A knife cut through my drunkenness, rending my flesh. Sheer rifts inside me split open, until, with a gentle swish, the blood gushed out of the rocky sides and filled the empty ravines. In a farmyard an old woman was whisking the surging blood, another adding flour, they whisked so hard that red spots splashed their wrinkled faces and made them laugh with their toothless gums. Their mouths were like the reindeer cow's quim when a bull hangs on her back, flaccid holes with female mustaches; and I wanted to go deep inside, into the darkness. Damnation! How I wanted to touch her! Hold her shoulders, lay my hand against the flimsy cloth, feel the warmth of her beneath it.

I approached, keeping close to the wall. My feet floated above the quagmire, scarcely touching the moss, gliding like sledge runners over the uppermost covering of snow crystals. Nothing could stop me now. And I laid my fingers so gently on her shoulder, and she turned, and I thought, Now it is going to happen, now we will float into the music, into Satan's sweaty throng. But it was one of the others she had turned to, one of the maidservants from Kenttä. They tripped out onto the floor together and the women's circle parted and let them in. The men's circle was moving in the opposite direction and without pausing I pushed my way in. I pried the men's wrists apart and joined the circle, a body among bodies. The singer was in the middle of a lengthy song cycle, tapping on a block of wood to mark the rhythm, the same beat as the stamping feet—two steps sideways, one step back—and it was surprisingly easy to find the rhythm. Everything was transformed into a heart. *Bo-boom-bo-boom-bo-boom.* First the men turned outward and the women inward, their backs to one another. And then, the most exciting part, we turned to face each other. And with every further move there was a different woman, young and on fire. When I glanced to the side I saw Maria coming closer. She took one step away, then two steps nearer in the same rocking pulse. Then we turned outward again. Back to back, fellows' sweaty paws in my hands. Inward, one more time. And there she was. Standing right in front of me. When she saw it was me, she looked down, first at the floor and

next at the front of my shirt. We took a step in the same direction.
For a second she was very close, just an arm's length from me.

"Maria," I said.

She looked up and met my eyes and she could see that I wished
her only good. But the moment was too brief. Immediately we each
took a step to the side and the rings slid apart, stretching out into a
chain.

The singer reached the last verse and the slow circling came to a
stop. It felt as though my insides were shaking. Maria hadn't been
angry with me. She must have been nonplussed to find me in the
ring of men, in this wall of muscles and chests, of powerful arms
and thighs. I was one of many. I was a man. Not a troll.

I saw her talking with a girlfriend. They tilted their heads together and laughed. I hoped that I was in her thoughts, and that
maybe she would throw me a quick glance. I carefully wiped my
hands on my trouser legs to make them dry and comfortable to
hold. The singer, who had taken another swig, broke into a new
melody, a brisk, rousing tune; the crowd grew visibly excited and
the entire building seemed to take a deep breath. A fellow stepped
forward unsteadily and tugged at Maria. It was Roope. She turned
aside to dodge him but he wouldn't let go of her wrist and tried to
pull her toward him.

At the same moment the door was flung open. A large figure
filled the opening and a smoky iridescent mist hugged his silhouette. In no time at all a sweet fragrance had spread throughout the
shed, an aroma I instantly recognized. It came from the stub he held
in his hand, the thing that was called a *siggar*. Nils Gustaf stood for
a moment, taking in the pulse of the music. Then he poked the
smoking implement between his teeth and started to clap the beat
extremely loudly. He seemed to form a hollow with one hand and
apply force with the other, making the noise rebound like a hard

ball. Meanwhile, he stamped the heel of his leather boot on the floorboards, not in time with his clapping, but in the intervals between, making each sound like an echo of the other. And in a strange way the sounds were in keeping with the song. They reinforced the rhythm and gave the music body.

Nils Gustaf strode forward for all to see. The whirling couples slightly drew aside to allow him into the middle. He shoved Roope away from Maria, pushed his hat farther down on his forehead, and performed a sudden little leap in front of her; surprisingly nimble for so large a gentleman. With startling alacrity, he clicked his heels together and slapped his hands against the leg of his boot with a rat-a-tat-tat; it was all done so quickly, you could barely see him move. It was as if the man were levitating, hanging freely in the air. As he spun round in a complete turn he managed to survey from beneath the brim of his hat not just Maria, but every single one of the womenfolk in the shed. And they looked back. Indeed, in truth, they stared. They had never witnessed anything like it. Nor had I. Who could have imagined a fellow could move in that fashion? It was undignified, it was provocative and sinful, it was quite clearly *knapsu*, the northern Finnish word for "unmanly," something only women do. But how it impressed the women! Not one of them could keep her eyes off him. They licked their lips and chewed their knuckles, as if they might start shrieking at any moment. It was the power of the music. All the clapping and stamping and high kicking got inside us and it heightened the music, made it almost sacred. It delighted the singer, who increased the tempo, and the ever-quickening tune made his tongue swell up, a shiny red glimpse visible in his mouth, as if he were bleeding while he sang, with a broad smile at the newcomer. Suddenly they were making music together, and the music expanded beyond the low roof, through the cracks between the shingles, and out into the falling night, toward the creatures of the forest.

With a flouncing swing of his leg, Nils Gustaf landed, bang, on the floor, at exactly the same second that the singer stopped, as if they were one and the same person. And the artist still had his smoking contraption between his teeth.

There was silence. Nils Gustaf walked up to the singer and ruffled his hair as if he were a little boy.

"In Hälsingland, that's where your legs can really spin!" he shouted in his foreign Swedish.

The singer gave a hesitant laugh and merriment spread through the audience. At the same time people felt inhibited. The visitor came from afar. What did the man want? Was he a government official?

"Have you danced the quadrille? Do you know this one? Up you come, everyone. The ladies here, like this. And the men on the other side. I'll give you the tune."

He hustled me out onto the floor with the other men. It was like being washed there by a wave. Then he began to sing a cheerful, snappy song in a strange dialect. The singer listened and was soon able to join in. Verse and refrain, verse and refrain. The artist in front of everyone, showing them the steps. The men into the center first, then the women. It was a little like the ring dance, and yet it wasn't. This felt more ceremonial, more genteel.

"Now you form pairs and turn clockwise."

Not many people understood his Swedish, so he grabbed the nearest person, who happened to be me. And then he found a woman and pulled her away from a truculent man. Laughing, Nils Gustaf planted a kiss on her cheek and led her to my side. It was Maria. He made us stand there, in view of everyone, and showed how I should hold her, and how she, this sweetness in human form, should put her arms round me.

"Now turn, and don't take such long steps. Yes, like that."

I was dancing with my beloved. Maria was holding me. She laid her hands against my body. And now she had no qualms about meeting my gaze. She was no longer afraid. And when we spun around it was so natural, as if we were in the same body. The couple next to us stumbled and had to start again, while we just seemed to fly. We soared along on the crest of a wave, on the very brink of the frothing spume. I had never known that dancing was like this.

"And then back again," he said, demonstrating.

As the couples rearranged themselves into new formations, he stepped forward and issued instructions on the execution of a two-step followed by a shuffle. And I could see that I would soon be next to her again. I felt a tingle of intense joy. A surging explosion of heat. My body seemed to have become too small for me.

THE ARTIST STAYED AT the dance all evening. I saw him trying to talk to the girls in his Swedish, with grand gestures of explanation, to which they shyly responded in their rural Finnish. When he went out later, I followed him at a distance. I saw him seek out a spot at the edge of the forest, where he opened his fly.

A ginger-haired man approached from behind with long strides. It was Roope. He was going in the artist's direction and at first I thought he needed to pee as well. But then I saw that he was carrying a wooden stick. He made no noise as he padded purposefully forward. Then I saw him lift the stick, raising it swiftly as if it were an ax. Before I could shout out a warning he aimed a terrifying blow at Nils Gustaf's head.

The artist could not possibly have foreseen the danger. And yet, somehow, he took what was almost a dance step to the side, just as the stick thudded against the ground. In a backward motion I had never seen before, he snapped his hand round Roope's wrist and twisted his arm so that it was pointing back and up. The stick fell out of Roope's fingers and onto the grass. The artist let go and snatched Roope's belt. Unceremoniously he opened the buckle and removed the knife and its sheath. I saw Nils Gustaf hold it to Roope's face and say something, but the sounds from the dance drowned out his words. With a powerful movement he threw the scabbard and knife far out into the trees. He unhurriedly buttoned up his fly and slowly began walking back to the shed.

The entire episode had been like a strange quadrille. Pulling a face and rubbing his sore arm, Roope got to his feet and, cursing, made his way into the forest to find his knife.

I tried to make sense of what I had witnessed. The artist had eyes in the back of his head. He could see behind him, while he was having a piss. He was scarcely human.

19.

THE LETTERS WERE SO SMALL, AND YET SO FULL OF FORCE. THESE slender, modest lines. With their tiny curlicues in the birth registers, newborn souls were transformed from soggy little bundles into baptized Christian parishioners.

By itself, each letter was frail. But when the pastor taught the young Sami boy to place them next to one another, something happened. It was like lighting a fire; one single piece of wood was of little use, but if you added another, it instantly grew hotter. The letters derived life from each other; in the company of others they began to speak. *I* and *s* and *ä* made *isä*, the Finnish word for father. But it could also mean God, our Father in heaven. The letters could do both a waltz and a ring dance; they could take each other by the hand in ever longer rows, and it was hard to understand how. You looked at lines and curves and saw only lines and curves. The letters by themselves were silent. But your lips could blow life into them. Turn them into objects, animals, names of people. And equally curious was the fact that they continued speaking even when you had closed your mouth. When you looked at the letters, they were converted into words inside your head. No, not words—bodies. My eyes look at "Maria," at the five letters, the five consecutive shapes, but in my heart and mind I see my beloved. Her cheeks, her shining eyes, her hands holding mine.

It was the pastor who taught the boy. The pastor who sat beside the boy and delightedly clapped him on the back and made him try again.

"*I . . . sssss . . . ääää . . . issäää . . . Isä!*"

"Now you can read." The pastor laughed.

"No, I can't."

"Look at this!"

"*J . . . u . . . Jussi . . .*"

"You see," he said. "The door's open, Jussi."

The door. Which door? I thought of all the parables I had heard in church.

"To heaven?"

The pastor's smile broadened.

"You'll see, Jussi. But you have to practice, you have to read as much as you can find."

And from that moment the world was full of letters. A kick-sledge seen from the front formed an H. A rake with all its tines was an E over and over again, just as a round-pole fence consisted of a row of Ns. A piece of string could be an O or an S, depending on the way it curled. Even people could resemble letters. A thin fellow with a large head was like a P. A stout woman with a wide skirt was an A. When you were digging in a ditch, the spade made the movement of a J. And when you cleaned the window, you made a Z. In the end I could be standing before an autumn birch that had lost its leaves and see letters everywhere among the black branches. *Novvu filit umnu . . .* I was reading the tree's language, the birch's language. All the gnarled branches in its crown were shouting at me. I was fearful and I wanted to forget it all, go back to my ignorance, when a birch was simply a birch. But it was impossible. One door had opened and at the same time another one had closed. I could never turn back.

I tried to express my disquiet to the pastor, but instead he brought out a book. His children had read it many times over and the pages were thumbed and worn. I seized it as if it were a piece of treasure.

The cover was made of slightly heavier paper, a light brown cardboard on the point of coming off.

"Sit down and read. The text is in Swedish. If any of the words are difficult, you can ask me."

I sat down on the floor with my back against the wall. Then I leaned forward and crossed my legs to form a little table on which I carefully propped the book. When I opened the cover there was a much thinner white sheet under it, which I also turned. And now the introduction. A picture of a man lying on the ground with his eyes closed. Another crouching beside him. Had he struck the one who was prone? No, now I could see the pitcher. He was holding out water so the man could drink.

S-a-m-a-ri-tan. It was hard to read. Sam-ari-tan.

"'Samaritan' means someone who is kind," the pastor said. "The Good Samaritan. It's a fine story. It's about helping others."

With painstaking effort, I plowed my way through the text. I hardly dared to turn the pages, I was so scared of dirtying them, even though I had been careful to wash my hands. I pulled a stalk out of the sennegrass and pointed at each letter, one after the other; I said it aloud and repeated it again and again until it sounded like a word. But the book was in Swedish and I had to ask the children what it meant. They laughed at my pronunciation and made fun of me until Brita Kajsa said something to them. It was a long time before I was ready to turn the first page. There were large pictures in the book that moved me profoundly. I studied the robbers at length, saw how they took everything the man had, even his clothes. And, what's more, they gave him a severe beating. On several occasions I had seen such things myself on the roads, the wickedness and malice, seen how the strong taunted and wounded the weak. I had seen old nags whipped to a pulp, dogs left with their ribs kicked in, paupers receiving into their outstretched hands not bread but gobs of spittle from those who passed.

But into the misery stepped this hero from Samaria. He stopped, even though he didn't need to. He helped the unknown man for no other reason than kindness. I could see him in front of me. He was like the pastor. And the victim, lying in the dust and about to perish, was me. What if the pastor hadn't taken me with him that day? Just passed by and left me by the side of the road? I would never have become a person.

For several days, I read in all the spare moments I had. I took the book out of the cloth I had wrapped it in and my finger slowly traced the words, one after the other. It was like walking through a vast forest. After a long hike I reached the last page, and as the trees came to an end, the cover closed. I took a good look at the book, held it up, felt its weight in my hand. The paper was frayed, the spine had a crack in it and was damaged. If you placed the palm of your hand on top of the white sheets of paper, the book felt strangely cool, chillier than wood. It reminded me of birch bark with its silvery smoothness. Now that I had finished reading, the pages were once again completely silent. I inspected the book from different angles, laid my ear to it, and listened. But now it was keeping quiet. And yet I knew what was inside, what would happen if I opened it and started reading again. It was incredible. Was the book alive? And if the book wasn't doing this, then where were the pictures and voices coming from? While I had been reading I had seen Palestine, I had been there. And the man from Samaria, now I believed I had met him myself. But where was all of this when the covers were closed? Perhaps the book was reading by itself in there? On the inside the words and letters were buzzing around like bees. Or perhaps they were more like seeds? Seedlings that needed earth to grow, wanting to put down roots in the moist loam that filled a person's head.

Shelves of books stood tall in the pastor's study. Black and brown spines full of tiny letters, books with many more pages than my childish book. When I looked at them, I felt my heart race feverishly. Could the pastor really have read all this? Did he carry this weight inside him, in the same way I now carried my one little story? Was there so much space in a human mind? Sometimes, when he was writing his sermons, he reached out, grabbed a spine from this compact wall, and leafed through the thin, silky pages until he found the right place. I could see a voice beginning to speak within him, see his lips trembling as if in conversation. Imagine having company like that! If you owned books, you would never be alone.

"I want to read," I pleaded. "To read more."

The pastor's daughter Selma found me another book. I tucked it into my shirt and held it next to my heart, as if I were carrying a baby. Even when it was closed, I could feel an occasional kick.

20.

O N SUNDAY THE CHURCH PEWS WERE ONLY SPARSELY FILLED. WE young people who had been at the dance tried to conceal our yawns while our elders muttered to one another about sin and immorality. The pastor warned of the temptations of summertime, that we should all constantly take care to avoid the demons that lured us onto the primrose path. Once again he cited use of alcohol as the root of greatest evil, and he condemned all the illegal liquor dealers operating their business in the area with no regard for the ruin they caused. I was listening with half an ear, as I had realized that Maria wasn't there. Until the very last moment, I hoped that she was just delayed, and every time I heard steps in the aisle, I turned to look. But she didn't appear. At the end of the Mass, the church door opened, but it was an elderly fellow, large and thickset, who sat down right at the back. When it was time for the announcements, I saw him rise, walk quietly up to the pastor, and whisper something to him. The man gave the impression of being nervous, he kept twisting his hat round and round and wiping his hands on the front of his shirt while his curled-toe shoes were tapping as if he were still out walking. The pastor listened and then gravely surveyed the congregation. He was silent for several moments, as his eyes traveled along the rows of pews, giving the impression he was looking deep into our eyes. Then he coughed and drew a deep breath.

"It is hereby announced that Jolina Eliasdotter Ylivainio has been missing since yesterday evening. Information relating to her may be submitted to me or to her father Elias Ylivainio."

The pastor appeared to hesitate, as though sudden enlightenment might be forthcoming from the congregation. Then he nodded to Elias, who walked softly back to his pew.

After the service I saw the pastor motion Elias toward him. They spoke in low voices at the front by the altar.

"When was Jolina last seen?" the pastor asked.

"Yesterday evening, before the weekend meal."

"Was she going somewhere?"

"I . . . I don't know."

"I heard that there was a dance organized yesterday," the pastor said.

"Well, yes. . . . Yes, she might have been going to the dance."

"Did she go on her own?"

"She didn't say she was going there. She must not have wanted to say anything."

"What was she wearing?"

"I didn't see her leave."

"A light gray dress," I threw in. "Striped apron, black boots. Hair in plaits, tied with slender red ribbons."

I glanced at the pastor, who seemed satisfied.

"So you recognized her, Jussi?"

"I know who Jolina is. She danced several times during the evening."

"With whom?"

"With various men. Roope, one of the foundry workers, was after her, I could see that. A large, ginger-haired fellow."

"He's been after her before," Elias said.

"And she danced with Nils Gustaf, the artist, as well. Though nearly all the women did."

"Nearly all?"

"The artist was such a nimble-footed dancer. He could skip and spin all over the place. I have never seen anyone dance like that."

"And what happened after the dance?"

"I . . . I don't know."

The pastor looked at me in silence. Then, with a "Hmm," he turned to Elias.

"Maybe she left with someone. If she doesn't turn up soon, we must start a search. Look for her around Kenttä and along the path home. The girl has to be somewhere."

"Does the pastor think . . ."

Elias paused before forcing out the rest of the sentence.

". . . that it's the bear?"

The pastor failed to respond. When Elias had gone, he said simply:

"Roope?"

"Yes?"

"I could see you had more to tell, Jussi. But you didn't want to say it while Elias could hear."

As always, he was right. I cleared my throat.

"Well . . . that fellow Roope . . . he was in a bad mood yesterday. He had been drinking brandy and was being a nuisance to the girls."

"In what way was he bothering them?"

"He was grabbing at Jolina and other girls."

"Brandy can cloud the judgment."

I recalled the rush and the heat and swallowed hurriedly. Could he tell that I had tried it too?

"Roope attacked Nils Gustaf. I think he was jealous of him."

"Oh?"

"Roope tried to knock him down with a wooden cudgel. But Nils Gustaf got away and brought him down. Then he threw Roope's knife into the forest."

The pastor looked thoughtful.

"This Roope," he said, "I didn't see him in church today."

"Likely enough he'll be sleeping it off."

"And Nils Gustaf stayed at Kenttä all evening?"

"Yes, he enjoyed being with the girls. He was an incredibly agile dancer."

"Really?"

"The best I've seen. He could leap and twist like a cat."

"And what about yourself?"

I was reluctant to reply.

"Is it a sin to dance?"

"What sort of thoughts did you have while you were dancing?" the pastor countered.

"I . . . I can't tell you."

"Well, where did it lead, Jussi? What happened afterward?"

"I . . . I'm just saying, people dance in church too. When the spirit moves them, when they reach their *liikutuksia*, during the pastor's sermons. Isn't that dancing too?"

The pastor gave me a sharp look.

"The intention, Jussi, was that you should seek out the perpetrator."

"A lot happened in Kenttä," I said cagily. "It was a remarkable evening."

"You can tell me about it on the way home."

21.

THE SEARCH FOR JOLINA ELIASDOTTER YLIVAINIO GATHERED momentum through the afternoon. One of her friends reported seeing Jolina walking in the direction of home after the dance. She was alone and seemed to be in good spirits. It was the last that was seen of the girl, as if the earth had swallowed her up. They combed the ground around Kenttä and along the path she was believed to have followed home. One of the farmhands investigated a storage barn, an *aitta* standing in a meadow, partly hidden from the marsh path. On finding the door locked, he was about to leave and carry on elsewhere. But when he peeped through a gap he could see that the door was latched on the inside, which struck him as odd. With the blade of his knife he managed to flick the latch up and open the door. When no one answered his shout, he started to look around inside the barn and suddenly became aware of low sounds from the loft. It sounded like the rustling noise of a small animal. He climbed up the ladder, expecting to see mice, or perhaps a stoat. There were some sacks piled in the corner, and when he lifted them he found Jolina Eliasdotter.

Her eyes were wide open. For one dreadful moment the farmhand thought she was dead. As he reached out to touch her, an eerie wail issued from her lips. It sounded like a hare caught by a fox. He spoke soothingly to the girl, but she didn't seem to hear. Her cry attracted others who came to help, and together they tried to maneuver her to the ladder. Shaking and pulling away, the girl didn't answer to her name and couldn't stand. Only after they had tied a rope around her waist did they manage to hoist her down from the loft. On a makeshift stretcher of poles and sacks they carried her home. When they asked her what had happened, she just covered her injured face with her arms and refused to respond. Her body convulsed as if with cold, and once she was safely home, she was wrapped in warm blankets and put to bed.

The message that Jolina Eliasdotter had been found was conveyed to the parsonage. The pastor was asked to bring the vessel for the last rites because they feared for her life. He and I immediately hastened to Elias's cabin. Many of those who had helped with the search were standing in the yard. After a brief greeting the pastor was shown into the cabin, where we met an oppressive silence. Elias was sitting at the kitchen table with his two adult sons. One of them stood and offered his chair to the pastor, while I sat down crosslegged on the floor. We had barely exchanged civilities when the door was flung open and in strutted Sheriff Brahe with Constable Michelsson in tow. Brahe gave a careless salute and wiped his hand across his sweaty brow.

"Where's the girl?"

The master of the house pointed to the bedroom. When the door opened we could see that the curtains were drawn, casting the room into semidarkness. Elias's wife Kristina, a slender woman with scrawny shoulders, was sitting on a truckle bed wringing out a wet flannel. In front of her on the floor was a pail of water. Jolina was motionless on the settle bed. The sheriff leaned over to look at her bruised face and the gray hue to her skin. The constable watched from the door.

"Is the girl asleep? Hello?"

Brahe was perspiring in the heat and snatched the flannel to wipe his own brow.

"Hello?" he said again. "This is Sheriff Brahe. What happened to you?"

There was no sign of reaction from the girl in the bed. He hesitantly stretched out his fingers. Finally, he took hold of her shoulders through the blanket and shook her.

The girl gave a croaky shriek and tried to free her arms but was hampered by the blanket. As soon as she got them loose she began to strike desperately at the sheriff. He caught her wrists and held them as the screaming continued.

"Listen to me. . . . I am Sheriff Brahe. Stop hitting me."

Jolina's body arched in a spasm and he deemed it wise to let go and withdraw. The girl stopped screaming but kept her hands clenched in front of her face, ready to beat and scratch, her eyes fixed, wide open.

"I've no time for this sort of charade," the sheriff said sharply.

He wiped off the drops of saliva on his uniform sleeves. Kristina had risen to her feet and evidently wanted to help, but he pushed her aside.

"Jolina," he said. "Is that your name?"

She stared up at the ceiling.

"Did someone hurt you, Jolina?"

Still no answer.

"Was it the bear? Did the bear attack you?"

"She won't talk to us either," Kristina said apologetically.

"Why won't you speak, Jolina? We don't have all day. Was it the killer bear? You can at least nod, can't you?"

A slight movement could be seen.

"She nodded," the sheriff said.

The mistress of the house did not venture to disagree. I was doubtful, but kept my misgivings to myself.

"I thought the killer bear had been captured," the pastor said.

"It might have been the wrong animal. We'll have to offer a new reward. Sooner or later it will bite the dust."

"Her arms," the pastor said.

"I beg your pardon?"

The pastor leaned cautiously over the bed. Her eyes were still open wide, staring fixedly. He murmured calming words as he knelt down to study her more closely. Her white skin was suffused with an ugly purple.

"Someone has restrained her arms," the pastor said. "Exactly as the sheriff did just now. I can see the finger marks here."

"They could equally be from a bear's claws," the sheriff said.

"Jolina," the pastor said kindly. "Sweet child, tell us. Who attacked you in the forest? Can you tell us, Jolina? Do you remember anything?"

Perhaps his gentle tone helped. She lifted her hands a tiny fraction from her lips.

"*Se oli mies*," could be heard.

"What did she say?" asked the sheriff. "What did she whisper?"

"That it was a man," the pastor said.

The sheriff looked skeptical, but Kristina had heard it as well.

"Tell me more. What did he look like?" Brahe said, reclaiming the initiative. "Did you recognize him? Was he known to you?"

He waited, and when she didn't reply, he repeated the question. She closed her eyes and turned her head away.

"Did you recognize the fellow? Was he big or small? What was he wearing?"

From her lips came a murmur. The pastor leaned forward and listened.

"*Se haisi konjakille*," he repeated. "He stank of brandy."

"That goes without saying," Brahe said. "But what was he wearing?"

Jolina lay still, her eyes still closed. Her pallor was increasing and she seemed on the point of fainting. The pastor straightened his back and looked about.

"A man who smelled of liquor," Brahe reiterated. "A farmhand on his way home from the dance. And the urge came over him when he caught sight of the girl."

"It is not dissimilar to the first assault," the pastor said. "Hilda Fredriksdotter was dragged into a barn, too, and subjected to strangling."

"Jolina hasn't said anything about being strangled."

"The sheriff can see the injuries to her neck."

"But Hilda Fredriksdotter was killed by a bear, wasn't she?" the constable interrupted, turning his watery blue eyes on Brahe.

"A bear," Brahe affirmed. "As the evidence indicated, unequivocally. I thought the pastor knew that."

"This is the second victim of the summer," the pastor reminded him. "A violent criminal is at large."

"A drunken peasant bastard," the sheriff declared, "who lost his head. She shouldn't have walked home on her own after the dance."

"I fear the fellow may strike again."

"Let us fulfill our office and you do yours, Mr. Reverend!"

The sheriff and the constable positioned themselves to form a wall between the pastor and Jolina. We offered no further objections and retired. She would hardly start talking while they were there. When I followed the pastor out into the yard, I realized how furious he was.

"Good-for-nothings," he hissed.

The farm dog came padding up to us and we let her sniff at our kneecaps. She was a Finnish spitz, small and light brown, with dainty little paws. The pastor pulled out a piece of dried reindeer meat and cut a slice off as a tidbit for her.

A couple of neighbors approached, curious about what had happened in the cabin. But the pastor wasn't in the mood for talking and turned his back, indicating he wanted to be left in peace. In front of us was the sauna hut; he opened the door and stepped inside. By the doorstep lay a bundle, which he poked with his walking stick. It appeared to be women's clothing, perhaps left there for washing later.

The pastor bent down to take a closer look at the pile. A kirtle, a bodice, and a simple blouse.

"Can you see, Jussi?" he whispered.

"What?"

"They must be Jolina's clothes. The ones she was wearing during the attack."

He carefully closed the sauna door behind us. Then he lifted the bundle up to one of the window openings and in the shaft of daylight he started to examine the clothes in detail.

The kirtle was woven from coarse wool and some pieces of straw had fastened onto the fibers. He turned the fabric inside out and inspected it in the light. A dark stain was visible, which wasn't yet dry. He brought his large nose closer and sniffed.

"Semen, Jussi. Are we to believe this comes from the perpetrator?"

He continued to investigate the garments with care. There was dust and dirt from the hut floor and in the hem of the kirtle the pastor found a tiny dried animal dropping. He pointed to a darker patch on the inside that I first thought was blood. But when he let me smell it, it had a sharp, slightly smoky scent.

"Do you recognize it, Jussi?"

"Fat . . . and tar . . . and something else. Not pine-tar oil, but more refined, somehow . . ."

"What on earth can it be?"

"From church," I recalled. "I recognize the scent from the church pews."

The pastor leaned forward again and took a deep breath with his thick nose. And then he nodded.

"You're right, Jussi. I think it's boot wax."

"Yes, that's it."

"Grease that people rub into their Sunday shoes."

"Grease that's been purchased."

"Exactly. You would hardly find poor people using this, or Sami with their soft-soled reindeer-skin shoes. Their footwear smells of reindeer bone and dogs' wet feet."

The pastor took a handkerchief from his coat to soak up as much of the grease as possible.

"But how could it end up on the inside of the clothes?" I asked.

"He pulled up her skirt and sat astride her. Write down what we've seen, Jussi."

I hurriedly found a pencil and a scrap of paper. Meanwhile, the pastor went on to look at the blouse. When new, it had been white, but years of wear and washing had given it a dull grayish tinge. In a number of places, the fabric had been mended, old tears had been sewn up, and a mixture of buttons used.

"The button by the collar has gone, write that down. You can see loose threads where it's been ripped off. And look, Jussi!"

I leaned forward and saw some round reddish-brown spots. They looked fresh.

"Blood."

"Note the pattern, Jussi. The drops have spattered. So they must have fallen from a certain height. On the inside, the drops are fainter and blotched, meaning that the blood hasn't gone right through the fabric. What does that tell us?"

"That it must have come from outside."

"Go on."

"It wasn't hers. The blood must have come from someone else."

"Namely?"

"The perpetrator?"

The pastor nodded and took a slow breath.

"So, the villain was injured."

The bodice Jolina had been wearing smelled strongly of her sweat. I could identify the reindeer's scent of fear at the wolf's approach. She had been facing the predator's jaws.

"*Kirkkoherra?*"

Suddenly I saw the sauna door open, and Kristina was standing there, a puzzled expression on her face. The pastor hastily gathered the clothes together into a pile.

"Were these Jolina's clothes? Was she wearing them when she was found?"

Kristina nodded nervously. The pastor tried to adopt a stern expression as he laid the bundle on the sauna bench.

"Please don't wash them before the sheriff sees them," he said.

"Brahe and Michelsson have already left."

"Oh well, you may do as you please, then. Presumably it doesn't matter. But perhaps we could see Jolina again?"

22.

THE ROOM SMELLED MUSTY AND STALE. JOLINA LAY STILL, WITH a sheet over her face as if she were already dead, but the slight movement of her breathing was just discernible. Her fear was palpable; the sheriff must have asked some painful questions. The mistress of the house, Kristina, sat on a stool with her arms wrapped round her thin body and appeared to be trembling. Elias and the sons stood in the doorway, their hands clasped.

In his warm, clear voice the pastor began singing the hymn "You Bore Your Cross, O Gentle Jesus," as he opened his etui with the small chalice and the pyx. Kristina quickly clasped her hands and pretended to sing too, though she didn't know the words. The pastor recited part of Psalm 25 from memory, a prayer for guidance and for deliverance:

"The troubles of my heart are enlarged: O bring thou me out of my distresses. Look upon mine affliction and my pain; and forgive all my sins . . ."

The singing and the holy words appeared to reach Jolina. Her breathing became deeper when she realized it was the pastor and not the sheriff who had returned. The pastor moved on to the confession, followed by the words of absolution, while the people of the household bowed their heads. Without haste the pastor continued with the ritual he had performed many times at the bedsides of the sick and the elderly. I could feel the room become fresher and smell better, feel the weight of death being displaced. At a sign from the pastor I went up to the window and took down the piece of material that was hanging there. The life-giving afternoon light streamed in. The girl began to writhe under the sheet as though the light caused her pain, as if the demons within her were in retreat. Next the pastor read the Eucharist Prayer, slowly so that every word would sink in, and after that the Lord's Prayer. And at the very first words—"Our Father who art in heaven"—Jolina drew the sheet away from her face with trembling fingers, and I saw her raw lips move silently.

When Jolina received the body and blood of Christ, the effect was unmistakable. Her body was seized by a forceful movement, a warm wave of unimaginable strength swept through the room, and the pastor was obliged to remain on his knees for several moments before he was able to gather himself for the final prayer. Kristina sensed his hesitation and proffered him the damp cloth. He took it and gratefully wiped his brow. Then he applied it gently to the girl's wet cheeks.

"Jolina," he said in a low voice. "Jolina . . . my dear Jolina."

The third time she heard her name she opened her eyes.

"The evil submits," the pastor said. "The power of darkness."

She didn't meet his eye, but it was clear that she was listening.

"We must stop the man of violence. He shall not do this again."

The pastor indicated to everyone else that they should leave the room. It was obvious they wanted to stay and listen, but he bowed his head in prayer until he heard the door close. He signaled for me to stay, and swiftly took out a sheet of paper and a pencil and handed them to me.

"What happened to your head?" he asked Jolina in so low a voice that no one outside could hear.

She showed no sign of answering.

"I can see a wound here on your right temple. May I push your hair back a little?"

He gently moved aside the hair sticking to her cheek. A nasty bruise on her scalp was visible. The pastor indicated I should make a note of the injury, which I hurriedly did.

"Would you be able to uncover your neck?" he went on, at pains to make his voice kind and compassionate.

Her gaze met the pastor's now, her pupils large and black.

"I only want to look. There's no danger."

The pastor was reluctant to touch her, after everything she had been through. But Jolina just lay there, rigid, breathing fast.

"If I may fold back the sheet just a fraction . . . There, now I can see better. You have injuries to your neck, I see. Does it hurt?"

She nodded now and took a deep breath.

"How did it happen? Do you remember?"

Jolina tried to say something, but her voice wasn't strong enough. Instead she raised her hands and bent her fingers into claws.

"Is that what he did? Did he try to strangle you?"

Her gestures became more emphatic; she demonstrated how the man shook her by the throat and how she herself gradually stopped moving.

"What happened, Jolina? Did he let go?"

"No," she suddenly whispered.

"But did you do something then?"

"Outside . . . on the path . . ."

"So the attack took place outside. The assailant squeezed your neck with his fingers. . . . But then something happened?"

She nodded uncertainly.

"Did someone come?"

"No, it was . . . it was me. . . ."

The throttling had damaged her voice and forcing out the words caused her obvious pain. Instead of continuing to speak, she lifted her arm and brandished it in front of her.

"You hit him? You hit him hard?"

She pointed to her head, to the back of her neck. And then the same stabbing gesture.

"I don't understand, Jolina."

She turned her head to the side, pulled her hair forward, and pointed.

"Did he pull your hair? Tell me, Jolina."

"Hairpin . . ." she said, in a barely audible wheeze.

"You removed your hairpin and you stabbed the man with it?"

She nodded quickly.

"Can you show me where you stabbed him?"

With a shaking finger she pointed at the pastor's left shoulder. I noted it down.

"In his shoulder, here? Thank you, Jolina. That is a very important piece of information. The hairpin, could I see it?"

A vague shake of the head.

"Did you recognize the man?" the pastor asked. "Do you know who it could have been?"

Jolina began to say something, but her voice lapsed into a croak. Instead she pulled the sheet up over her mouth and nose.

"He had covered his face? With a cloth?"

Another nod.

"Did you notice anything else? How he was dressed? Was he a tramp? Or maybe a farmhand?"

"*Hhhhh . . .*" she wheezed, and started coughing. Then she tried again.

"*Hhherrras . . . mies . . .*"

I nodded silently. *Herrasmies*. A gentleman.

"Thank you, Jolina. God bless you."

Her lips contorted, her face tensed. She held her breath for several seconds, her body contracting in spasm. The pastor remained beside her, silent. Then he bent forward and made the sign of a cross on her forehead with his finger. And again. And a third time. He spoke in a whisper and I could hear only snatches. That it was not she who had sinned. That she had saved her own life by defending herself. That Jesus Christ walked by her side and at any time she could reach out her hand to him and receive his help.

Eventually I heard someone timidly opening the door. It was Kristina, who looked anxiously through the crack.

"Sleep beside her tonight," the pastor said. "There is room for you both on the settle."

Kristina nodded.

"And I would like to borrow this. You'll get it back later."

He took the damp cloth that had dabbed Jolina's brow and folded it into his pocket.

THE SHIELING AT KENTTÄ was gray and silent. There was no music to be heard here now, just the lowing of ruminating cows in the distance. An empty bottle lay in the grass. The pastor picked it up, poured the last drops onto his palm, and sniffed it with a scowl. He walked over to the shed and looked inside. In my head I could still hear the stamping of the ring dance and the lithesome singer's tune, and I could see Nils Gustaf's elegant steps. And when I closed my eyes I could still feel Maria's waist beneath my hands.

The pastor muttered when he saw a hair ribbon that must have come off in the swirling dance. He came back out and walked toward the edge of the forest.

"Was it here that Roope attacked Nils Gustaf?"

"Yes, it was right here. But how could you know that, Pastor . . . ?"

Without a word he picked up a short, thick piece of wood from the grass. He gave it a tentative swing and held it in the way Roope had. He looked around intently and then began to follow the tracks into the forest. I followed close behind and could see him leaning forward, his eye sweeping the ground just as it did when he was hunting for rare plants. After a while he came to a halt and pointed at a blueberry thicket in which some of the stalks had recently been snapped. He parted them carefully, pushed his hand down into the soft moss, and brought out a knife in its sheath.

"It's Roope's," I confirmed.

"It's easier to find what you're looking for in daylight," the pastor said dryly.

He placed the knife in his coat pocket and looked about.

"We need to search along the path Jolina took. You can go first, Jussi. Shout if you find anything unusual."

"Yes."

We walked slowly along the Kenttä path. The pastor stopped every now and then to examine something that had attracted his attention. There was evidence of the revelers everywhere and the path was well trodden. We found several bottles, clods of ash where people had raked out their pipes, and a wad of spit the color of chewing tobacco on the leaf of a *Trollius europaeus*, the globeflower. I heard the pastor call out. When I turned, I could see him pointing into the forest.

"What do you think of this, Jussi?"

"What?"

There was the clear outline of footsteps in the cushiony moss.

"There . . . there are some big footprints," I said. "And smaller footprints next to them. A man and a woman must have walked through here."

"And a third person has walked here, to the side. Strange."

The pastor followed the impressions in the moss. I sensed the eagerness in him, almost like a tracker dog's excitement. Farther on, where the ground became softer, he stopped and pointed. The outline of a woman's boot could clearly be seen.

"Make a sketch of this, Jussi. Wait, here's a piece of paper. Draw the imprint as accurately as you can. Try to include every detail."

I sat there drawing for some time, fighting off the mosquitoes. Meanwhile, the pastor walked on.

"Look, Jussi. The man and woman walked next to each other the whole time, with the third person walking nearby. The distance between his steps is short, as if he were sneaking along behind them. You can see how he took cover behind bushes and tree trunks!"

I hurried after him and handed him the sketch.

"And this is where their pursuer stopped and hid."

The pastor indicated where the moss behind an uprooted tree was squashed flat. The footprints were no longer distinguishable in the moss. He bent closer to inspect more carefully the sprigs of wild rosemary growing there.

"The pursuer stood here for quite a long time watching something that must have piqued his interest. Aha! Look at this, Jussi!"

A little farther on, a blueberry thicket had been flattened.

"They must have lain down here. I assume it was a man and a woman. Don't you agree, Jussi? They lay here embracing while someone was hiding over there watching. But who can they have been?"

"Jolina and the attacker?"

"Maybe. But the barn where Jolina locked herself in is quite some distance from here. Could she really have run so far after the assault?"

The pastor knelt down. He gently picked up a little brown stump.

"Look at this! Can you see what it is, Jussi?"

He gave the object to me. At first I thought it was a tiny fir cone, or possibly an animal dropping. Until I saw that it was burned at one end.

"*Siggar* . . ."

THE PASTOR WAS TIGHT-LIPPED and thoughtful as we continued toward the barn where Jolina had been found. He questioned me again and again about which men had danced with Jolina, whether any of them apart from Roope had appeared to act aggressively or oddly, and who among them was dressed as a *herrasmies*. I tried to recount what I remembered, but I had the feeling that I was disappointing the pastor. I had seen Jolina with the other girls, she had been one in the crowd. But everything seemed to pale into insignificance beside Maria.

After we had walked quite some distance, we saw a man coming toward us along the marsh path. It was Elias, Jolina's father, and he had the dog with him on a leash. Elias made me think of an ox, with his broad torso and his stooping posture. His head seemed to lack a neck, as if it grew straight out of the top of his body. He was unwilling to meet the pastor's eye, but turned his face from side to side as he spoke.

He started to walk in front of us to show us the way to the barn. After a while he veered off into the forest, where, beyond a small marsh, there lay a hay meadow with a tall storehouse. It was timbered in the traditional way, with a loft above jutting out.

"Was it in here Jolina was found?"

"Yes."

"And the door was latched on the inside?"

"Yes."

"Has the sheriff been to see it?"

"He has, and the constable."

The pastor gave me a knowing look. There were unlikely to be any clues in there now, other than those left by Brahe and Michelsson.

"Did they look outside as well?"

"Well, they walked about."

"Did they search very far?"

Elias couldn't understand what the pastor was driving at and just scratched his mallet-shaped chin.

The storehouse had been left unlocked. The pastor entered and climbed up the ladder to the loft.

"So up here was where she was lying?"

"Yes, over there by the wall. Under the sacks."

The pastor bent down and picked up some mouse droppings.

"These got caught in her skirt," he whispered to me. "But I see no blood here."

We climbed back down. The pastor asked me to lock the door on the inside with the crosspiece that was propped up next to it. I positioned it in the slots and heard him rattle the handle.

"That should have kept her safe," he said. "Was Jolina familiar with the storehouse?"

"Everybody in the village is."

"She must have run here to hide. But the assault took place elsewhere."

"The sheriff thought—" Elias began, but broke off.

"What?"

"That she'd arranged to meet a man here. But Jolina would never do that!"

The man's voice had suddenly become shrill, and he looked as though he wanted to hit something.

"We'll soon know," the pastor said gently.

"Jolina isn't that sort of girl!"

When the pastor walked up to the dog we had tied to a birch tree, the mutt stood up and patiently licked her lips. He took the cloth bearing the scent of Jolina out of his jacket pocket and the dog eagerly buried her nose into it. The pastor took the leash and followed the dog back along the path.

"Seek!"

The dog pulled hard on the leash and we half ran over the uneven ground. A short distance along the path she stopped and started sniffing in the verge. Just a few paces in, among the short birch trees, we came across an area where the grass had been compressed. It looked very much like an elk's resting place, and I thought at first it was indeed an elk scent the dog had detected. But she thrust her nose in and started scrabbling vigorously with her front paws. The pastor let Elias take the leash while he crouched down and examined the ground. In among the vegetation was something shiny. He carefully freed the object and lifted it up. It was a long, thick brass pin.

"Do you know what this is?"

"It's Jolina's hairpin," Elias said.

The pastor scratched at some rust-colored marks and tested it with his tongue.

"Blood?" I asked.

He nodded.

"Jolina stabbed the man with the pin. That was how she managed to escape. Then she ran to the barn and barricaded herself in.

"It's hers," Elias repeated. "It was a gift for her confirmation."

He reached out to take it, but the pastor folded it into a handkerchief.

"The sheriff has to see it. May I quickly borrow your shirt as well?"

"My shirt?"

"Yes, your shirt. I need to polish my spectacles."

Elias looked nonplussed and hesitantly removed his shirt so that the pastor could polish his glasses. Meanwhile, I observed the pastor eying Elias's upper body. His shoulder was unharmed, with no pin marks to be found.

"Thank you," the pastor said, returning the shirt.

With his spectacles on his nose, he bent down and scrutinized the ground.

"I think you're right, Elias, that Jolina hadn't arranged to meet anyone at the barn," he said. "This was where the attack took place."

The pastor began to go through the flattened blades of grass, bending them over gently and looking at them closely from every angle.

"Here it is," he said, holding up a button. There was a white thread still in the hole.

"I could see there was a button missing from her clothes. The perpetrator ripped the collar open to get to her neck."

The button was folded up in the handkerchief along with the hairpin. Then he crouched down in the grass and sniffed around. He indicated that I should do the same, and all of a sudden I thought I could detect the smell that had been clinging to her skirt.

"Boot grease," I whispered.

"So Jolina set off home after the dance. And then?"

"The fellow followed her."

"Possibly. He might have been dancing with her and now he wanted something else."

The pastor looked thoughtful.

"Remember, someone sneaked after the man and woman earlier. Who probably saw them lie down to . . . embrace. We can assume that he found the sight arousing. The desire of his flesh was stirred. What do you think, Jussi?"

I blushed and mumbled in agreement.

"Afterward he crept away and ended up here."

"The same man?"

"He was excited by the scene he had witnessed. He had been drinking as well and his judgment was impaired. Maybe he was recalling how he attacked Hilda Fredriksdotter and now wanted to do the same thing again."

I made no reply. The pastor was humming to himself as he took note of the surroundings.

"The marsh path has quite a long straight stretch just here," he said. "Which would enable you to see a person from a distance. The perpetrator must have concealed himself here in the grass. Though not precisely here, for he would have risked being seen. If you wanted to hide, Jussi, which place would you have chosen?"

My eye was drawn to the opposite side of the path, where there was a dense growth of small fir trees. I pointed to them and felt slightly nauseous.

"There."

The pastor agreed.

"We have to try to think like the attacker. Get inside his head. Let's have a look, Jussi."

Elias stayed where he was with the dog while we walked over. Behind the firs we found a gray tree stump covered in lichen. The ground in front of the stump had clearly been trampled on.

"Exactly as I suspected. This was where the fellow sat and waited. And look at this. Still fresh."

The pastor held up a branch of fir that had been lying on the ground.

"He cut this off to gain a better view," I suggested.

"No, look more closely. You'll notice the twigs are damaged, and I surmise he was sitting here waving it about."

"At the insects."

"That's right, Jussi. The man had been sitting here for quite a while when Jolina arrived. What can that mean?"

"He hoped she was on her way home."

"But why Jolina in particular? He knew there was a dance in Kenttä, so maybe he was waiting for any woman who happened to come by. When a group of several girls passed he let them be. He was waiting for someone walking alone."

Something by the stump had caught the pastor's attention and he leaned forward.

"But what's this?"

He gingerly picked up something tiny between his thumb and forefinger. At first I thought it was a sedge stalk, before realizing it was a tiny wood shaving.

"Help me, Jussi. Let's collect them."

We started carefully turning over the moss and lingonberry plants, and found several small wood chips.

"What is it?" I asked.

"You've seen this kind of thing in my study."

I turned the minuscule shaving over; it looked as though it had been removed with a knife. There was also the residue of something else, darker, gray like graphite.

"Pencil lead!"

"So the man was sitting here . . . sharpening a pencil," the pastor murmured. "He was sitting here writing. The monster sat here and wrote while he waited for his victim."

"Or . . ." I muttered, "or he was sitting here drawing."

The pastor folded the shavings in a piece of paper and waved to Elias.

"Don't allow any stranger to visit Jolina," he said. "A villain is at large here."

As we walked back to the parsonage something came to the pastor's mind.

"The injury Jolina had on her right temple—what do you think about that, Jussi?"

"The man must have hit her."

"Yes. And?"

"With his hand. His fist."

"Let me try to hit you in the same spot, Jussi."

I stared at him without understanding.

"Are you going to hit me, Pastor?"

He nodded calmly. He raised his right hand and aimed but stopped just short of my right temporal bone.

"That feels awkward, Jussi."

"It would be easier if you hit with your other hand, Pastor."

"My thoughts exactly. You recall that Hilda Fredriksdotter's hair had been pulled out on the same side of the scalp. The right."

"So, you think the perpetrator is . . . is left-handed, Pastor?"

The pastor puffed with satisfaction on his pipe.

"Good, Jussi," he said. "Good thinking."

23.

People are greatly in fear of the Devil. Especially when he comes in the guise of a wolf or a snake. But he is far more dangerous in human form. And most dangerous of all in the form of an angel. For when Satan himself transforms into an angel of light, it is hard to escape him.

—LARS LEVI LAESTADIUS

THE MISTS GRADUALLY DISSIPATED. BRITA KAJSA GENTLY STROKED the pastor's cheek.

"You slept so fitfully," she whispered. "Your writhing around made the bed shake."

"I was dreaming about a bear."

The pastor's wet cheeks glistened in the dim light.

"A bear?"

"Yes, there was a gigantic bear under our bed, wild and ferocious. The bed was moving up and down as he tried to get out and I was fighting back with all my strength."

"You're soaked with perspiration."

The pastor was breathing hard, as if he had been running.

"I think I was battling the Prince of Darkness. I feel his presence every day. He wants to destroy all the good we have achieved. Stamp out our faith here in the north."

"But we'll fight back."

"Every Sunday I think the devil has sneaked in among the lambs. He is one of the silent men in the pews, head bared, looking at the cross. Can my utterances bring him to a halt? Can my preaching penetrate the dragon's scales, reach into the ogre's hardened heart? Which words can make the evil among us stop?"

Brita Kajsa lay quietly for a moment.

"We have Jolina," she said, by and by. "She was attacked by the villain but managed to outwit him. I think she could identify him."

"But the man was wearing a mask."

"His smell. His way of moving, his breathing when he's excited, the feel of his hands against her body. Women remember things like that."

"She appears to be paralyzed with fear," the pastor said.

"Jolina is strong. Give her time and she'll get over it."

"Jolina did in fact contrive to injure the man."

"How?"

"She stabbed him in the shoulder and drew blood. I think that ensured her escape and survival."

"Then just look for a man with that sort of wound!"

"It is the sheriff's business, for all that."

"Tell everyone we're on his trail. Spread the word in the village. Maybe that will scare him off."

The pastor nodded thoughtfully.

"Yes, maybe then he'll stop. Maybe he will."

24.

THE PASTOR INVITED ME TO ACCOMPANY HIM TO THE SHOP IN Pajala. In common with market days in Kengis, the shop was where you could hear most of the village gossip. The inquisitive would install themselves here hoping to pick up some juicy piece of local news about fornication and brawls, sibling quarrels and robbery, sickness and sudden death. Naturally there was talk of poor Jolina, attacked by an unknown man. What had she actually been doing at the dance? Why did she not stay home, like all properly behaved girls? Was it simply her beau she had met that evening, who had finally had enough of her taunting rebuffs?

The pastor asked if he might take a look at the pencils. There were two types in the shop's range and he bought one of each. Then he asked if he could see the boot wax. The merchant, Henriksson, opened a tub of the smelly fat and praised its water-repellent qualities. The pastor dipped his finger in, held it to his nose, and then let me sniff it, before wiping his finger on a handkerchief. I saw him put it discreetly into his coat pocket.

"The price is a touch high," he said.

"But it's the best quality. This wax will never turn rancid. Surely the pastor won't begrudge himself," the merchant said fawningly.

"It must be the well-to-do who buy this?"

"The mill owner himself is one of the customers. And the pastor's sexton too. Ask him what he rubs into his church boots. Well, look who's here! If it isn't the sheriff himself."

Brahe walked through the door and gave a guarded nod when he saw the pastor.

"The pastor is looking at boot wax," Henriksson simpered. "Perhaps the sheriff could recommend its application?"

"How goes it with the investigation into the villain?" the pastor asked, in a voice just loud enough to make everyone in the shop fall silent and listen.

"We're on his trail."

"Is there anything in particular the general public should know?"

"He appears to have been a passing vagabond. A type seen in the area."

"But could such vagrants afford this fine shoe wax? There were traces of it on Jolina's clothes."

Brahe had nothing to say.

"The sheriff did make an examination of her clothes, didn't he?" The pastor was persistent.

"Obviously, obviously."

"So you also know the perpetrator was injured?"

"Injured?"

"Yes, a puncture wound. Jolina managed to stab the man in the left shoulder, resulting in his blood on her clothes. It might be useful for people hereabouts to know that."

"Of course."

"Because then they might be able to find out if there's any fellow with a fresh puncture wound. I doubt it's had time to heal yet."

"So the pastor went through the girl's clothing?"

"Yes, but you said you did as well. Let us suppose all the men in the area could be examined. One of them might display a puncture wound on his left shoulder. Or does the sheriff have specific evidence that points to a vagrant?"

I detected the pastor's pleasure in revealing the sheriff's incompe-

tence, and how greedily the listeners hung on his every word. The
information would soon be spread throughout the entire parish.

"Moreover, I believe Jolina will be able to identify the guilty
man as soon as she has recovered."

"But the man was masked," the sheriff said.

"There are other distinctive features," the pastor said, staring defiantly at the sheriff. "Women are adept at noting details that often
escape men."

The sheriff took a step toward us. It looked almost as though he
intended to assail the pastor. I hastily pulled him out of the shop by
the arm.

"Was that wise?" I whispered.

"Now people know that we're not looking for a tramp."

"But Jolina might have been placed in danger?"

"When this gets out, the culprit will know we're on his trail.
Then he would hardly dare attack anyone else."

We left the courtyard with our wares. A woman dressed in black
was standing by the gate. With her shoulders hunched, she looked
as though she were cold. She appeared to have been waiting for
quite some time and as soon as she saw the pastor she hurried toward us. A pointed nose was sticking out of her shawl, a drip on the
end of it. The pastor took the woman's claw-like hand and greeted
her warmly.

"*Jumalan terve*. God's peace."

She was overcome by emotion, and her words sputtered into
dribbling froth. Stammering, she held out a piece of folded material, but when the pastor started to open it she snatched it back and
clasped it to her chest.

"Do you feel unwell, ma'am?"

"It's . . . it's my boy."

"Your son?"

She turned and hurriedly shuffled away. The pastor rushed after her.

"Tell me what is preying upon your mind."

"My boy is sick. Very sick."

"Stay for a moment. Let us pray for your son. What is his name?"

She increased her pace.

"Stop!" the pastor said, more sharply.

At that, she halted, her white lips tightly closed. The pastor tugged the piece of fabric out of her icy hands and carefully unfolded it. It was a child's vest, so small that it must belong to a baby.

"Do you want to give it to me, ma'am?"

"No," she whispered.

"First you gave it to me, and then you took it back."

"The lad needs to . . . he needs to wear it."

Then the pastor understood. Tears glistened in the corners of his eyes.

"Only Jesus can heal," he muttered, with forced composure.

"Jesus," she echoed. "*Jeesuksen Kristuksen . . .*"

She grabbed his arm again, convulsively, as if to draw him into her own body, swallow him up. He freed himself as she made a deep bow and pressed her greasy, damp brow against the back of his hand.

"Let us pray," he forced out. "What is wrong with the infant?"

"Measles."

In his mind the pastor could see little Levi's swollen face and even today could still hear the boy's fast, feverish breathing. He had offered a thousand prayers for the child's soul, a thousand and a thousand more.

"Dear Jesus," the pastor mumbled, "dear Jesus, hear our prayer."

The woman began to rock back and forth, back and forth. Her pointed nose was like a beak. A bird pecking seeds out of the mud. The parson stood with closed eyes, while more and more awakened souls inquisitively joined the tight circle that was form-ing. *Jeesuksen Kristuksen* . . . A miracle was about to happen. A child was going to be saved. Afterward, several of them would report that a gust of mild air could be felt, a breeze that came from above bearing the scent of honey.

The pastor was aware of people pushing from every direction. They all wanted to warm themselves. It was he who had kindled the flames that were spreading over the land of the north, he who kept stoking the fire until the whole of Finnmark was ablaze. But what if the revival were merely ignited brushwood that flared up furiously but was immediately extinguished? And all that was left behind was the blackened earth.

Had he tricked them all? Perhaps it was better to lead a lukewarm life? Tepid but persevering? Smolder like the *Phellinus igniarius*, the fungus known as the fire sponge, producing almost no warmth, giving off a faint wreath of smoke that never ends. Not to do very much, but to do it all the time. The pastor who claimed to despise all those who were priests only in pursuit of material gain, with their dutiful biblical utterances to the pews of the replete bourgeoi-sie, their grinding litanies that brought no sign of change. Step by step they made their laborious way up the mountainside, when they should have been running. That was what the pastor thought.

The revival caused a great hullaballoo. Church folk seemed to enjoy a good racket. Sinners' hearts racing, faces contorting with passion; the patter of curled-toe shoes, as an entire congregation jumped in *liikutuksia*. Old men and women pushing forward and seeing not a simple village priest, but Jesus.

What if the only thing he had accomplished were idolatry?

25.

THE PASTOR KEPT A FEW PACES IN FRONT OF ME ON THE WAY home from the shop. I could see he was despondent. When he was in a good mood he was happy to reason with me; he would raise his elbows and form words with his hands, as if he carried his thoughts like an armful of unformed bread dough, a fermenting lump that had to be constantly kneaded and knocked back to prevent it from dropping to the ground. But today his arms hung stiffly by his side.

Most people behave like reindeer. They want to walk with others, move forward in a herd. If a female grunts, the others will start to grunt too. If a male gives out a warning signal, they all run, even if they haven't seen the danger themselves. The reindeer navigates by fear, its enemies the wolverine, the wolf, the bear, and the lynx. A human being is also afraid, created that way by our Lord. Luther's call was to love and fear God. But we love and fear each other with the same intensity. And most of all we fear losing one another. Being alone, being separated from the protection of our herd.

But the pastor was different. He seemed to represent an alien species. When all around him were shouting, he was silent. When everyone pointed in front, he turned aside. When he was mocked or threatened, he appeared more steadfast in his conviction. He saw what he saw, took note of it, and lodged it in his mind. Opposing the authorities didn't faze him. Brandy was an obvious example, for everyone loved brandy. Swigged by peasants and enthusiastically refilled by innkeepers, whose pockets clinked with silver coins.

How could brandy be anything other than a good thing? The first mouthful spread warmth and happiness, the second imparted good humor and the desire to talk. What was wrong with that? Even Jesus drank wine, didn't he?

But the pastor saw that which had surrounded me as a child. Drunken bodies lying in the filth, trousers full of excrement, and porridge-like vomit all over the deerskins. Waking up to the horrors of streaming red eyes and a tongue curling round the neck of a bottle for the last drop of poison. The herd of reindeer carried on, but the pastor turned aside. He was the most courageous man I had ever met.

I also walked alone. But in my case it wasn't courage, it was the lack of it. I could do nothing else. My child-lips were damaged where the blows had struck, my young arms bruised by cruel pinching. And the worst of all punishments was her way of pulling my hair at the nape of my neck, where it hurt the most. As if she were ripping up turnip greens, yanking and pulling until blood trickled out, as if she wanted to tear off my entire scalp in one gluey lump of skin.

My sister wasn't beaten as often. She wasn't as wicked as I was. She never argued, just looked at me with her huge eyes. She didn't learn to crawl in the usual way, but by bracing with her tiny hands she pulled herself along on her backside in a comical, bouncing way. That was when they started calling her the runt hare. I remember how red and sore her bottom was. Splinters and twigs scraped her skin and the mosquitoes and ants sucked her blood and excreted their waste until the skin between her legs was like an enormous ulcer. She scratched off the purple scabs and screamed with pain. I used to turn her onto her stomach and spit some phlegm onto it, big gobs that I rubbed in like ointment. When she was older she was given a ragged tunic, but never anything to help her bum. When she squatted to relieve herself, the inflamed crack was exposed, red and chapped like an ax cut. I taught her to stand astride the embers of the fire once in a while and let the smoke rise until a shimmering film of tar settled over the wound, to keep the insects away, at least. But she still scratched day and night and bits of her came off and fell into the mat of needles.

"Runt," croaked the witch. "Come here, runty."

And my sister hopped over to the stinking bosom to receive something chewed up straight from the hag's mouth, turnip maybe, or some sinews of reindeer shoulder, or perhaps just grain. Spittle and grain from the mouth of evil, that was the bread on offer.

My sister had two names, the most beautiful names of all: Anne Maaret. But the witch never used them, she just called her the runt. "Look at the runt, look at what she's doing." But I used to say her real names. When we were alone I would whisper them softly under the mountain birches. "Here, Anne Maaret," I would say, blowing the names gently into her damaged ear. "I have saved some bread for you, Anne Maaret."

When I decided to run away, I tried to take my sister with me. I shouted and hectored, I pulled so hard I nearly dislocated her arm. But she was too small. I couldn't save her. I will never forget her desperate sobs while she clung to the witch, clutched at the frock on the snorting pile of rancid lard and lousy hair that I could never bring myself to call my mother. I left my sister, the only person who was fond of me. Since that time I have traveled life's road alone. I am not afraid of being lonely. I took my knife and cut myself free from the human body because I had to.

These were the thoughts in my head as the pastor and I wandered homeward. Two wild reindeer, which no lasso could catch. He invited me to go with him into his study. He silently took out his knife and began to sharpen both of the pencils he had purchased.

We compared them with the shavings from the scene of the crime. It was easy to see that these were different. The culprit's pencil didn't come from the shop in Pajala. The shoe wax, on the other hand, smelled the same as the grease that had stuck to the girl's kirtle.

26.

THE PASTOR'S ENEMIES CONTINUED TO MAKE HIS LIFE DIFFICULT. A report was sent to the chapter accusing him of refusing to conduct a service for a woman after childbirth. The report was anonymous, but the pastor knew local innkeepers were behind it. On the occasion of churching ceremonies, beer fests would usually be held for the new mothers and their babies, and that meant there were significant profits. But since the pastor's arrival revenue from the sale of alcohol had diminished markedly, and now the innkeepers wanted revenge. And, despite an appeal, the pastor was sentenced to pay five hundred riksdalers in compensation to the woman, a substantial sum that he was obliged to settle.

Instead of using their silver to buy brandy, the Sami and peasants began to donate it to the school or to help the poor. This too aroused suspicion and envy in many quarters. Surely it was going into the pastor's pockets? Didn't some of it end up with his children and relatives? New accusations were sent to the chapter about the pastor's accounts. They tried to wear him down, bespatter his name with dirt. Some of it stuck.

In the end the chapter felt obliged to act. The decision was taken to make a visitation and Bishop Israel Bergman from Härnösand boarded a ship and commenced the long journey north to Kengis Church. After several days' sailing across the Gulf of Bothnia, he arrived at Haparanda and stepped ashore at the mouth of the Torne. There he took a seat in one of the long river boats typically used in the district and was poled upstream by wiry, Finnish-speaking boatmen. They knew every part of the long river and every rapid, pool, and bend had a name. They swerved to avoid stones you couldn't see, they knew of resting places where pitch-filled pine soon crackled with warmth. It was as though the river were a creature unto itself, fantastically long, with its head resting in the mountains and its toes dipping into the Gulf of Bothnia. The men caught grayling on the towline during the journey, the bishop emptied the nets, and they ate the fish, piping hot, tender, and delicious, with their fingers. The bishop had to eat more quickly than he was used to, as the other men had a knack for dispatching their food at speed. Their hands were as tough as cowhide, they never wore gloves; their grip on the poles and the oar shafts was so hard that after thousands of miles' use the timber bore the indentations of their fingers.

The farther north the bishop traveled, the lighter the summer nights became. When they stopped overnight in Övertorneå, he took the opportunity to visit the church with its ornate baroque organ from Stockholm. With his own hands he held the walking stick used by Russian Cossacks to beat the priest Johannes Tornberg to death. That night, as the bed seemed to rock like the river beneath him, he couldn't sleep. He lay listening to the relentless whine of a mosquito under the eaves, and he thought about the remarkable man up in Kengis whom he was on his way to see.

Bishop Israel Bergman and the pastor had become acquainted during the latter's student years in Härnösand. Bergman was a mathematician, and had impressed his students with his sharp intellect while also clearly caring about his young charges. He was particularly concerned for those who, like himself, came from small Norrland communities, such as the parish of Attmar outside Sundsvall, where he was born. As a professor of astronomy, he was deeply fascinated by the stars, and on one unforgettable autumn evening he gathered his students together in his garden at home. There he had rigged up a tall device that resembled a gun barrel, but which he explained was an instrument for gazing at stars. One by one he bade the young men to sit down on the observation platform and gaze out into the vast universe. The students would never forget the moment they were able to contemplate the planet Saturn with its extraordinary ring system. They were infected by Bergman's excitement, when he explained that the small dots of light near it were not stars at all, but the planet's own moons orbiting the celestial body. But it was something else that made the biggest impression on them: when it was the would-be pastor's turn to observe the planet, the eyepiece was totally dark. He assumed that someone had moved the telescope's tube, and requested Bergman's help with adjusting the focus. The teacher enthusiastically explained that it was not the telescope that had shifted. Rather, what had moved was the thing under our feet. The celestial body we call Earth was rolling through space like a giant orb. For one dizzy moment, it made the young man's head spin and he had to support himself on Bergman's shoulder, which amused the professor.

As a teacher, Bergman demonstrated a dry humor that he had probably acquired in Uppsala's academic circles. Lateness was something he especially disliked and would earn a student the moniker "Service Canceled." As for him, he was in perpetual motion; there was always something to write, a thesis to read, a board meeting to attend. He claimed that was why he had never married; he simply hadn't had time.

Now, many years later, when he entered Kengis Church, he still displayed his somewhat crooked smile. He was five years older than the pastor, and age had left its mark on them both. The bishop's hairline had receded over the crown of his head and the thin tufts that remained had gone gray. He had a thick nose and a narrow, delicate mouth. But his gaze was still sharp and critical. Experienced educator that he was, Bergman had instantly taken in the place and everyone present, and from their seating he had identified hierarchies, alliances, and those individuals who could cause trouble.

It wasn't often that a bishop happened to pass through Kengis, and many people had come out of curiosity. The pastor's enemies and their wives had gathered in the pews at the front: the foundry owner Sohlberg, Forsström the merchant, Hackzell the bailiff, and Sheriff Brahe. Fellow believers had assembled farther back. There were far more of them, but for the most part they were poor, ignorant folk. The bishop seated himself in an imposing chair with padded cushions and ornate armrests. The pastor had requested something simpler for himself, a homemade kitchen chair. Bishop Bergman slipped on his spectacles and took out his papers and documents, which he placed on a drop-leaf table, covered in honor of the occasion by a white celebration cloth. He opened the proceedings, mindful that he should create a good atmosphere. However, it was soon obvious that several of those present had difficulty understanding his Swedish and his academic turns of phrase. In a calm voice he outlined the reason for his visit and began to list all the complaints made against the minister for this parish.

"Let us start with the accusation that the minister has not recorded honestly the donations to the school and the poor. After my arrival I went through the accounts in detail and have found nothing untoward. The amounts have been recorded accurately."

One of the innkeepers raised his voice.

"The minister said here in church that everyone who has gold, silver, or valuable clothes should give it all to him."

"Is that true?" the bishop asked.

The minister was prepared, and read out the announcement he had made during the church service.

"'If anyone is minded to offer alms for the school and the poor, this will be received by the undersigned. If it be gold, silver, or clothes, they will be converted into money for the school and the poor . . .'" he read.

He knew, of course, that the bishop himself organized collections for impecunious students in Härnösand. And, indeed, Bergman had no objection to this announcement.

Someone nudged Brahe, and he stood up and declared:

"The pastor doesn't follow Lutheran teachings! He's started doing his own kind of confessional."

"And in what way does the confessional contravene Lutheran teachings?"

Brahe stole a glance at the others and reiterated that it wasn't Lutheran. But in what way it might be heretical, he couldn't quite explain in theological terms, and the minister couldn't help but smile.

Next, they came to the matter of disorder during church services. In their complaint, the foundry owner Sohlberg and several of the others had denounced the fact that the awakened, and especially the women among them, were permitted to disturb the services with shouting and shrieking, and even dancing in pairs at the altar and in the aisle. All this impeded their attention to the sermon. In addition, the minister had encouraged the youngsters in particular to berate, condemn, and arouse the so-called "unawakened." What's more, in both his sermons and his conversations, the minister used language that was foul and shocking.

Bergman had the details of the complaint explained to him. By "disorder," the complainants meant all the *liikutuksia* that might occur during services. The congregation would be seized by profound emotion manifested in a kind of ecstasy. Frail old people would be up on the points of their curled-toe shoes, performing wild jumps and waving their arms about as if they wanted to fly. Burly farmers broke down in the most heartrending tears, their bodies swaying like trees in a gale. The minister didn't consider that he had ever encouraged this conduct himself, and his wife Brita Kajsa was never seen to join in. But it was also true that he had never forbidden or sought to stop it. The agitation arose from a deep spiritual force and was proof that the churchgoers' conversion and remorse were not playacting, but reached deep into their hearts. The commotion could even be seen as a sign of the Holy Spirit's presence, in the minister's opinion.

When it was the turn of Forsström the merchant to speak, he described how distasteful such a service was. People would shout and wail so much it was impossible to hear the sermon. You would be jostled in your seat or showered with spittle from the lost souls wandering to and fro in the aisle. Did not every member of this community have the right to listen to the service in the same orderly way as the rest of the kingdom?

The bishop turned to the awakened and asked if the hubbub troubled them. They replied in unison that it did not. On the contrary, *liikutuksia* strengthened their devotion. The debate continued for a while, until, when hostilities appeared to intensify, the bishop intervened. Having weighed up the pros and cons and noted something down, he reached a decision.

"Since this excitement appears to be of a spiritual nature, we cannot suppress it by force. But to avoid causing offense to others, the people concerned must leave the nave when it occurs."

Although disappointed whispering could be heard among the awakened, the burghers of Pajala were visibly pleased.

"On the other hand," the bishop went on, "there is nothing to prevent the pastor holding a special service for the awakened after the regular service."

And so it happened. Henceforth, the minister held two services on Sundays. One for the insouciant well-to-do, and after that, one for the awakened.

Toward the end of the visitation the bishop inquired as to whether there were any unlicensed premises in the region selling alcohol. None of the assembled company answered, so the minister asked to speak.

"Since we often see persons intoxicated, there must be inns, of course."

"Perhaps the sheriff knows where these inns are?"

Given that one of the innkeepers was sitting next to him, the sheriff shifted uncomfortably.

"I know very well . . ."

The bishop went on to deliver a sharply worded address on sobriety, in which he warned of the consequences of drinking.

"Those to whom it applies, take this to heart!"

After the meeting, a number of the awakened went up to the bishop and praised his courage and wisdom. One of the old women stretched out her arms and held him in a fierce embrace, her streaming tears moistening his chest. The bishop couldn't understand her Finnish and seemed thrown off guard by all the enthusiasm, but was clearly pleased with his performance.

27.

HAVING GIVEN THE MATTER DUE CONSIDERATION, THE PASTOR did in the end decide to have his portrait painted. A day or two later, with great fanfare, the artist Nils Gustaf arrived. A couple of crofter boys came along as bearers and were weighed down with bags and boxes and strange tripods. Nils Gustaf was welcomed with a substantial meal, over which respects were exchanged, though there was still palpable apprehension in the air. The pastor declared himself embarrassed by his own self-aggrandizement, but the parish might derive pleasure in seeing him preserved for the future. Nils Gustaf pointed out that such embarrassment was found only in the greatest of characters and it was of the utmost importance that this record should be made. The pastor's portrait could hang in the sacristy and be a source of support and inspiration for all future ministers. Perhaps this would even be the start of a tradition for every minister to be depicted in oils, so that the pastor would be the first in a long and imposing line.

After that a sizable deposit changed hands. The artist counted it carefully and then placed the money in a leather purse. That done, work on the preliminary sketches could commence.

One of the bearers was ordered to fetch a wooden casket the size of a smallish tabletop. Inside it lay some large sheets of paper and a box of charcoal sticks. The pastor was then invited to take up any position he chose in the courtyard. I noticed how stiff he was, this being a situation quite alien to him. Nevertheless, he persevered, advancing his toe slightly, lowering one shoulder, sticking out his chest. The artist viewed him from different angles, squinted up into the sky to assess the light, and bade the pastor make one-eighth of a turn while he circled round his subject. He went up to the pastor every now and again and adjusted something as if he were a doll, lifting his wrist, moving a wisp of hair from his brow, pulling out the tip of his collar. It all lasted a considerable time. Only then did the artist move over to the tripod, ease one of the sheets out of the casket, and secure it under a wooden batten. Next he held up the carbon stick and screwed up first the left eye and then the right eye, while shaking his head to and fro. Then, in an explosive flick of his wrist, the charcoal sliced through the air several times before diving down to the paper. There was an audible screech. It sounded as though he were squeezing a she-cat, making her spit on the paper. After only a few seconds he stepped back, sweat pouring down his face, and changed the piece of paper. The pastor in a new stance, trying a new coat, the French Legion of Honor received after La Recherche Expedition pinned on carefully by Brita Kajsa. A chair for him to sit in, in different positions. Finally, they went inside, into his study, where the light was softer and the shades of color more pronounced. The artist picked crayons out of a tin; waxy, oily crayons in yellow and purple, ice-blue and rosy red. After several further sketches he pulled out a large handkerchief, wiped his neck and cheeks, and concluded by blowing his nose loudly into the fabric.

"I think we have it," he announced.

Ceremoniously he laid out sheet after sheet on the floor. Some depicted the pastor full length, on others only one or two details were visible. His nose, for example, had an entire charcoal sketch to itself; it was large and bent in a distinctive way, an essential element for an accurate likeness. The pastor, Brita Kajsa, and those of the children who were at home had to appraise each sketch as Nils Gustaf pointed to it with his walking stick.

"I fancy a half figure, seated. The face in half profile to allow for a proper rendition of the nose, the eyes looking straight at us. We see a person on the road, someone who has taken a momentary rest. Imagine the play of light to the right at the back, an arbor perhaps."

"A what?" Brita Kajsa said doubtfully.

"A portion of the pastor's wife's delightful garden," the artist hurriedly explained. "You see how the vegetation forms a window of light where the sky can be glimpsed. You understand the symbolism?"

Brita Kajsa was won over by the unexpected praise and displayed an air of benevolence seldom witnessed in her. The pastor pointed at the table.

"So I'm sitting outside? The desk is going to be in the garden?"

"It is symbolic. In one hand, a magnifying glass, in the other, one of God's beautiful creations you have just been examining, a mountain plant. And by the herbarium, instead of a brandy glass we'll place your wooden cup, filled with fresh spring water from a babbling mountain brook."

"That is also symbolic," said the pastor, nodding thoughtfully.

"Just like the broken bread on the table. No wafer, but a hearty and nutritious potato loaf! And two fishes on a plate. And we'll prop the rifle against a birch tree in the background. You can see the branches, can't you? The pattern they form with the metal of the gun?"

"A cross!" I whispered.

The cross of Christ in Brita Kajsa's garden. It was a stroke of genius and filled us all with excitement. The artist moved the sheets of paper around, showing how the parts would coalesce into a hitherto unseen whole. It would be a full account, a unique picture, as deep and multifaceted as the pastor's own life.

"This is going to take some time, isn't it?" The pastor was thoughtful.

"Naturally it will require a number of sittings. We'll have many opportunities to exchange our thoughts. I have some folk paintings I would like to complete first, some local scenes, nothing formal."

"Dance scenes, perhaps?"

"Yes, I was in fact inspired by the dance setting a little while ago. Such heartwarming rusticity."

"Which ended badly."

"Yes, that was dreadful. To think that a violent criminal could lie in wait out there for a suitable victim."

"And you didn't notice anything yourself?"

"Such as . . . ? No, thank heavens."

The artist solemnly took his leave and the pastor accompanied him a short distance along the road. The bearers were bent under their load and disappeared in the direction of the foundry at Kengis, where the artist's cabin was.

"Did you see how he was sketching?" the pastor said in a low voice.

"Yes, it will be outstanding. The pastor's painting."

"I was thinking of something else. Did you see how he held the crayon, Jussi?"

"In his left hand."

The pastor pulled off his tie as we watched the walkers merge into the summer greenery.

28.

DURING THE HAYMAKING SEASON, I WAS HIRED AS A DAY laborer in the parish. The weather was favorable, and with no rain expected the hay would dry from one day to the next. I was sent out to one of the waterlogged bogs that had been divided up between the villages generations ago. The master was a withdrawn, sullen fellow who communicated with his ill-tempered wife in sidelong glances and gestures. They argued constantly or, more accurately, she walked around snarling and swinging her rake in a lethal manner, while the muscles in her husband's shoulders were knotted so tightly that he resembled a T. Their adult sons had left home, leaving only the daughter, as irascible as her mother. In the evenings they lay down in the hay barn while I rolled myself up in a blanket on the ground outside and listened to them continue their quarreling. They never called one another by name, but they had a large repertoire of epithets they spat at each other, words such as "swine," "pismire," "lard-bladder." I soon acquired the nickname Räkä, or Snot, and I could well understand why the family had so much difficulty getting hold of hay makers that they were forced to hire a stranger.

When it was time for a meal break, we gathered by the hay barn. There was a wooden barrel inside that had been driven there on a sledge earlier in the year. The lid had swollen and stuck, and the master had to tap an ax around the edge until it loosened. Filled with expectation and displaying a rare grin, he lifted the lid. Inside was a hairy blanket of mold. With his tobacco-stained fingers he lifted it off to reveal a fatty sludge streaked with yellow. His wife and daughter waited with bated breath, in one of the few moments they showed any kind feelings to one another. I saw the wife pick up her wooden cup, dip it in until it was full, and then take a slurp.

They called it *piimää*, in other words sour milk. But this was something quite different from the sort served fresh in the parsonage. I had never tasted anything so vile. It was musty and rank. Over the months in the hay barn the substance had fermented and putrefied until it was dead, and then it rose again and started re-fermenting. In the end it was so acrid, the noxious elements seemed to cancel each other out, leaving an overwhelming taste of graveyard. That was the food on offer, and that was what I forced into me as I retched involuntarily. But the strange thing was, you got used to it. By the second day it was easier. And on the third day, when the barrel was thumped open again, I could feel my mouth filling with saliva as soon as the stench reached my nose; and then I realized that I was beaten. I shakily held out my cup and it was returned to me full to the brim with the slime, and when I let it fill my palate, a song began to grow inside me, a poem, a sensation that my entire brain was addled, and instantly I wanted more.

THE WORK ITSELF WAS heavy and sweaty. The insects were irksome, especially the horseflies, so I kept my shirt on even though it was soaked through. Naturally I had been given the worst scythe: it was difficult to get it really sharp and it seemed to skew as it struck, so there was none of that swishing sound you would make if you were blowing grass away with your lips. I cut swath after swath nonetheless, smeared resin over my blisters, and downed gallons of water. As I was the lightest among them—I weighed less even than the daughter—I was the one who had to strap on the marsh skis and cautiously tramp farthest out on the undulating flark. Despite my skis, the water reached above my ankles, the surface rolled like waves on a great lake, and if I fell, or if I put my foot right through it, I would never be able to stand up again. In the black depths beneath me I felt the icy fingers of the netherworld dwellers groping for me, creatures who wanted to drag my hot, perspiring body into the kingdom of the cold. I thought about Hilda Fredriksdotter, about how she lay in the bog facedown, about what horrors must have filled her eyes down there.

Before I fell asleep I would pick up my birch-bark knapsack, carefully fold back the leather binding, and open a book. It belonged to Selma, the pastor's daughter, who had lent it to me, and I never touched it without washing my hands in the stream first. *Apostle of the Wilderness* was its title. It was about a young man like myself. Who went out into the great forests. Where he built himself a wooden house. And caught fish and snared wild animals. And then he met a woman who made him believe.

The more I read, the more the letters faded away. When I had turned back the cover, the doors had opened onto a world I could step inside. I entered, and became Aaron. I felt the suspense when the wolves advanced, when the arrows were unleashed and the only thing holding the wild animals at bay was the flaming torch in his hand. And the word of God. Carried in safety through the perils by the torch and the word of God.

The first pages had been almost impenetrable. The letters were very small and it was in Swedish, to boot. Every sentence had to be endlessly chewed over. But then it became less difficult and by the second chapter I was hooked. I shaped my lips so that my mouth could feel the meaning of the words, that made it easier. But I made no outward sound; it all happened in my mind. A different world was lying in my knapsack during the day, waiting for me like a trusty friend. Someone I could converse with at night, listen to, take by the hand and follow. It was the best book I have ever read.

Without my noticing, the woman had come to stand beside me. She must have been on her way to pee before she retired. I had been so immersed in the book I hadn't heard her footsteps. Now she was staring at me as I lay on my bed of spruce twigs with the nighttime mosquitoes buzzing round my head, staring at the cover, at the too-white paper I was awkwardly trying to conceal. This was something unexpected. Something she had never seen before. Her lips blubbered noiselessly for a moment, wet with spittle, while her brain worked overtime.

"You'll go crazy," she said eventually. "Satan's little *noaidi*. Crazy. If you read, you'll go crazy."

At first I was going to hide the book away. But then something happened: I turned into Aaron. I swung the torch at the wild animal. I turned my eyes firmly to the page and stepped back in. This was my hour of rest; the working day was over. This had nothing to do with the old hag.

And Aaron awaited me, his muscles taut. He was face-to-face with a bear, holding his hunting spear in his hand. It was difficult to see how this would turn out.

29.

WHEN I RETURNED TO THE PARSONAGE AT NIGHTFALL A FEW days later, the pastor was in the sauna. He stuck out his steaming mop of hair and waved to me.

"The stones are still hot, Jussi!"

I was unsure; normally I would bathe last, after the family, the visitors, and the servants. But he seemed to be eager and in a good mood, so I put my knapsack away and went in. It was the first time I had seen the pastor naked. He was surprisingly hairy, not smooth-skinned as we Lapps and Tornedalians usually are. His genitals were strikingly large and hung slightly askew. He spread out a piece of sacking on the wooden bench so that the soot wouldn't blacken me and poured a few ladles of water over the pile of stones.

"Really and truly," he said, giving a pleasurable groan, "isn't the sauna God's greatest gift to mankind?"

I could only agree with his sentiment. My shoulders ached. My thighs ached. My arms, my blistered hands, even the little muscles in my toes hurt. But gradually I felt the pores in my skin open and small drops of perspiration squeeze out; and I was rendered permeable and wide open to the miraculous healing powers of the steam from the *löyly*. My ears started to ring and my temples to pound, as the blood vessels expanded to let the blood sweep through. This blood, which was so filled with salts and strength.

By this time the pastor had been sitting there for a good while and was radiating a rare gentleness. He handed me his *vihta* and asked me to beat his back with the bunch of fragrant silver birch, in particular the area a handbreadth below his shoulder blade, where his age prevented him from reaching. He moaned with pleasure, while I beat with all my might. The summer scent of birch filled the sauna, the leafy twigs skipping across his thighs and chest, and soon the pastor gave me the same treatment. He beat as hard as a catechist, just as I wanted him to, lash after lash so that the marsh mud came off and washed away through the slats in the bench.

Afterward we sat in silence. The prickling heat was over and the stone oven was emitting its protracted secondary warmth, like a large, curled-up animal.

"I have been in paradise," the pastor said.

"Ah," I said.

"In paradise. I didn't know it had its place here in the north. It's called Poronmaanjänkkä. Below Jupukka Mountain. I didn't think such floral splendor was possible up here."

He half closed his heavy eyelids in his usual manner when withdrawing into himself. It was as though the pictures flowed out of him and attached to the dark sauna walls, as if he were illuminated by an inner source of light.

"Orchids!" he exclaimed. "The entire bog! Rich violet, pale pink, deep red. As if the Creator had splashed paint from the whole palette with his brush. It was a sea, Jussi!"

"A sea?"

"I had only intended to stay for a short while, but I couldn't leave. The food ran out, I was bitten to death by mosquitoes, but I could hardly drag myself away."

"The pastor must be exhausted!"

"Not like you, my boy. Were you paid your wages? Did the old fellow keep his promise?"

"I got a few coins. And I read as well."

"Read?"

"A book I borrowed from Selma. *Apostle of the Wilderness*."

"Indeed. Indeed. And what do you think of it, Jussi?"

"It was . . . it was . . ."

"Yes?"

"Never before have I read anything as good."

"Apart from God's word?"

"Yes, of course. But this book . . . it was . . ."

The pastor nodded pensively at my stammering. He placed his fingertips together and propped his elbows on his knees.

"Such books as these are called novels. I am a little afraid of them."

"But it was about faith."

"Yes, I know. But all that power. The collective power of words when they are piled up like that. Do you think it's altogether a good thing, Jussi?"

"Aaron fights the wild animals and becomes a believer. He starts to preach God's word."

"Exactly, Jussi. Just imagine those words in the service of the devil. A novel from evil's perspective. A story about evil deeds, about death and corruption."

"Books like that will never be written."

"I fear that time will come. That such things will even become common."

"Books about evil?"

"Yes. About murder and death. About the effects of wickedness."

"But . . ."

My thoughts were in turmoil. Could books be dangerous? I tried to pull myself together.

"But if . . . if you describe evil, and then show how evil is outwitted? In the novel you can follow the devil being fought and in the end being wrestled to the ground."

"By whom?"

"By the rest of us! By good people, righteous people. The pastor could write a book like that."

"A novel?"

"In the service of goodness. It would reach out to people. It might be in the interest of salvation."

The pastor looked at me sharply. For a moment I thought he was angry. But his voice was thoughtful.

"I have actually considered it already, Jussi. I have been thinking about it for quite a while. To write a book in which you can see evil being conquered."

"As opposed to what happens in reality."

"Perhaps that is precisely why people like to read them. Novels about crime. Maybe you should write one yourself?"

I grinned at him, expecting to meet his teasing smile. But I couldn't find it. Instead he laid his arm lightly on my shoulder.

"And you have to learn to speak," he went on.

"I can speak."

"No, Jussi, you talk. Speaking is something quite different. To soften a grudging heart with words. To gnaw one's way in, even when the listener is unwilling and resists.

"Does the pastor mean preaching?"

"We will be having guests this week. The brothers Juhani and Pekka Raattamaa and the preacher Per Nutti are coming. Be among them and listen. I'm sure you can learn something."

He ladled on more water so that we were enveloped in a long heat, the heat you never want to leave. And he added, as if it were a trifling detail of scarcely any import:

"You'll be there for the questioning in the afternoon?"

"Is the pastor at a church inquiry?"

"No, not that sort of inquiry. I'm expecting someone, a young woman. Her name is Maria."

30.

I SAT ON A THREE-LEGGED STOOL, IN CLEAN CLOTHES, SWEATING. Perhaps the sauna was still working its effects on me, for I had to constantly wipe my arm across my wet brow. We were sitting in the pastor's study, waiting. He was wearing his spectacles, with their peculiar glass prisms attached to long stalks of shiny metal. They slid down his large nose as he studied our notes. Now and then he peered out of the window.

When the knock at the door came, I stopped breathing.

"The pastor has a visitor."

And there she stood. My beloved. It seemed as though she had a circle of light around her head, a halo, and her feet scarcely touched the floor. I was forced to cough into my clenched hands and waited for her to blow away, dissolve like a picture in smoke. She looked at me and it hurt; her gaze seemed to come from inside a painting. My fear was such that I couldn't smell her scent; perhaps there was none, perhaps she was in a different world. I wanted to put my hands around her waist again, to cling to her sweetness; I wanted to breathe her in and never breathe out again. I had to cough one more time to make a hole in the world where the air could get in. She remained standing in the doorway and curtsied, her eyes darting between the pastor and me.

"Come in, come in," the pastor said, indicating the visitor's chair awaiting her.

I stood up hurriedly, drenched in sweat. When she sat down, so did I, and I fumbled for the paper and pencil with trembling hands.

The pastor had given me strict orders not to speak unless I was addressed directly and to write down exactly what I heard.

"Maria, you are engaged as a maid, are you not?" he began.

"Yes," she squeaked, so quietly that we could hardly hear her.

She had changed into her finest Sunday clothes for the visit, as if going to a church service. Undoubtedly she had spent a long time scrubbing herself, and her neck had turned red. Small golden curls were peeping out from under her headscarf and I wanted to twirl them round my finger. Tuck them between my lips. I thought I would write something about it, her sweetness, but it was just a scrawl. I crossed it out and wrote "maid" in stiff, uneven handwriting.

"Maria is a pretty name," the pastor said.

"It's my mother's name as well."

"And Maria loves dancing, so I've heard."

Giving me a furtive sidelong glance, she blushed intensely, her neck flaring up as if covered in gnat bites. I was furious. Now she would think I was the one who had been telling tales to the pastor.

Maria sat in silence, her cheeks burning. The pastor stared hard at her, tormenting her, wanting her to feel the agony of sin.

"There is nothing wrong with dancing," he said after a pause. "Did Maria believe I thought there was? I know people say I'm severe, but I actually enjoyed dancing in my youth."

I gawked at the pastor, scarcely believing my ears. Would that rather stooped body manage a waltz? No, he was lying!

"However, one must heed the dangers," the pastor added hastily. "Dancing can arouse the desires of the flesh. Like a sauna, it can make someone hot. And that person might walk off to cool down?"

She attempted a nod, but her neck was so tense her head barely moved. Once again the pastor waited, knitting his eyebrows. I wrote a jerky "sauna."

"And what about after the dance? When everyone walked home-ward?"

"Yes?"

"Was Maria alone then?"

"Yes."

It came too fast. The pastor placed his fingertips together and flexed his fingers. Perhaps he was emulating one of his old professors in Uppsala.

"So no gallant escort accompanied Maria home along the path?"

"No. . . . No, no one at all."

With shaking fingers, I wrote down "no one at all."

"None of the other girls?"

"No."

"Is Maria absolutely sure?"

She swallowed and gave a brisk nod. I wanted to shout at the pastor to be quiet, to stop tormenting her.

"I walked . . . I walked home on my own."

"Did Maria notice anyone following her?"

"Who might that have been?"

"A man."

"No. . . ."

"Did Maria see the lad Roope during the evening?"

"Yes, he was there. But he wasn't very nice."

"In what way, not very nice?"

"He . . . he'd been drinking."

"I understand," the pastor said. "So he didn't follow Maria?"

"I didn't see him."

"And what about Jolina? Did you notice if any fellow followed her?"

"No, I didn't see her."

"Not at all?"

"Yes, earlier in the evening. But then she disappeared."

"And Maria wasn't afraid to walk home through the forest on her own? I mean, in the light of what happened to Hilda Fredriks-dotter?"

She looked defiantly at the pastor, and then at me, before shaking her head. Red blotches spread across her neck. The pastor smiled and rose to his feet.

"I thank you, Maria, for this conversation. By the way, may I show Maria something before she leaves? I have been experiment-ing with sowing potatoes. Something quite blessed has grown. Come with me and I'll show you."

She followed him out into the garden and I saw them wandering around Brita Kajsa's vegetable patch. They bent down and he showed her some of the plants. With his hands he gently pushed the soil aside and uncovered the white rootlets. The pastor looked com-pletely relaxed, and joked with her, while she showed every sign of being anxious to depart. As for me, I couldn't take my eyes off my beloved. With a hasty curtsy she took her leave and hurried away. I couldn't remove my gaze from the swing of her hips, the curls of hair on her bare neck, the hands, slender but strong, smoothing the cloth of her kirtle.

When she had gone, I walked over to the pastor, who was wiping his fingers on a tuft of grass.

"Well, Jussi?"

I cleared my throat and attempted to arrange the words in the right order in my mouth before I replied.

"She appeared to be slightly nervous."

"Do you think so, Jussi? Nervous?"

The pastor gave me a sardonic look.

"Perhaps she had cause."

"And why did the pastor want to show her the potatoes?"

"The potatoes? Well, Jussi is finding it hard to think today. He only has eyes for the young lady's pretty shape."

I blushed and was about to step onto the potato patch. The pastor cried out and pushed me away.

"What the——"

Bruised, I saw the pastor put his hand inside his coat and take a piece of paper from the inside pocket. He was pointing at the ground, just where I had been about to set my foot. In the soft soil you could clearly see: the perfect impression of her boot. When he unfolded the piece of paper, I could see it was the drawing I had made of the shoe print at Kenttä, the footstep we found in the clay.

"Look at this, Jussi. This cut in the sole matches. And the pattern of wear and tear on the heel is identical. I would say that the imprint comes from the same shoe."

I could only nod in agreement, as I recalled the depression in the moss where the lovers had lain. The man's *siggar* butt.

"You thought Maria seemed nervous," the pastor said grimly. "Is it so strange that she lied to our faces? She and Nils Gustaf lay together there on the hill in the forest. While a pursuer hid himself and spied on them."

"Does the pastor think it . . . it was the assailant?"

He gave no answer and instead gently stroked the potato plant, fingering the thick, fluid-filled stem.

"The potato . . ." he said. "I believe it can have a significant bearing on Tornedalen's future. As long as it ripens."

I pointed at one of the white flowers that had closed and was beginning to turn into a berry.

"This one's already on the way."

"Nonsense," the pastor said. "The berries are poisonous. Never trust outward beauty, Jussi. The edible part of the potato plant is something else entirely. I'll show you when the time comes."

As we returned to the cabin, he spoke good-humoredly about his climate studies and how the same plant species could assume quite diverse guises according to its particular habitat. This could result in ambitious botanists discovering new species that they hoped would be named after themselves. The pastor contemptuously called them "species-makers." Rather, it was vital always to examine one's conclusions critically.

I had things other than plants on my mind.

"What are we going to do about the sheriff? Shouldn't he know?"

At a stroke the pastor's good humor vanished. He stopped and kicked at the grass like a horse.

"What do we have to show him?" he exclaimed. "Some notes and a couple of sketches."

"And our deductions," I said. "What we have thought out."

"Thoughts," the pastor muttered. "Complicated thoughts often seem to be the last thing justice is interested in."

31.

THE ENTIRE PARSONAGE WAS SWEPT AND SCRUBBED, BEDDING was aired, and quilts shaken out in the fresh air. The pastor himself decorated the house with beautiful summer blossoms, and the sweet smell of newly baked bread rose from the oven.

The guests arrived on foot in the afternoon. I had met them when we lived in Karesuando and recognized them from a distance. Juhani Raattamaa was blond with a neat line of beard down the side of his cheeks and along his jaw and a mouth that resembled a kerf. His face was warm and jovial, as the pastor walked up to welcome him with outstretched arms. Plodding behind Juhani came his older brother Pekka Raattamaa. His face was angular and beardless and his expression warier. It was not only in appearance that the two brothers differed; Pekka was older by several years and sometimes had the air of wanting to quell Juhani's enthusiasm. Tjalmo the dog ran around the guests, barking happily, as they both embraced the pastor and exchanged their greetings of peace. The day was cool with chill winds from the north, but the men were perspiring after their walk. Juhani in particular was panting and wiping the end of his long nose, which wouldn't stop dripping. Both men were strikingly well dressed, considerably better than the pastor was. Their coats were of fine cloth and their Finnish boots looked newly sewn. Pleased to have arrived, they removed their carrying straps and rubbed their sore shoulders.

Later on that day Per Nutti arrived, another of the pastor's renowned preachers. He was wearing his Sami tunic and seemed unaffected by the journey, despite having hiked all the way from the coastal region of Norway over the high mountains in the north. The pastor came out with Juhani and Pekka and they exchanged warm salutations. Brita Kajsa emerged into the yard too, with the brood of children, the youngest, Daniel, in her arms. The daughters curtsied and the sons bowed while the pastor and Per Nutti both began to puff on their pipes. Juhani handed a ladle to the thirsty Nutti, with the words:

"He that believeth on me, out of his belly shall flow rivers of living water."

"John 7:38," Nutti answered, and gulped it down with gusto.

"The sauna is warming," added Juhani, "so the kingdom of heaven is truly nigh."

"Enough preaching," Brita Kajsa said, and shooed them all toward the cabin. "First of all we shall have full stomachs."

I followed them into the parsonage, eager to listen to these famous gentlemen. Ever since the revival had gained pace, they had been the pastor's crying voices in the barren north. It hadn't always been easy. God's word had been met with derision, menace, and even fists. I had heard them preaching up in Karesuando in both Finnish and Lapp and seen them reach into people's hearts. Juhani was one of the pastor's first catechists; he organized a mission school for the village children whenever he passed through, and conveyed God's word to the adults in the evenings. But he had seldom noticed me, cowering in the farthest corner of the parsonage. Now I could smell their damp clothes, the sweat and pine-tar oil, and I noticed how both they and the pastor were animated and excited, almost as though anticipating a lovers' tryst. Once in the kitchen, Juhani turned round hastily to take something from his bags. It took me by surprise and I had no time to react. Our heads collided so hard there was a sudden crack, forehead against forehead, like the sound of an earthenware dish breaking. Without a word he looked at me, rubbing his poor skull. The others were seating themselves round the kitchen table, unaware of what had happened.

"*Anna antheeksi*," I whispered. "I'm sorry."

The whack seemed to have made Juhani giddy, and he shook himself. He was standing so close I could see the short stubble that had grown on his sunburned cheek since his morning shave. I sensed he was seeking inspiration for something to say, something funny, something clever or witty that would ease the tension between us.

"Woodenhead! You have a wooden head, *puupää*."

"I'm sorry," I said again.

"But at least with one of those you'll escape death by drowning," he said.

I rubbed the bump and realized he was inviting me to a duel. I frantically tried to think of a good rejoinder. Had I been a speaker, I might have succeeded; if only I had the gift of speech . . .

"I don't have the gift of speech," I said, blushing slightly.

With a quick movement he took hold of the scabbard hanging from my belt. He drew out the knife and brushed the blade's edge with his thumb.

"The tongue is no gift," he said. "The tongue weighs nothing, you have it with you all the time. But only you can make sure it is kept sharp."

With an elegant flick, which he must have learned in Kuttainen, he flipped the knife in his hand so that I could take it by the handle and slide it back into the scabbard. Now it was two–nil to him. This was a duel I would never win.

PEKKA HELPED WITH THE fire in the sauna. He grasped the pastor's hand-forged ax, praising its fine balance. Clearly all the blacksmiths in Kengis knew their craft. With proficient swings he chopped the wood and carried it in. As the flames flickered and the sauna slowly reached its full temperature, I sat and listened to the guests' conversation. My head was pounding after the knock, but in a good way. It was as if Juhani had forced an opening in me, a gap through which the world could enter. The men sat crouching over their Bibles filled with bookmarks, and they swiftly thumbed through to the verses they were looking for. The conversation was about the revival movement, the earthshaking wave that started up in Karesuando and was spreading over North Calotte to both the east and the west. But all was not well. There was still serious discord in Kautokeino. Per Nutti related how Ole Somby, Aslak Haetta, Rasmus Spein, and a number of the other awakened had been thrown into the jail in Tromsø and Alta. Around twenty Sami had been convicted for breach of the peace and blasphemy at the trial.

"Blasphemy?" the pastor said.

"Both Haetta and Somby shouted out in church that they were Christ and God."

"That can't be true, surely?"

"It is, according to numerous witnesses."

"Christ and God!" Juhani exclaimed, aghast. "We must travel to Kautokeino and talk some sense into them."

They went on to discuss their "work in the vineyard," as they called their revivalist preaching. They had been through village after village on the Swedish, Norwegian, and Finnish sides. I heard several stories about the miracle of salvation and their opinions on various theological matters. I didn't always understand, but I could see how earnest they were. How much salt of the law was needed before you could proclaim the sweet honey of the gospel? Did salvation happen in the same way in all people? What actually were the signs of grace?

It was clear that the situation in Pajala was a matter for concern. Juhani asked the pastor if the seed had begun to bear fruit, but the pastor replied grimly that the ground in the Kengis region was harder than rock. The Pajala burghers' denouncement of him to the chapter meant that now he was obliged to hold two services, one where peace and tranquility could reign, and one for the awakened souls that the Holy Spirit was allowed to attend. And in the columns of the newspapers the assault continued, compelling the pastor to spend a great deal of time writing submissions in his defense. The only advantage Pajala had over Karesuando appeared to be that the potato grew better here.

"So the gentlefolks of Pajala want to stay asleep," Pekka said.

"It probably accounts for many of the workers as well," the pastor said. "If they just get their jug of brandy, they're happy."

"Perhaps the children of Pajala are our hope," Juhani said. "Is there anything greater than seeing a little boy or girl who can read the Lord's name for the first time?"

Juhani told them about his teaching, how he would bring together the children in one village at a time and organize a mission school for several weeks. Many of their parents were illiterate and some could do no more than scratch their mark. Nevertheless, they permitted their children to learn the alphabet, and every time a child learned to read, a miracle happened. On the last day of the school, he would gather all the children and parents for worship and let some of the children read out God's words in their own voice. It would bring tears to the listeners' eyes and several of the adults would ask if they could learn to read too.

Brita Kajsa sat down at the table and joined in. It was education that would eventually give the people up here their freedom, she said. The poor would no longer be poor if they could read and write. Armed with knowledge, the Finns and Lapps too could train to become teachers, scientists, or doctors, and they would have control over their own future. And in this way the future would prosper in Lainio, Kangos, and Tärendö, indeed in the whole of the north. Free, God-fearing people who didn't give their last farthing to the liquor dealers.

"Instead they donate it to schools," the pastor said. "Our enemies are trying to use it against us by saying we pocket the money ourselves. But Bishop Bergman has personally approved our accounts."

Pekka agreed that education was a good thing, but it had to involve a degree of rigor. He had noticed how some children wanted to hold the pencil in their left hand, not the right. Since the left side was the devil's, these children must be reprimanded and taught to write with the correct hand. Juhani concurred, the right hand was preferable, and he thought that if children learned correctly from the start, they would continue to use their right hand for life. His way was to encourage these children to always hold their left hand clenched behind their back while they were writing.

"There's another thing," Juhani said gravely. "I need to tell you about prayer meeting we held in a courtyard in Kitkiöjärvi. Some women arrived in a state of high anxiety and agitation. They asked me if I could tell whether they had the true faith. I answered, as we always do, that only they could look into their hearts. One woman in particular was deeply disturbed. She was a recent widow, suffering the pain of sin, and she begged me again and again to help her, weeping inconsolably. I remember her appealing for deliverance."

"If you are honest before God, you will feel it," the pastor said. "Feel it with your whole body."

"Perhaps we need something more," Juhani said. "After I left, I heard something shocking. Following the meeting these women had secretly carried on. And one of them had herself granted the widow absolution."

The men looked at each other, speechless.

"One of the women," Per Nutti finally said.

"Yes."

"Read the absolution in God's own name?" the pastor exclaimed.

"We'll have to seek her out," Pekka said. "We'll have to issue a sharp warning."

Juhani looked hesitant. It was obvious that he and his brother had already discussed the matter many times.

"I have thought about this," he spoke slowly. "What if the woman did the right thing? What if our revival has only got halfway?"

"Do you mean we should start offering forgiveness?" Per Nutti said doubtfully.

"Maybe she was showing us the way? Maybe we already hold the key to the kingdom of heaven?"

The pastor sat in silence for some time. Outside, the roar from the Kengis waterfall rose and fell, and the sheep could be heard bleating in the meadows.

AT NIGHTFALL, AFTER THE sauna, the men sat down on the porch. The pastor bade me fetch the twist of tobacco and I cut the dried leaves into pieces for them to fill their pipes. The clouds puffing up soon held the gnats at bay. Juhani inquired if there was any news about the dreadful killing the entire Kengis region was talking about.

"They say a killer bear has been slain. Is that so?" Pekka Raattamaa asked.

"I fear the situation is worse than that," the pastor said.

In a low voice he told them about the dreadful attacks, how one young woman had lost her life and another was lying on her sickbed. He gave an account of our investigations, how we had found traces from the cow-girl Hilda Fredriksdotter in one of the hay barns on the bog, which indicated that she had been taken by force. Strands of hair had been pulled out of her head when a man assaulted her in the hay.

"And why would a bear attack a cow-girl? Why not attack one of the cows?"

"Yes, it sounds strange," Per Nutti agreed. "But if it was a she-bear, maybe she was protecting her young?"

"The girl had strangulation marks on her neck," the pastor said. "And someone tried to strangle the other girl who was attacked too."

"So there's an assailant at large here in the forests?"

"So it would seem."

"Does the pastor have any ideas about who it might be?"

"We found an unusual plant in the hay, which we believe may have come from the murderer's clothes. A tiny mountain plant that doesn't grow in this area. Who travels between the mountains and Kengis?"

"Sami like us," Nutti said.

"And preachers like us," Juhani said.

"Tradesmen and peddlers," Pekka added. "Tax collectors. All manner of officials."

"A fellow whose path takes him past Kengis," the pastor mused. "Who cannot control his urges. Who creeps up on girls and then silences them."

"The last attack took place the evening of the dance," Juhani said. "Music excites the desires of the flesh. I have always feared the seductive powers of dance."

"Maybe not the dancing," the pastor said, "as much as the liquor."

"Dance and drink go hand in hand," Pekka Raattamaa said. "I have personally seen the most violent of acts happen under the influence of drink at a dance. An inadvertent push, a thoughtless word. The recollection of some old grudge stirring, maybe. Brandy can arouse the wildest rage."

"So true," the pastor agreed.

"But couldn't it be over now? The perpetrator might have moved on to other areas?" Juhani said.

The pastor looked doubtful.

"I don't know. . . . Recently I've felt darkness gathering around me. As if someone is spying on me. Someone waiting for the opportunity to break me."

"May God protect you." Pekka made the sign of the cross, casting a quick glance over his shoulder.

"I understand why the evil one comes here," Per Nutti said. "Is it not precisely in our regions he wants his work to be done?"

The men stared at him in astonishment.

"Here in the north is where the battle is being waged," Nutti pointed out. "We are in a time of visitation of the Spirit. The Lord's presence up here is stronger than anywhere in the world."

"Of course," Juhani agreed. "The front line is here in the north, and here the battle is at its height. It's the revival that is luring the devil and his cohorts here."

I could feel that the temperature had dropped and darkness seemed to be falling around us. Unseen demons came flying through space and gathered under the roof.

"I fear this is just the beginning," Pekka said. "They want to destroy the movement."

"Who?"

"Our enemies. All those who fear the truth."

"Our enemies . . ." the pastor said thoughtfully. "All the enemies out there, or the ones within ourselves?"

The door to the parsonage flew open and Brita Kajsa walked past the men bearing a water bucket.

"Women's sauna!" she said impatiently.

Her daughters and the maid were eagerly waiting for their sauna too, and slipped past us into the sooty temple. We moved into the pastor's study so that the youngest children could sleep peacefully in the cabin. I settled down in the corner, my chin resting on my knees, like a sitting shadow, while Per Nutti quietly resumed.

"I heard a story in Norway: four years ago, in 1848, Antin Pieti and Mattis Siikavuopio traveled over to preach the revival to Norwegian Sami. At the winter market in Skibotn they stood among the people and began speaking. Loudly, in the midst of jingling purses and bottles of liquor, they spread God's word, but they were met with ridicule and apathy. Despondent, they carried on along Storfjord, where they met two fishermen, Mons Monsen and Hans Heiskala. It was here, after speaking together, on the thin strip of coast between the ocean's immensity and the steep mountainsides, that the fishermen became believers. They were the first in the region to be seized by the revival. Their neighbors and friends were scornful and distanced themselves and no one would listen to them.

"One day, when the fishermen were out in their boat, a terrible storm blew up. Monsen and Heiskala had to abandon their tackle and attempted to reach land, but the wind and waves threatened to smash the boat. They feared they would perish in the ice-cold sea. Panic-stricken, they prayed to God, and held on for dear life for so long that their hands went numb, until, by some miracle, they managed to land at Polfjellet. Soaked through and half frozen, they were taken in by a kind family. And there, in front of the warm fire, they reported that what had saved them was their firm faith. The men's story and their calm conviction affected the listeners deeply. Despite having come so close to death, they were filled with peace and trust. The entire family became believers there and then, and that was the beginning of the great awakening in Lyngen."

"Thank the Lord," murmured the pastor.

"Yes, Antin Pieti is indeed a mighty preacher."

There was a gleam in the pastor's eye as he went on:

"You've listened to Antin Pieti. You know how he leads people to living faith, don't you? By speaking slowly!"

"That's true. He certainly doesn't hurry," Nutti agreed.

"His sermons take hours." The pastor smiled. "I mean, truly hours. He speaks so slowly he could bring a mountain to salvation."

The men burst into laughter at the pastor making fun of one of his own.

"As for me, I speak too quickly," Juhani said with a laugh, "so I need to preach to the birds and the flies."

"I've often wondered about one thing," Per Nutti said. "When Jesus comes to our region, is he going to be bitten by mosquitoes too?"

It came as a relief to hear these distinguished people joking with one another. Only Pekka remained impassive. He smiled, yes, but his face looked like hammered steel.

Evening slipped into night, and it seemed the men didn't want to end their conversation. The room was filled with their hushed voices and pipe smoke, as they spoke of people they knew, of acquaintances who had become believers, of how to respond to the dissent and discord that were threatening to split the movement. They had completely forgotten I was there, and I sleepily sat in my corner, smiling. I felt like a child listening to these trustworthy, fatherly voices. In their arms I felt utterly calm. And this was how I fell asleep, leaning against the pastor's large bookcase, supported and strengthened by words, with one blessed bump on my head.

32.

I T WAS WONDERFUL TO SEE THE PASTOR'S MOOD CHANGE. HIS recent melancholy was dispelled, he was full of vitality, not to say exhilarated. Or perhaps the correct word is "confident." Even though the pastor was the strongest one among us, I had seen him become worn out, his back increasingly bent, weighed down by an overwhelming burden. But now that burden had lightened, thanks to our friends. They fortified each other, like four smoking logs in a hearth that were pushed together on the embers and flared up again.

Four apostles, I reflected. Four evangelists. Four horsemen in the holy war.

"You're always in the corner, listening," the pastor said to me down by the river.

"I'm learning all the time," I answered.

"You learn everything I show you," he went on. "How is it going with the Gothic script?"

"I can read Gothic script as well now."

"You see, you see! But speaking, Jussi, speaking is the hardest."

"Yes."

"I think the difficulties are to do with the voice itself. The nature of the voice. It comes from within us, from the depths of our heart. It rises by means of pressure in the lungs, through the throat and vocal cords, and is forced out like a cloud of invisible droplets of saliva."

He curled his hand around the cloud of saliva, outlined its shape in the air, how it rose and then dispersed.

"We are ashamed of the things that leave our body," he said. "We all have to answer the call of nature, but we want to withdraw to do it. We would rather be left alone in the privy. In Härnösand, you know, they even latched the door with a brass hook, as if the professors' bowel movements were a shameful secret. But they could certainly speak. Sometimes I think that is the real purpose of education: to overcome one's embarrassment at speaking."

"It's worse when there are many people listening," I said.

"And so you must practice when you're alone. Stand here and look out across the river. What do want to say to the river?"

Was the man joking? I looked out across the wide surface drifting past and mirroring the sky. The roar of the rapids could be heard from farther down.

"Say?"

"Yes, it's not sufficient to think. Words that are only thought become crumbs; they may be enough for the moment, but they're forgotten just as quickly. It is only when they are uttered by the mouth that we see what they are worth."

"But it's possible to write down your words."

"In that case people must first be able to read. Come on—the river. She's listening. She is waiting to hear what you're going to tell her."

Without another word he turned on his heel and left. I was alone. When I was sure he could no longer hear me and that no one else was there, I turned to face the water.

"*Väylä*," I said. "River . . ."

It felt peculiar. I peered in all directions to make sure no one was listening.

"The greatest sin," I continued. "The greatest sin people can commit is not to love their children."

The river murmured gently in reply.

"Not to love their children," I repeated. "To bring forth children into the world and do them harm. To want to hurt them, to give them no comfort when they suffer."

The witch's blowsy face appeared before my eyes. Her sneer made me fall silent and feel afraid. If I contradicted her, she would hit me hard. Pull the hair on the back of my neck, hurt me as much as she could.

"What have you done with Anne Maaret?" I said. "Bitch. If you've harmed the girl, I'll kill you."

I wonder what she is doing now. My sister. I wonder if she is still alive.

33.

Early the next morning a visitor arrived at the parsonage. I was still lying in my straw sleeping bag on the floor when I heard a knock on the porch door. I swiftly pulled on my trousers and opened it. Outside stood a woman I didn't recognize at first. Her face was contorted and wet as a dishcloth. Then I realized it was Kristina, Jolina's mother. She was treading up and down on the spot with small, halting steps. I was immediately seized with a feeling of foreboding.

"The reverend must come . . . must come . . ."

"He is still asleep. Has something happened?"

Kristina tried to tell me, but she was sobbing so violently that I couldn't understand what she said. I hurried in to the pastor, who had been woken by the noise we made and was sitting on the edge of his bed in his floor-length nightshirt, rubbing the sleep from his eyes. He started to dress, but I could see from his slow movements that he wasn't properly awake.

We followed Kristina out into the yard, where she tugged at the pastor's overcoat until, with mild force, he loosened her grip. Then she set off along the village road with small scurrying steps, the torn hem of her skirt flapping around her ankles. Now and then she turned and waited until we caught up.

The cold night air was still lingering and the grass and leaves glistened with dew. You could feel that summer was over. The birch trees would soon turn yellow, before shedding their leaves. The plants' time was over and, as always, it made me melancholy. The silence of winter would soon follow. The stems and leaves would turn black and bow to the ground and their hard seeds would be tossed out into the wind. The rustling stalks would be pressed down like letters of the alphabet under the white sheet of snow and lie there hidden all winter long.

We reached Kristina's cabin. The master of the house, Elias, saw us and came out onto the porch step with his adult sons. Motioning with his arms, he led us across the yard, past the barn and the privy, and up to where there was a patch of forest. On the ground we found an oblong bundle lying on a rag rug and covered by a blanket. I feared the worst when I saw that it was the shape of a human body. Apart from the buzzing of flies, there was no sound.

The pastor slowly knelt down. He cautiously took hold of the edge of the blanket and pulled it to the side. With a cry of horror, he let it drop and recoiled, his hand over his mouth. The sight was so hideous that he could barely utter a word.

Jolina's once-pretty face was covered with a bluish-black discoloration. Her lips were parted and her tongue was so swollen that there scarcely appeared to be room for it in her mouth. Elias had laid heavy coins on her eyelids, but when the pastor lifted one of them the eye was half open and bloodshot, as if she had beheld the devil. It was painfully obvious that the girl was no longer alive.

"I cut her down," Elias muttered.

He pointed to the big pine tree beside them. Only now did I notice a piece of rope dangling over one of the hefty branches. The other end was tied several times round the trunk of the tree itself. The pastor looked at the ground underneath.

"Was there a stool here when you arrived?"

"No—she must have climbed up the tree and jumped from there."

"God rest her soul," the pastor murmured.

He studied the huge pine tree and then sank to his knees. Pensively, he picked up some bark chips.

"My wife woke early," Elias went on. "It was as if she knew something was wrong."

"Yes?"

The pastor turned to Kristina, who was holding her apron over her mouth. She turned away, unable to look at her daughter's body.

"I thought I'd look in on her. It was then I realized the room was empty. Jolina must have crept out while we slept."

The pastor folded the blanket back, to expose the torso. Jolina was dressed in a nightgown that went down to her ankles; it looked old and had a grayish tinge.

"Did she usually sleep in this?"

"Yes."

"And her feet? She's not wearing any shoes."

Elias shook his head. The pastor looked around and discovered a severed piece of rope, tied into a noose, that had been thrown onto a lingonberry thicket.

"Was this . . . ?"

"I cut it off." Elias caught his breath. "I hoped she was still alive."

His voice broke and this big man fought back his tears in a fit of hoarse coughing.

"Do you recognize the rope?"

Elias shook his head.

"It isn't ours. She must have borrowed it."

"*Voi tyärparka*," Kristina sobbed.

"Yes, poor girl," the pastor mumbled.

"Will Jolina go to hell?"

The pastor couldn't bring himself to answer. He steadfastly clasped his hands together and said the Lord's prayer, as he had done when he gave her the Eucharist. Elias and Kristina bowed their heads, but I found I couldn't join in. Words. They were just words. Incapable of protecting her.

"A Christian shouldn't do this to herself, should she?" the man said.

"No, she shouldn't."

"Even if things are hard. You have to try to hold on."

It sounded as though he were aiming the words at himself. The pastor turned to the man's wife and shyly put his hand on her shoulder. She gave a start, unused as she was to being touched.

"Tell me what happened when you found her."

"I . . . I was calling for Jolina. I looked in the barn and the woodshed. And then I saw something hanging at the edge of the forest. I knew at once it was her."

"Yes?"

"I ran inside and shouted for Elias and the boys."

Jolina's brothers nodded silently.

"What happened then?"

"Father cut her down," the elder son muttered.

"We laid her on the rug here," Elias continued. "I thought . . . that maybe you can't take them into the house."

"You can."

"People who've taken their own life, I mean."

"You can lay her in the sauna for the time being. So the sheriff can look at her."

"We haven't sent for him."

"It's probably better if you do. Let's carry the body in now. I can see flies are starting to gather."

Elias bent over the body and waved away the insects. He covered it awkwardly with the blanket and then he and his sons lifted the lifeless corpse. I could see that her limbs had begun to stiffen; her arm was protruding, fingers splayed, as they carried her into the sauna. In a dignified manner, the men laid Jolina on the bench, whereupon the pastor sank to his knees by her head and prayed. With his eyes half closed and his back more bent than usual, he was lost in deepest devotion. I turned to Elias and his sons and whispered:

"I think we should leave the pastor in peace. Arrange for the sheriff to come while I stay and keep the pastor company. And please bring a tallow candle."

Kristina immediately came with the candle for the dark sauna, we lit it, and then, with bows and curtsies, they left. I carefully shut the door after them. The pastor swiftly stood up, took off his coat, and rolled up his sleeves. I took out pencil and paper and made myself ready.

"We have to hurry," he whispered. "Poor girl."

With great care he pulled back the blanket covering her and moved the candle closer.

"The neck," he began. "The neck has been damaged by the rope. But notice the marks too."

"Yes."

He held his hands out and measured with his fingertips. They matched the bruises in an uncanny way.

"Just like Hilda Fredriksdotter. The monster strangled her with his bare hands. She was presumably already dead when he hoisted her up into the tree."

"So . . . she hasn't committed suicide?"

"These are injuries we recognize, Jussi. Crescent-shaped indentations in the skin of the neck."

"From the culprit's nails."

He cautiously lifted off the coins and gently pulled back her eyelids. Jolina's empty pupils were hideous to behold. He studied the bloodshot whites of her eyes in the light from the tallow candle.

"The small blood vessels have burst. That, too, indicates strangulation. Make a note, Jussi."

"But how can the pastor know?"

"It's ordinary science. I had a friend at Uppsala who was a medical student. Write this down, Jussi. She has bruises on her arms, typical assault injuries."

"The perpetrator held on to her?"

"Jolina was strong, she tried to defend herself. But this time, unfortunately, she was not wearing a hairpin. Can you help me?"

I placed my hands under her thighs and lifted her the way he showed me. For a moment he appeared to hesitate. Then he took hold of the nightgown and slowly pulled it up.

"Look at the legs. What can we say about them?"

"They look fairly unharmed."

"Exactly. No scratches or marks. And what does Jussi make of that?"

"What do you mean, Pastor?"

"This too runs counter to suicide. Her skin would show signs, if she had slithered up a massive pine tree wearing only a nightgown and then clung to a branch."

He raised her foot. The leg was rigid, so he had to crouch down to study the sole.

"Her heels, on the other hand, are scraped on the back. Both of them. Do you see?"

"The body was dragged."

"Good, Jussi. The man strangled her after knocking her to the ground. Then he grabbed her under the arms and dragged the body over to the tree. That was when her heels were damaged. He had prepared the rope in advance. He threw the rope over a branch in the pine tree and placed the noose around her neck. Then he hauled her up by the other end until the body was hanging clear. I found some fresh slivers of bark on the ground that must have been loosened by the friction while he was hoisting her up."

The pastor told me to write this down while he drove away the buzzing flies. He gently closed Jolina's eyes and replaced the coins, before covering the body with the blanket.

"Let's study the surroundings."

We went out and I followed him to the far end of the cowshed. The privy had been erected there, a simple gray building.

"I think Jolina must have been on her way here to relieve herself. It was nighttime and no one noticed her slip out. The evildoer was hidden and prepared. Perhaps he had kept watch for several nights, patiently waiting for the right opportunity."

The pastor looked around and noticed an aspen grove at the edge of the forest. He walked over to it and nodded.

"This was where he was standing."

The pastor leaned forward and put his nose to the ground. Something in the moss caught his attention.

"Now, what's this?"

Between his thumb and forefinger, he picked up something very small and slender. I bent down.

"Pencil shavings?"

"No, not this time. This is something different."

I raised my eyes and identified it at once. Some newly made knife scorings were visible in the aspen's bark. They formed a well-known shape.

"A cross," the pastor murmured. "The fellow stood here and carved a cross in the bark while he was waiting."

"Why a cross?" I asked.

"Maybe it was intended for me."

"What do you mean, Pastor?"

"I issued a warning to the wrongdoer when we visited the shop. What if he was there in the crowd listening to my words?"

"So the cross . . . ?"

"Might be a threat. He wanted to retaliate."

"But who would be so cold-blooded?"

"The snake, Jussi. The snake's venom is dripping upon Pajala."

34.

WE HASTILY RINSED OUR HANDS AND ENTERED THE CABIN. Kristina had prepared some breakfast, which we gratefully accepted, having had no time to eat anything at all before we left the parsonage. I spooned up a little fish gruel while the pastor posed his questions.

"I was thinking about your dog. Did you hear her bark in the night?"

"No, the dog's gone."

"What do you mean, gone?"

"She's always loose. So sometimes she runs off."

"I see. When did you last see her?"

"It must have been the day before yesterday," Elias said in a low voice. "She's been so unsettled since Jolina's troubles. She's been barking and making a noise at night."

"I think she's been guarding us," Kristina said. "I thought I saw someone creeping about outside myself."

"She's been growling at the door for several nights," Elias agreed. "We usually let her out to guard the place. We thought it might have been the fox."

"But this last time she stayed away?"

"She'll come back soon," Kristina said. "She always appears after a while."

"Perhaps we ought to look for her anyway," the pastor said. "Her name is Siiri, isn't it?"

"Yes."

"A fine name for a dog. Siiri."

WHILE WE WERE EATING breakfast we heard the rumble of a horse and carriage approaching on the marsh path. Shortly after, a wagon rolled into the yard and some men climbed out. Into the cabin stumped Sheriff Brahe, followed by Constable Michelsson and the country doctor Sederin, who happened to be in the area. The little group smelled of punsch, despite the early hour, and the sheriff immediately took control, with Kristina rushing around to give him assistance. The doctor Sederin was a bulky gentleman who appeared to be bothered by his back and supported himself with a walking stick. His round spectacles were continually slipping down to the end of his swollen red nose and every so often he pushed them up with a clumsy shove. The doctor greeted the pastor stonily, doing little to disguise his dislike. Old soak that he was, he hated the pastor's sobriety campaigns, which threatened to render Lapland dry and deprive him of the only remedy for Arctic ennui.

Once informed of the situation, the three men pushed into the sauna to inspect the corpse. It was so cramped that the pastor remained in the doorway. Sheriff Brahe showed his distaste when he saw the body and wiped his hands on a handkerchief.

"Damnation! They go so blue when they hang themselves," he muttered. "Ugly and swollen. A pity, on such a sweet girl."

"Take a closer look at her neck," the pastor suggested. "And you, Michelsson, can help the doctor to examine her feet."

"I see the pastor's still here, then. Perhaps we might attend to our duties in peace, if the pastor will excuse us."

Dr. Sederin needed something to sit on and was offered the sauna stool. It could hardly have been the sight of the dead woman that made him light-headed, for he must have seen far worse in his day. But after the previous day's revelry with Brahe, he would very much have liked to lie down on a settle.

"The tongue is blue. The face swollen. And the neck disfigured by the noose. The girl has clearly hanged herself," the sheriff said.

Nothing pleased Sederin more than to agree. With a great effort he pulled out a small writing pad and recorded a suicide in his medical Latin.

"The marks on the neck don't match the noose," the pastor objected.

"And how do you know that?"

"The bruises have been caused by fingers. They can't have come from the rope."

"They might be a result of the earlier attack."

"No, these are fresh. The skin also has new injuries that appear to come from fingernails, several small indentations."

The sheriff took a step toward the pastor, grabbed the collar of his coat, and very nearly lifted him off his feet.

"Bloody pastor," he hissed, "Satan's black coat. You're humiliating me in front of the parishioners!"

He shook the pastor, who was short in stature. The sheriff's wheezing breath reeked of the morning's drams.

"The sheriff doesn't scare me," he mumbled.

Then everything exploded in a haze of red. The pastor was flung backward against the sauna wall, the back of his head slamming against the sooty logs. Even the doctor fell headlong, landing on the floor as the stool overturned. The sheriff had aimed for the pastor's teeth, but the pastor had managed to turn away, so that the fist hit his cheekbone. Dazed, he sank down on his backside and held his arms up in defense. I tried to stand between them, but the sheriff shouldered me to one side and then stood astride the pastor, as if he were going to kick him. At the same moment the constable noticed the corpse had begun to slide off the bench and he reached forward to stop it, just in time.

"Now shut up, bloody pastor! Shut up!"

Brahe pulled off his cap and rubbed his trembling mustache. Then he shook himself like a huge dog.

I bent down and helped the pastor to his feet. His gaze was unsteady and he was spitting something that might have been blood. Both reeling, we staggered out into the yard, where the family and neighbors were waiting with looks of astonishment.

"It's nothing," the pastor muttered. "Nothing."

I cautiously led him over to the doorstep where he could sit down and get his strength back. He was visibly shaken and sat for a long time with his face in his hands. I felt so distraught I could hardly stand still. In the end I took out his travel Bible and stuck my thumb in at random. The page opened on Luke 15. The parable of the lost son. The one who had journeyed in a far country but returned to his father. *But the father said to his servants, bring forth the best robe . . . and bring hither the fatted calf, and kill it; and let us eat, and be merry: for this my son was dead, and is alive again; he was lost, and is found.*

At this point, a man came running out of the forest. When he approached I realized that it was the younger of the sons.

"*Kirkkoherra . . . Kirkkoherra . . .* "

The pastor didn't seem to have heard. I tentatively nudged his elbow and he looked up in confusion.

"Reverend?"

"Yes?"

"We've found the dog."

THE POOR MUTT LAY curled up, with her paws extended. A trickle of blood had come from her nose. Her lips were drawn back revealing her eyeteeth, covered in blood-streaked saliva. The dog lay concealed under a dense fir tree, almost invisible. It was the swarms of flies that had led the son to lift the branches. I stayed in the background while the pastor gently stroked the coarse fur, running his fingers over her ribs. The body was stiff and had already started to smell; it must have lying been there for some time.

"Siiri," the boy moaned, trying to hold back his grief.

The pastor rose and turned back to Elias and Kristina.

"Do you hunt foxes?"

Elias cast a glance at his wife.

"Yes, now and then."

"How?"

"We have an iron trap."

"Do you ever use poison?"

"No, but the neighbors might. Does the pastor think that Siiri swallowed some?"

"I've seen foxes killed with strychnine. But they show more signs of convulsions. What a pity for such a fine dog."

"Yes," the younger son sobbed, hiding his mouth behind his closed fists.

"We'll have to burn the mutt," Elias said. "So other animals aren't tempted to eat it."

"Have you had any visitors in the last few days? Who's been here to see you?"

"What does the reverend mean?"

"I think the perpetrator has been trying to get to Jolina ever since the attack. He poisoned the dog so she wouldn't bark."

"But who . . . who can have . . . ?"

"It could be someone you know well. Someone you see every day."

Elias's lips trembled, his fingers clenching and straightening in frustration, again and again.

"We should pray for the dog," the pastor said quietly.

"Pray for a dog?"

"A prayer of thanksgiving. For all the joy she has brought in her blameless life. Give thanks to God for creating her."

At this the son crumpled and burst into a fit of uncontrolled weeping. He couldn't get any air, it sounded as though he were suffocating. Elias raised his right arm, clearly intending to give the boy a clout, his fingers tightening into a blunt instrument.

"We'll put our hands together," the pastor said hastily. "Clasp thine hands and lift up thine heart to God. Lord, we thank thee. . . ."

Everyone reverently calmed down. The pastor and I, Elias and Kristina, and both their sons. No one touched anyone. This was what grief looked like, here in the north.

But in the midst of all the thanksgiving and prayers for forgiveness, I noticed how the pastor's voice was shaking. We both perceived the dreadful truth. The pastor had made it known that Jolina could identify the perpetrator. That was why she had been silenced. If the pastor had kept quiet, then Jolina might still be alive.

35.

THE FUNERAL OF THE ILL-FATED JOLINA ELIASDOTTER WAS A grim event. Most of the people in the region were of the same opinion as Sheriff Brahe, that the girl had hanged herself. The brutal attack on the night of the dance had meant she couldn't bear to go on living. And rumor had it that she did not die alone. No, the miscreant had left her with child. And thus it was—the poor girl hadn't only killed herself, but an unborn child as well. She had ended up a child murderer. Thus the road down to the torturous fires of hell was, on this occasion, dead straight. Stories such as this were gratifying to spread at kitchen tables and useful for the youth to hear, not least for all the girls who showed an interest in going dancing, where one thing could all too easily lead to another.

The more often the incident was recounted, the more numerous the macabre details. The girl was said to have taken poison before she hanged herself. She wanted to be quite sure the child would die too. And she gave birth to the dead fetus while hanging in the noose. The poisoned mite had oozed out of her and the dog had obviously caught the scent. It had arrived and polished off the child, thereby ingesting the poison. Yes, the dog had been found dead too. They had to burn the animal afterward, for clearly it couldn't be dumped in the forest with what was in its stomach. And the child, it had become a dweller of the underworld. A lost soul who prowled along the footpaths at night, screaming, who would never be at peace. Unbaptized, unchristened. So it was for the offspring of whores. Eternal unblessedness. May God have mercy on the wretched pair.

I observed how the pastor called for peace for Jolina Eliasdotter. Both he and I knew the truth, that she was the victim of a cold-blooded man of violence. The pastor's preaching offered consolation to the family, he spoke of the dark forces surrounding us, that we must have the Lord's help to stand firm. From the church pews rose the stench of mistrust. For the congregation, there was a child murderer lying in the coffin, a sinner who had done away with herself. Sheriff Brahe and Constable Michelsson could be seen whispering, their heads together. Elias and Kristina could barely move, like black-clad tree stumps, exposed to everyone's eyes. Not once were they seen to weep. In their hearts they must have felt a mounting pressure, an inner scream that sooner or later would cleave its way out, like a beak. Questions kept going round and round in their heads; if only they had brought her up a different way, been able to bend her in another direction while there was still time. If only she hadn't gone to the dance that evening. Then she would still be alive.

I rattled off the confession but my tongue was a dead fish, lying in my mouth with its belly on the bottom. My lips were pretending to form the torturous vowels, but inside I was struck dumb. I glanced toward the front pews and met Constable Michelsson's eye. I saw him write something down on a piece of paper and show it to Sheriff Brahe, who gave a quick nod and looked briefly in my direction. It was clear that they were talking about me. A cold breeze blew up, a chilly draft passed through the church. Yet all the doors and windows were closed. I glanced at the pastor, who had lost his thread midway through a sentence. He squared his shoulders beneath the ecclesiastical stole and it seemed as though he had felt it too, as he anxiously looked around. It only lasted a second, before he cleared his throat and carried on where he had left off. But his voice was suddenly unsteady and without its usual strength. I thought I could sense movements along the church walls. Strange shadows that had invaded the church, invisible beings that wished us ill. As if the pastor could hear my thoughts, he grasped the large wooden crucifix on the altar and pressed it to his lips. I could see his mouth mumbling something.

At the same moment a cry went up from the pews.

"*Oohooloom ohhoo!*"

Immediately another joined in:

"*Herra Jeesuksen Kristuksen, aaiiaaiiaa . . .*"

Arms in black coat sleeves were raised, crippled fingers clawed at the air as if they were tearing at fabric.

"*Oohoo hoo*," echoed the first girl in her owl-like way, while a third woman began to rock, which set those nearest to her going, until the whole row was swaying in the pew.

The pastor put his arms around the crucifix as the noise in the church grew. I saw him close his eyes and take sharp intakes of breath, but without losing his composure. The women's side was now in full swing and even a couple of the wrinkly old men sat wailing and twisting their caps on their knees. A small boy was frightened and burst into tears, but when none of the adults noticed, the boy crossed his arms over the top of his cropped hair as if afraid of being hit. On all sides black-clad bodies moved like trees in a gale, standing up like tall, swaying tree trunks threatening to fall. The pastor let go of the crucifix; he was right at the front, with his back to the congregation, at the prow of this lurching ship. Now a prolonged rattle could be heard. It was coming from the board on which the hymn numbers hung; one of the hooks had come loose, the one holding up the sixes. A jangling shower of brass fell to the floor. The leaping members of the congregation were filling the aisle now, embracing one another, the tears of sin splashing around them. Some of the numbers were lying on the floor by the font, showing the figure 666. I could feel a fat man breathing down my neck, smelling of sour lard and sulfur. Another grabbed my elbow and clung to me, as if we were jolting along in a horse-drawn cart. I twisted away from the fellow; it was a cross-eyed farmhand with snot dripping from his nose. He gave a stifled sob, his arms trying to swim upward with groping, lopsided strokes, and he was shouting "*Äiti, Äiti* . . . Mother, Mother . . . !" I leaned forward and supported myself on the pew with both hands, held on in the gathering storm. The pastor was still standing motionless by the wooden crucifix on the altar. He was frozen, immobile; this seemed only to increase the congregation's excitement. You could feel the Holy Spirit's presence fill every corner of the church; you could almost see a light mist and smell the aroma of freshly baked bread. There was a sweet fragrance, too, of God's grace, and now people began to shout as well. Shrill screams, rising like tongues of fire in a baker's oven. I noticed the man beside me panting and straining as if he were in a latrine and something far too hard was on its way out. Perhaps this was a birth, the crown of a baby's head forcing its way out down there? He fought to hold the creature back but it was too strong, too wild, and soon it would burst out through his pelvis.

I was holding on so tight that my knuckles were white. When I looked around, I saw Michelsson and Brahe staring at me. They were stiff as pikestaffs, like seabirds on a stormy ocean. I tried to glare back, but I couldn't, so I turned to the front, a ball of fear inside me. My head ached, a pain as if someone were beating me, thumping me from above with a fist, a log, a brandy keg. With anything lying within reach in the Sami tent. Throb after throb, like a pounding thunder, throb, throb, throb. . . .

36.

I STAY HIDDEN IN THE BUSHES. AN HOUR PASSES, TWO HOURS. WHEN someone goes past on the track I flatten myself against the ground until the footsteps have faded away. The gnats bite. A column of ants pesters me; the tiny soldiers march up my ankles and bite me red-raw. I have to see her soon. Why isn't she coming? Isn't she going to the barn? I shall give up soon, it's been long enough. But she just might still come. I hold her round the waist, we dance so pliantly, my skin tingles with pleasure with every touch. The fabric of her dress. Her wrist. The feel of her outstretched fingertips.

And now she is coming out. Standing there. My beloved. The cabin door closes behind her and she is carrying a birch-bark knapsack. Where is she going? I creep behind her at a distance. She is barefoot and in a hurry. Is she going out into the forest? Does she have supplies for the shieling girls? No, she is following the marsh path. Perhaps I could catch up with her? Offer to carry her knapsack? But then she might scoff at me, and I feel my courage failing. And all of a sudden, she is gone. Disappeared. I press ahead and peer around the next bend. Has she turned off, up toward the foundry? Yes, by all the forces of good, there she is. She has stopped behind a barn. I am giddy with excitement, my heart is on fire. She takes off her clothes. For a second I see her naked shoulders, pure white. And then she puts on something red, a red dress. And she lets her hair down, loosening the plaits so her hair is all curly. She is so pretty. Is there someone in the barn, someone waiting? I am silent, completely still, my mouth quite dry. Then I see her walk farther on.

She passes the barn and goes up in the direction of the manor house. Crosses the courtyard, and then turns toward a little cottage. She knocks on the door. Someone opens. Light of foot, she slips inside.

Confused and doubtful, I stand there for a while. My beloved. I wait, but she doesn't come. A watchdog at the manor house barks at me, a deep, weary bark, until it starts to flag and rests its nose on its paws. The manor house is like a reclining giant, its large window-eyes staring at me. I notice an enamel bucket by a woodpile and it gives me an idea. I leave my hidey-hole and fetch it. The river is rushing past below. I am dressed like a farmhand and I pull my cap down over my eyes before hurrying along to the water to fill it. Now that I have a job to do, I can cross the yard. I walk slowly, pretending to be on my way to the vegetable garden to do some watering, but it is the cottage I am advancing toward. The dog comes to life again and barks in deep, ill-tempered coughs. I put the bucket down and wipe the sweat from my brow. It is only theater, in case someone should observe me and start to wonder. I approach the little cottage and glance through the windows as I pass, but I don't see her. I wipe my face the whole time with my grubby neckerchief, rub it back and forth to keep my face hidden while I look behind it through the windows.

And now I catch a glimpse of her. The room is lit by the afternoon sun and I can see her red dress twirl. Maria is dancing, spinning around alone on the floor. Her hair swings about her head. She stops suddenly and appears to be listening to instructions from someone. Now she repeats the movement, a fraction slower. And a large figure walks up to her. He is still holding the brush in one hand and with the other he adjusts her billowy curls, shaping them. And she lets it happen. He alters the angle of her upper body and she gives a little smile. He smooths the fold in her dress, his long fingers running over her waist and bosom. And she seems to enjoy his touch. I feel sick, but I can't leave. At any moment they will catch sight of me. I wipe my staring face again and again, rub my eyes as if they were made of glass. Now I am aware that one of the farm maids is approaching. I walk swiftly over to the vegetable garden and empty the bucket over the turnips and rutabagas, splashing the water everywhere. Then I dash off before the girl can inspect me more closely.

"You there," she shouts, "come here!"

I put the bucket down and hurry away without looking back.

"So, HE'S PAINTING A portrait of Maria," the pastor says.

"Wearing a red dress."

"With her hair loose?"

"The pastor must put a stop to this."

"And how does Jussi suggest that happens?"

"The pastor will have to talk to her. Tell her not to go there."

"And the painting? Is it any good?"

"It was obscured from my view."

The pastor ponders. He blows little puffs of air through his lips, maybe in an effort to dislodge a tobacco flake.

"So, Nils Gustaf attended the dance in Kenttä and a very pretty girl caught his eye. He asked her if she was willing to sit as a model for a painting in her spare time. What's worrying you, Jussi?"

"Nils Gustaf is left-handed," I remind him.

"That's correct."

"He is a *herrasmies*."

"And?"

"Maybe he takes pencils with him to do some sketching while he's sitting alone in the forest waiting for someone to come past."

The pastor gives me a thoughtful look. He slowly runs his hand through his unshorn hair, as if he needs an unobstructed view.

37.

O F ALL THE ARTS THE PASTOR TRIED TO TEACH ME, SPEAKING proved to be the hardest. If reading and writing were an adventure for me, a walk amid the mountain peaks where the views became ever more magnificent, speaking was like digging out a bog. The more you shoveled, the more sludge came slurping up. Every word a slop-filled spadeful. Squish. Squash. Squelch. And despite the bog extending farther and farther, despite the words being laid in long strings along the edge, it was still just mud and peat.

My voice lacked something. As was so often the case among the Sami, the pitch of my voice was quite high and it was also rather grating. You never heard Sami talking with the chest tones from deep in the thorax that you heard in the sheriff or Nils Gustaf. With us the timbre was more up in the head and throat, and this was especially evident in the *joik*, our traditional form of song. For us northerners, feeling was the most important thing. For the Swedes it was volume. The pastor told me that, when he began his studies for the priesthood, he too had problems making himself heard; how his voice could scarcely fill a classroom, let alone a church, and that his lecturers had pointed this out.

To a large extent, of course, it was to do with shyness. If you wanted to become a speaker, you had to overcome your fears, something requiring a great deal of practice. The pastor advised me to consider listeners as a herd of reindeer, a trick he used himself sometimes. Reindeer were large and, with their horns, could look quite dangerous. But the only thing they were actually concerned about was eating grass. If your voice was too low, they just carried on eating. If you shouted and waved your arms about, the herd scattered to the four winds in terror. But if you spoke calmly you could see the animals lift their muzzles and prick up their ears, and very gradually you could increase the volume and vary the sounds. Their interest was piqued, and one or two would even take a step forward. Then the rest would follow suit. If you could just get the flames alight, you could soon lay on branch after branch. During some sermons, the pastor had experienced a mutual exaltation grow between him and the congregation, the listeners responding to him wordlessly, and the feeling that he was becoming their tongues and lungs.

"At such moments you can feel the Holy Spirit," the pastor said.

"So all the weeping, all the leaping and shrieking . . . ?"

"It comes from God."

Dogs were good to speak in front of, as well as cows and sheep. Who could be shy in front of an animal? A useful exercise was to stand in front of a farm dog that was barking furiously. And then calm it down by talking. If you shouted back, it just aggravated the dog's rage. But if you did the opposite, if you started to whisper the quietest prayer, you could see its anger turn to curiosity. On several occasions the pastor had preached dogs to sleep, their noses on their paws, an achievement often in his mind when he stood in front of enraged innkeepers or scornful townswomen.

I tried to follow his advice. I spoke to crows and spiders. To a newly caught grayling. To suckling pigs and dragonflies and clucking hens. When I found a baby crying in a leather pouch, I sat down next to it and talked it to sleep. The mother was suspicious when she returned, but I even spoke to her. It was difficult and required all my concentration. I searched for fine words, water-smooth pebbles, sleek shapes of beauty, and nervously I placed them in a row. She sniffed and walked off, the baby slung across her chest, but she looked back several times and seemed to want to stay. I had made something with words and for the first time it had worked. I had reached into her heart. It was like learning to walk; I was stumbling and falling, traveling clumsily over bumpy ground.

I was obviously able to speak before—if speaking was defined as the noise animals make. Give it to me. Move. Look at that. Let's go.

Most human utterances were of this simple kind. Expressing ideas, making them develop into trains of thought—that was something else. The road to salvation, for example. The pastor had been preaching about this all his adult life, and yet there was always more to say. And the remarkable thing was that the words changed when they were written down. The same words, in one case made from the letters of the alphabet, in the other from sounds. What separated them? The Bible was written down, but you had to chew the text over to reach inside. Let it pass through the mouth and be transformed into the living word. What did this transformation consist of? Ostensibly, saliva and muscle movements. A little hot air expelled. And at the same time something happened that couldn't be explained, but it deepened the experience. Listening to a good speaker was like eating. Like receiving nourishment straight from a mouth.

Juhani Raattamaa paid another visit to Kengis, after his travels between prayer meetings in the valley's southerly villages. During the pastor's service Juhani sat hunched over in the pew as if he were gathering his strength, and when it was time for the sermon, the pastor did a remarkable thing. With a sign to Juhani Raattamaa he called him up to his side and declared that this man would be speaking in his place. Whispers were exchanged in the pews, especially between the burghers. Could he do that? Let a layman preach in church? Did this not violate the Conventicle Act?

The pastor had foreseen the objections. He calmly handed a piece of paper to Juhani and explained that today's sermon had been authored by himself. It would simply pass through Juhani's lips. Juhani took the piece of paper and warily raised his eyes, as if expecting protests. When none came, he licked his lips to soften them, opened his mouth, stretched his vocal cords, and filled the church with his melodious Finnish.

"The world has never really loved Christians, and in every place where true Christianity has manifested itself it has been the target of anger and persecution."

Not once did Juhani look down at the piece of paper. The pastor stood beside him. It was as if the pastor were talking through Juhani, as if Juhani Raattamaa were his mouth. The words rose up to the church roof like winged bodies and from there they sailed down over the men and the women, the old folk and the children, over the newly awakened with their tear-streaked cheeks and over the unrepentant with a hip flask in their pockets.

"And the Lord called unto him the apostles and sent them forth two by two and gave them power over unclean spirits."

It was biblical. And I was filled with trust, that this evil summer was now over. That the devil would finally be driven from our region by the pastor's general, that we would have peace.

My beloved hadn't come that day. The women's side was full of maids and servants, and on the way out I asked some of them if they had seen Maria. They just shook their heads and quickened their pace as if I had said something improper. So I went on to comment about the pastor's sermon, the one Juhani had delivered, and wondered if it had moved them. The women became even quieter, so I let them disappear from sight. They whispered to one another, casting timid glances over their shoulders to see if I was following them. I thought of them as ptarmigan. White-clad winter ptarmigan with shrill laughs. How were you supposed to talk to them? In what voice, what tone? There was still so much to learn.

38.

As the late summer progressed, so did Nils Gustaf's work on the pastor's portrait. Occasionally the pastor gave up all his duties, his steady stream of visitors and urgent writing tasks, and walked to the artist's cottage by the Kengis foundry, where he made himself available to sit for an hour at a time. With elegant gestures, the artist set out his tools. His large frame swayed to and fro in front of the easel as if performing a quaint dance. The brush looked like a reed in his huge hands and it was remarkable that he could form the most delicate of lines with his large fingers. For the most part the palette lay on a table, but sometimes he brought it up to the window in order to get the shade exactly right. It was as if he wanted to collect the light in the oil, let the sun drip in like melted butter. At the start of the sitting he usually lit a cigar, which would lie smoldering in a porcelain dish throughout the hour. The thin smoke caught the light and intensified it, making the atmosphere more alive. As for the pastor, he sucked on his pipe from time to time.

The pastor studied Nils Gustaf's hands. The thumbnail shone in a way that was reminiscent of a crescent moon. It looked as though he were trying to imagine it being pressed into a woman's neck, while she choked and tried to twist away.

Was it possible that these same hands could capture the softest shimmer of light in one moment, only to wound and strangle in the next? Could such extremes coexist in the same psyche? While the pastor sat absorbed in these thoughts, he heard the cottage door open and one of the girls from the foundry came in with a silver tray. On it were some delicious little fried pastries.

"Crullers." The artist smiled. "I asked the cook to bake some. The recipe is supposed to come from Gustav Vasa's household."

He handed a copper to the girl, who shyly mumbled her thanks in Finnish. It was obvious from her appearance that she must be a descendant of the Walloons at the foundry; her eyes were brown, and her plaited hair dark and thick. When she took the coin, he snatched her wrist and pressed a kiss on her neck. The pastor could see she didn't like it. Blushing, she hurried out, while Nils Gustaf proffered the still-warm pastries.

"Cinnamon," the pastor noted. "But is there brandy in there too?"

"Only a few drops for flavor."

The pastor hesitated and stopped chewing. He silently put the cake to one side.

"A delight," Nils Gustaf said with a laugh. "I mean that girl. I've been wanting to paint her, but she keeps digging her heels in."

"But you think you can persuade her?"

"I have my own ways to make girls soften."

"And if she doesn't?"

"She will."

"A woman's strengths should not be underestimated," the pastor said. "Some people think a woman is superior to a man."

"Do you believe that?"

"In certain respects, yes, I do."

"Maybe the pastor means a woman's guile? Her power to ensnare? Her way of offering a man forbidden fruit?"

"I mean that without my mother I wouldn't be here."

Nils Gustaf gave an unconscious grimace.

"No, that's certainly true. A woman has to bring us forth."

"In my childhood home in Jäkkvik it was my mother who held

the family together. Without her sacrifices, Petrus and I would never have survived. Father was away for long periods. He was doing business of various kinds."

"And perhaps with other women?"

"Do you think so?"

"A man has to have women. Even the pastor must understand that."

"And if he doesn't get them?"

"There's always a rose somewhere to be picked."

"And if she declines? If she offers resistance?"

"What at first appears to be reluctance usually turns into desire when it comes to the moment of truth."

"But if the man wants it but the woman doesn't, should he make use of his physical strength?"

Nils Gustaf drew on his cigar and gazed into the distance.

"The pastor thinks of his mother with love. I wish I could do the same."

He exhaled, rounding it off with a short bout of spitting, and watched the wreath of smoke rise to the ceiling.

"I was an unwanted child. To this today I don't know who my real father is. Her brother had to look after me. He was a lieutenant in the cavalry, always ate his dinner in uniform. I was expected to follow in his footsteps. Now, with the passage of time, I understand him better, but then it was difficult. He wanted to make his sister's bastard child respectable."

"Was he harsh toward you?"

"I remember my paint box. It was my most cherished possession, and when he realized that, he confiscated it as punishment. Every little misdemeanor led to a ban on painting. It wasn't until I started painting horses that he relented on that point."

"Horses?"

"Horses at a walk, horses over hurdles, cavalry charges, hunters, parade horses, a team of four to whose driver I gave some of his own features. And thanks to this he finally let me paint. You see, he liked horses more than he liked people."

"And your aunt?"

"She had enough to do with her own children. For the whole of my upbringing I felt as though I'd forced my way into their home, that I was taking up space that belonged to the real family."

"Didn't she ever show any motherly feelings?"

"I never received any warmth. On the other hand, they were careful about my clothes, because I represented the family in the outside world. Sometimes I think she was scared of me."

"Scared of a child?"

"I was big for my age. She used to take her children out of my way. At times she seemed to think I wanted to hurt them."

"Did you want to?"

"I kept to myself. It was worse when I started school, when I learned the word 'bastard.' Then I had to take advantage of my size."

"You learned to fight?"

"Top-sawyers' kids or whoever the hell they were, I gave the whole lot of them a good walloping. Even when they were older, even when there were several of them. I had fights all the time I was at school."

"And as an adult?"

"When I have to. Doesn't the pastor too? Or does he always turn the other cheek?"

The pastor gripped his pipe and pretended to clean it on his sleeve.

"I have a temper," he said. "But I do everything I can to resist coming to blows. I don't want to be like my father."

"I understand. But that's still preferable, to have a father who hit you. Rather than not having one at all."

"Your mother never said who he was?"

"She came to see me now and then. Always stylishly dressed in voluminous gowns, a thick layer of powder in the corners of her mouth. When she'd gone I tried to sketch her from memory."

"Your first portrait?"

"I don't remember her ever touching me. My stepfather gave me to understand she was ill."

"Was it serious?"

"Supposedly. But I don't know. Maybe she just wanted an excuse not to hold me."

"And she never told you who your father was?"

Nils Gustaf gave a sardonic smile.

"It was an excellent idea, wasn't it? The bitch is still alive, you see. Maybe I should look her up and threaten to strangle her if she doesn't tell? Squeeze her neck harder and harder until in the end the old battleax understands what she has to give me. Or do you have a better suggestion?"

The pastor gave no answer.

"Good," Nils Gustaf said. "Maintain that expression. That exact expression."

AT ONE OF THE sittings Nils Gustaf took a break to visit the privy out in the garden. The pastor was left in the cottage alone. He wrestled with his conscience for a while before getting up and walking over to the large wooden trunk standing in one corner. It was locked. With mounting apprehension, the pastor looked for the key and finally found it in a waistcoat that was hanging up. He unlocked the lid and stood there speechless. The trunk's interior was divided into a large number of compartments. There were liquids and powders in a variety of sealed bottles and jars, several of which bore labels with gaping skulls. There were metal boxes, glass receptacles and measuring tubes, meticulously graduated scales with weights, all the equipment you could possibly need in a chemical laboratory.

On the desk was correspondence about artists' materials and commissions for portraits. One letter was an invitation to an exhibition in Stockholm in the winter. He was clearly having some success in the finer salons. In the penholder were a quantity of pencils. The pastor examined them and put one of them in his pocket.

"Did you find anything interesting?"

The pastor hastily turned. The doorway was filled with Nils Gustaf's mighty form. He came to stand next to the pastor, who was pretending to look through some canvases.

"The mountain theme!"

"Yes, I spent a time up by Lake Torneträsk before I made my way down here to Pajala. Do you like them?"

"You must have walked a long way to find views like these."

"I borrowed a tent. To experience the midnight sun over the mountain heath was sublime!"

The pastor nodded quickly. The artist went over to a painting that had been placed to one side to dry and turned it round.

"What does the pastor think of this?"

"It . . . it is exceptional!"

The pastor stared dumbfounded at the picture Nils Gustaf was holding up to the light. It was pinned to a simple wooden frame and was still not completely finished.

"Can the pastor see who it is?"

The woman in the painting was radiant. Her body appeared so light, as if she were floating. The golden hair spinning around like clouds, the dress red as blood, the face shimmering in the darkness of the barn. Her beauty was striking.

"Maria," the pastor murmured.

"It took some time to get her hair loose. But I succeeded in the end."

The pastor looked grave.

"A painting like this can hardly be shown to the people."

"In Stockholm it can."

"But should it?"

"The girl's beautiful, Pastor. She's the prettiest I've seen. My painting captures but a dim reflection of the real Maria."

The pastor stared at the picture for a long time, as if trying to retain it inwardly. Then he turned to Nils Gustaf.

"You are not awakened?"

"Not in the pastor's sense, no."

"Do you wish to be? Shall I tell you about the divine grace I myself encountered during a period of great despair?"

Nils Gustaf smiled.

"No," he said.

But then, while he was mixing the colors, he added:

"Actually, yes. I can paint you in the meantime. I can reproduce it in the picture."

For a moment, the pastor was obliged to close his eyes. To step inside, wander deep into his limitless forests.

"That woman was called Maria too," he began.

This was a lie. The woman in his innermost heart was called Milla Clementsdotter.

"It happened the winter after my pastoral degree. I was on a long visitation, and arrived at the village of Åsele one January evening. The winter darkness weighed on the landscape and a similar darkness prevailed in my soul."

"Yes, those are the times you crave female company."

"Those are the times," the pastor said, "the times under the sparkle of the starry heavens, that divine grace can reveal itself. . . ."

39.

WE ALL FELT THE NIGHTS GROW NOTICEABLY CHILLIER. THE animals sped up their preparations for the long polar winter. People, too, hastened to reap and gather and fill their storehouses.

Although it was only the end of August, the pastor noticed the first signs of frost damage on his potato plants. The tips of the leaves had shriveled and turned black. In concern he took the little trowel and raked around the roots. Soon he glimpsed something yellow in the brown clay soil. Squatting down in the garden, he very gently picked up the hard tuber and dug a little farther. He immediately discovered more of these fruits of the earth, six larger ones in total, as well as two the size of peas still attached to the root system. He gathered them all and examined them with interest. He rubbed off the soil with his thumb and saw that they had a thin skin, and under the skin a light-colored, yellowish flesh. He bit into one, expecting it to taste like an apple, because the consistency reminded him of freshly fallen fruit, but found it tasted mostly of water. With the little harvest in his cupped hands he walked over to the well and rinsed it clean.

"Come here, Jeana," he called to his daughter, who was playing with the dog.

He cut a piece off for her; she chewed it quickly and then spat the mush out onto the grass.

"Don't trick me, Father!"

"It's a potato," he hastened to tell her. "I got the seeds from a student friend in Uppsala."

Now that the tubers had been washed, small indentations were visible in them. They were similar to the ones he had planted last summer, when little purple shoots had sprouted out of them. Maybe he ought to give the whole lot to the pig?

He carried the potatoes in to the kitchen table and examined them through a strong magnifying glass. He split one of the tubers and discovered that the inner structure consisted of a hard, cream-colored flesh that was shiny and slightly wet. On the fireplace was an iron pot with some hot water left at the bottom. He dropped the potatoes in one by one and brought it to a boil. Nothing happened. No change in color, no contraction or wrinkling of the skin. On the other hand, a rather agreeable smell was rising, suggestive of moist bread. He prodded them now and then with a needle to see if the consistency was changing, and after a few minutes the tubers started softening. Soon the needle went right through. Full of anticipation, he served them up on a plate and put them on the table, just as Brita Kajsa came in. She gave off an odor of farmyard, and her forehead was glistening with perspiration from her labor.

"Sit down," the pastor urged her, looking for a spoon. "Now we'll try our crop."

She frowned when he presented the round, steaming shapes.

"Are they turnips?"

"No, not turnips. They're our newly acquired solanums."

"You've harvested them?"

"Just the first few plants. The dog refused to eat the fruit. But now I've cooked it."

Brita Kajsa cautiously cut the potato into pieces. She took a small bite and let it rest on her tongue. The pastor hurriedly did the same. A small smile spread across his wife's face.

"Not bad," she said. "Possibly needs a pinch of salt."

She sprinkled a few grains from the saltcellar on top. The pastor reached for the butter dish that had been left there, scooped out a knob, and let it plop down. The heat made the butter melt and mix with the salt. He rolled the piece of potato in the sauce and put it on his tongue. As an undreamed-of tenderness dissolved in his mouth, he shut his eyes and smacked his lips with pleasure.

"We need to be sparing with the butter," she said.

"Yes, but taste it first. Mix the potato with butter and salt."

Brita Kajsa did as she was told. The pastor watched her close her lips, chew tentatively, and then pause. Without moving, she looked at her husband.

"Oh!" she exclaimed.

At first he thought she had burned her tongue, but instead she gave him a look that demanded to know if this could be true.

"Potato?" she asked.

"The tubers I put in the ground. Six of them came from one single plant."

"It tastes heavenly."

"It does indeed."

"It's so good it's probably poisonous."

"In that case we might die this very minute."

The pastor cut up the next potato. She did likewise; they were both eating from the same plate.

"Six from one single plant?"

"Yes, and there are more out there."

"Potato," she said again. "From the solanum plant?"

"At first I thought I'd give them all to the pig."

"Are you out of your mind?"

"But then I remembered hearing that it had to be cooked. And when you eat it with butter and salt . . ."

"Well, the butter isn't entirely necessary."

"From just one of the tubers I got six back. Imagine if we get the same crop from the others! We need to share the knowledge. I'll announce it to all from the pulpit!"

"People prefer turnips."

"Shouldn't we encourage them to plant some all the same?"

"As an extra crop, maybe," she said.

"This taste!" the pastor said excitedly. "Fresh, newly cooked potatoes. I really believe I won't ever forget it."

"As long as it doesn't make us ill!"

"Then we'll die in bliss."

"You said there's more out there?"

"Certainly, there's more out there. We can cook some for the children too."

"I can feel something moving in my stomach. Maybe it's like the toadstool. The poison creeps up on you after a while. . . ."

"We'll lie down and rest, Brita Kajsa. It's just the feeling of being full."

"Yes, God help me!"

"Potato," he repeated. "Who could have imagined this? Isn't creation filled with the sweetest miracles?"

As soon as they lay down, Brita Kajsa's stomachache passed. She didn't usually get enough peace to rest, but this time she shut her eyes and nodded off. Soon the pastor could hear her heavy breathing and see her purple, veiny eyelids twitch slightly. The pastor dozed off too and dreamed of a future in which every farm in the north had large, leafy potato crops. A sixfold return in the harvest of these delights, was that really possible? Such an outcome would finally banish starvation from the Tornedalen vale of tears.

40.

I WAS BY THE WELL, CLEANING SOME AUTUMN SALMON THE PASTOR had received as a tithe. I tossed the guts to Tjalmo the dog, who sniffed them with suspicion before warily trying them. The tithing should naturally have increased after the pastor moved to Pajala. The poor crofters up in Karesuando had difficulty delivering the tax they owed and the pastor never wanted to insist. Here in the Pajala region there were some prosperous farms, but nevertheless the inhabitants gave less than they ought. And you could well understand the reason. Since the revival, the pastor had stopped serving brandy to those who came to him with their butter, their cheeses and turnips. This was matched by a conspicuous disinclination to pay. It was easy to overlook your obligations if you didn't receive your dram in return.

The fishes' flesh was badly damaged and covered with cuts and gashes. At this time of the year, as autumn approached and evenings began to draw in, the salmon were caught with gigs. An iron stand was mounted at the front of the boat, on which kindling was lit, so that the flames shone out over the waves. The fish were drawn to the light, forming a shoal so dense the water looked as though it were boiling, and the men stabbed at the glistening backs with large spears.

As I was rinsing the fish Tjalmo leaped to his feet and started barking. It was Nils Gustaf arriving on foot.

"Is the pastor available?"

I washed the slime off my hands and went into the parsonage. The pastor interrupted his writing and followed me out into the yard. Nils Gustaf grinned and flung his arms wide.

"Pastor, do you have anything to say about the light?"

"The light?"

"Yes! What does a man of the church say about the light?"

"That it's God's creation."

Nils Gustaf's smile widened even further. It was obvious there was something brewing.

"Can anyone hold on to light? Touch it, catch it?"

"I don't really understand. Do you mean the painting, is it ready?"

"No, I mean the light of the world. Come and see!"

Nils Gustaf set off along the village path without delay, the pastor and me hurrying behind. With a wide sweep of his arm the artist traced the heavens' curve.

"Look up there. All the clouds sailing past across the sky. Do the clouds exist? We can't touch them, can't get close to them. And yet we say they exist."

"They consist of water vapor," the pastor said.

"And think of the rainbow. Does that exist? Or the full moon? Do you believe they exist, Jussi?"

"Yes."

"You can't touch them. And you say they exist even so?"

"Yes."

"Why can we see them, then?"

I couldn't think of a reply. Nils Gustaf clicked his tongue delightedly.

"Because we have light! If the moon were dark, we humans would never have spotted it. It's because of the light that we can see it."

We had reached Kengis Church and Nils Gustaf pointed to the façade.

"Take the church, for example. Does the pastor think it exists, here and now?"

The familiar profile of the church's parvis rose up.

"Yes," the pastor. "It's all here."

"We believe it because our eyes can see it. The church enters the eye with the aid of light, isn't that the pastor's thinking?"

"You could put it like that."

"I could take out my sketch pad and draw a likeness of it. I'd draw for a while and we'd soon see the church on the paper. It wouldn't be exactly the same, but we'd see what it represents. Now, Pastor, have the goodness to behold your church."

"Yes?"

"It's standing there. Do you see it?"

"I see it."

Nils Gustaf waited, a cunning expression on his face. For a second I wondered if he was drunk. He slowly put his hand inside his coat and pulled out a cardboard portfolio. He opened it with care. Inside lay a small, square piece of glass, which he held up in front of us. The pastor looked quizzical, put on his spectacles, and leaned toward it.

"It's the church!" he exclaimed.

Nils Gustaf nodded eagerly.

"It's beautifully drawn," the pastor said, impressed.

The artist raised his hand.

"Not drawn."

"Painted, I mean. You've painted it."

I leaned forward, too, to get a better look. The picture was smaller than the palm of the artist's hand. And yet all the details were depicted with remarkable precision. The church could be seen with all the details reproduced exactly, the position of the windows, the pitch of the gable timbers, the wooden cross adorning the roof. Nils Gustaf lowered his voice as if about to reveal a secret.

"I didn't make the picture."

"You didn't?"

"No, the fact is no person made this picture. Can the pastor explain how that is possible?"

The pastor turned the piece of glass over. There was no lettering, nothing to give any clue.

"The light," Nils Gustaf said.

"The light?"

"What the pastor is holding right now," he said solemnly, "is frozen light."

The pastor cautiously extended his finger and brushed over the glass plate. The surface was shiny and hard.

"So it's supposed to be some kind of wizardry?" he asked.

"You could say that. You could indeed say that. Now, if you please, come with me."

The artist climbed the steps to the church. The door was unlocked and he showed us onto the porch. By the wall he had rigged up a tent of dark blankets. He disappeared inside for a while; we heard the clink of glass receptacles and detected the sharp smell of chemical fumes. Then he crawled out of the tent and showed me a wooden apparatus with turned legs and attachments.

"Could Jussi help me with the tripod?"

I lifted it while he undid a brown leather trunk with brass fittings. Inside lay a square black box, which he carefully picked up.

"Perhaps the pastor could bring out a chair for us? Preferably one with a high back."

The artist went out onto the parvis and I followed him. When we had walked about fifty paces he stopped. I handed over the thing he called a tripod; he folded the legs out and secured them with screws and braces until it was stable. Then he unfastened the strange black box, opened it up, and attached the contraption into the screw holes on the top of the tripod.

The pastor came out of the church, dragging a heavy seat from the sacristy. I hurried over to help him. The artist indicated we should place it a short distance in front of the church.

"Now I want the pastor to sit on it. Lean your head against the back. It's essential to sit completely still. There mustn't be the slightest movement.

"Shall I just sit?"

"Wait for me to prepare everything first."

Nils Gustaf unfolded a piece of black cloth and pulled it over both himself and the tripod. All that protruded was a little tube with a glass-covered eye. The artist raised his right arm.

"Is the pastor sitting quite still?"

"Yes."

"Don't move for as long as my hand is in the air. Make sure that you look straight at me the whole time!"

I heard metallic sounds from some kind of mechanical apparatus underneath the blanket. His right hand signaled that the work was in progress. The warm sun shone down on us. A cow was lowing on one of the farms. I saw a bird pass swiftly overhead, its shadow flitting across the pastor's face, but he sat like a stone. Finally, the metallic sound was heard again and we saw the arm lowering.

Nils Gustaf emerged panting from beneath the piece of cloth, as if he had been holding his breath for a long time. Without further explanation he hurriedly dismantled the box, still wrapped in the black cloth, before carrying the bundle back to the porch.

"Shall I bring the tripod?"

He had no time for a reply. I lifted the wooden frame off the ground and saw the three marks left by the legs. I carried it to the church steps supported on my shoulder, then helped the pastor haul the heavy chair back. We were both equally confounded by what had just happened. Vigorous activity could be heard inside the tent on the porch. We saw the blanket billowing out as the artist crept around in there. There was more clinking of glass and metal and I could hear lids being unscrewed and liquids being poured. Clearly a complicated process was being performed and soon there was the smell of smoke as he heated something up. Eventually his heavy boots appeared as he clumsily backed out of the tent. Inside I glimpsed dishes, bottles, and long tweezers. He was holding something close to his body, as if sheltering a fragile nest. With obvious excitement he stood up and held out his hand. There lay a glass plate, still shiny with moisture. At first I saw only the gleam: a glistening drop was forming on the underside and swelling, before it fell like silver. But when I changed the angle of my view, I could see that there was something there, a pattern, a picture.

The artist walked out onto the church steps and held the glass plate up to the light. And now we could see. There was Kengis Church, just as on the first glass plate. But this time, outlined against the church, was a figure in dark clothes, a human shape dressed in a long coat, with unkempt hair that had been pushed back. The lips were large and pronounced, the nose curved. And above them two dark holes that must be eyes. I looked at these eyes and they stared back without blinking.

"You're sitting beside your church, Pastor. Now you are preserved forever."

The pastor was trembling with delight. He could barely stand still.

"I read about this when I was in Uppsala!" he exclaimed. "This must be a camera obscura."

"Even better, Pastor. This is something totally new. A friend of mine ordered the apparatus from France. The technique is called 'daguerreotype.'"

"A machine that catches light. . . ."

"Here, Pastor. Have the glass plates as souvenirs, the first to be taken in Pajala. Remember the day when the pastor was the first person in the north to be depicted in this way. Take care of the picture. Keep it for all time."

"That I shall," the pastor mumbled, carefully holding the glass between his fingers as if it were a tiny sheet of ice. "Thank you, I certainly shall."

He pulled a handkerchief out of his pocket to protect it.

"And the image won't disappear over time?"

"It is said to be permanent."

"Longer than a human life?"

"Yes, perhaps. Wouldn't that be remarkable? One day, when we're both long gone, in an unknown future, people will be able to look at the pastor, see him as if he were alive. Like being preserved in an herbarium, you could say."

The pastor could not drag his eyes away from the picture.

"If the art of the daguerreotype becomes widespread," he asked, "if it can be performed by anyone at all, how will that affect you?"

"What do you mean, sir?"

"Will the world need portrait painters then?"

Nils Gustaf didn't look entirely comfortable with the thought.

"It will take some time before that age comes."

"But one day it might happen. When all have their own equipment, when all can produce their own pictures and show them to each other. Will that be the end of the art of painting?"

"Do you know what, Pastor? I think you might be right. That age might be approaching."

"And what sort of age will it be?"

"One of light," he said. "The age of light."

The pastor nodded, still clearly in a daze.

"Could you show me the process?" he asked. "Before you pack it all away. . . . I thought I could detect the smell of lead?"

"Mercury vapors," Nils Gustaf corrected him. "Come in and I'll demonstrate."

I left the men on the porch, in earnest conversation. Disquiet was mounting inside me, a sense of danger.

The age of light. Lucifer.

Was this what was awaiting mankind?

I KNEW IT WAS TIME. I had heard the voice singing within me for a while. It was *matkamies*, the wanderer, and I must set forth north-ward. At the side of the roads the fireweed, *Epilobium angustifolium*, released its swirling puffs of seeds, which stuck to clothes and, in a certain light, looked like snow. Gathering in flocks, the birds pre-pared to take their leave. The wasps, infuriated at their impending death, wanted to gnaw on flesh. At night the skies opened a shining channel to the cosmos, to let the chill of outer space descend over the meadows. At the start, autumn was just a gentle incline, but then it gradually became a steep downhill slope, until a precipice just ahead would plummet into white obscurity. There was a sense of haste in everything that lived, an urge to get away. I found my birch-bark knapsack and in it saved some bits of bread; I had men-tioned to no one what I was going to do. On the last evening, the pastor laid his arm around my shoulder, wanting to give me advice, it seemed, searching for the right words, his eyes averted. He could discern my state of mind, understand that the time had come once again. But this was something we had never been able to speak about. That night, when everyone had fallen asleep, I crept out as though I were simply going to empty my bladder. And they didn't see me again.

41.

THE PASTOR SAT ON THE PORCH STEP BUSYING HIMSELF WITH HIS morning pipe. As soon as the smoke rose, the gnats, the plague of August, dispersed. He heard the door open and Brita Kajsa sat down next to him. Like the pastor, she had grown stiffer with age, and the weasel-like nimbleness she had when they were sweethearts had disappeared over the years. But her mind was as quick as ever. Now that her morning chores inside were finished, she could at last allow herself a short rest.

"Jussi left last night," Brita Kajsa said.

"Mm."

"Didn't he say anything to you?"

"I knew it was time. I noticed his unease."

"What's pulling at him so terribly?"

"He'll come back."

"Do you think so?"

"He usually comes back."

The pastor surveyed the cloudy August sky.

"The years are passing."

"How's your stomach?"

"Better."

"Doesn't hurt?"

"No, it doesn't hurt. And you?"

She shrugged her shoulders slightly.

"I'll be all right," she said. "Though the years are affecting my joints."

"Mm."

"Why did the Lord create such bad joints for people? The pastor could preach a sermon about it sometime."

"There's not much in the scriptures on the subject of joint pain."

"Lots about leprosy and blindness and the lame and the crippled and locusts and floods, but nothing about aching old women. Didn't the Lord miss a chapter there?"

"Perhaps Brita Kajsa should preach about it herself?"

"Aren't we women supposed to be silent members of the congregation?"

"It wasn't I who gave that order."

"The pastor's preachers are all men. Pekka and Juhani, Erkki Antti and Antin Pieti and all the others. If you don't make a woman a preacher soon, the revival movement will be run by men far into the future."

The pastor considered her words.

"One problem . . ." he said, and hesitated before continuing, "is that women often lack the requisite education."

"Well, give it to them, then. Allow women into the seminaries and seats of learning and let's see whether they learn to think."

"Then there's the acoustic question. A woman's voice is by nature weaker and can't be heard as well in a church."

"We'll have to raise our voices, then," she said, "to be heard."

"It'll probably be a while before that time comes."

"Wasn't it a woman's words that inspired the revival?" she said. "Your young woman in Åsele, who displayed a deeper understanding of the order of grace than all the reverends and Bible professors you've listened to over the years? It was a simple, uneducated Lapp girl who kindled your spiritual fire."

"Yes, I'll never forget Maria. . . ."

"Milla was her name. Milla Clementsdotter."

"Yes, she was baptized Milla."

"Milla Clementsdotter would be an excellent preacher."

"She would, certainly," the pastor agreed. "Indeed she would."

"Or why not one of our own daughters? Nora or Sophia?"

"Allow them into the pulpit?"

"You could teach them to speak. Like you train the men around you. Like you trained Jussi."

"But Jussi is different."

"Because you found him by the side of the road."

"Because . . . because he reminds me of Levi."

The pastor remembered Levi's curly hair, how he shook with laughter when you rubbed your nose into his stomach. Of all the children they had lost, Levi was the one he missed the most.

Brita Kajsa began to knead her thumb into the tightening tendons in her neck.

"And how have things been going in Kautokeino?" she asked. "I heard that the Sami who held a service were sent to prison."

"Yes, but most of them have been released now. I would like to think everything will soon calm down."

"But the pastor sounds doubtful."

"The sheriff still hasn't got hold of Ellen Skum. She's absconded and her relatives up in the mountains are sheltering her. In addition, the Sami incurred heavy legal expenses. They might be forced to sell all their reindeer in order to pay."

"But what will they live on, then?"

"Unrest and bitterness are rife up there. They thought they were fighting for good."

"Are they continuing to disrupt church services?"

"I heard that Stockfleth has moved. The new one is called Fredrik Waldemar Hvoslef, another priest who only does it for the money."

Brita Kajsa tentatively took her husband's hand. From inside the cabin came shrieks from the girls, who were arguing about something.

"I'm worried," she said.

"So am I."

"There are evil forces at work," she said in a low voice. "I fear they are preparing for a battle."

"With us?"

"With the Sami. With the revival movement. With everything we hold sacred."

The pastor looked into her serious face. Years had dug deep furrows at the corners of her mouth and the skin around her eyes was loose and gray. And yet in the early morning light she seemed to radiate an inner glow. If the pastor was a suddenly flaring piece of birch bark, then Brita Kajsa was the pine-tar stump, the bit that could smolder for hours during the winter night and save the life of the shivering, curled-up wayfarer.

"I have to go to Kautokeino," the pastor decided. "I'll go as soon as I have time. But first we have to find the evildoer. We have to stop him. Now that he's had a taste of violence, there's a big risk he'll strike again."

"May the Lord go with us," she murmured.

Louder shrieks and thuds could be heard from the cabin. Brita Kajsa rose, straightened her kirtle, and went inside. As soon as she opened the door, the girls fell silent.

PART THREE

❖

The prettiest women
Caught by your brushstroke
The treasures you hide
Deep down in your poke
In honor of art
Let us raise a toast
He who is strongest
Will sup up the most

42.

THE AUTUMN RAIN WAS TEEMING DOWN, COPIOUS AND COLD, occasionally turning to snow. I was half lying in the corner of the room while Tjalmo dozed with his back against my thighs. I had arrived in the night while everyone was sleeping, crept in and lain down to sleep in my usual place. Now the pastor was standing staring down at me.

"*Sieki täälä*," he finally managed to say. "So you're back, Jussi."

Not a word about where I had been or what I had done. But I could see he was pleased.

We sat there quietly, happy to escape the foul weather. This was a day for indoor work. Brita Kajsa gave me an extra ladle of porridge, though I said I didn't need it, her way of welcoming me back. And the daughters giggled because I was talking strangely, almost like a Norwegian. I gave them my last piece of stockfish and let them chew on it and taste the sea. Meanwhile, the pastor sat picking at his morning meal as he browsed through old gazettes sent up from Stockholm. *Aftonbladet* was written across the front page of the newspaper. Maybe he was looking for material for Sunday's sermon.

Suddenly Tjalmo leaped up. Steps could be heard on the porch, followed by a heavy pounding at the door. Nora opened it, and in the entrance to the kitchen stood a man so drenched, so dripping with rain, it looked as though he had been swimming in the river. Not until he removed his hat did I recognize him. It was Heino, one of the workers at the foundry. Nora showed him into the cabin.

"Come in and get warm, Heino," the pastor said calmly. "There's porridge and a knob of butter."

"The pastor must come," the fellow said, gasping for breath after rushing through the storm.

"What's so urgent?"

"It's best if—"

"Tell me!"

"The pastor knows the fellow. The artist who lives by the foundry. He's locked himself into the cottage. We've knocked on the window, but he won't open."

"I'm coming."

Heino nodded with relief. His face looked frozen, his forehead and cheeks shining from the rain. He gazed out into the yard, at the rain beating at the windowpanes. The pastor abandoned his half-eaten bowl of porridge and went to fetch his coat. I shot to my feet and picked up his bag, which I wrapped in a piece of felt to protect it from the worst of the weather. Then off we set.

After only a few moments we were completely soaked. My leather tunic was greased to withstand rain, but I could still feel the wet seeping in through the seams. The wind was violent, driving the rainfall toward us like water in a river. The flurries of snow obscured our vision and sometimes visibility vanished altogether, like a fog. The pastor tried to obtain more details about what had happened, but the answers he received were vague. Heino just increased his speed until we could scarcely keep up. The water ran down my trouser legs and into my curled-toe shoes and every step made a squelching noise. I did my best to shield the pastor's bag, my fingers ached, and I was freezing and perspiring at the same time. It reminded me of mountain ordeals in my childhood, when we were on the move with the *goahti* covering in a sledge pulled by my swearing father, while I did my utmost to keep up in his wake. I rapidly wiped my hand over my face to sweep away the mixture of rain and sweat. Heino glanced back, looking concerned that we were taking too long. Luckily the foundry wasn't far from the parsonage and we could soon see the large outline of the manor house rising over the meadows.

We rushed over to the cottage where Nils Gustaf lived. By the wall on the leeward side, out of the rain, huddled a figure; it was the dark-haired girl the pastor had met at one of the sittings for his portrait. At the sight of us, she curtsied. The pastor gave a brief nod and stood on tiptoe to reach the window. He shaded his eyes with his hands and peered through the glass.

"You take a look as well, Jussi," he said.

I put down the bag and did as he requested. The room inside was as I remembered it from peeping into it before. There was the easel, and canvases hanging here and there from hooks to dry. Nils Gustaf's bed was in the corner. Two betrousered legs were sticking out slightly, as if the man lying there were about to get up. But despite our vigorous knocking, there was no sign of movement.

The pastor went around to the door and tried the handle. The door wouldn't budge. He examined the hand-forged Kengis lock.

"Does he usually lock the door?"

"Yes, when he goes out."

"And at night?"

"At night as well."

"There's a brandy bottle in there," the pastor went on. "Maybe he's just drunk?"

"I thought so at first. But he's not moving. Surely he should have woken up eventually?"

The pastor thought quickly.

"Go and wake the foundry owner," he said.

"He's left for Matarengi."

"So be it."

"And the key's in the lock on the inside. The door can't be opened from the outside."

Bending down, the pastor looked through the keyhole and confirmed that was the case. He banged on the door again, but there was no reaction.

"If the door can't be opened without a key, we'll have to break it down."

"But—"

"Nils Gustaf might have been struck down by illness. I'm afraid it could be serious."

The maid was sent to the woodshed and returned immediately with a short-handled ax, which she gave to Heino. He hesitated.

"I take full responsibility," the pastor said.

Heino took aim and hacked at the doorframe. The door itself was too valuable to damage, but the frame soon broke into pieces and enabled us to prize off the striking plate. When the door swung open, a sour smell of turpentine and old wool met us.

"Stay by the door," the pastor said. "You too, Jussi."

He removed his boots and carefully brushed off the wet bits of hay from the shoe lining that were stuck to the soles of his feet. Paying particular attention to where he placed his bare feet, he edged forward toward the bed. I could see his eyes taking in the surroundings, as they did when he was looking for his plants. When he reached Nils Gustaf he leaned over him and felt his wrist, standing motionless for a moment as he searched for a pulse. Then he straightened and shook his head.

"May the Lord have mercy. . . ."

A shudder went through my body. The people from the house looked at each other as the words sank in.

"Is Nils Gustaf . . . ?"

The pastor took a handkerchief out of his pocket and coughed into it, wiped his mouth, and folded it up.

"I'm afraid so," he said, struggling to keep his voice steady. "His limbs have already stiffened. Someone must send for Michelsson and Brahe. The rest of us will stay here and keep watch."

The maid turned and ran to the manor house, her kirtle flying.

"Jussi, give me my bag. And I want Heino to stand by the door. Whatever happens, don't let anyone enter."

Through the doorway I handed him his bag, from which the pastor withdrew some paper and a pencil as I took off my curled-toe shoes. When I walked in he indicated that I should follow his footsteps and we padded across to the bed in silence.

Nils Gustaf was lying on his side facing the wall. His face looked hideous, his lips parted and twisted as if in a protracted scream, his cheeks and chin discolored with livor mortis. He was fully clothed, with plain leather slippers on his feet, and his legs sticking out over the edge of the bed were stiff. His left hand was inserted partly into his mouth, as though he were trying to rip out his tongue, and his right hand was clutching the bedspread. He must have died in agony. The pastor opened his shirt and laid his hand on his chest, to feel if there was any life left there. He cautiously tried to bend one of the artist's legs. Glancing at Heino, who was following what we were doing, he changed from Finnish to Sami.

"Cold and rigid," he said in a low voice. "He must have passed away yesterday."

"Mm."

The pastor ran his fingers over the soles of the slippers.

"It started to rain in the evening. A far as I remember it was around six."

"That's right."

"His slippers are wet on the underside. And the coat feels damp.

Nils Gustaf must have gone outside at some point after it started to rain."

"For an evening walk?"

"In that case he would have put on better shoes," the pastor said. "And the coat isn't buttoned properly. Maybe he took a brief turn outside. To empty his bladder. And when he came back . . ."

"He must have been taken ill suddenly," I suggested. "He felt bad and lay down on the bed."

"Continue, Jussi."

"A stroke, maybe? Or his heart?"

The pastor rubbed his stubbly chin.

"Why are there two glasses on the table?" he asked.

"Two?"

"Write it down, Jussi. It looks as though someone paid him a visit yesterday."

"But who was it?"

"The easel is up. Perhaps someone who wanted his portrait painted?"

The pastor went over to the easel. A piece of paper was propped against it, covered with charcoal lines. A rough sketch of the upper part of a body could be seen.

"It looks like a man," I said.

Next the pastor examined the empty glasses. He leaned forward and sniffed at them like a dog. On a shelf next to the bed was the stand the artist had put canvases on to dry. The pastor pulled them out one by one and inspected them. He spent a long time on one of the paintings and I couldn't help squinting over his shoulder.

It was the portrait of the pastor. He was sitting in the garden beside his herbarium studying a tiny plant between his finger and thumb. The light fell obliquely from behind, giving off a glow around the pastor, almost like a halo, until I realized it was pipe smoke, rendered by the artist with astonishing skill. But the thing I found most striking was the unexpected expression on the pastor's face. In it there was such heartfelt longing, something that was fragile and mournful. Nils Gustaf had laid bare part of the pastor's soul, and what we saw in his eyes was not the irascible fire-and-brimstone preacher, it was a person filled with doubt.

"He didn't have time to finish it," he muttered.

He seemed almost embarrassed.

"What did you talk about during the sittings?"

He was silent for a moment, lost in thought.

"About women," he said then. "Women we'd met."

"It's magnificent," I said.

"It's not finished," he said again.

"A picture like this can never be finished," I said. "It will continue to be painted all your life. And afterward too. Paintings by all those who think they know the pastor. Layer upon layer throughout history."

"God forbid."

"But this one . . . if I may say . . . Nils Gustaf's painting will, I believe, always be the best."

"It can't hang in the sacristy," he said. "It's not finished."

I wanted to disagree, but kept quiet. The other paintings looked more conventional; they were of the foundry owner Sohlberg, Forsström the merchant, and Hackzell the bailiff, and they looked finished, though there might have still been a layer or two of varnish left to put on. The pastor looked around and signaled that I should start writing.

"Write down that the door was locked from the inside. And all the windows were hasped on the inside."

Turning to Heino, he changed from Sami to Finnish.

"Is there a cellar hatch someone could have got in through?"

Heino shook his head.

"Or one into the attic?"

"Yes, outside, on the gable end."

"But I can't see one in here in the ceiling. Could anyone get into the cottage that way?"

"No."

In a far corner stood the daguerreotype apparatus, screwed onto the tripod and covered by a dark blanket. The trunk with all the fittings and chemicals lay open on the floor. The pastor bent down and we could both see that the receptacles and glass plates had been taken out of their compartments and now lay scattered all over the place. He stooped closer and studiously examined a side compartment, which appeared to be slightly askew. The pastor tentatively pulled at it, and discovered that it could be moved aside. A concealed space opened under the compartment. But when he felt with his fingertips, it was empty.

"What does Jussi think could have been in here?"

"I don't know . . ."

"It's easy to push the compartment open and there's a little wear here, by the locking device, you see? In other words, it appears to have been opened and shut many times. And the bottom has a slight discoloration on the inside."

The pastor pressed his nose against it, drew a deep breath in, and then indicated that I do the same.

"Metallic," I said.

"I agree," the pastor said. "The green deposit is verdigris from copper, I think. But why is it only on the bottom, and not on the sides higher up?"

He glanced at me, but whichever way I considered it, I couldn't work out the reason.

"Tell me."

"Because the coppers were rattling at the bottom and the notes were on top."

"Of course!" I exclaimed, impressed by his ingenuity.

"It was in this secret compartment that Nils Gustaf kept his money. I surmise it was a substantial sum; presumably that was why he was so careful about locking the door to the cottage."

"Where's the money now?" I asked.

The pastor patted the dead man's coat pockets but found them empty.

"He hasn't put it in his pockets, anyway."

"Could he have hidden the money somewhere?"

"Jussi will have noticed that the secret compartment wasn't completely closed. The mechanism appeared to have been damaged, making me think it was forced. And Nils Gustaf would hardly have broken his own secret compartment. There remains only one possibility."

"The pastor thinks it was . . . a thief?"

"A thief . . . and maybe worse than that."

The pastor put his fingertips together in an attitude he sometimes adopted when he was preaching.

"I think the money was taken by the person who murdered Nils Gustaf."

"Murdered!" I exclaimed.

Despite the fact that we had switched to speaking Sami again, Heino noticed my alarm. I lowered my voice to a bewildered murmur.

"But . . . but the door was locked. Locked from the inside. And the key was in the lock on the inside?"

"Undeniably."

"No human being can steal money and commit murder . . . and then make off with all the doors and windows closed from the inside."

"Carry on, Jussi."

"If a person hasn't done this . . . it must have been something else . . ."

With my fingers I made the Sami sign for the devil, whose name I didn't want to utter. The pastor gazed at me pensively, then turned his eyes to the light from the window and the pupils narrowed to pencil points. I felt a long shudder down my spine. Satan. These were the forces we were dealing with.

THE SOUND OF A horse-drawn carriage rolling into the yard announced the arrival of Sheriff Brahe. He strode into the cabin in his customary obstreperous way, closely followed by Constable Michelsson. It was immediately obvious that they begrudged having had to go out in the rain, and their mood was not improved by seeing the pastor and me in the cottage.

"And what the devil are you doing here?" the sheriff snapped, pushing past us without a greeting. I could tell by the smell of sour brandy and his bloodshot eyes that he was suffering from the effects of the night before. Sopping from the rain and with mud on their shoes, the men traipsed around the cottage and poked at the stiff body.

"Mother of God, what a stench!" Brahe said, and opened the window. He thrust it wide open and rested against the windowsill, breathing heavily.

"Why did you send for us?" he shouted with an accusing stare, before sinking into a spindle chair. "The poor chap has died in his sleep."

Heino cast a sideways glance at the pastor. The pastor appeared to hesitate, before leaning forward and calmly saying:

"I don't think Nils Gustaf's death was natural."

"What do you mean?"

"There are signs that—"

"Isn't it the case that the room was locked from the inside and all the windows were hasped? Or have I misheard?"

"No, that's correct."

"The chap fell ill in his sleep. Shall we assume a stroke?"

Brahe cast a challenging look at Michelsson, who nodded in agreement.

"Into the grave double-quick with the unfortunate fellow, his body might be infectious," Brahe went on.

"But what if the man has been killed?"

"The cottage was empty when you entered?"

"Indeed. But Nils Gustaf appears to have had a visitor yesterday."

The sheriff eased his collar, looking for a second as though he felt nauseous, until with evident repugnance he began to unbutton the artist's clothing.

"There are no injuries as far as I can see. No blood or signs of struggle. How could he have been murdered? By a creature that can walk through walls into a locked house and kill a man without it showing. Is that what the pastor believes?"

Sheriff Brahe looked around scornfully.

"Tee-hee," Michelsson giggled, to demonstrate his support for the sheriff.

Over by the door, Heino looked inquiringly at the pastor, expecting a sharp riposte. Meanwhile, Brahe was riffling through the as-yet-unframed canvases on the drying stand. He held one of them up.

"Look what a master he was!"

The ferocious she-bear was up on her hind legs, roaring. In front of the beast stood a fellow in a sheriff's uniform bravely raising his saber. The body of the bear seemed about to leap out of the picture, blood and saliva dripping from her gaping jaws. The sheriff's saber glinted like a flash of lightning.

"Such a skilled artist!"

Michelsson agreed. The sheriff suddenly noticed the brandy bottle on the table, reached out for it, and took a good swig. The pastor looked outraged and for a second seemed to be on the verge of wresting the bottle out of his hands. But Brahe just gave a smug smile.

"We'll hang this painting in our office. Won't we, Michelsson?"

"Yes, Sheriff."

"And now we want everyone to leave the cottage at once. The pastor as well! Michelsson and I will begin a methodical investigation of the circumstances pertaining to this death, and we don't want to be disturbed."

"May I take the glasses?" the pastor asked.

"The glasses?"

"Or would the sheriff like to examine them first?"

Brahe gave a dismissive wave of the hand and the pastor picked up the two glasses with the utmost care, using a handkerchief to protect them from his fingers, and then gently placed them in his bag so they wouldn't topple over. It was clear to us all that Brahe wanted to be left alone to empty the bottle of brandy in peace and quiet.

"What's the Lapp boy writing over there?" he suddenly said.

I tried to hide the paper, glancing desperately at the pastor, but it was too late. Brahe snatched it off me and started reading, his forehead creasing into a deep frown.

"This is just bosh! What's the good of that?"

"Jussi is practicing his writing," the pastor said calmly.

"But the words don't mean anything. This is just twaddle!"

He crumpled up the piece of paper and tossed it into a corner. Putting on a submissive, almost sheepish expression, I picked it up, while the sheriff waved us away with irritation, as if we were flies.

I straightened out the ball of paper and stored it in my pocket. Sheriff Brahe couldn't read Sami.

43.

BACK AT THE PARSONAGE, THE PASTOR INVITED ME INTO HIS study, shut the door behind us, and motioned for me to come up to his desk. I had to sit on a stool, which was low, and as a result the top of the desk was at the height of my chest. He took out a little folded piece of paper and opened it gingerly. On it lay some tiny flakes of wood, so light they could have been scattered by my breath.

"What's this?" he asked.

When I leaned closer, I recognized it.

"From a pencil that's been sharpened with a knife. Is it the shavings we found from Jolina's attacker?"

"Precisely, Jussi. These are the flakes we found lying among the aspens where we think the perpetrator was standing. And look at this."

He took a pencil out of his pocket and sharpened it with his pocketknife over another sheet of paper.

"They look the same."

"Look carefully."

He handed me a magnifying glass and I held my breath as I tried to focus.

"They could have come from the same pencil."

"I agree, Jussi. The shavings must come from the same sort of pencil and, as you recall, we found no pencil of this type in Henriksson's shop."

"No."

"I took this one out of the artist's penholder on one of the occasions I was sitting for him."

"The pastor stole it?"

"Let us say I borrowed it for investigative purposes."

"But that means . . . it was Nils Gustaf who attacked the women?"

"I suspected him for a long time. His boots were oiled with the same kind of shoe grease we found on Jolina's kirtle. He possessed poisons that could have been used on Jolina's dog. But nonetheless I had my doubts."

"Why?"

"Nils Gustaf's psychology. He liked talking about women during our sittings. He both adored and despised them and was hardly one to respect a refusal. But would he really lurk in a hiding place and assault them?"

"Who else would sit outdoors drawing? Perhaps he was harboring a man of violence deep down?"

"Yes, perhaps, Jussi. Perhaps we all carry such fiends within us. But I took the opportunity to examine Nils Gustaf's torso when we were in there. And there was no sign of a puncture wound. The man who injured Jolina must have been someone else. Find your notes and read out what was on his table."

I hastily started reading.

"Two empty glasses with traces of brandy. Next to a brandy bottle, one-third full. Memorandum book, receipt book—"

"What about the memorandum book?"

"There were orders for paintings in it. Who'd ordered them, the sums agreed—"

"Skip the obvious," the pastor interrupted. "I only want to know whether Jussi noticed that the page with the most recent order had been torn out?"

"Was it?"

"You recall the sketch on the easel, don't you? It's conceivable that someone visited Nils Gustaf and said he wanted to order a portrait. The order was written down in the memorandum book and signed. A commission fee was paid and placed in the secret compartment, whereupon a bottle of brandy was produced to celebrate the agreement."

"So the page that was ripped out . . . ?"

"On it Nils Gustaf had written the customer's name, and the visitor must have torn the page out before he left."

"Why?"

"Don't you understand, Jussi? The visitor already knew the murder would take place."

"But why did the pastor say nothing to the sheriff?"

"I tried, Jussi, didn't you see I tried? And I would very much like to examine the memorandum book and the receipt book more closely."

"What does the pastor mean?"

"The impression made by a pencil is usually left on the piece of paper underneath. Let me show you."

The pastor brought out two pieces of paper and laid one on top of the other. Without me seeing what, he wrote something on the top one. Then he gave the sheet underneath it to me.

"Shade it with the pencil lead, Jussi. Shade the surface carefully."

I did as he said. Little by little, almost like magic, the hitherto invisible text began to appear.

"I think the perpetrator's name can be deciphered from the memorandum book," he said.

"But the door was locked, wasn't it?"

"Where's the piece of paper, Jussi? What have I written?"

The pastor's large nose was quivering, the moisture in his nostrils glistened. He reminded me of an aging dog when it was time for food. His eyes were cloudy, the bristly eyebrows drawn together, individual hairs sticking out as they often do in old men. I got the impression the pastor found himself in a shadow, in a forest full of dangers, and I had a sense of foreboding, an instinct that I had to save him before it was too late. My hand wanted to grab his old coat, hold on to it, drag him back into the daylight of the study. Something bad was going to happen. There were forces we should leave alone. All this went through my mind as I read his words:

Now we'll get the bear.

The pastor turned his face to me and it was transformed, so mild and friendly that I was embarrassed. He touched my head, stroked it as if I were his child.

44.

THERE IS ONE BOOK I OFTEN BORROW FROM THE PASTOR, WHICH I have read many times. It is about Carl, a man who lives in sin, a drunkard and a thief, a thoroughly detestable human being. His mother weeps and tries to talk some sense into him; his brother lends him money but he never pays it back, devoting himself instead to buying brandy and playing cards. Carl stands at the abyss, already one step over the edge, until finally the inevitable happens. One evening he is grievously assaulted when he isn't able to pay his gambling debts; his assailants take his clothes and he is left in the gutter naked and bleeding, as the last of his life ebbs from his wounds.

Suddenly a beggar girl appears and offers him the only thing she owns, a gunnysack that she has filled with straw. With gentle hands she wraps the sack around Carl against the cold and then kneels down and prays softly for him, appealing to God to heal his wounds. And the bleeding stops. Soon a policeman comes past to offer assistance, and Carl is taken to a home for the poor, where he is given a bed and provided with care.

When, much later, he has recovered, he starts to inquire about the girl who saved him. But no one knows anything about her, no one has seen her, so he goes out into the city to search for her. He asks everyone he meets, he describes her, but she is nowhere to be found. And at that moment, when he realizes he will never be able to thank the person who saved his life, he is crushed. This is how Carl achieves salvation, and henceforth he dedicates himself to helping the poor.

At the end the book talks about Carl's good deeds, how he opens a home for abandoned children, delivers speeches so that listeners in their thousands are saved, proudly shakes hands with the president. The book ends with an assurance that this is all true and actually happened in the American city of Philadelphia.

I love this book and I know several passages by heart. I can see the events inside my head as clearly as if I had been there when they took place. I open it at a page near the end and see Carl receive forgiveness from his brother on his deathbed, the light filtering through the window, the last thing Carl experiences in life being the scent of spruce twigs and milk. Then I open the book at the beginning, where young Carl attacks the farmhand Bob Holley with a spade when Bob tries to prevent him from stealing from the storehouse.

And even though Carl at no time gives up the search, he never finds out who the poor girl was. The girl who saved his life. He can never, ever forget her.

The strange thing about the book is that you can read it backward, so that Carl starts off good but turns out bad. You can also jump back and forth, and then he is good—bad—good—bad, in a constant state of flux. Between these covers is the long lifetime of one person, and I am conscious of holding time itself in my hands. Time that can start, jump to the end, begin again, go back. In real life time always goes in the same direction, but in a book something else can happen. And it feels quite creepy. On the pastor's shelves I see the books' spines, standing side by side, and all of them are filled with different sorts of time. The time it has taken to write the book, the time evoked in it, and then the time it takes to read it. And with a dizzy feeling I realize that in a given mass on the bookshelf, the books must contain more time than a human life encompasses. The books' experiences are greater than an individual person can ever embody. There are more ideas than you can ever think up in a life-time. Even if your entire life is spent in a reading spree, one book after another without stopping, there is a limit to how many you can fit in. The thought of large buildings filled with more books than anyone will ever have time to read is breathtaking.

"Such buildings exist," the pastor said. "They're called libraries."

"No!" I said.

"I've been in them."

"No."

"In Härnösand. In Uppsala. There are libraries in lots of places."

"That must be dreadful."

The pastor looked at me quizzically, not understanding what I meant.

"So much time," I stammered. "No one could ever read them all."

"No, hardly."

"Only . . . God."

"Yes, God, obviously. Maybe that's the purpose of libraries, that we should witness God's greatness in them."

"But if libraries exist, do we need churches?"

The pastor fell silent and I was afraid that he was angry. But when he turned to me there was something else in his eyes, something wandering, vague. Something like fear.

45.

THE DAY AFTER THE BODY OF NILS GUSTAF WAS FOUND, THE pastor invited Constable Michelsson to the parsonage, telling him to come alone, unaccompanied by Sheriff Brahe. The pastor requested my presence and showed us both into his study. Michelsson courteously doffed his cap as soon as he entered and energetically ran his hand over his balding head, as if to comb the hair that wasn't there.

"Sit down, sit down," the pastor said.

We each took a chair, while he sat down at the desk.

"It's a good thing the weather's improved," the pastor said conversationally, in a bid to lift the atmosphere. "How has the haymaking been?"

"Oh yes! Mother and Father have got the barns full."

"Your parents live some distance away, don't they?"

"Yes, in Pello. My older brothers are still at the farm."

"So Michelsson is the youngest?"

"Youngest of eight."

"And you are still unmarried?"

"I . . . I am betrothed to someone in Pello. My mother has chosen for me—a girl from a good family."

"How appropriate."

"The girl and I were both pupils of Juhani Raattamaa. He was the one who taught us to read and write."

"Well, well, well."

"A very kind and clever man."

"I am so pleased to hear that." The pastor smiled. "And now Michelsson is the parish constable. That must involve a lot of writing?"

"I assist the parish in taking the minutes for various official functions."

"I've heard that Michelsson is highly regarded for his beautiful handwriting."

"Oh?"

"Yes, so everyone hereabouts says."

The pastor swiftly produced a blank sheet of paper.

"Would Michelsson like to show us a sample? Write a few lines for my enjoyment."

The constable flinched and suddenly looked worried.

"But I can't . . ."

"I have quite illegible script," the pastor lamented. "Sometimes Jussi has great difficulty deciphering my scrawl, don't you? Look, just a couple of words!"

Michelsson squirmed but finally stepped forward to the desk, rummaging through his coat pockets. He pulled out a pencil and leaned over the sheet of paper.

"One second," the pastor said. "I'll sharpen it for you."

He quickly took hold of the pencil and shaped it into a point with his pocketknife. The shavings fell onto the desk and he brushed them into a little heap. When Michelsson got his pencil back and wrote down a few words, his hand moving in elegant curves, it was clear what an accomplished writer he was. I knew the pastor wished to put the constable to the test, but we could both see he was using his right hand. The pastor held up the piece of paper and read.

"'Our Father who art in heaven, hallowed be thy name.' Yes, I really do have to concur, I have seldom seen a script so easy to read and at the same time so graceful. But the pencil is of the highest quality, I can see. Where does the constable obtain pencils like this?"

Michelsson put the pencil back in his pocket and seemed rather embarrassed by the praise.

"It's the sheriff who purchases them."

"Aha, Sheriff Brahe!"

"He's got a whole box of them. I think he buys them in Haparanda."

Giving me a quick look, the pastor folded the pencil shavings into a piece of paper. I noticed his excitement, although he was trying to hide it.

"And what's he like to work with, our sheriff?"

"A very experienced man," Michelsson replied warily.

"But he avails himself of the bottle fairly often."

"I know the pastor disapproves of drinking."

"The poison of alcohol clouds both vision and thought. But I am pleased Michelsson himself is abstinent. I can see you as a very able future sheriff."

"Oh . . . thank you, Pastor."

"In due course, naturally. But I have an eye for enterprise, and a person's inner character makes a greater impression on me than titles and uniforms. And I always convey such opinions to the influential people I meet."

In surprise, I cast a furtive glance toward the pastor. Never had I heard him flatter anyone in that way, and I could see how proud and self-conscious the compliment made Michelsson.

"Let us hear your thoughts on Nils Gustaf's tragic passing," the pastor said.

"Um . . . the building was locked, so Sheriff Brahe thought—"

"I didn't mean what the sheriff thought; I have no trouble figuring that out. Let's hear instead what Constable Michelsson himself observed."

"Well . . . the fellow was lying on the bed fully clothed. Death must have been sudden."

"Anything else?"

"There were some canvases on a dryer. There was the beginning of a sketch on the easel. There was a brandy bottle and glass on the table."

"How many glasses?"

"One, I think."

"One?"

"I don't remember exactly."

"There were two glasses," the pastor said. "Weren't there, Jussi?"

I picked up my notes.

"That's correct, two glasses."

"Doesn't Michelsson write things down during police investigations?"

"Yes, afterward," Michelsson stuttered. "At my desk afterward I try to remember the most important points."

"Memory can be deceptive," the pastor said. "I suggest that henceforth the constable write down all observations on the spot. All possible details. Even what seems irrelevant at first glance can later prove to be highly significant. Carry on reading, Jussi."

"On the table there was a receipt book and a memorandum book," I said. "On the painting support there was a cursory portrait sketch."

"I just said that," Michelsson pointed out.

"Now that the constable knows there were two glasses, what are his thoughts?"

"That there . . . there may have been a visitor."

"A visitor who gets the artist to make a sketch and take out his receipt book. Maybe the visitor came to order a painting."

"Who could that be?" the constable asked with a look of puzzlement.

The pastor scratched his chin.

"Let me change track for a moment. Was it not the case that Sheriff Brahe traveled to the mountains at the beginning of summer?"

"To Kvikkjokk," Michelsson confirmed.

"A most beautiful place," the pastor said. "Petrus and I lived there for some years at the home of our elder brother Carl-Erik. May one ask what Brahe was doing in Kvikkjokk?"

"He was investigating reindeer-stealing."

"Thus the work entailed walking across heathland?"

"Of course."

The pastor brought out a dried stalk and held it up.

"Does the constable by any chance know what this is? Please don't touch it."

Michelsson bent forward to have a better look.

"Grass," he said.

The pastor grinned.

"Grass it certainly is not. No, this is Arctic heather, *Cassiope tetragona*. An extremely common mountain plant, often found on treeless heaths."

"I am not as well versed as the pastor in botany."

"No, I'm not asking you to be. But the salient point is, this plant does not occur in our region."

"Oh, doesn't it?"

"So explain to me, therefore, how I could retrieve it from the hay in the barn where Hilda Fredriksdotter Alatalo was attacked."

"She was slain by a killer bear."

"No, Jussi and I don't think so. We found blood in the hay and ripped-out hairs. The poor girl must have been lured in there, attacked, and fought for her life before she was strangled."

"The sheriff shared the reward out among the bear hunters, didn't he?"

"May I ask the constable to look at this?" the pastor said, showing him an envelope. "These are the parings from a pencil sharpened with a knife. We found them near the place where Jolina Eliasdotter was murdered."

"What do you mean, murdered? She hanged herself," Michelsson said, glaring at the pastor and half rising.

The pastor didn't take his eyes off him.

"Compare these with the ones I just cut from Michelsson's pencil."

Michelsson leaned closer and with trembling fingers picked up some of the wood shavings and stared at them.

"From the pencil I got from the sheriff?"

The room was completely still, the air so thick it was hardly possible to move.

"So the pastor is implying . . ." the constable murmured.

"In June, Sheriff Brahe visited the mountains where the Arctic heather grows, as you have told us yourself. He has in his possession pencils of the same sort of which there were traces at the scene of the crime. He also shows, as I'm sure Constable Michelsson has noticed, great interest in young women."

"I could never believe that Brahe—"

"Jolina's kirtle was marked with a wax the sheriff uses on his boots. And she reported she had been assaulted by a *herrasmies*, a gentleman."

"But didn't she refuse to speak after the attack?"

"Only while Brahe was there. Presumably she recognized him, in spite of the fact that he was masked when he assaulted her. Perhaps that was why he felt compelled to strangle her later and try to make it look like suicide."

"No, that's impossible!"

"Did Michelsson notice whether Brahe appeared nervous and on edge around this time? Did he purchase a rope, perhaps, of the same type Jolina was hanged with? Jolina also reported that she had managed to injure the perpetrator in the left shoulder with her hairpin. If Michelsson has the opportunity, he might take a look. Maybe during a sauna—see if Brahe's shoulder has the mark of that type of puncture wound."

Looking queasy, Michelsson stood up and supported himself on the top of the desk, breathing heavily.

"The pastor should serve as a sheriff himself," he said.

"Searching for clues at the scene of a crime is not unlike looking for plants. You have to have an eye for the deviant. And besides, I've had a great deal of help from Jussi."

The constable gave me a sideways look as the pastor rose to his feet and took his hand. Michelsson muttered a hurried farewell and departed.

The pastor meticulously folded an envelope and placed it in a drawer.

"Well, what do you think, Jussi?"

"Why did the pastor do that?" I asked.

"What?"

"The pastor revealed . . . everything!"

"If the fox is hiding in his lair, maybe he needs smoking out."

"And when he comes out?"

"Then we'll get him."

"A sheriff?" I said doubtfully. "How do you arrest a sheriff?"

The pastor lit his pipe and drew on it vigorously, sucking in his cheeks.

His nostrils widened with pleasure. Presently two thick puffs of smoke were emitted and transformed into spirals that twisted together in a sweet-smelling cloud. It was clear he was in a very good mood. He asked for herbal tea and I went out into the kitchen and prepared a steaming infusion of *Epilobium*. When I took it in to him he had put on a strange brimmed hat and pulled up his coat collar as if he were cold. His sharp profile had a look of deep concentration, so I put the cup down and silently withdrew.

46.

M Y BELOVED. WHERE COULD SHE BE? IN THE EVENING, WHEN I lay down on my straw sack, I could see her in my thoughts, wearing her red dress, floating. My disquiet was mounting. Had something happened to her? As the parsonage prepared for the night's rest, I crept over to her farm, where I sheltered at the edge of the forest. The late summer twilight descended very slowly, as if the evening light were running out through a tiny hole on the horizon. I thought of the hourglass standing on the pulpit, filled with white sand, the little stream trickling down into the deep and the glass bulb above becoming empty darkness.

In the high brushwood by the meadow I settled down like a cat, with my pointed ears and my pink button nose. The gnats plagued me; I pulled up my collar when they stung my neck and I crushed the tansy's yellow flower heads and rubbed them into my wrists and neck. The spiced aroma was as good a protection as wild rosemary, but some of the little brutes still crawled into my ears or got stuck in the mucus in my eyes. End-of-day stillness fell over the village, the dogs broke off their endless barking, and the cows stopped lowing now that their udders had been milked dry. I heard a mouse running across the grass below in short, rustling spurts, before it came to a stop, its whiskers trembling, in fear of the constant threat of the fox's teeth and the owl's claws. All the time the perpetual roar of the waterfall could be heard in the background, like the blood pounding inside your ear when you lay your cheek against a reindeer skin. A thousand tiny trembling bristles of fur, that was how water can sound. There is no sound more beautiful.

And suddenly she came out into the yard. The quick steps of a woman, a skirt she lifted so that the evening dew shouldn't wet the hem, the briefest glimpse of her ankles. And I knew I had to speak to her. I ran across the meadow, waving, and she stopped, her eyes wide, black with fear, a scream rising up. And still she was more beautiful than all the angels in heaven. I saw the smoothness of her cheeks, her arched eyebrows, her lips drawn back, the tip of her pink tongue. Then she recognized me and the fear receded. I sensed that something had changed, her color seemed stronger, or maybe it was the way she moved, as though her feet had grown bigger.

"Maria . . ." I whispered.

"Go," she said curtly.

I reached out, I had to touch her. But she backed away and I felt the merest hint of rough cloth.

"Maria, you remember when we danced, don't you? We could walk into the forest, lie down in the moss. No one need see us."

Although she was unwilling, I took hold of her wrist. It was so unutterably soft and smooth, the skin on the inside of her arm so delicate and shiny. She looked away, her lips tightening.

"He died," she whispered, barely audible.

"Yes."

The soles of my feet were so hot, I had to stamp up and down on the spot and I was holding her harder than I really meant to.

"Maria, you are more perfect than all the angels in heaven—"

"You don't understand, Jussi!" She stopped me.

I tried to embrace her but she pulled free, the jolt so unexpected I staggered. She hurried toward the privy, but before she could reach it I saw her bend double like an old Lapp biddy, take a few faltering steps, and hold her plaits back. Then it came pouring out of her, in more than one gush, warm yellow slime pouring onto the grass with a bitter stench. She coughed and spat and cleared her throat in an effort to cleanse her mouth, wiped her hand over her lips. Then she gathered herself and realized I was still there.

"Go!"

I stayed.

"Go home, Jussi. This is how it is now."

I didn't move. She opened the well cover, hoisted up an ice-cold bucket from the world below, and rinsed her face. I saw her hands, pure white in the gathering darkness, like fishes' bellies. Soft, smooth pike.

47.

My heart was pounding so hard it was difficult to breathe, my thoughts rampaging as I followed the uneven village path through the twilight. Get away, just away. Leave everything, set out on the roads of the big wide world, disappear far to the north, beyond the edge of the Arctic Ocean.

You don't understand, Jussi.

The clatter and trampling of a horse's hooves could be heard approaching and a wagon came careering along, accompanied by the drunken shouts of the two men driving it. I took cover in the brushwood to let them pass without seeing me. The wheel axle creaked, the horse snorted and gave off the smell of stable as they rolled past me, and the men argued about money, about card games and debts, so drunk they nearly fell off their seat. I stood still under the half-moon. I didn't want to speak to anyone.

A dog barked. It had been lying in the cart and now it flew up with a howl, a huge lupine creature. It leaped down onto the ground, long-legged as a wolf, and rushed after my scent. I fled as fast as I could, but I stumbled in the undergrowth and, terrified, tried to heave myself into a tree. But it was too late. The dog's jaws ripped my trouser leg, I could feel its teeth tear at my shinbone; I tried to kick it off, but the dog hung on like a snarling shackle.

"*Mikä saatana!*" I heard the men yell.

"*Olen ihminen,*" I shouted as loud as I could. "I'm not Satan, I'm a person!"

They reined in the horse, which was nervously stamping the

ground, and I heard rustling as they forced their way through the thicket.

"Stand still or I'll kill you!" the driver shouted. "Damn it, I'll kill you!"

"Call the dog off!" I screamed.

The animal opened its jaws to get a better hold and I managed to free myself. Something warm was running down my shin. The driver swung his knife to and fro while the dog bounced up and down between the trees.

"Off! Call it off!"

I felt a hand grab my belt, the driver hauled me from the tree trunk, and I fell onto the moss. The dog went for my face, and as I shielded it with my arm I felt its fangs sink into my forearm muscle.

"Drop, Seppo! Drop!"

And then I saw that it was Roope. The dog refused to let go, even though he was dragging it off by its hind leg, and not until it was dangling in the air did it finally loosen its jaws. Roope flung the dog to one side, where it pitched head over heels onto the grass with a yelp. I lay where I was, whimpering.

"Who the hell is it?"

Roope, so drunk he was drooling, grabbed my collar.

"What the devil! It's the little *noaidi*. What are you doing out in the middle of the night?"

"You'll pay for this," I gasped. "My clothes are ruined."

"Pay," he crowed. "Oh yes, I'll pay. Think yourself lucky you didn't get your stomach ripped open."

"Who is it?" the other man shouted.

"It's the bloody *noaidi*. The bastard was hiding here."

"Why was he hiding?"

Roope turned back to me.

"Yes, why were you hiding, you rat? Why were you skulking in there?"

"Don't you see? It's him!" said the other man.

"Who?"

"The one who attacked Jolina. It must be him!"

"The swine!"

"Christ's sake! He was lying low waiting for women. Now we'll get him!"

Roope looked at me, his eyes narrowing.

"Do you know what we do to the likes of you? Do you?"

Then came his fist. The blow hit my mouth, my face exploded, I heard the crunch in the roots of my teeth and could taste blood filling my palate. I raised my curled-toe boot and kicked back as hard as I could, making contact with Roope's groin. He grunted like an ox and then he hit me again, even harder this time so I fell headlong. Roope picked something up, a heavy stone, lifted it, and aimed: he was going to dash my— I just managed to twist my head to the side, the stone smashed above my ear, almost forcing my eyes out of their sockets, and now the dog was back again, on top of me, trying to tear me to shreds. With the second crack a blaze of colors erupted, and now I could no longer move.

"Bloody hell! We'll castrate the swine. We'll beat his prick to a pulp."

They glanced back at the marsh path, where a figure was approaching. He must have been sitting in the cart with them. His face hidden behind a scarf, he pulled out something sharp and with a powerful blow he sank the point into my left shoulder and twisted. The heavens crashed over me.

After that I remember nothing.

48.

The first time I wake, a surging torrent sweeps me forward. A humming, screaming pain. I realize my face is full of flies, a buzzing swarm. They are crawling all over me, and when I lift my head they fly up like a shiny blanket. It is difficult to breathe. Clots, membranes. I spit, but my spit gets stuck. I roll onto my side, retching. There is no strength in my arms, and for a moment I think they are broken. Then I see my blackened muscles, crushed, and the teeth marks of the dog.

They have pulled my trousers down to the knees. And between them—no, I don't want to know. I roll onto my back again and gasp for air, while the flies return to land on the clots of blood. For a long time, I can't move. I know this is wrong. This is very wrong. Something has been torn apart and has trickled away between my thighs. There is an oozing gouge. But it is there, it is still there. I struggle up and try to see. They have done something down there. It is hollow there. They have crushed me, staved me in. Did the dog eat it? I pull my trousers up but the cloth sags and I feel bolts of lightning filling the world with white-flashing darkness.

The second time I wake, I need to pee. I lie motionless for a long time, holding it back, trying to stop what must come. In the end I have to let go. A stream of venom eats through skin and flesh and I scream as my thighs come away from my body and lie like rotten steaks that will soon be carried off by the beasts of prey.

THE THIRD TIME, I am woken by thirst. A burning thirst now that everything has turned to a crust. The sun has passed its zenith and the day is sitting back in its chair. I dream that it is raining, a teeming rain filling my mouth like a constantly flowing stream. Swallow the stream, swallow, but nothing has the power to assuage. Thirst is the worst torment, the last sensation before darkness descends, and I can hear the roar in the distance again. There the waterfall thunders, water crashes over rocks, huge volumes of water foaming in my face, I can feel it. Just once more in this life, I must see water. I push up onto all fours, snorting like a calf. Grab hold of a sapling pine, brace myself with my knees, and stand up, swaying to and fro. I don't see the marsh path, don't know where I am. But I hear the roar. With one hand I support myself against the tree. With the other I hold my trousers up and propel myself slowly forward.

But it doesn't work. My knees give way and I slump facedown in the berry thicket. I lie there for I don't know how long. The sun begins to set and I see a silhouette against the evening sky. And then I hear his voice.

"Jussi? Jussi, is it really you?"

It is the pastor, ye Good Samaritan.

49.

I WOKE BETWEEN WHITE SHEETS. AT FIRST EVERYTHING WAS unfamiliar, but then I saw the bookshelves. I had been put to bed in the pastor's study. My was head full of confused recollections, of a jolting stretcher, a bottle of water held to my lips, careful hands taking off my tattered clothes and washing the blood, vinegar on my wounds burning like fire.

"Jussi?"

The pastor fetched a basin and a rag and proceeded to gently bathe my gaping flaps of skin, to lay on clean strips of linen and tie them up.

"Ooh . . . aah . . ."

A throbbing drum was beating in my body, banging until I almost burst.

"Are you hungry, Jussi? Wait, I'll get you something."

No, I felt no hunger. But the pastor hurried out to the kitchen, found a bowl, mashed something up, and mixed in some butter.

"Eat, Jussi. It's fresh potato. Can you manage to chew?"

Sharp twinges shot through the open root of my tooth. It was like being stabbed with horseshoe tacks, nailed with heavy hammer blows. But when I waited awhile the softness came, of the butter, the holy butter, and the sweetness called potato. I sucked it in and made a space for it at the back of my mouth, where the pain was less severe, where my mouth was warmer and my tongue at its widest. Moaning, I made it into a paste, flattened out the mush, and kneaded it again and again, and with every heartbeat there came light. My mutilated cheeks were flaming red from inside, veins and teeth were showing, and I tried to make time stop. But my body wanted to swallow, my body sucked down the blessed mash and made me want to sing. My chest heaved, my belly tightened round this little pearl of nourishment. Then the second spoonful joined the first. It still hurt, but at the same time I wanted to cry with relief. And with the third mouthful my body knew it would live, once again it would rise from the dead.

They sat around my bed and prayed. I saw Brita Kajsa, Nora, Selma, and I felt a cool hand placed on my forehead. They said I had a fever. I felt sweat seeping through my skin, or maybe it was pus. When I needed to pee they lifted my hip and slid a bowl underneath, and I passed my water and screamed. It hurt so much I wanted to die. I knew what devastation was down there, but I ignored it. Didn't want to think about it. Didn't want to think. . . . I rocked and moaned. I must have reeked of putrefaction. They changed my sodden nightshirt, a thing I had never worn before, and carefully eased on a fresh one. Then they let me be and I turned my head and shut my eyes and what was left of me rose up into the blood-drenched sky, into the light of blood.

THE FOLLOWING DAY I woke unnaturally early, before the day had even got its name. My stomach was churning and I struggled up. My legs couldn't carry me, but I had to go. Bent like an old man, I shuffled across to the privy. It came out of me in a violent spurt. Tjalmo was scared and backed away on stiff paws, terrified by my stench. I filled a bucket from the well and staggered into the cold sauna. I sat there shivering as I washed my bruises and wounds, the ribs in my chest hurting almost unbearably every time I breathed. I crouched with my legs apart and shuddered, my whole body shaking. I dried myself with my bare hands, shook off the drips, brushed them from my hair and loins. I didn't dare to feel between my legs. I raised my arms to form a V, an invocation, and for a long time I stood like that, trembling. Come thou and take me, I thought. Come, I am ready. Like a child. A sacrificial lamb.

When the village awoke I was sitting outside on the steps. Cows were lowing, wanting to be milked. A dog gave tongue and others answered. A fox ran across the meadow, slipping like a red pearl through the grass. Chimneys smoked, doors creaked, tin pails clattered in milkmaids' hands. Soon I heard voices from inside the parsonage and Brita Kajsa emerged onto the step, brushing her hair and throwing away a gray clump when she had finished.

"Another day . . ." she said.

"Mm . . ."

She laid her hand on me to see if I had a fever.

"Does Jussi feel better?"

"It's my stomach. . . ."

"We have some of yesterday's soup left. Cold broth. Will you manage that?"

I followed her in and was given a cup. Solid rings of fat floated on the surface and I drank with my upper lip, sipping it drop by drop. The pain in the root of my tooth still made me reel. Brita Kajsa gave me a piece of bread that I dipped in the liquid and sucked on inside my cheek, which was better. Dipped and sucked, trying not to make such a disagreeable noise. The daughters averted their eyes from me, from my face that didn't look human. Yet they wanted to show compassion, asked if I wanted more, if they could fill my water cup. I drank from the corner of my mouth, clamping it tightly, and the water spilled over my nightshirt. The pastor was next to me and noticed, rescuing the ladle before it thudded onto the floor.

"Who hit you, Jussi?"

I could feel the nausea mounting as he took hold of my arm.

"I could kill the monster!" he said. "Rip him to shreds. Was it one of the farmhands? You recognized him, didn't you?"

"I . . . I don't remember."

"Yes, you do, Jussi. Just say who it was!"

I pointed silently to my mouth, to the bloody shard of front tooth.

"May I look?" he asked.

We went out into the morning light in the yard, where he steered me into a beam of sunlight and asked me to open my mouth. With a blade of grass, he picked away the clots of blood until the tooth was free. He brushed the bare nerve and I cried out.

"We must go to the doctor," he said.

Shaking my head, I stumbled over to the woodshed. Hanging on the wall over the workbench in the corner were some iron pliers with narrow jaws, which I handed to the pastor, pressing them into his hands. But he refused.

"I can't do it," the pastor said.

He had to. I wouldn't give in. When he walked toward the parsonage, I followed him. Finally, he sighed and grasped the pliers. I sat on the ground and opened my mouth, then I changed my mind and lay down. The pastor sighed again and knelt astride me.

"Is Jussi absolutely sure?"

I nodded and squeezed my eyes shut, opened my mouth wide, and raised my chin to the sky. Felt the steel take a crunching grip. The contact made me shake and arch my back. He tried to pull, but he couldn't. The stump of the tooth wouldn't budge, his hand slipped, and he banged my lip.

"I'm sorry, Jussi. It won't work."

I screwed my eyes shut, opened my mouth wider. The blood was running down my throat. I coughed, it spattered everywhere. The pastor changed his method. Instead of pulling, he started to wiggle it, prizing the tooth back and forth. Each time it was like a church bell clapper, a heavy pendulum finishing me off. Metal, blood, and rusty iron. I felt something drip onto my face. It was the pastor's tears. He was weeping and levering, and with a wet crack the long roots finally came free. I lost consciousness and for a moment everything turned black. Then I turned on my side and coughed and coughed and watched the grass become speckled with red. The pastor put something sharp in my hand. Then he hurried away, wiping his face with his shirtsleeve. I heard splashing by the well as he washed the pliers. Then a thud from the woodshed as he replaced them. I held up my tooth. It was white in the sunshine and I ran my fingers over the edges of the enamel. My mouth felt as empty as a shoe, empty and shrunken. As if everything had dwindled away. All that was left was a deafening release, as if inside a church bell. I was drawn up into it, and I faded away.

And an immense building towered up. The door opened and a large throng of people came streaming out. They made their way to a nearby cottage, where a figure with horns on its knees was dancing. He made them all join the dance. It suddenly stopped and they made a long chain. He pulled them toward an abyss of fire and smoke. And there the people plunged down into the deep, fathers and mothers with children in their arms. I was dragged by the figure to the very edge. And a handsome youth came by and asked my name.

"Jussi," I answered.

"I am Jehovah," he said.

The youth picked up a book.

"I will write your name in here. And then you will eat this."

He held out a little box of food.

"Now tell people how dangerous it is in a stormy sea," he said. "For otherwise they will land down there where the agony never ends."

50.

I CAME TO MY SENSES ON THE HAY IN THE BARN. MY MOUTH WAS A snout of hardened blood. I made a hole in the crust and tried to spit and I cautiously touched the gap where the tooth had been. It stung but wasn't quite so unbearable now.

Taking small steps, I walked down to the riverbank. As long as I didn't drive my heels in too hard, I could manage. I crouched down by a stone, dipped my hands in the flowing water, and kept rinsing my mouth until the water stopped turning red. The streaks of blood curled away, growing thinner and thinner, until soon there was only water to see. I sat there for a long time, listening to the waterfall intone, its sound filling my ears. It was like the murmur of countless voices and I thought they were prayers. All humanity's laments and powerlessness. Perhaps this was what it sounded like to God, a cacophony that never ended. Sometimes our Lord stuck his finger into the flowing currents and plucked a drop from farthest away, and examined it closely before placing it on the tip of his tongue. And that was the moment a miracle happened somewhere on our earth, and a person received solace.

With my legs wide apart, I staggered back to the parsonage. A little crofter girl was walking toward me along the path and shut her eyes in horror when she saw my battered face. Openmouthed, she turned tail and scampered back, her bare feet drumming on the ground. In the yard I went up to Tjalmo, who cowered and backed away with a warning bark.

"It's only me . . . it's Jussi . . ."

For the moment the cabin was empty. On the kitchen table was the writing box with sand that one of the daughters had been busy with. I sat down next to the flattened sand and was filled with a strange disquiet. With an unsteady hand I took hold of the pointed wooden stick and bent forward. Then I wrote the first thing that came to me. *Piru.* The devil's name in Finnish. I brushed it out and wrote *saatana.* I swept that away, too, and then wrote *vittu.* And then *kulli.* Cunt and cock. *Perkele. Helvetti.* Demon. Hell. All the words you must never use, I wrote them and then wiped them out, writing and flattening, writing and flattening. And then I looked at the sand. It was smooth and golden and like sunshine. No dirt to be seen. No wickedness, no ugliness, just light-colored writing sand.

Imagine if life could be like that too. You crawled in your mire, your mouth cursed and vilified, your heart filled up with lies, your backside shat and farted, your prick ejected its whore-spunk into wet crotches. Then God passed his leveling board across the earth, ironing out all the scratches and indentations until there was only smooth sand. What did that say about the world? That at heart, deep down under all the wars and atrocities, it was still, in spite of everything, fundamentally good?

I gazed at the smooth sand for a long time and I could sense the apprehension inside me, as if a feeling of nausea were mounting. What was the point, if in time everything was erased? If my life was forgotten the moment my body was lowered into the earth? And the same for all the people I had around me, all the hardworking villagers, the wonderful woman I loved, and even my revered pastor. If we were all to be swept away and disappear, what was the point of sitting here on a rough-hewn stool with an aching mouth and the taste of blood? Why not go straight down to Kengis waterfall and be washed away?

I picked up the writing stick and took a deep breath. The point dug into the uppermost grains, formed a little dip, a furrow.

I. And then *am.* I had to think long about the third word, but finally I wrote *human.*

> *I am human.*

And several more words instantly followed.

> *I am from the mountains.*
> *I have a sister.*
> *Her name is Anne Maaret.*

The writing box was full of sentences. There wasn't room for any more. For a moment I stared at the letters, shut my eyes, and realized they remained inside me. I brushed them away and started again.

> *Our mother did not want us.*

It was dreadful to write it, but I knew it was true. She never wanted to have us. Not the runt hare. Not the devil-boy.

I wrote and then I smoothed it over. But the words were still inside me, remained in me even though they had been rubbed out. Letters were so strange. So I carried on. Page by page. The introduction to the story of my life, the life I lived in my body. Life as it was and how it felt. And I thought that what I was doing, these words, would one day be a book.

THE CURIOUS THING ABOUT writing is the way it gets inside your soul. You see a turbid stew, dip a wooden spoon in, and start to stir, go in circles, dig around. Rising up out of the murk something lighter appears, perhaps a turnip. Or a chewy piece of meat with the bone still in, sharp and scraggy. Or maybe a leaf, like the ones Brita Kajsa grows and calls lovage, with the taste of tanned hide and resin. Where does all the food come from? Who has put it there? Is it me?

Writing brings anxiety, makes you feel almost sick. And yet you keep on searching through the dregs. There, a child's face with black lips where small teeth have chewed deep notches. And there a little Arctic dog, dark all over apart from the white patches on its forehead as if it had an extra pair of eyes. It is thin and almost lifeless, as happens with the smallest in the litter. But if you do as the witch usually does and spit things into its mouth, it will swallow everything, scraps of food, sooty sinews, pan fat from the hearth. And as it swallows, it perks up. Its little tail wags to and fro with pleasure when you come back to the spruce-twig basket where it sleeps. You make a bed on moss, to make it warm and soft. You let it lie snuggling in your armpit at night when the witch isn't looking.

But one day when you return, its hind leg is crooked. It drags strangely, and when you try to put it straight, the puppy squeals like a mouse. Something has happened. Anne Maaret says it was the witch. It was something she threw, maybe a log. You hope it will heal and you bandage the little leg, but then you see there is something wrong with its ribs as well. It takes several days for the puppy to die, nearly a week. On the last night the fever gets worse and its breathing is so fast, but by dawn it becomes only slower and slower. Why didn't I take the puppy with me? Why did I leave her there alone? I had called her Lihkku. It means Lucky.

Now I write the puppy's name in the sand. It is the first time her name is in letters; no one has ever told Lihkku's story before and of how she died. But now she exists. In just the same way as I do in the pastor's parish register. When you are written down, you can never be forgotten.

And then I brush the sand smooth and clean until it looks like a fresh sheet of paper. The writing has gone. Perhaps the pastor's register will be gone one day too, just as all texts will be eaten away in the end, crumble to nothing and vanish. But what is written down will still exist. I know it, I feel it. Everything that has ever been written will last forever. So extraordinary is the power of the letters of the alphabet.

THE DOOR SLAMMED AND the pastor's daughter Selma returned. She asked what I was doing but I pretended not to hear. Then she leaned over and took the wooden stick, which must still have been warm from my hand. With her plaits dangling in front of her, she scratched a playful message to her father. A comment about how slowly he was walking, that she had been at home for ages.

"No peeping," she said, and nudged me away.

But it wasn't her words I was trying to read, it was my own, the ones I had just written in the same sand. And I could see they were still there, all of them.

51.

BRITA KAJSA LOWERED HER HEAD TO THE TABLE WHILE I OPENED my mouth. She placed the cooking pot next to her and stirred it with a wooden spoon.

"Open wider," she said.

I opened so wide it felt as though my head would split in two. She put a wooden needle into my mouth with a wad on the tip and pressed it into the hole left by the tooth. It stung and I felt sick with the strong scent of resin mixed with lovage and camphor, plantain leaf, rust, bistort, and whatever other indescribable things she had found on her shelves.

"Keep still," she said, as I convulsively bit on the pin.

She dipped the wad into the pot and repeated the procedure. The wound had to be cleaned three times. I was aware of blind patches crossing my vision. The daughters thought it so disgusting that they left. They knew I screamed sometimes, I couldn't help it, and my scream was the worst of the worst, like the sound of vomiting into a church bell.

Then she pulled my trousers down. I looked away. She tried to be careful, soaking off the dried-on bandages with lukewarm water. I bit my arm to take away the pain.

"Imagine you're a fish," she said soothingly. "A fish at the bottom of the river and you're quite still as the water flows around you . . . hold still, now . . . there. . . ."

My gums turned black, maybe because of the tar. Between my legs it felt as though someone had carved a cunt. A deep, bloody mouth-hole. I collapsed in the corner and lay motionless, as if my spine were balancing on a razor-sharp edge. I was hovering just above the floor like someone crucified. The edge had to remain exactly on my middle vertebra, the hardest place of all in a human body. Only at that precise point was I able to withstand it.

52.

THE NEXT MORNING THE SUN WAS STREAMING DOWN ON KENGIS Village. I had chosen to sleep in one of the outhouses so as not to disturb any of the household with my groans. The pain made it impossible to lie still and all through the night I writhed like a worm on my straw-filled mattress. In the middle of the morning I forced myself to get up, giddy after not a wink of sleep. With short, shuffling steps I made my way to the parsonage cabin and hobbled inside. I could tell there was a visitor by the strong smell of man's sweat and tar that met me, and a rough, familiar voice.

Sheriff Brahe was at the kitchen table, sitting astraddle, shoveling in the soup Brita Kajsa had warmed up. Michelsson kept him company at the end of the table. The men looked at me, without a greeting, and then resumed eating. The pastor seemed uncomfortable, pacing back and forth with his hands behind his back, now and then casting a glance out of the window.

"What sum . . . had you paid?" the sheriff managed to utter, between bites.

"Unfortunately, it concerns a considerable sum," the pastor conceded with visible hesitancy.

"Was it your own personal money?"

"Yes. I paid a commission fee and at a later date a larger sum while the painting was in progress. The final payment I made sometime before the artist's death."

The policemen exchanged doubtful glances and Brahe cleared his throat.

"Just to be clear, was church money involved?"

"It concerns my own savings," the pastor said, with an unsteady voice.

Brita Kajsa's jaws were clenched, and her hands looked as though they were about to strike something. When she realized that I had come padding in, she hurriedly turned and pretended to rearrange the kitchen shelf. She picked things up and put them back, until she found something that needed wiping.

"It wasn't only the pastor who put up money. The artist must have received appreciable sums for all the commissioned paintings he was working on."

"Yes, presumably."

"But where's the money? We searched his home but we didn't find it."

"He must have hidden it, mustn't he?"

"Yes, but where?"

The pastor gave me a quick sideways look and hesitated.

"In the trunk," he then said. "The one where he also kept his chemicals for the daguerreotype apparatus. As Sheriff Brahe will doubtless have discovered, there was also a secret compartment."

"A secret compartment?"

"It was probably where he kept his money. But when we entered the cottage, the compartment had been opened and emptied."

"Why did the pastor not report this before?"

"You kicked us out before I had time to show you."

Brahe held his breath for a moment, his color rising.

"So, the pastor is the first to arrive at the cottage, takes himself inside, and spends a good while in there. What were you actually doing?"

"I was praying for the soul of the deceased."

"And then you dug around. Eh? Suppose you examined the

trunk and happened to find the secret compartment with the artist's savings?"

"Is the sheriff suggesting . . . ?"

Brahe didn't reply at once. He poked out a sinew from between his teeth with his fingernail and smacked his lips. His eyes were black, like fish eyes.

"I'm not suggesting anything at this stage, I'm just thinking aloud. The pastor was with . . . him over there?"

The sheriff rose to his feet and walked slowly toward me. Michelsson immediately stood up too, and followed two steps behind. I was seized by involuntary fear, a feeling like an icy pike swimming in my stomach.

"In the devil's name! Have you had a beating?" he asked, grabbing me with his large hand. "Did you meet the killer bear?"

I could feel Michelsson wrap his arm tightly round my neck from behind. With a violent tug he ripped open my shirt to reveal my shoulders. Then he leaned forward and pressed his finger onto an infected red wound on my left shoulder.

"But take a look, Pastor. The boy's got a wound just here. Didn't you say that Jolina Eliasdotter Ylivainio had stabbed her attacker in the left shoulder?"

"Yes, with a hairpin. This wound looks wider."

"Hairpins come in many different widths."

"Of course. But this wound is fresh. It must have been inflicted very recently."

"So, you're defending him? You're defending the little devil?"

The sheriff pushed me just as Michelsson let go his grip. In my weakened state I couldn't keep my balance or prevent myself from stumbling and falling to the floor. My crotch exploded, and I rolled onto my side, coughing saliva across the floorboards. The men watched my pitiful crawling and the sheriff made as if to kick me.

"Where have you hidden the money?"

The pastor tried to stand between us, but the men unceremoniously shoved him aside.

"Well, we'll have to search the house," Brahe decided. "Where does the youth keep his things?"

"Leave the boy alone!" Brita Kajsa screamed.

The pastor made an effort to keep the peace and gave the sheriff a hard look.

"We will of course assist you. Jussi's knapsack is here. But I want to have a written search warrant."

When Brahe dug a pencil out of his inside pocket, the pastor handed him his pocketknife and Brahe proceeded to sharpen the point with it. Meanwhile, Michelsson had taken a piece of paper out of his constable's portfolio and the sheriff rapidly scrawled a few lines. While the pastor was taking the paper from Michelsson, the sheriff emptied my knapsack onto the floor, scattering my few belongings. It was easy to establish there was no money. Moving on, he began a rough-handed search of me, going through all my pockets and feeling to see if any notes could have been sewn into the lining. When he found nothing there either, he looked around the cabin with suspicion.

"You are not to touch my study," the pastor said firmly.

Almost in passing, he picked up his walking stick and held it in front of him. The policemen could easily have overpowered this undersized man, but something in his expression made them desist. Instead they went across the yard over to the outbuildings. I could hear them rummaging about in the barn, rattling containers and buckets and traipsing up a ladder to get to the hayloft. Brita Kajsa and the pastor supported me over to the settle to sit down. My legs wouldn't hold me up, and I blacked out for a moment.

"I haven't . . . stolen . . ." I managed to say.

"I know, Jussi."

"When they attacked me, they stabbed me . . . they stabbed me with a nail . . ."

"We'll let them get on with it," the pastor muttered. "They won't find anything."

Brita Kajsa gave her husband a skeptical look. She made a start on clearing the table, but the pastor stopped her. Astonished, we watched him study the china they had been eating from, and the leftover food. He carefully put his fingers into the two glasses Brahe and Michelsson had been drinking from and lifted them up in this awkward manner, without needing to touch the outsides. He carried them over to the stove, where he put them down. Then he swept up some of the finest ash into his palm, raised his hand up to his lips, and blew very gently. The ashy powder floated toward the glasses and on into the hearth. The pastor lifted the glasses in the same clumsy way as before and showed them to me.

"Can you see, Jussi?"

He held the curved glass surfaces up to me. The ashy powder had stuck to the greasy fingerprints so they could be seen very clearly.

"You can see their fingers."

"Look carefully, Jussi."

"There are lines in the fingertips. Round patterns."

"Exactly. And when you study them, all the patterns are different. You can tell them apart. The sheriff's thumbprint is completely different in appearance from the constable's. Can you see?"

"Yes . . . yes, I can see."

The pastor reflected for a moment, before tearing off two slips of paper, on one of which he wrote *Brahe* and on the other *Michelsson*. He put each in its respective glass. Then he fetched two more glasses from his study, which were protected by handkerchiefs, and placed them next to the first. I recognized them.

"They're the glasses from Nils Gustaf's cottage, aren't they?"

"Quite correct."

"But one of them has gone blue!"

The pastor nodded. An astonishing bright blue color gleamed from the dregs of brandy in one of the glasses.

"Prussian blue, it's called," he said. "I've carried out a little test, but it's too soon to say more."

Brita Kajsa opened the kitchen cupboard and began searching among her herbs.

"Try to rest now, Jussi. I'm brewing alder-bark tea. It's bitter, but it will help."

While she busied herself with the tea, I heard strange puffing noises from the floor. With some difficulty I turned onto my side to see better. The pastor was back and had fallen to his knees in the middle of the kitchen. At first I thought he was praying, but then I saw he was picking something up with small, pincer movements, as though he were gathering rare flowers down on the floorboards. Then I realized: what he was gathering in the palm of his hand were the shavings from the sheriff's newly sharpened pencil.

53.

THE BODY HEALS SLOWLY. WOUNDS CLOSE. SCABS GRADUALLY fall off and leave white scars. When I run my fingers over them, the skin is harder and almost without feeling. My ribs take a long time to mend. Night after night I am woken by sharp stabbing pains whenever I turn over carelessly in my sleep. But eventually I can draw cautious breaths without it hurting. The worst is my mouth, where the craters close up, but their edges remain black. The taste of blood goes, leaving the taste of something bitter.

The pastor turns his face aside whenever I breathe on him, so I know I stink and I try to keep my mouth shut. In the shop I place my hand in front of my mouth when I ask for something. I think I look like an old man without my front tooth. Women turn away when I forget myself and open my mouth, and I know I will never get close to them. I am forced to chew the hard pieces of bread on one side, with my back teeth, gnawing them like a cat. The *s*-sound is almost impossible to pronounce; it comes out like "*fff*," until I discover that I need to move my tongue nearer to my eyeteeth. It sounds sharper that way, but still not good. I will never be like Raattamaa and stand by the pastor's side in church and read his sermon, the congregation would mock me. I practice doggedly, to make my speech more distinct, so that I can at least make myself understood. I try talking with my lips nearly closed, that way I don't have to hold my hand in front of my mouth.

I often have the thought that I want to remain in the world even after my death and I don't know where this desire comes from. Maybe it has to do with the letters of the alphabet. My forefathers couldn't write. They lived out their lives working, and then they disappeared. I know my grandmother was called Anne Maaret, the same name given to my sister. And that my grandmother's mother was called Stina Inghilda. But that is all. I have a vague memory of my grandmother, of meeting her in Kvikkjokk. We slept outside, it was summer, I remember a smoking fire to get rid of the mosquitoes. She was so wrinkled she looked like a chopping board that has been much used for cutting meat. Her hands were cold and dry, like pieces of wood. I must have been four. She ate something, chewed it for a long time with her empty gums, and then leaned forward. I opened my mouth and she spat a gristly slime into it. It tasted slightly sweet from her spittle, and of something brown as well, like bark. I knew it wasn't edible, it was dead. Long strands stuck in my throat and however much I swallowed they just got longer. In the end I wanted to die. They bent double with laughter, all of them sitting there on the reindeer skin, laughed while they drank and drank until they lay like bits of offal in their dirty leather clothes.

I think she died after that. My mother never told me, but we never went to see her again. So I think the old woman died. My grandmother Anne Maaret. And now nothing at all remains of her in this world. Well, yes, maybe something she sewed, maybe there are still some of her traditional fur boots tramping around out there. Or a fine shoe band woven by her. But no one knows now that the band was once hers. That she was the one who wove it with her cold, wooden fingers. And it didn't worry her, she felt no need to stay. Nor did her forefathers, not one of all those shadows wandering away in the darkness. They lived and disappeared, lived and disappeared, like waves on a breezy mountain lake breaking onto the beach and washing over the pebbles. For a moment, you see the film of water, smooth and formless, reflecting the sky, before it all disappears beneath the next foamy wave.

I feel uneasy when I think about this: that I too will be washed away like water, leaving not the slightest trace. Am I the first of my people to feel like this? Is this thought new for us? To want to remain? Not in heaven, but to leave something of yourself for posterity? To be immortalized, like the pastor, in an oil painting at the Salon de Paris. To start a revivalist movement that changes the way people think. To give your name to a newly discovered plant. To write a book.

My master has achieved all of this, whereas I have accomplished nothing. I have lived like my forefathers, that is all. I have walked in their footsteps. Like a reindeer I have trotted after the reindeer in front of me in the snow. But now I think that this won't be enough for me. Something has happened with the world and it isn't the way it was before. From this day on man must live, not through others, but through himself.

My THOUGHTS FLOWED ALONG these lines and they tormented me, so clearly did I see my worthlessness. I couldn't even get close to the woman I loved. How then could I touch the mind of an unknown person with my words?

I tried to speak to the pastor about it.

"Does this longing of mine to be remembered come from the devil?" I asked.

He looked at me gravely.

"You are forgiven for your sins, Jussi. In the name and blood of Jesus Christ."

"That's not enough," I said.

For a second I thought he was going to give me a clip round the ear.

"Or is it necessary to be like everyone else?"

"What do you believe yourself, Jussi?"

I didn't reply.

"Who actually beat you, Jussi?" the pastor asked. "Who beat you so badly that you were more dead than alive?"

"Roope," I said. "Roope and another man."

"So there were two of them?"

"And a third came, wearing a mask. He didn't want me to recognize him. He was the one who stabbed me in the shoulder."

"Sheriff Brahe and Constable Michelsson seemed to know you had an injury there."

"Yes," I said. "That occurred to me as well."

"We have to report Roope!"

"That can wait."

"You mustn't be afraid of him."

"I'll be going soon anyway."

"Pardon?"

"Nothing, it was nothing, Pastor. It was nothing."

54.

Now that the harvest was finished, it was time to overhaul the tools. Since I was capable of only light tasks, I was assigned to repairing the hay rakes. The pain meant I couldn't sit in the normal fashion, but had to kneel and cautiously support my behind on my heels. With a knife I whittled tines to fit the holes exactly and then I knocked off the old, broken ones. It was a job for an old man, someone for whom everyday manual labor was too much, and I could see how the farm maid and the pastor's daughters felt sorry for me. Even though I was young, I had become an old man, with a bent back, bad on my feet, and no balance. I was like the pastor. While he could look back on an outstanding life of battles and victories and fame, my life was over before it had begun. I had achieved nothing of value. I thought about my sister, who had stayed in the north to look after the old folk. Time after time I begged Anne Maaret to come with me, to flee from the stinking garbage inside the tent, escape their spluttering wrath when the effects of drink wore off. But even though she was so young, barely more than a child, she had already become like a mother. She knew that without her the old people would perish. I refused to sleep inside with her when I visited, I made my bed outside by the fire. It reeked of fox piss out there, but that was better than inside the tent with the fleas and the rags.

I was so deep in thought I didn't notice the visitors until the dog barked. Two figures were approaching, dressed in black as if on their way to a funeral. They were walking up to the parsonage, two women, and something about them made my heart pound. I hurriedly took cover between the pastor's crops, behind the lush, green wall he called potatoes. The rake was still on the grass; they might stop and cast a curious eye around. No, it was quite clear there was something else on their minds. The woman in front was stockily built and advanced in years. She was wearing layer upon layer of cloth, one jersey over another, one skirt over another skirt, headscarf and coat, and a black shawl around her shoulders so thickly woven it looked more like a blanket. The only thing protruding was a hand, clutching a gleaming white handkerchief. It wasn't clear what purpose the handkerchief served, sometimes it dabbed the corner of her eyes, as if there were tears to wipe away, sometimes it fluttered around like a signal of some kind. It was writing in the air, forming letters, a *U* and an *N* and a *Z*, white script in the woolly gray damp of autumn.

Behind the old woman came a younger figure. Her clothing was black too and the headscarf was pulled right down to hide her face. Yet there was something that made me gulp and catch my breath, I wanted to rush forward and touch her. I recognized her and was instantly roused. Even though her face was covered, I knew it could only be her. I recognized her way of moving, the way her hips swayed—as when she carried the milk pails—the rounding of her shoulders, the angle of her neck, that lightness in her step I had seen when she was dancing in the artist's studio, and during the dance in the shieling, when we had come so close.

But at the same time I could detect that something was different. Something had happened to her, there was a stiffness, or maybe a weight. I had never met the woman who walked in front. Was it Maria's mother? I didn't even know which village Maria came from. But it was clear that the older woman was in charge, that she had an errand. It had all the air of a ritual, the white script of the handkerchief against the gray sky, the disaffection of the two women, the coolness between them. When they reached the yard, I saw Maria peer around. I lay flat on my stomach and slithered closer to the potato shaws. When the women entered the parsonage, I followed and opened the front door very slightly. I could clearly detect their scent—the aroma of the hay barn on the old woman, but on Maria the flowery foam of meadowsweet. They stood at the entrance to the kitchen and I heard the pastor chatting about harvesting to make them feel welcome. I moved silently into the pastor's study, where I immediately looked for somewhere to hide—the bookshelves, the desk, the chest, the drop-leaf table. I heard the pastor's voice approach, the door opened, and the three of them stopped in surprise. They found me at the folding table with my nose deep in a book.

"Sorry," I mumbled, pretending to be startled.

"Is Jussi in here studying?" the pastor exclaimed.

He sounded unduly cheerful, obviously trying to lighten the serious mood of his guests.

"I felt a burning need to read something," I said apologetically, and rose stiffly to my feet.

"*Loca Parallela Plantarum*," the pastor said with a wry smile. "Doesn't Jussi find the Latin somewhat impenetrable?"

I closed the book at once, casting a quick look at the flyleaf. It was the pastor himself who was the author.

"Yes," I muttered.

"We'll get to grips with Latin, Jussi. Latin will be our next foray."

The women stared at me, the old woman's face full of mistrust, the handkerchief pressed to her mouth as if to hold back the scorn welling up. But Maria looked at me with such a beseeching expression, almost with desperation, that I was forced to look away.

"So what has occasioned the ladies' visit?" the pastor went on, drawing up a chair for each of them.

"We don't want that *noaidi* child . . ." the old woman said.

She jerked her head in my direction and moved the handkerchief to the other corner of her mouth. Her lips were narrow and white, they reminded me of scythe blades when she spoke.

The air in the room grew even more charged and difficult to breathe. I left without answering and quietly closed the door behind me. In the kitchen Brita Kajsa was busy with a soup pot, peeling vegetables with a short knife. The smell was so good from the melting lard and herbs, from the table beer fermenting in its trough, from the wort and newly churned butter bubbling with freshly chopped onion.

"Cut flowers wither fast," she said, with a meaningful nod toward the visitors.

"What?" I said, though I had heard.

"What?" said Johanna, one of the pastor's daughters, holding her hand in front of her mouth to mimic me. "What, what, what?"

I hurried out. The last of the insects were whizzing around in the evening light. No one paid any attention to me sneaking around the corner of the house, to crouch and sit down underneath the study window. I took my knife out and pretended to be cutting my nails, straightening the ragged edges and trimming the frayed cuticles. With my ear pressed to the wall. The visitors' voices went through the timbers and straight into my back. I could hear none of the words, but I could feel the vibrations. The old woman must have relinquished the handkerchief and now the words were pouring out. The pastor was silent, letting her carry on. Soon he would suggest they pray together, but as yet it was too soon. Maria's voice was so weak, it could barely be felt in the pauses before the old woman took up her monologue again with mounting intensity. It was like seeing a staircase leading down into the abyss, every step taking the visitors ever more steeply down into the flames. And the pastor let it happen. He let the sinners smell the sulfur in their nostrils and see the damned, screaming in the depths. Their torment was unspeakable, bloodthirsty worms crawled over their skin, gnawing holes and burrowing inside. It was the heart Satan wanted to reach. The heart's core. And the pastor thought that was right, and he offered no consolation. Not yet. Instead he let the women's terror grow. Their hard shell had to split open. Their pride, their self-righteousness. Their complacency.

And now the old woman really did crack, she fell apart. I heard the wails through the wall, deep like a man's, and rising, and now I could hear the words as well.

"Whore, whore . . ."

Again and again until the screeches turned to gurgles, and then the pastor's voice of thunder.

"Get thee behind me, Satan! Be gone!"

The parsonage seemed to shake as if something from the netherworld were forcing its way out, a gigantic snake's head lashing and biting. And now another voice rose, sharp as a dagger, shrill silvery cries from a bird of prey plunging to the floor, beating its wings as bodies dived on top of it and held it fast, pressing the room together like the covers of a book. Smoke could be seen seeping out of the window frame, there was the smell of fire, an awful odor of scorched feathers, or maybe it was teeth on fire.

The wailing changed to deep sobs. I pictured the pastor praying. He fell to his knees beside the women, all three thrown to the floor. The pastor invoked God, appealed to God to have mercy on them all. God, who had power to destroy and punish, who with the simplest flick of his fingernail could tip them all down into the flames. The sinners were balancing on the very edge. Now there was only salvation for the one who could bare her heart, proffer it, naked and pulsing, in her hands.

Thy sins are forgiven thee. In the name and blood of Jesus Christ. Such was the ritual. I dismissed the idea of peeping through the window, terrified of what I might see. The timber wall behind was silent now and I crept away, back to the porch, and waited. It felt cold. The sun was approaching the edge of the forest, I could just see it through the branches, a red spot in my line of vision that turned bright green when I shut my eyes. They were talking for such a long time! Maybe they had gone out into the kitchen for something to eat? No, through the window I could see Brita Kajsa sitting by the chimney breast and she too appeared to be waiting. Her fingers were busy with herbs, ripping dried leaves from the stalks in her apron. She could never really be at rest, never just sit and look out of the window. Every moment had to be used.

But now she rose to her feet. She had heard the study door open and she would be asking if the guests would like supper. Her face gave no hint of what she thought of the din she had just heard. The pastor came into view and it was obvious the visitors wanted to leave for home. I grabbed the broom, to have something in my hands. The door opened, I stopped sweeping and bowed to the old woman as she hurried past, her face blotchy and swollen. The handkerchief had disappeared, in its place she held a small piece of paper. They were always on the pastor's desk and he used them to scribble down appropriate words from the Bible for confessants. A sour smell of sweat enveloped the old woman, forcing its way through all her layers of clothing. Underneath she must have been dripping wet.

Maria walked behind the old woman, her mouth hidden behind her hands. I saw her back shaking with despair in silent, uncontrolled weeping. She teetered forward, almost losing her balance on the porch, and I instinctively held my arm out to support her. She flinched with alarm at the sight of my scarred face and then, quick as a wink, leaned toward me, her face right next to mine, her eyes completely dry. Instead of tears, there were bruises, as though she had been hit, and I was seized with fury. She pressed her cheek to mine and whispered:

"I'll go wherever you want, Jussi."

The old woman turned round, but Maria had already caught up, her hands covering her face once more. They left the yard and I watched the two women turn off the village road and disappear. The scent of my beloved's hair was still in my nose. *Filipendula ulmaria*, meadowsweet. But a hint of onion too, and of sulfur. I had to lean against the porch for support.

I'll go wherever you want.

Her cheek against mine. Forever.

55.

SELMA CAME OUT AND SAID DINNER WAS READY, TO WHICH I shastily answered that my stomach was out of sorts and I felt unwell. I went into the cowshed and stood in the half-light, swallowing hard. The cows, newly milked and calm, stared at me without a pause in their constant chewing. I rubbed their hard noses, rested my fingers on the rounded horn buds, felt the smoothness of the cowhide as I stroked the fur. The huge eyes encircled by muscle gazed at me, the muzzles wet, with one or two stiff bristles. A cow lifted her tail, emptied her bowels, and the pat of dung plopped to the floor with a pleasant, pungent smell. I took the rake and scraped the muck, still so warm that it was steaming, into the manure gutter; all the blades of grass that were transformed into shit and milk. Some of it was swept into the gutter and the rest served up in a fine pitcher at the dinner table. Exactly like the human race.

I heard footsteps coming from the parsonage, most likely Johanna carrying out the slop pail, so they must have finished eating. I waited a little while longer. The pastor usually did a last stint at his desk before going to bed, putting the final touches to his correspondence or taking a look at the bills. Replete and slightly sleepy, he would be relaxed and might be in the mood to exchange a few words. He would doubtless still have the visitors on his mind. The old woman's shrieks, the girl's obstinate defiance. Maybe he would like to share his thoughts with someone?

That was what I was thinking when I entered the parsonage. Brita Kajsa was putting more wood in the stove so that the massive wall could store the heat throughout the night. Like a shadow I slid noiselessly across to the study. The door was ajar and I pushed it farther open without knocking. The silence inside was alarming.

I found my master bent forward with his forehead on the desk. For one dreadful second I thought he had left us. A stroke, a hemorrhage that caused the rock to break and fall apart.

Then I realized that he was sitting there praying. His eyes were just slits, as if they were looking into another world. I sank down beside him, knelt on the bare floorboards without daring to touch him. From his mouth, brown tobacco juice had dribbled onto his writing paper. It had formed the letter U. Maybe he tried to raise his arm, his hand, but his body remained motionless, as if he were asleep. Like a leveret clutched in the huge talons of an eagle. He looked like someone being borne away to be eaten.

I stayed where I was and waited, picked up a book, read, but took nothing in. My knees hurt and I cautiously changed position as twilight fell, and as we were both immersed in the deepening blackness of the autumn night.

Suddenly a wave seemed to go down his spine and like a ghost he sat up straight, his upper body leaning against the back of the chair for support.

"Ah, it's Jussi."

I stood up, stiff and frightened. He was back, as if he had just woken up. But then I recognized his wry smile.

"Well, Jussi, what did you hear when you were eavesdropping out there?"

The blood drained from my face.

"Noth-nothing, Pastor."

"Who else would have been sitting by the wall? The grass underneath the window was flattened, and besides, you dropped something."

I instinctively felt for the knife on my belt. It was still there.

"The pastor is mistaken," I lied, with a little more daring.

He held something up between his thumb and forefinger. With his other hand he grabbed a tuft of my hair and tugged.

"A strand of your hair caught on the wood when you pressed your ear against the wall," he said. "I can see that the color and length match."

"I'm sorry," I whispered.

The pastor dropped the hairs on the floor.

"What did Jussi manage to gather?"

"Please forgive me."

"Just tell me what you heard."

"'Whore,'" I whispered doubtfully. "The old woman shouted at Maria. That she was a whore."

"Is she?"

"Maria . . . no, never. No, not Maria."

"Jussi is taken with her."

"I don't know."

"That's why Jussi was eavesdropping. Because surely Jussi doesn't have the bad habit of hiding outside every time I hear a confession?"

"No, no."

"Then, if I may, I'll ask a straight question. Has Jussi been intimate with Maria?"

"We have . . . danced together."

"I mean in the carnal way. If so, I need to know."

My thoughts spun, and then I recalled her suddenly vomiting in the yard.

"I . . . There is nothing I would rather have done than be intimate with her."

"So what stopped you?"

I didn't know how to answer. If only I had dared to ask her. If only I had been able to carry her pails. If only I hadn't been a young *noaidi* . . .

The pastor lit his best pipe, the enormous one with a bowl as big as a child's skull. He let the smoke percolate through his nostrils with tiny peeping noises.

"You have to take stock," he said then. "She is not the person you believe her to be."

"What does the pastor mean?"

"I have a duty of confidentiality as a priest. But it made me worried, Jussi. Or rather, fearful."

"Not for Maria?"

I'll go wherever you want, Jussi. Wherever you want . . . Till death do us part . . .

The pastor's eyes closed to slits again. I couldn't look at him and instead I walked over to the window. Outside, the night sky was darkening and the thickening clouds threatened rain on its way. He shook himself and seemed to brush away an invisible spider's web. He changed position, the chair creaking under his weight. With a trembling hand he lit the oil lamp standing on the desk. I studied his profile in the light from the flame, his large potato-shaped nose, which some of his children had inherited.

"Autumn's coming," he murmured.

"Mm."

"A cold autumn after a grim summer."

"The summer's been hard," I agreed.

"Peace be with Hilda and Jolina. And peace be with Nils Gustaf. And you yourself, Jussi, with your dreadful injuries. Shouldn't I have been able to stop the evil?"

"The pastor has done everything he could."

"Shouldn't I have felt the devil's presence better than this? Shouldn't I, as priest, have been the first to expose him?"

"The wiles of the devil are boundless."

"That is true."

"He finds our weakest points."

"Yes, alas," the pastor agreed. "It's about the human being's inner construct, our psychology. Even I have weaknesses, no matter how strong I like to think I am. In every fortress there is always a hole, a back door unlocked, a cellar window someone forgot to hasp. While the master of the house sits at the table buttering his giblets, robbers are sneaking in and waiting for night."

"We are all only human."

"Yes, but how? In what way am I human? Where is my weakest place? That is what I reflect upon."

He puffed and offered his pipe to me, but I shook my head.

"Pride," he said dryly. "My damned pride."

I was startled by the profanity. He removed the tobacco juice from the corner of his mouth and wiped his hand on his trouser leg.

"We are all proud," I said, barely audibly.

"I had pictured my portrait handing in the sacristy. Mine would be the first in the long line of pastors' portraits. Henceforth I would hang there like Abraham for all Pajala inhabitants to see."

He smiled apologetically, his teeth a dirty yellow.

"Nils Gustaf's murderer is sure to be caught one day," I said.

"I fear you are wrong," he said thoughtfully. "I am afraid it will all get much worse."

"Worse?"

"What if our suffering has essentially been caused by the revival? By the force of the revival movement? I fear that the evil we have hitherto experienced is but a foretaste of something much darker."

I stared at the pastor, aghast. He looked terrible, his eye sockets appeared to go right into his skull. The coal-black pupils looked as though they had been cut out of the earth, they had seen everything. I had a premonition of what he would look like when he was dead, how I would stand by his bier and hold his icy hand. With a shiver I dismissed the image, but the unease lingered on. The pastor lowered his voice, filled with anxiety.

"Stay indoors from now on, Jussi. Stop sneaking around outside. I fear a storm is brewing."

56.

NIGHT ADVANCED SLOWLY LIKE A DREAM, DAWN'S ARRIVAL almost imperceptible as the last mists lifted over the region. My beloved stepped onto the porch, dressed for the cowshed, and I could see immediately that she wasn't herself. Her steps stiff, she plodded like a sow, and when I crept nearer I could see her face was swollen from crying. I reached the barn door in front of her and held it open. Maria stared at me as if I were a ghost. When I slipped inside quickly, so as not to be seen from the cabin, she came in after me and the door creaked shut. The smell of cattle was strong and sweet. The air was warmed by the mass of bodies and I heard them stamping and banging into the walls of their stalls as they caught my unfamiliar scent. The udders were waiting, their veins taut, waiting for her nimble fingers.

"Maria . . ." I whispered, with my hand in front of my ugly, scarred mouth.

She avoided my eyes. Shyly, I moved closer, my elbow nudged hers. Suddenly she gave a start and threw her arms around me, sending a stab of pain through my ribs.

"You came," she whispered.

"I've been waiting here all night."

"Why?"

I hesitated. It was difficult to speak, and yet I had to.

"What you said . . . I'll go with you, Maria. Wherever you want."

"No, you don't understand, Jussi."

"Yes . . . I can say the child is mine," I muttered.

She pushed me away, staring at me in dismay.

"But how do you know . . . ?"

"I'll marry you," I said, with as little breath as possible.

She saw my mouth, my nearly-toothless jaws.

"A whore?" she whispered back.

"You're not a whore."

"He promised . . . that we would get married."

"Who?"

"It doesn't matter now."

"I can marry you," I whispered. "I'd like that, Maria."

Gently, she embraced me. Her soft cheek against mine, discolored and scarred. I couldn't move.

"Where would we go?" she whispered.

"North. To Norway."

"Norway? But when?"

"We can leave now."

"No, that's not possible."

"This evening, then? You do the milking, then pretend to go to bed. When everyone else has gone, I'll be waiting for you out here."

"This very evening?"

"We can walk all night. Then no one will catch up with us."

"But you're injured, Jussi. Someone has hurt you."

"We can walk side by side into the land of Canaan."

"You mean you and I . . . ?"

"Even unto Bethlehem, if it be so."

She let go of me, as if she were almost giddy. Swallowed, and nodded eagerly.

"Tonight," she whispered, and caressed the sensitive skin under my chin with her fingertips. Then she hastily looked around and reached for the milking stool, worn smooth with use.

57

As I HURRIED BACK TO THE PARSONAGE, I COULD STILL FEEL where she had touched my skin and I carried with me the warmth of her, the scent of her. The village was stirring, I could hear doors opening, the clatter of tools, I could see smoke rising from the cabins and barn kettles. Stopped by no one, I made my way to the pastor's woodshed, crept inside, and sat down on the chopping block. I cut away a piece of birch bark, trimmed the edges with my knife, and then got out my little pencil.

I am human, I carefully wrote in the dim light.

I used the tiniest letters, to fit in as much as possible.

I come from the mountains. It was difficult there. My sister is still there . . .

Writing was hard, my vision blurred. I wiped my eyes with my hand, timidly looked up. I could hear footsteps and just had time to hide the sharp-edged piece of bark under my shirt when the door opened.

It was Brita Kajsa, who jumped and gave a little cry.

"Oh, it's Jussi."

I nodded, gathering an armful of firewood and balancing it against my side.

"Take it into the cabin." She motioned with her head. "And there's some porridge if you're hungry."

I meekly went in with my load, thinking that now the journey had commenced in earnest. The first steps in a very long journey. One day it would be a book.

I PRETENDED TO EAT THE porridge, but saved it in a small bent-wood box, along with some tough bits of dried fish in my knapsack, so difficult to chew that I would have to soak them in water later. As long as we were prudent the food would last two days, maybe three. Then we would have to see. I packed the fire striker and a ball of thread. Along the way I would be able to whittle a fishing rod and sharpen a needle of juniper wood to thread through a worm. When the fish bit the worm the needle would lodge sideways and I would be able to pull the fish ashore and then we could grill it over the fire at night. The pouch of salt should last a few months. And in Norway it was easy to get hold of more. There were still plenty of berries in the forests. I took an old blanket. As for me, I could sleep in the clothes I was wearing, but Maria needed help to keep warm at night. I would sit and tend the fire in the forest, stay awake all night while the firelight played on her rosy cheeks. They were sure to come after us and we would have to be careful. Start using different names, profess to be on our way to relatives on the Arctic coast.

I hid my knapsack in the cowshed, up in the loft. Then I treated the wounds that still hadn't healed. They looked worse like this, in the daylight. The pus was seeping out and I made a face at the nagging pain. I scooped up cobwebs and laid them over the wounds, as I had learned from the old Lapp women, spat on them and protected them with bandages. If the pain got worse I would have to burn the wounds clean with the blade of my knife, make the steel red-hot and press it on. There was a sour taste in my mouth from the tooth stumps. And it was still bad between my legs. But it would be all right. It had to be all right. They would search for us in the south, but we would go north, to meet the cold. Now I had to sleep. Gather my strength. In only a few hours, a few brief, short hours, I would hold her hand. And never let it go.

58.

EVENING CAME AND THE PARSONAGE STARTED TO SETTLE DOWN. I made an effort to act normally, washed my face at the well, and huddled up on the floor by the door on my straw-filled mattress. I pretended to have already fallen asleep by the time the pastor read the evening prayer, and I saw the last candle be blown out. I lay motionless for a long time, until everyone stopped tossing and turning and I could hear their breathing become slow and steady. I rose like a shadow, picked up my boots, and stole to the door as quietly as possible. Tjalmo thought I was going out for a pee; she stretched and yawned so that I could see her white eyeteeth in the dark, then she curled up in her corner by the door. Like a shadow still, I fetched my knapsack from the hayloft and set off along the village road. It was as if I had never existed, I just dissolved into the darkness.

The cold sky was clear and starry, a crescent moon hanging on the horizon as a guiding light. I tried to avoid the holes in the road. Every misplaced step sent pain shooting through my body, but I still managed to make good time and every step brought me closer to my beloved. We would walk side by side all night, for as long as we were able. When dawn began to break, we would take shelter under a fir tree and lie down close together. I could hardly believe it was possible.

I could soon make out her farm between the trees. I took up my usual post at the edge of the forest, not wanting a dog to start barking. The yard appeared to be empty. Or perhaps she was already waiting in the semidarkness? I sank down into the grass, which was slightly damp with dew. Like a cat, I raised my head and strained my eyes. The windows in the house were dark, no sound to be heard. I resolved to wait. Still with my knapsack on my back in readiness, I settled down. The crescent moon sailed slowly up above the forest and in the distance I could hear the roar of the Kengis waterfall. The noise wasn't constant, but rose and fell like far-off breathing. There was the sound of an animal approaching through the undergrowth. I listened to the gentle rustling, until it caught my scent and froze. I raised the back of my hand to my lips and sucked in the skin so that it made a little mouse-like squeak. The old trick worked and I saw a young fox peep out hopefully. But then he spotted my shape and disappeared back into the shadows.

Suddenly I heard the front door open and someone came out onto the porch. A figure moved across the yard and seemed to stop, to hesitate. I couldn't see who it was in the gloom and didn't dare to shout. Instead I began to inch nearer. Yes, it was a woman. My heart was pounding. The figure looked around, unsure. It had to be Maria. I moved forward as quickly and quietly as I could, holding my arms up as a shield against the saplings whipping at my face. Should I whistle so she would know I was there? No, there was too much of a risk that it would wake the others. Now she looked around again and I thought she whispered something. Was it my name? Then she turned and hurried back to the cabin. No, she changed course toward the barn. She opened the door and slid in through the black gap. I waited to make sure no one was following her. No, everything was still quiet. Taking a deep breath, I stepped out into the yard and sped silently across to the door of the barn. I looked around one last time. There was no one about, no light in the cabin. I silently grasped the door handle and pulled open the heavy door.

There she was. I sensed her outline, watched her walk toward me.

"My beloved," I whispered. "My heart's desire . . ."

She threw her arms around me. But they were hard and sinewy, they clasped me so hard I groaned with the pain.

"I've got him!"

A man's voice, a man's smell, the rasping skin on a cheek as I tried to twist free. The barn door was thrown open, heavy feet lumbered closer, and I saw the flickering light from a lantern. Strong hands grabbed me and hurled me to the floor. I felt my knapsack being torn off me, my arm yanked backward at a painful angle.

"We've got the swine!"

I recognized the voice all too well. Sheriff Brahe. In the light from the lantern I could make out the men from the farm, the master and both sons, each armed with an ax. And next to me, dressed in Maria's blouse and kirtle, stood Constable Michelsson, tightening his grip on me until I moaned with pain. His face was contorted in a triumphant grin.

"Jussi, Jussi, now you're really in the shit-pot!"

I heard the clinking of metal and rattling of chains and felt my knife being taken out of my belt.

"You are under arrest, Jussi," Brahe said, barely able to conceal his glee.

"Get the wagon ready," Michelsson shouted.

The master of the house hurried off to harness the horses. The older son advanced, an ax shaking dangerously in his hands.

"*Voi saatanan . . .*" he mumbled, over and over. "*Voi saatanan piru . . .*"

"What have you done with Maria?" I whispered.

The kick hit my shoulder blade, followed by a wad of spit. Then I felt a burning pain as my arms were wrenched backward.

The night would be a long one.

PART FOUR

❖

The priest in his church
Alone in prayer
Nobody hears
What he lays bare
Before our Lord
We bow and esteem
Jesus above
May sinners redeem

59.

THESE ARE MY PEOPLE, THE PEOPLE OF THE NORTH. IT IS FOR them that I preach. They are so few in number, so dispersed. If the city dweller is an anchor, then the Northman is the wind. He weighs nothing. He moves with no trace, makes no noise, no fuss. If you take a pinch of writing sand and fling it across the room, the sand will disappear. It is there, but you can't see it anymore. So it is with the people in the north. They gather in large numbers only when the signs are auspicious. When the salmon are passing. When the wild berries ripen. When the capercaillies play in the glades of the ancient forests and the seabirds lay their eggs. Then they walk together and reap from the abundance until it is time to move on. Northerners' homes are made from the forest, from the forest's bones and heart, from wood and skins, from stones that are laid round the hearth to warm tired bodies long after the evening fire has gone out. They wander across heaths and swamps, they paddle along winding streams, they travel on skis faster than by horse, they carry their knife, their wooden cup, ready to face anything, they carry the knowledge of how to survive the winter. They know death, they know that the one who stops wandering will die, and that a knife wound, a broken bone, a sudden cough can be the parting sign. They know grief. They know that for every living person there are ten dead, for every child twenty dead are waiting, that it is the thinnest child that usually survives while the fat one gives up when the breast gives out. They know that happiness is a net dragged in, heavy with fish. A bucket filled with fresh berries. A well-tanned reindeer hide. A squealing puppy. A marrow bone newly split, still warm from the slaughter. They know that love is lying by the fire with a friend, turning away from the dark, nestling close together and telling stories through the endless winter. The best way for people to keep warm.

ONE DAY DURING MY term of service in Karesuando I received a visit from two very determined gentlemen. They came to my parsonage wanting help in procuring Lapp skulls. They were young and ambitious, their clothes seemed still to be quite new, despite their long journey; perhaps they had several changes of clothing in the trunks their bearers put down to catch their breath. Authentic Lapp skulls. The lecturer wore spectacles, for all his youth, and had the hands of a noblewoman, smooth and hairless, with pointed fingers. As part of his research at Copenhagen University he had examined authentic Negroid skulls, fingered the prominent eyebrow ridges and studied the even, flat shape of the nasal bone. In his logbook he had kept a careful record of the measurements; what he lacked was a comparison. Perhaps the Lapps were closely related to the Negro race? Could one not discern a certain southern pigmentation in a number of the specimens?

The assistant was a few years his senior and had a croaky voice, his head was bald and shiny, and he moved his arms incessantly while he spoke, as if laboriously grinding out the words from a reluctant barrel organ. He said he had tried to wash a Lapp child clean while it greedily stuffed its mouth full of sweets, and under a thick layer of grease and soot a dark, almost African skin tone had emerged.

I advanced the notion that the child doubtless played outside all the time, instead of sitting in a reading room, nose in a book. Both men gave me a long stare, as if transfixed, before deciding I had made a joke, and then laughed in that formal, academic way in which they avoided showing their teeth.

So, Lapp skulls, then. They were extremely keen, making clear that I would be generously recompensed for my assistance. Would there be somewhere out in the wild where a person of Lapp descent might have met his death and been buried? I explained that since the advent of Christianity, Lapps were buried in churchyards, just like the rest of us. This answer troubled the gentlemen, not to say depressed them. Were Lapp corpses never discovered eaten by wild animals, the body perhaps chewed up beyond recognition but the skull left more or less undisturbed? I said that of course such things could happen, but sooner or later these unfortunates would be found by their family and friends, who, by means of the clothes and baggage, would generally be able to confirm their identity and put them to rest in the family grave.

What about a criminal, then? Even Lapps must commit an act of violence once in a while, a dreadful murder punishable by death? Maybe the executioner could be asked when the next murderer or assassin was going to the block? The authorities could be contacted in good time and give permission for the body to be donated to science. Well, primarily the head.

I replied that access to murderers was highly unpredictable in these parts, and that I wasn't aware of any such trial currently. Perhaps they could contact the judicial services themselves and supply a suitable box filled with salt for this purpose?

They went so far as to attend a funeral. The coffin was open, as is the custom, and these fine gentlemen pushed to the front and bowed their heads reverently, while excitedly noting that the deceased was most decidedly of Lapp stock, an old reindeer herder now lying there in his ceremonial finery. I saw them approach the widow, standing with her children and immediate family. The researchers took her hand, something she was unaccustomed to, and she couldn't understand their flowery condolences, translated by the sexton. I don't know what they thought they would do next, but when they found themselves immediately surrounded by a large group of curious kith and kin, they deemed it wise to retire.

They were exceedingly disappointed. I helped them collect all manner of everyday implements, such as objects carved from masur birch or reindeer antlers, the magnificent handiwork the Lapps surrounded themselves with. I explained at length about Lapp mythology, which predated Christianity and still left an impression on their minds. The men managed to get wind of a place of sacrifice on a migration route and caused a great deal of damage by using spades to dig deep holes. Maybe they were hoping to discover a silver treasure trove, even though the offerings at this place traditionally consisted of reindeer antlers or bundles of reindeer hooves.

Finally, I guided them to the site of the old church at Markkina. Some ten years or more previously the church had been pulled down and moved and the settlement abandoned. But the churchyard remained. And I can barely describe the zeal that seized the men when they realized where they were. Literally trembling with anticipation, they gripped their spades. After glancing in all directions to assure themselves there were no unauthorized witnesses, they selected a grave where the earth had sunk in and they started shoveling. It wasn't long before they struck rotting wood. With great care they began to uncover their find, which proved to be a buried reindeer sleigh. In it lay a male person, stretched out on his back, his hands clasped as if in prayer. Both the sleigh and the leather costume clearly indicated this was a nomadic Lapp, a male of short stature. As soon as there was enough room in the hole, the two men climbed down and continued digging with smaller trowels and brushes. They folded back the cloth covering the face and sighed with pleasure.

It was a well-preserved specimen. The soft bits, such as the eyeballs and flesh on the cheeks, had fallen in. But the rest of the skin remained, as did the eyebrow hair. The jaw had fallen open, revealing the teeth, which looked healthy and in good condition; the man must have died relatively young. On his head was a Sami headdress, painstakingly cut and sewn. The men tried to remove it in order to assess the state of the skull, but it was stuck fast. After cautious wiggling and jiggling, they managed to lift the hat off. They examined the skull and were delighted to find it intact. No fractures, no distortions from the prolonged pressure of earth. The excellent condition of the corpse caused problems for the two men: the skull was firmly attached to the torso by tough ligaments and was difficult to detach. It would be necessary to take part of the spinal column as well. With a cracking sound the rib cage was broken away from the vertebrae, to which end a small ax served the purpose well. A fusty smell had now begun to rise out of the grave, from the soured fat and bone marrow, and I saw fit to stand back while the work was completed. The spoils were placed in a sack of heavy material and labeled with a handwritten tag. A wooden cup and other objects were taken from the grave as well. I walked down the path to the Könkämä River, washed my hands, and rinsed the top of my head and the back of my neck. I felt the curvature of my own skull, its weight, and I had the impression it was loose, that only my hands were preventing it from falling to the ground.

When I returned they were in the process of digging up another grave. They were hoping to find a female specimen this time, which would provide a valuable comparison.

I stood pondering the final day. The moment when Christ would resurrect us all, according to the creed I so often preached. In my mind I saw the graves being opened and the dead standing up, and the headless bodies being obliged to stagger all the way down to Uppsala and Lund to try to put themselves back together.

As the men had promised, I received a generous remuneration. Thirty pieces of silver. I gave it all to the parish.

THEY EVEN COME TO Kengis, these men, always men, who are captivated by the north. Their eyes gleam. They want the midnight sun and magnificent views, they want to meet rare creatures such as wolverine and lynx, they want to listen to drums and traditional songs, they want to hear hunting tales of bears brought down by spears, of wolf packs besieging entire villages, and when the day's adventures are done they want to drink French brandy with mill owners and managing directors and entice farm maids into the sauna. For them Norrland is a kind of India. They come here to perform heroic deeds, gaze at the world's end on the sheer black cliff of North Cape, paint dramatic scenes to be exhibited in London or Paris, make astounding scientific discoveries, preferably with great physical hardship. For them Norrland is an unbaptized land. It wasn't really here until they arrived. The folk here are not people, not people to the extent they are themselves. They have a predilection for standing on the highest points of the terrain. They measure all around them with sextants, barometers, oculars, and chronometers, they collect treatises in Latin and compose accounts of their travels with sumptuous accompanying plates printed on costly paper. They fall out with one another over who was here first, who walked the farthest, who discovered the most. But they never compete over who carried the most. Because the peasants always did that. Silent men, short in stature, nameless, tortured under their bearing poles for mile upon mile. They carried the gentlemen's instruments and punsch bottles to the ancient resting places, they withstood the pain in their backs and joints and at the end, by the shore of the Arctic Ocean, they received their few coins.

The vastness and wildness of Norrland was what they all sought. Mountains to conquer, mighty waterfalls, anything that could, one day, deliver a medal from the hand of the king. The small life, on the other hand, passed them by. Infant diseases, peasants' coughs and cramps, the outstretched hands of the have-nots. All the cultivation attempts that failed, all the starvation and suffering in lamentable huts. And the alcohol, the snake poison, this caustic piss that burned out homes with its venom and left behind devastated tents and abandoned children.

WAS I NOT ONE of the gentlemen myself? With my natural history collections and herbarium sheets, with my examination of soil and rich fen and all my cataloging? Yes, in many ways I too was lured by the devil of ambition. To discover a new plant, to scour flora collections and realize that it has never been described before, that I was the one to find it first. That zealousness could make anyone at all a slave to nefarious passions.

But one thing distinguished me from them. I was born here. My mother was of Lapp descent, Lapp blood flowed through my veins. The mountains were my childhood neighbors. I was no occasional visitor. One day my body would rest in this northern soil. These were my people, this was my country, my final home.

60.

I AM FIFTY-TWO YEARS OLD NOW AND MARKED BY THE AUTUMN OF life. Aging came so unexpectedly. My eyes are dim and wreathed in wrinkles. Where previously I could read by one tallow candle, now I need two. As a young man I could eat until my stomach bulged like a storm-filled sail, whereas now I am full after only a few bites, and my bowels answer nature's call but every three days. My hands that could draw every leaf vein on a plant now tremble when I dip my pen in the ink. My back is bent and my children point out that I lean forward when I walk, as if in a perpetual headwind, though I think I am upright. Sometimes words fail me; I pause and search for the name of a member of the parish, I know her name perfectly well, but it won't surface. Work takes longer to perform and even simple tasks tire me. My life is on a downward trajectory. Earth to earth approaches. Life has passed so quickly, far too fast. It was not so long ago that I stepped briskly across the watery bogs of inland Västerbotten with my vasculum full of rare plants. An eternity opened up before me, expanse after expanse of mountain waiting with new discoveries. I was unmarried, childless, ambitious. At night I could barely rest, my legs still wandering energetically in my sleep. My thoughts were only of myself, of the triumphs I was convinced awaited me, honor's sweetness that would soon be conferred upon me from lecterns and directorates. And I did indeed achieve success. But it was to be of a very different kind. The honorary academic titles were bestowed on other, meeker candidates. While I was the one who would touch people's hearts.

THEN I FOUND MYSELF in the wilderness. At the age of twenty-eight I stood with my dead daughter in my arms, Emma Maria, just one week old. The little infant body still had a hint of warmth, her eyes were not fully closed, they held a glimmer as if from inner candle-light. We sat there quietly, Brita Kajsa and I, as the tiny body stiff-ened and the infant soul departed. It is hard to keep your faith at times like this. Nora, our daughter begotten in sin before we had entered marriage, still lives and is strong. But Emma Maria, the most innocent of us all, the one who had no time to sin in thought or word or deed, was taken.

I too have felt death's hatchet draw near. Ten years ago in the summer my dear brother Petrus died from hemorrhage of the lungs. And I myself was struck by a cough and fever so severe that I thought I had tuberculosis. Convinced my days were numbered, I thought my life had been in vain and served no useful purpose. I had not made the most of my talents, had devoted my time to satis-fying the devil of ambition and neglected my spiritual develop-ment. How easy it is to get stuck in the sweet dough of life, to clap each other's tailcoated backs, to be bedecked with laurel wreaths and medals. And still the success is never enough, ambition is only hungry for more. How easily I could have become one of these art collectors or writing-desk botanists who only lives to have his name perpetuated in the botanic registers.

Eventually my run of illness ended. After some months I finally felt my strength return and was able to rise from my sickbed. And yet it gave me no pleasure. The world seemed to lack color. Dark thoughts pursued me and I tried to escape them. I obtained a copy of Carl Nordblad's *Health Primer for the Common Man*, in which he prescribes an hour of daily walking, and I began to follow this for-mula. Every day I strode round the church building, circuit after circuit, I paced round the holy place until a trail was formed, worn down to the grass roots in a brown footpath that surrounded the church. And I could feel this physical exertion actually doing me good. My thoughts were still somber and bleak, but the exercise strengthened and energized me. My ailing lungs were exposed to fresh air and they recovered. And I thought about all the sedentary town dwellers in our kingdom, how well they too would feel with exercise. The villagers, however, all the farmhands and maids who dragged and lifted and walked many times more than I did every working day, they thought I had taken leave of my senses. Behind my back they started calling me Wandering Lasse.

My ruminations left me no peace. Was I saved? Yes, I believed in God, didn't I? I rattled off the confession with the parishioners and dispensed forgiveness for sins as if I were dishing out sugar lumps. Sinners went to church for comfort and a pat on the head. Then all of them went home and carried on drinking and whoring and snaffling money and calling themselves Christians. We took a brandy, we dallied with the maid, we added a few pennies to the bills. Sober boozers, virtuous fornicators, honorable thieves. Could people like that call themselves believers?

That was when I went to Åsele. And God awakened me. He came to me and spoke to me in a woman's voice. He showed me Milla Clementsdotter, this holy mother of God, who took me into her womb and embraced my shriveled husk and gave me life again.

My work in god's vineyard will soon be over. I must have only a few years left. How many? Twenty? Or maybe only ten? Autumn is approaching and I can feel the night cold. One winter's day my life will end and my body will be buried in the earth of the north. I want to believe that I have achieved a little good. There have been a few articles and books, and my extensive herbarium will stand. But in a hundred years all this will be forgotten. Some small detail from my sermons might have lodged in an old crofter-woman's mind. It won't be more than that. The only thing that will remain, the only thing that testifies my life and work, will be the name of an unimportant plant. I will be a plant on the southern slope of a mountain in the vast Torne Lappmark.

I bow my head so my hair hangs like a shadow over my brow, I clasp my nicotine-stained hands together. But no one answers. How can I face the world's pain? Where can I find the strength and grace? The sky is cold over the land of the north, the empty curve of a giant eyeball. Not even the stars are twinkling tonight.

61.

BRITA KAJSA WOKE ME EARLY IN THE MORNING. HER EYES WERE wide open, her hand on her heart. I felt paralyzed with fear. My wife was ill, she needed my help. Awkwardly I tried to get up, but she held on to me, pinching my shoulders painfully.

"They've got him," she gasped.

"Who?"

"The neighbor's maid came to tell me. Jussi's been caught red-handed!"

"Our Jussi?"

"He assaulted a girl. But this time they managed to arrest him. He's been put in jail."

Her chin was wrinkled and thrust out as she tried to say more but couldn't. All I could do was embrace her. I could still remember the dream she woke me from, I had met Linnaeus himself. He had let me browse through his herbarium, and there I had found an unknown plant, completely new to science, the leaves similar to *Taraxacum* but the flowers like *Dryas*. But now a sheet of ice was drawn over my happiness.

Before long the night's events were on everyone's lips. Aha, it was the pastor's *noaidi* child who attacked the women. The monster! Many people said they had suspected Jussi all the time; he was described as weird, he was from a Sami family and he had a craven, evasive way about him. People had noticed how he avoided eye contact and his voice was low and he mumbled as if he were trying to hide something. In church he had been seen staring across the aisle to the women's side, making the girls shudder when they felt his lecherous eye. It was obvious this man had for a long time harbored evil instincts within him. Roope could testify that the prisoner had previously been caught skulking beside the village road. Roope had happened to be passing in his cart and thanks to the dog's vigilance Jussi had been sent packing with a proper bloody nose and at least that night an attack on another woman had been prevented.

I made my way to the prison in Pajala but wasn't allowed in. The sheriff explained that he and Michelsson had interrogated the prisoner all night and there would be no interference from outsiders. When he had the confession finished and signed, that might be the time for the priest to deal with his sins, but at the moment it was too soon. He reluctantly allowed me to leave a passage from the Bible for Jussi on a piece of paper. I chose Isaiah 51:14.

"The captive exile hasteneth that he may be loosed, and that he should not die in the pit."

Brahe carelessly folded the paper and said it would be given to Jussi at the appropriate time. Whereupon he showed me out in no uncertain manner. I heard the key turn in the lock when the door was shut.

I looked up to find the villagers staring at me inquisitively. Everyone knew that Jussi had been living with us at the parsonage. Why hadn't I noticed anything? One of the old women squeezed out a few tears and asked if I would give some words of comfort at this difficult time, when the devil himself had been captured in the village. I said something noncommittal. When the woman grabbed my coat and held on to me, I almost struck her. At the last moment I came to my senses and she let go, a look of terror on her face when she saw the fury in my eyes.

I returned home and sat down to write Sunday's sermon in an attempt to calm my stormy soul.

———

IF YOU, THE GOOD Samaritan, do not help this wretched man, who lies half dead at the roadside, then he will surely die forever. And the dogs and all the wild creatures of the forest will seize their opportunity and tear him apart and ravage him. Gnomes and forest demons will rejoice and laugh. . . .

JUSSI, MY JUSSI . . . THE poor boy who had been hiding by the path like a little reed. And I picked him. I dug him up by the roots and made a place in my herbarium, a tiny plant ripped out of its home soil. Perhaps I did wrong? Perhaps he would have been happier to have stayed in his meager frost-bound earth. I taught the boy to read and write, but what else did he get in my presence? Not a woman, not a friend. Perhaps I frightened away everything that might have been good for him? His peers were scared of the nasty priest. They wanted to avoid my critical looks, my scathing writings and restless obsession. The peasants sensed that Jussi was different from them. So they beat him to a pulp. They battered him between the legs so that no more like him could come into the world.

Jussi, my Jussi . . . you poor boy. I saved you at the side of the road not once, but twice, I held you like a son to my breast. Did you let the devil build a nest in your poor heart?

I thought of all the times Jussi had just disappeared. He had gone off without a word and then been away for weeks. As if he were driven by powerful external forces. I too had noticed his staring looks at the women's side in church; he must have felt the desires of the flesh, for he is a young man after all. And at the same time he had been plagued by his timidity and awkwardness. I had never felt shy in front of the fair sex, I had always been able to joke and jest with the girls. But if, like Jussi, you felt strong desires but hardly dared say a word, and if you couldn't find a way to approach women, then in time an ever greater inner pressure would result. A fire that blazed more and more intensely until it was forced to break out in a frenzy.

What was the psychology that turned this humble village boy into a violent criminal?

I was obliged to put my sermon aside for a while. In despair I bowed my head over my desk and clasped my hands. But rational thought was beyond me. Instead I was transformed into an empty vessel. From all directions thoughts shot up like sprouting weeds, poking up like twine. The knot in my stomach wouldn't loosen and the sharp light of an inextinguishable lamp burned in my chest.

Only much later did I gradually feel my heart lighten. And suddenly it happened. As if the river flowed into me. The long and mighty Torne with its foaming Kengis waterfall flooded through me and sluiced all the dirt and filth. All the gray lice and nits, all the impurity and murk was washed away in the current. Finally, the only thing left was a rounded mirror of water. An eternally circular O.

While it was happening, I was no part of it. I don't know how long it went on. It was a state I couldn't describe, because at the time I wasn't there.

And without being shocked, I knew that this was death, that this was what it looked like.

62.

I HURRIED TO THE PLACE WHERE JUSSI HAD BEEN ARRESTED. THERE were a number of the overcurious already assembled in the yard, keen to acquaint themselves with the gossip. In the midst of them stood the master of the house pointing toward the edge of the forest to indicate where the assailant had come from. He and his sons, together with Sheriff Brahe, had hidden in the cabin with all the lights extinguished and had kept watch through the window. They had waited until darkness fell, then given the signal to Michelsson, dressed as a woman, to walk toward the cowshed. As he did so they could see a shadowy figure come creeping out. At the door to the cowshed the offender threw himself on top of the person he thought was the farm maid Maria, but instead fell straight into the constable's arms. Sheriff Brahe and the people inside the house had immediately rushed out and helped with the arrest.

I walked up to the barn door and studied the ground.

"So Michelsson tackled him head-on about here, on this spot?"

The farmer demonstrated the hold and how the man arrested fought like a wild animal to get free.

"So Jussi fought back violently?" I asked.

Yes, he had even tried to cut Michelsson's throat. The sons nodded. But at the last moment they managed to kick the knife away.

"How could you see the knife in the dark?"

On that, the witnesses were uncertain. But after a while they agreed they had seen a blade glint in the moonlight. And thanks to their speedy intervention, they had prevented a bloodbath. The accused had struggled frantically, and even though they were all strong men, they had only just managed to get the better of him. Not until the attacker was dealt a few salutary blows did he submit.

I opened the barn door and let the light stream in. The floor consisted of rough, hand-sawed planks. I bent down and examined the wall of the nearest cow stall.

"Was one of you injured?" I asked.

They shook their heads. Sprayed on the wood in long arcs were dark oval splashes of blood.

"Was this where Jussi landed? On the floor down here?"

"Yes, his head was lying at that end." One of the sons pointed.

I crouched down and examined his frayed boots. There were dark spots on the leather uppers. He must have kicked Jussi until he bled. I bent closer to the floorboard and discovered a tiny bit of skin with some strands of hair stuck to it. They must have slammed the back of his head against the floor while he was down.

"And then you took him out into the yard? Did he go voluntarily?"

"No, we had to drag him."

The grass outside had been trodden down by all the visitors and it was impossible to see any drag marks. But by the door I found something. It was a couple of small, grayish lumps, and when I squatted down I noticed a familiar smell. It reminded me of something at home, but I couldn't for the life of me think what.

"Did you hold Jussi on the ground?"

"Yes, we did, we guarded him. Father fetched the horse and harnessed it for the wagon. That took a while."

"Did you eat anything while you were waiting?"

I scraped up the gray clumps on my finger and showed them to the men, who looked blank. I put out my tongue and licked cautiously. The taste was familiar too, but I still couldn't place it.

"Did you eat any bread, by any chance?"

"No, but we had a drink. The sheriff had his bottle with him."

A ripple went through the crowd, for everyone knew my abhorrence of alcohol. But I was pondering the taste and now I knew what it was, something that came from my own home: Brita Kajsa's porridge.

"That's porridge down there," I said.

Only then did the son remember.

"Oh yes, we went through his *laukku*, his knapsack. And there was a birch-bark box. We thought he might have hidden money in it, but when we opened it the porridge spilled out."

"You mean Jussi had a knapsack on his back?"

"Yes, a *laukku*. An old one, very shabby."

"With porridge wrapped up inside?"

"And other stuff as well. A fire striker. An old blanket. A pouch of salt and some dried fish."

"And where's the knapsack now?"

"Sheriff Brahe took it."

I stood in silence, considering the situation. Then I turned to the cabin and raised my arms to make my way through the mob. People stepped aside to let me through and I entered the large cabin without knocking. I thought at first that the house was empty, but then I thought I could hear the sound of quick footsteps.

"Is anyone there?"

No answer. I carried on to the bedroom. The door was shut, and when I tried to open it, it appeared to be locked. But a muffled rustling suggested someone's weight was against it on the other side. I braced myself with my shoulder and pushed. It opened a crack, so I pushed harder, slowly forcing the door wide open.

I went in and found her standing with her back to me. She was hiding her face in her apron and I could see her shoulders shaking.

Tentatively, I touched her shoulder, at which she jackknifed, her upper body snapping against her thighs.

"Maria?"

Her weeping made no sound. When she came to the parsonage with her enraged mother, she had been stiff-necked and uncommunicative, but today she displayed an entirely different side.

"Tell me, Maria. What happened?"

She shook her head. I brought my hand to her neck and her tightly plaited hair.

"Jussi was carrying his knapsack," I said. "In the middle of the night he brought tools and implements and a blanket. Isn't that strange?"

"Don't know," came her faint reply.

"Had you arranged to meet? Did you and Jussi intend to sleep beside each other?"

"Don't know."

"And how did Sheriff Brahe come to be here, keeping watch? Someone must have summoned him, someone must have said that Jussi was on his way here."

"Don't know, don't know."

"Was it you, Maria?"

She twisted as though her whole body were in pain, as if she were strung up from a hook. I raised my voice and gave it a sharper ring.

"Jussi is accused of attempting to attack you. But if you say that you had agreed to meet of your own free will, he will be released."

She shook her head violently, making her plaits swing to and fro, and she covered her ears with her hands to block out my words. I felt my powerlessness growing. I grabbed her wrists roughly and prized them apart. She stiffened, twisted round, and stared straight at me. Her eyes were dry and empty, like an angel's.

"Don't know."

We looked at one another as if from different planets. Her beauty was striking, her clear blue eyes saw right through me, a lock of golden hair curled round her ear.

"He is very fond of you, Maria. You can save him. Just one word from you and he will walk free."

But it was as if she weren't there. Perhaps she wanted to protect the unborn child, the little flame that had been kindled in her stomach, the child that had no father.

"Don't know," she whispered again.

"Get thee hence!" I hissed back. "In the name of Jesus Christ our Savior, be gone!"

Her face darkened, she was about to vomit; inside her the toad's feet and coiled tongue writhed, and soon it would come screaming through her mouth and rend me apart.

Steps could be heard from outside and someone trod heavily on the porch. I let her go and turned away, bitter acid rising in my throat.

The father of the household entered the cabin and found me in the kitchen, drinking from a ladle of water. I praised the water's quality and was told it was his grandfather who had dug the well. He had gone straight down into a spring that never dried up, even in late winter.

I also remarked on the excellent condition of the house, which improved his mood still further. Yes, they knew how to build a house in his family. In fact, it was a family trait, woodwork demanding both precision and patience, in his opinion. But, so as not to appear too arrogant, he pointed out some small defects in need of repair, and we agreed that for a homeowner there was never a shortage of things to do.

I led the conversation to the events of the previous day and was told that Sheriff Brahe had arrived in the early evening, accompanied by Constable Michelsson. The farmer had no idea who might have summoned them, they just turned up. The sheriff had explained that they were going to set a trap and the family had followed his instructions. All the lights were put out, so it looked as though everyone had gone to bed. The constable dressed in the girl's milking clothes. And then they just had to wait.

"What was Maria doing while this went on?"

"She was told to stay in the maids' room."

"What sort of mood was she in?"

"The sheriff told her to keep calm."

"So she was upset?"

"Yes, it wasn't very nice for her."

"But the policemen knew that Jussi was coming. Did Maria tell them?"

The farmer shrugged.

"At least we got the monster."

I glanced at the bedroom door. It was closed, but nevertheless I lowered my voice so that Maria shouldn't hear.

"Maybe Jussi was lured here? Maybe Maria had asked him to come?"

"I don't know about that."

"How long has she actually been working as a maid here?"

"Since last spring. But she's going to stop now."

"Is she?"

"The girl's mother doesn't want her to stay. And neither do we. The mother thinks that one of us men has been with the girl."

"And what do you think about that?"

"No, absolutely not. Neither I nor my boys have touched her. I can swear on the Bible. . . ."

"But the girl is certainly very pretty."

"She has to stay until the autumn jobs are done. Then she can leave before it starts to show too much."

"I understand."

"The pastor probably knows the girl has been running around the village. Been painted and everything. She doesn't even know who the father is herself."

"Or she doesn't want to say."

"Well, it's neither of my boys. They were as annoyed as I was when the mother came here implying such things."

I thought of the son's blood-spattered boot. The spray on the wall. How many nights had they seen Jussi sneaking around out here this past summer?

63.

IT TOOK MICHELSSON AND BRAHE TWO DAYS TO GET JUSSI TO confess. Only then was I allowed into the poky cell that served as the local prison. Jussi lay on his stomach on a wooden bench with no mattress, just crude, rough planks nailed together. His hands and feet were chained and I could see that the links had chafed ugly wounds into his skin. Instead of his own clothes, they had put him in a sack-like tunic that smelled disgusting. Behind me I heard Michelsson slam the door and lock it, and doubtless he remained standing outside to listen. I looked at Jussi, appalled. At first I thought he was asleep, and then I saw violent tremors shake his body. I quickly took off my coat and spread it over him against the cold. I gently stroked his filthy hair and felt clotted lumps come loose.

"It's me, Jussi. . . . It's the pastor."

He didn't answer. Could he be unconscious?

"How do you feel? Don't you have a blanket to lie on?"

Very carefully I took hold of his shoulders and turned him onto his back. He let out a groan. I flinched when I saw his injuries. They had struck him so hard his eye had swollen shut.

"Can you hear me, Jussi? It's the pastor."

I saw his lips part a fraction.

"Water," he whispered.

An overturned jug was lying by the end of the bench. There was still a splash at the bottom and I put a drip onto his lips. He opened his mouth so that I could pour the rest in.

"Jussi, is it true you've confessed to the attack?"

He forced his eye open a crack to reveal a wet glimmer.

"They . . . they forced my hand."

"What do you mean?"

"They pressed it against the paper."

"Did they force you to write, Jussi?"

"Maria and I were . . . Maria knows . . ."

"I went to see her to find out."

"Then she must have said . . . ? We'd agreed we would meet."

His shaking worsened and I anxiously stroked his brow as the rage welled up inside me.

"Water!" I roared, and heard Michelsson draw the bolt back. The hinge creaked as he half opened the door.

"Fetch some water," I said again. "And blankets, the man is frozen to the core."

"The sheriff ordered a hard bed," the constable said. "No bedclothes, that's the rule in cases like this."

"And you've beaten him half to death!"

"He resisted arrest."

"Did you, Jussi? Is he telling the truth?"

"We have witnesses," Michelsson said smoothly.

"But fetch more water, for God's sake."

"It was the prisoner who tipped the jug over. That's what happens to people when they suddenly realize their guilt. They're so distraught they refuse to eat and drink. But after a few days the convict usually cooperates."

"And how can you be sure of his guilt?"

Michelsson stretched and rubbed his neck.

"It was me he attacked. I dressed in the maid's milking clothes when we laid the trap. In the dark he took me for a woman. And besides, he signed the confession."

"A written admission?"

"He confesses to the attempted assault on the farm maid Maria. And to the earlier attack on Hilda Fredriksdotter—"

"But you claimed Hilda was slain by a killer bear!"

"—and the attack and subsequent murder of Jolina Eliasdotter."

"Sheriff Brahe was of the opinion Jolina had taken her own life!"

"Sheriff Brahe has changed his mind."

"And how is that possible?"

"The suspect has confessed to everything. The summer's scourge is over and the guilty man has admitted all his deeds."

Michelsson glanced at Jussi, who lay motionless.

"And what about Nils Gustaf, the artist? Who killed him?"

"In Dr. Sederin's opinion he died following a stroke."

"So you're letting that murderer walk free!"

The constable's expression was full of regret.

"May I look at the confession?" I asked.

"The sheriff has that in safekeeping. And at the moment he's taking a nap. The interrogation has been demanding. And in addition . . ."

Michelsson leaned over Jussi and pulled off the coat I had laid over him. He pulled the dirty tunic down a little and pointed to Jussi's left shoulder, where a stab wound could distinctly be seen in the center.

"But this wound is fresh!" I protested. "It can't have been inflicted by Jolina. He got this when Roope and his gang gave him a beating."

Michelsson shrugged regretfully. I tried to give him the empty water jug but he shook his head resolutely and hustled me out of the cell.

"No prolonged visits. Sheriff Brahe's orders."

The constable's pale blue eyes were cold and expressionless.

When I tried to force my way back to Jussi, he stood in front of me. From his belt he loosened a wooden club, a good foot long with a metal head. With an angry crack I slammed my cane on the floor.

"I'll be back, Jussi! Do you hear me? You won't be left on your own."

"You forgot something," Michelsson growled when I turned round.

With a jerk he tossed my coat over to me.

"But the poor boy's freezing to death!"

"Rules have to be followed," he said dryly. "The pastor has to realize that in here the law applies."

I grabbed my coat and as I hurried away I heard the wooden door being shut and bolted. Bitterness simmered inside me and I had to strain every nerve to contain my thoughts.

Back at the parsonage I swiftly collected together all the evidence Jussi and I had gathered during the summer. There was the mountain plant we had discovered in the barn together with the strand of Hilda's hair, there were the pencil shavings, the boot grease, and the notes we had taken. For a long time, I sat studying the empty glass from Nils Gustaf's kitchen table with the marks of sticky fingers. Eventually I carefully packed it all into a leather bag, which I carried outside to the shed. I had to find a place the mice wouldn't get to. No one saw me climb up a ladder and push it in at the top of the gable wall behind one of the roof trusses. No one would find it there.

64.

I N THE MIDST OF ALL OF THIS, MY DAILY DUTIES HAD TO CONTINUE.
I made a visit to the sick and to the old woman Wanhainen, who
lived with her simpleminded son in a modest farm down by the
river, and suffered so badly from breathlessness that she could barely
rise from her bed. She was unwilling to call a doctor, as that would
cost money she didn't have. But she wanted to talk about her son.
Believing the end was close, she was deeply distressed about how
the simple boy would fend for himself. Throughout our entire conversation he sat staring at us, his eyes watery and his mouth open.
Even though she asked him to close it, it opened again straightaway
and long threads of saliva trickled slowly down onto the front of
his shirt.

I could do little more than listen to her anxieties and anoint her.
She confessed her sins with tears rolling down her face; she thought
she had often been too hard on the boy, she hadn't had enough patience. I could see her repentance was genuine and granted her absolution according to established practice. From my etui I lifted the
wafer and the wine and gave her Communion. Her shriveled lips
sucked noisily and for the moment she seemed to be comforted.

When I prepared to leave, the boy wanted to come with me. I indicated that he needed to stay with his mother, but he took hold of
my coat and refused to let go. He shuffled after me, barefoot, and I
was obliged to return to the farm. I could see he was hungry, but
the woman assured me they had just eaten, though there was no

sign of plate or spoons. I gave him a drink of water from the ladle and tried to slip out, but he was instantly at my heels.

"You'll have to tie him up," the old woman said wearily.

She pointed to a rope by the door. I had taken it to be a dog leash, but it turned out it was intended for him. The woman advised me to secure one end to the settle she was lying on and then to wind the other end round his chest. If I tied the knot at the back, I would have time to get out of sight before he managed to free himself.

I was forced to do as she said. The boy resisted—this was not the first time it had happened to him—but with my adult strength I was able to fasten the rope. Then I wished them both God's peace and set off hotfoot.

When I got home Brita Kajsa came out to meet me in the yard. She was so upset she could barely speak.

"They . . . they searched through everything. Your papers, your things."

"Who did?"

"I wanted to stop them but they said they had the law behind them."

"But who was it, Brita Kajsa?"

"The sheriff, of course. And that pale, ginger fellow he always has in tow."

"Constable Michelsson."

"They took your personal notes. They wanted me to sign for them, but I refused."

Her voice trembled with rage and I nodded pensively.

"That's what I expected."

"What are you accused of?"

"They want to get at Jussi. They knew that we'd gathered evidence. Did they search the study?"

"The whole house! They rooted through the cupboards and chests, in the truckle beds, they even dug around in our bedding."

"Have they gone now?"

Brita Kajsa nodded. I asked her to wait inside the cabin while I slipped out to the shed and groped for the leather bag behind the roof truss. It and all the evidence we had gathered were still there.

65.

THE NEXT DAY I VISITED JUSSI AGAIN IN THE PRISON. HE WAS still exhausted after his ill-treatment and was lying on the hard bench with his eyes closed. Michelsson stayed and rattled the keys. I explained that this time I was here in my capacity as priest and wished to speak to the prisoner in private.

"But the sheriff has given orders that—"

"A prisoner has the right to private confession," I interrupted sternly.

Something in the tone of my voice made him slink away after he had locked us both in.

"Jussi, there's going to be a trial."

He nodded. A secretion had dried in the corner of his mouth, the wound from the tooth I had pulled out still hadn't healed.

"I thought I should stand at your side, Jussi."

"Why?"

His voice was hoarse and weak. His forehead was hot when I felt it, he clearly had a fever.

"Because I failed you. Because I wasn't able to protect you."

"But the pastor—"

"There's one thing I need to know first, Jussi. Can you answer me honestly?"

"Yes."

"Was it you who attacked the girls?"

He stared at me and made an attempt to sit up. I held him down on the bench.

"You were the one, Jussi, who sneaked after Maria and Nils Gustaf the night of the dance at Kenttä. I recognized your footprints, small curled-toe shoes, flat soles, behind the uprooted tree where you hid and spied on them. The person was left-handed like you, Jussi. His feet were small, and the footprints indicated a gait I recognized as yours from all our wanderings together. In addition, you'd crushed the wild rosemary, as is your habit. The sprigs were still on the ground. You crushed them and rubbed them in against the mosquitoes. I could still smell it in your hair the following day."

"But I—"

"What were you doing, Jussi?"

"They . . . I saw them lying together."

"Maria and Nils Gustaf?"

"Mm."

"That must have been difficult for you, Jussi. Maria was your beloved. I have given this much thought. Maybe that was when you decided to hurt Nils Gustaf. Did you visit him and put poison in his cognac?"

Jussi shook his head feebly.

"You must have been filled with rage, Jussi. And also seized by desire. Could it be you felt as though you were a wolf, Jussi? You had to get hold of flesh. So you hid farther along next to the path. While you were waiting you took out a pencil and sharpened it and then you sat there and wrote. What were you writing, Jussi? Poems, maybe? Short rhymes about the woman you love, about her betrayal and deceit. How she's going off with someone else. When you've been sitting there a while, you suddenly see a woman walking along the path. You're inflamed with anger and sorrow and you've been drinking brandy. She's alone and she's approaching the place where you're hiding, without suspecting the slightest danger. You take a handkerchief and tie it over your face."

I stopped speaking and let Jussi suffer. His eyes were bright with fever, the shackles clanked when he tried to sit up.

"Jussi, I know you were prowling around out there all summer. Despite my warnings. You still went there and waited for Maria. In the middle of the night. It looks bad."

"I—I only thought . . ."

"You took your knapsack with you, Jussi. Why? You'd packed some food as well, some of Brita Kajsa's porridge you'd saved from the morning. You took a blanket, a fire striker, and other things people usually take on their wanderings. I think you were intending to leave."

He closed his eyes and nodded.

"Did you want to bid her farewell, Jussi? Feel her body one last time before you departed? Put your hands round her neck and squeeze harder and harder, even though she fought against you? Soon she'd be lying there, motionless. And you'd be done with it all. With Maria, with Kengis, with your stupid old priest. You'd disappear along the paths, never to return."

"No . . ." Jussi moaned.

"It wasn't like that?"

"No," he said again. "It was both of us who . . . Maria and me . . ."

"Who what?"

"We were going to go together . . . to the north . . ."

Jussi made as if to grab my arm but the chains were in the way.

"You must believe me, Pastor. . . . I didn't attack the women!"

"But why didn't you tell me you were planning to leave, Jussi? Why did you want to go without a word? Didn't you trust me?"

"Yes."

"I could have married you both, Jussi. I could have entered you into the book as husband and wife. You're like a son to me, there's nothing I would rather have done for you."

I saw the tears in Jussi's eyes as he turned his head away.

"Jussi, my dear Jussi."

"I hoped that we . . . I was going to tell everyone that the child was mine."

"And where did you think you would go?"

"To Norway."

"But Maria tricked you, Jussi."

"No . . ."

"She never intended that you should be hers. The sheriff found out about it all. He was the one who set the trap, and Maria was the bait. She had Satan inside her, Jussi, she knew what awaited you."

"No, no!"

Jussi's body convulsed in a silent spasm. I could hear noises outside and I reached for my etui and lifted out the chalice.

"Hurry up, Jussi. There's some bread here, baked by Brita Kajsa. The body of Christ given for you. . . . Eat it quickly before they come!"

I broke the soft bread into tiny pieces and fed him. Then I loudly recited the "Our Father," in case Michelsson was standing outside listening. I opened the wine cruet, today filled to the brim with creamy milk, which I let Jussi empty.

"The blood of Christ shed for you. . . ."

"Aah . . ."

"Have trust in our Savior, Jussi. He can set you free."

"The Savior doesn't exist," he whispered.

"Yes, he does."

"I've never been able to believe in that."

"But we've prayed together, Jussi. I've seen your tears during the services, I've seen your heart open."

"I've tried, Pastor. But there's nothing there."

"Jesus exists!"

"He died. He's dead."

"If God is dead, then man is nothing more than a wild animal. You're heading into the abyss, Jussi! Give up this bravado!"

"It's not bravado, Pastor."

"What is it, then?"

"It's just me."

"What do you mean?"

"The bit of me that's left. That's still here even though they nearly killed me."

"But for God's sake, Jussi! Is this the way we should face life's difficulties? By being us?"

"Forgive me, Pastor. I really tried. I wanted nothing more to be your son."

66.

THE PAJALA DISTRICT COURT SAT IN ONE OF THE MAJOR MANOR houses in the parish. The judge, Ragnarsson, was a thin, eagle-like man, with a long nose not dissimilar to a door handle. He sat hunched over as if his neck ached, chewing on a pastille. We greeted one another and he explained that he had recently given up smoking and was using lozenges as a substitute for the pipe stem. Overzealous smoking had led to heartburn and dizziness, and after much agony he had, with his wife's support, taken this difficult step.

"Personally, I find tobacco beneficial to the health in many respects," I said. "American Indians are said to use it as a medicinal plant."

I saw him instantly seized by a craving for his pipe and realized I really should have resisted the repartee. I turned to greet Malmsten the secretary instead, who could barely get up from his desk. He was overweight and had a dreadful cold, sniffling and continuously wiping his nose on a dirty handkerchief. The grunting coughs emitted from his throat throughout the entire trial would invite comparison with the eating sounds of a pig. Malmsten was bilingual, in contrast to Ragnarsson, who came from a coastal community, and I reminded them both that witnesses and plaintiffs in this region expressed themselves primarily in Finnish. It was agreed that the secretary Malmsten would be enlisted to interpret when required.

The prosecutor Anders Petrini was a swarthy gentleman in a redingote and expensive pigskin gloves. Despite that, his handshake was cold. It was obvious he was suffering, after the exertions of the journey and the privations of the north. He complained that the food in the inn was dull, with little flavor, and asked if people hereabouts hadn't started to use pepper yet. I invited him to the parsonage, but he declined when it was made clear to him that I would be the one assuming responsibility for the meal.

"Well, this will soon be over," he said hopefully, eager to leave the place as quickly as possible.

A large number of people had been allowed into the public seats, and extra benches had been supplied, on account of the enormous interest. There was a damp whiff of mothballs—several of the burghers were wearing suit jackets and pressed trousers in the hope they might make the acquaintance of the distinguished guests. I was wearing my cassock but had removed my collar to indicate that on this day I was not representing the church. Sheriff Brahe arrived in his usual ebullient way, hailing people to left and right, keen to emphasize his importance. After all, it was he who, thanks to his wealth of experience, had managed to catch the miscreant. The public packed into the benches, awkwardly shuffling their boots on the floorboards as if they were in church. The iron stove in the corner was replenished and soon the emanating heat made people ease their collars and loosen their ties. The wife of one of the merchants brought out a fan in the Spanish style, and started fanning herself ostentatiously. She wanted to show the assembled gathering that she was the first woman in Tornedalen to have visited Santiago de Compostela in the footsteps of Saint Brigid.

Now a clatter could be heard from the front door and the defendant was brought in. His hands and feet were in chains and he was pushed up to the defendant's place rather than making his way under his own steam. The constable walked on one side of him and a burly prison guard on the other. The chains were removed and I could see ugly abrasions on his wrists. Jussi was supposed to stand up during the trial, but I begged that in his weakened condition he be allowed to be seated. A scratched old wooden stool was found for Jussi to sit on, his legs trembling. The ill-treatment had clearly taken its toll and if anything he had lost even more weight. His eyes had sunk into their sockets, giving him the look of a timid animal. Unfortunately, the agonies he was suffering gave him the appearance of the monster in human form the public expected to see. A wolf that had had its teeth pulled out. Ragged and cowed.

Ragnarsson stroked his prominent nose several times, as though he were sharpening it, and then opened the proceedings. The farmhand Johan "Jussi" Sieppinen was accused of the murder of the maids Hilda Fredriksdotter and Jolina Eliasdotter. In addition, he was accused of the attempted assault on another girl, and of the theft of money from the deceased artist Nils Gustaf at his dwelling at the Kengis foundry. Thereupon Ragnarsson handed over to the prosecutor Petrini, who stood up and gripped his lapels. For a moment of dramatic silence, he looked at Jussi, who avoided his eye. He solemnly cleared his throat, picked up a sheet of paper, and read out more or less word for word the description of the offenses.

Jussi was presented as a cunning and violent criminal. He had lived a life apart from others and avoided mixing with his peers, all in order to hide his true personality. Under the shy and timid exterior lurked a villain who couldn't hold back his murderous tendencies. Strong sexual desire combined with unbridled savagery within drove him onto the road to seek out women walking on their own. Under cover of the forest trees he unleashed his depravity and forced himself upon the cow-girl Hilda, after which he strangled her and concealed the body. Following the summer dance at Kenttä, he attacked the unaccompanied maid Jolina Eliasdotter, who managed to escape. He later strangled her to prevent her from identifying him. Finally, he attacked a person he believed to be the farm maid Maria, but who in fact was Constable Michelsson in disguise. Thanks to the intervention of Michelsson and Sheriff Brahe, another act of violence was averted and the felon was arrested.

I watched Jussi while the allegations were read out. He showed no reaction, stared at his knees, and appeared to be in a different world. Only when Petrini had finished and sat back down did Jussi shake his head, almost imperceptibly. Ragnarsson turned to me and asked for our response to the accusations. I declared that the defendant pleaded not guilty. I pointed out that in Sheriff Brahe's earlier opinion the first girl had been slain by a killer bear and the second had taken her own life. My statement was placed on record, whereupon the real battle could begin.

It was a pitiful affair. The prosecutor called various witnesses, all of whom confirmed Jussi's odd behavior, how he stared at women during my services in church and how he had forced himself on Maria during the dance at Kenttä. The foundry worker Roope was called to testify that Jussi Sieppinen had previously accosted Maria.

"She met Jussi on the marsh path once. I saw him try to take her bucket of fish."

"Where were you then?"

"Farther along the same road. I saw Jussi start to tug at Maria. He was wild and crazy. She dropped the bucket and just screamed. I took my belt off and threatened him and he backed off then. If I hadn't arrived, who knows what he would have done?"

I refuted all of this with facts that should cast doubt on the allegations. No witness had seen Jussi commit the murders. Nothing found at the scenes of the two crimes pointed to Jussi, and Sheriff Brahe himself had initially assumed it was the work of a killer bear. Instead, a number of things suggested a different perpetrator. There was a risk that the true culprit was still at large.

I lifted up the leather bag I had stowed away in the shed, and continued:

"At the time of the attack on the maid Jolina Eliasdotter I examined the ground where the offender had hidden behind a tree. There I discovered minute wood shavings and drew the conclusion that they had come from a pencil sharpened with a knife."

I took a folded piece of paper out of the leather bag and held it up.

"It transpired that the shavings came from a type of pencil that cannot be purchased in any of the shops here in the Pajala region. However, I did manage to ascertain that such pencils are sold in Haparanda. Sheriff Brahe is one of the few people here to possess such a pencil."

Brahe hastily looked around. With an expression of sneering disbelief, he tried to throw me off balance, but I would not be checked.

"On Jolina Eliasdotter's clothes there was a mark that appeared to come from shoe grease. There is a very characteristic smell, and the wax is for sale in certain shops only. The price means that only the well-to-do are in the habit of purchasing it. And Jolina Eliasdotter told me that the man who attacked her was a *herrasmies*, a gentleman."

I unfolded another handkerchief and invited those nearest to me to smell the shoe wax from the scene of the crime.

"And I would like to refer to an old student friend of mine from Uppsala, Dr. Emmanuel Sundberg. He has made an unparalleled discovery that will probably be of immense assistance in future police work. May I ask that all those present observe their fingertips?"

The prosecutor wanted to interrupt me, but Ragnarsson let me continue.

"As you can see, there is a pattern. It may be compared to a whorl of tiny ridges. Emmanuel Sundberg has called these papillary lines. Each time we touch a smooth surface we leave an impression of these papillary lines. They might seem invisible, but if you coat them with very fine powder—ash, for example—a clear pattern emerges."

I brought out a small etui and opened it. From it I carefully lifted out a glass by spreading my fingers inside it. In this awkward way I held the glass up for all to see, without touching the outside.

"Dr. Emmanuel Sundberg's research hitherto has demonstrated that each fingerprint is unique for every individual. By comparing the prints from this glass, for example, with a suspect's fingerprints, the culprit could be tied to the scene of the crime. This glass bears such fingerprints. The glass comes from the artist Nils Gustaf's kitchen table the morning he was found dead. The last person to visit the artist drank out of this glass. And with the help of the papillary patterns I have managed to obtain the visitor's identity."

"What does this have to do with it?" Petrini exclaimed.

"The defendant is alleged to have stolen money from the artist. So the court needs to know that these fingerprints do not belong to Jussi Sieppinen. Let me show you one more object. . . ."

Once again I ducked down into my leather bag and brought out a cardboard portfolio. I gingerly opened it and held up a small shiny glass plate.

"I would like to show you this as well. This is what is called a daguerreotype. Nils Gustaf had an apparatus that could reproduce the image of a person through the direct action of light. A lens to refract the rays, working with particular chemical substances, can produce a light-portrait. I am holding just such a portrait in my hand now. It was mounted in the deceased artist's daguerreotype apparatus and must have been taken the evening he died. The image was therefore never developed. But earlier Nils Gustaf had demonstrated to me how the process worked. By exposing the plates to mercury vapor I have been able to produce a glass slide of the man who visited the artist the same evening he died."

With more than a touch of triumph, I held up the glass plate.

"Well, who is it, then?" A buzz went through the room as people stood up to see better. "Who is it a picture of?"

"The image is very much like a portrait, but so small that a magnifying glass is needed to discern the detail. If the judge would like a closer look, I have brought—"

"Papillaries and light-pictures!" Petrini exclaimed. "Whatever next! Heavenly revelations?"

Several opponents of the revival burst into jeers on the benches, while others merely looked puzzled. Sheriff Brahe tried to grab the glass plate out of my hand, but I managed to put it back in my pocket. The drinking glass, however, I wasn't able to shield, and it was snatched from me and passed around the benches so that the papillary patterns were very soon completely obliterated. The court adjourned for deliberations, and when it reassembled Ragnarsson called for silence. The murmuring abated and the gathered company once again had to squeeze themselves onto the crowded benches.

In a firm voice Ragnarsson declared that he had considered the defense's submission. And scientific methods could of course be adopted in the investigation of criminal cases. But the scientific methods must be in general practice. And never before to his knowledge had a trial involved either papillary patterns or light-pictures. The court must therefore disregard these and the evidence must not be included in the transcript or be allowed to influence the verdict.

The plaintiff Jussi Sieppinen crumpled and the tendons in his neck tensed as he bowed his head. Those closest to him thought they heard him mumbling eerie Sami rhymes. I stood up angrily, pulled out the glass plate, and held it up so that everyone could see a dark figure in the middle. I pointed to the human shape in silence, then folded it back into the handkerchief and looked around. My eyes were so bitter that a shudder went through the crowd. At the same time a commotion could be heard at the front door and everyone turned to look. An old woman dressed in black pushed into the room, elbowing her way through the throng.

"A blessed miracle!" came her shrill cry. "He healed me! Hallelujah! He took me in his arms and gave me back my life, brought me back from the valley of the shadow of death. . . ."

The old woman shoved forward to the podium, but the pastor was not her goal. Instead she fell to her knees, tears streaming down her face, in front of the defendant, Jussi Sieppinen. She managed to press her wet face against his thighs before the guards arrived to stop her. She struggled fiercely and kept up her howling as they dragged her away.

"Jussi gave me back my life, Jussi came with the miracle of healing, hallelujah. . . ."

People on the benches were glancing furtively at one another. Everyone could remember the old woman coughing up blood after a service and Jussi carrying her out onto the church steps. There was no doubt, she had been dying. "*Noaidi* arts," people were whispering, their horrified gaze on the gaunt youth sitting with half-closed eyes.

Sheriff Brahe tried to laugh off the tension in the room, getting Michelsson to join him in a strained titter.

"Tee-hee, tee-hee . . ."

"God help us," I mumbled in Finnish to Jussi, slumped on his stool.

The secretary Malmsten did not bother to translate.

67.

I LEFT THE COURT BITTERLY ANGRY. A NUMBER OF THE SPECTATORS grabbed me, stood in my way, and wanted to delay me to discuss their thoughts on the trial. I broke free and shouldered my way through the crowd. Jussi had been unshackled for the duration of the hearing but was clapped back in irons before he was taken away by the guards. I managed to give him an encouraging smile, but my face must have looked more like a gaping skull.

The verdict would be announced later, and I knew the outcome was uncertain. Jussi had sat there shaking uncontrollably at times, a sign, I knew, of starvation and ill-treatment, but to the onlookers it appeared like fear and guilt. He had denied all the charges but refused to look anyone in the eye. The badly healed scars, the bruises, and the nearly-toothless mouth he covered when he spoke made him appear an untrustworthy tramp. An orphan Lapp boy who couldn't control his actions and had given in to greed and sexual appetite. My feeble attempts at logical reasoning had fallen on deaf ears.

At first I intended to go home, but my feet seemed to think differently. In the end, I took out the stiff priest's collar, fastened it round my neck, and set off briskly in the opposite direction. I had an uncomfortable feeling someone was following me, but when I turned around, the path was deserted. I soon saw the farm and entered the yard. The cabin door opened and the mistress looked out.

"They . . . they're all at the trial," she blurted out.

"I know."

"Both the master and his sons. They've been called as witnesses."

"I wanted Maria to be a witness," I said, "but she didn't appear."

"I'm afraid Maria is ill."

The woman nodded toward the bedroom. The door was ajar, to let in the warmth from the kitchen, and I could see that it was almost dark inside.

"She can't tolerate the light, so I've covered the window."

I went quietly up to the doorway and listened. There was no sound, not even of her breathing.

"It's the pastor," I said softly.

There was a movement; she must at least be awake. The air was stale and musty, a sour smell that put me in mind of a tannery, meaty hides soaking for a long time in acids and animal fat. I quietly closed the door behind me so the mistress wouldn't hear our conversation. I let my eyes adjust to the dark. The faint gray daylight filtered through the gaps around the blanket hanging over the window.

"It's the pastor," I said again. "I've come straight from the trial."

She didn't answer. In a couple of strides I was at the window and pulled down the blanket to let the daylight stream in. Her large pupils were directed toward me and then instantly shrank to the size of pinheads. Something seemed to have happened to her skin, it was lackluster. Her face was gray and swollen, dark bags had appeared beneath her eyes. I had the impression she had been waiting for someone.

"I have such a headache," she whimpered, and turned away from the light.

Her work clothes were lying on a stool. I lifted them off and sat down beside her. She needed the dark, just like the bedbugs do when you lift the sheet. There was no doubt that she felt ill.

"Jussi is going to be condemned," I said.

"Who?"

"Jussi, the man you betrayed."

"I can't . . ."

Her voice was indistinct, almost slurred, and for a moment I thought she was drunk. But it was the headache, and her breathing was so shallow that scarcely any air passed her vocal cords.

"This is serious now, Maria. You could have saved him. You could have told the truth, and then he would have walked free."

"I don't understand. . . ."

I wanted to grab hold of her and give her a hefty shake, like a money box from which you shake coin after coin.

"You and Jussi had arranged to meet that night. You tricked him into thinking you would go away together. Why don't you want to admit the truth?"

Her body began to rock from the waist up, as if she were about to break in two, and I held her firmly, pressing my simple wooden crucifix against her brow.

"In the name of Jesus Christ, admit what happened. You disclosed to Sheriff Brahe that Jussi was going to pay you a visit!"

She tried to push the crucifix away, and retched as nausea overwhelmed her. I knew that Christ was torturing her demons and I brusquely held her flailing arms.

"You must drive Satan out, Maria. You are Jussi's last hope. He wants to take care of the child, Maria. He wants to do it all for you!"

With surprising force, she knocked my hands away, and the crucifix slipped out of my grasp and onto the bed. She snatched it and flung it violently onto the floor. I picked it up, wiped off the dust from the floor on my cassock, and discovered to my annoyance that it had an ugly new crack across the crown of thorns. I put it back in my breast pocket, swiftly fell to my knees, and clasped my hands.

"Get thee hence, Satan! In the name of the Holy Trinity, flee this woman's body—"

As the nausea rolled over her, she closed her blue eyes, her face twisted in a grimace, and she shook her head.

"It's too late."

"It's never too late for Jesus Christ," I insisted in my earnest priest's voice, so often adopted in the course of my duties. "The Lord's arms are always open, ready to embrace you too. But you have to take the last step yourself, Maria. Try to overcome it, Maria, try to force it out."

Maria's body contorted, she raised her upper body and her thighs, and then came the hideous scream, a knife piercing the eardrums, by all that is holy, and Jesus Christ burning in my breast pocket, the smell of excrement and blood escaping from under the quilt, and I saw something black slithering away, a rat's tail, a lizard-like hind end, a movement under the bed, quick as lightning. All the time I prayed and drowned out the guttural grating of the devil, pursued it with divine oaths until it fell silent, until the girl was finally filled with calm.

The expression on her face had changed. For a moment I thought she was well, that now she could save Jussi from his pain and suffering, that the miracle had happened by the power of the Holy Ghost.

"Thank you," I murmured. "Thank you, Almighty God. . . ."

When I offered her the wafer, she thrust my hands away so hard that it was crushed and fell in crumbs onto the sheet.

"Go," she said hoarsely.

Then she turned to the wall and pulled the stained sheet over her head.

68.

LUCIFER. THE FALLEN ANGEL EXPELLED FROM HEAVEN'S all-embracing light. From the whiteness of the heavenly kingdom that is so difficult to picture. Like the glare of the sun on frosted snow at the end of March, the strongest light in the land of the north a person can ever see. A sparkling brilliance from all sides, lifting the traveler a yard up from the earth's surface, on the frozen crust itself, so white and pure not even skis leave marks behind them, black ski tips against sun-snow writing paper across the glittering infinity, and the only sound the crunch of crystals.

And now he wanders here among us on the shadowy autumn paths. Lucifer, the spurned, who wants to extinguish the light of the revival. He follows my steps and I feel his presence behind my back. When I turn, he instantly takes cover, and the only movement is the wind playing in the branches.

"Dear Jesus . . . Lamb of God . . ."

DARKNESS GATHERED IN THE treetops, the outlines blurred in the drizzling mist. In my hand I carried the leather bag with my evidence, my assembled thoughts. Worth nothing. I couldn't save Jussi, that much was painfully clear to me. While the real killer would walk free.

Instead of returning home to the parsonage, I continued to the lofty building of Kengis Church. Drips falling from the shingle roof made it look as though the church were weeping. I followed the wall toward the sun and breathed in the faint aroma of the roof tar the crofters had applied that summer. The wall paneling was sawed by hand, the nails forged at the foundry, the timbers dragged here by horses from the wide expanse of forests. The church had been built with the wood and iron of this region. Hardy workers' hands had chiseled and hammered it into shape. And now it stood here like a mother's open embrace. A rib cage protecting the heart of the parish. I walked all the way around it, placing my hand against the wooden wall at intervals, and I thought I could feel a gentle warmth coming through my palm. At the entrance I drew out the huge key and unlocked the door. The hand-forged hinge creaked as I stepped into the shadows of the porch. I carried on into the semidarkness of the church itself, the late afternoon light filtering through the windows and making the pews look like the timbers of a ship. In the mighty silence I walked reverently up to the altar. No parishioners sat shuffling the soles of their shoes, no one coughed or sneezed, no one whispered or admonished little children. No clocks rang. And yet I thought I heard a voice speaking. There were no words, just a sense of solace. I touched the altar cloth with my forehead, felt the handwoven pattern against my skin, smelled the lingering scent of sweetgrass, *Hierochloe hirta*, from the linen cupboard. I quietly sank to my knees, my head bowed, and clasped my hands. The prayer was slow to come, but I allowed myself to remain in the emptiness. Eyes closed, I faced my darkness, my despair. I was here, in the valley of the shadow of death. Powerless and abandoned, like a child. Not even tears came. I had done my utmost, but it was too little. I could only feel the autumn, this dark towering immensity surrounding me.

Then the darkness vanished too.

Time stopped.

But for a mouse.

A mouse in the church vault, a tiny, intruding whisper.

I looked up.

I turned my head slightly, to where the scratching was coming from.

And at that moment, the world around me exploded in a flash of yellow light.

YELLOW, GOLDEN, GOLDEN YELLOW. Vivid golden light, yellow, yellow, yellow. I could hear a noise inside me too. Within my body. A sound as though submerged, an underwater bang. Glittering gold and pattering water. And now the pain flooded in, the hideous pain, and I sank to the floor, the whole church on top of me.

The next blow struck my back. Hard across my shoulder blade, which split apart and fused together, all at once. And now the pain made me want to throw up, now that it had closed in. I rolled onto my back, defenseless, my limbs twitching like a beetle's legs trying to find a foothold, but there was only air. Over me loomed a specter, pushing his knee against my chest, tearing at my coat and searching through my pockets.

"I knew . . . it was you, you devil," I gasped.

A fist pounded mercilessly against my mouth, my lips were beaten bloody on my teeth, and a dull saltiness filled my mouth. Strong hands snatched something out of my inside pocket, unfolded a piece of cardboard, and triumphantly held up the glass plate.

"You left too many clues," I continued.

The specter leaned forward, his eyes black holes.

"Shut up, bloody priest!"

Constable Michelsson's voice was full of hate. His knee forced me down as I lifted my head and tried to fill the air with talk.

"Who would suspect you? I can address you informally, can't I, now we know one another? A blameless officer, with strikingly fine handwriting, so correct and polite. But we humans all have a weakness, a flaw. And this has led to your undoing."

"What do you mean?"

His voice was sharp, but I had piqued his interest. He wouldn't kill me. Not yet. I nodded and slid my fingers into my coat pocket.

"Love, Michelsson. Consuming, despairing love. What is it about women that scares you so?"

"Be quiet!"

"You wanted to get close to them, but something prevented you. You came home from the mountains in the summer, after investigating the reindeer-stealing with the sheriff, and then lust led you into the abyss. You went out into the forest and violated Hilda Fredriksdotter and murdered her. The urge had been aroused and now it only intensified. Soon after, you assaulted the maid Jolina Eliasdotter, but she managed to wound you and escape. You were afraid she had recognized you, despite your mask, and later you strangled her. But the whole time your eye was on Maria, the prettiest of them all."

"She has nothing to do with this."

"But with her it was different. You wanted to be with her. But you had to have an excuse to speak to her. You told her that, being the constable, you'd found out who the murderer was, the one who'd attacked the women. Wasn't that what happened?"

"Everybody around here thought it was Jussi."

"During one of your encounters, Maria mentioned something to you about Nils Gustaf's fortune. While he was painting her, she had seen where he hid his money. It whetted your greed and you couldn't stop thinking about this hoard. In the end you managed to obtain a strong poison."

Michelsson shook his head.

"The pastor forgets that the cottage was locked from the inside!"

"That's true. It took me a long time to solve that puzzle. We knew someone had visited Nils Gustaf on the night of his death. I found fingerprints on both brandy glasses and took them home, as you recall. When you and Brahe paid me a visit later in the parsonage, I kept your glasses and compared the papillary patterns. And there was no doubt, the prints from Nils Gustaf's cottage were identical to yours. I also managed to decipher your signature in the artist's receipt book. You presumably told him the purpose of your visit was to arrange to have your portrait painted. At the appropriate moment, when he turned his back or maybe when he went outside to empty his bladder, you pocketed his money. It must have been a very considerable sum. You knew that when he eventually discovered the theft, suspicion would fall on you. But you had already drawn up your plan."

"There are no witnesses to this!"

"While you sat there drinking French brandy, Nils Gustaf rigged up his daguerreotype apparatus. He made everything ready and asked you to pose, without moving. But you didn't understand what he wanted to show you, that your picture could actually be captured on a glass plate. Meanwhile, you surreptitiously poured prussic acid into his glass of brandy."

"Pure blather!"

"I got to know a chemist while I was in Uppsala, a fervent admirer of his Swedish predecessor Carl Wilhelm Scheele. It was Scheele who discovered this substance. My friend taught me how to test for its presence by adding iron salts. A compound is then formed with a bright color known as Prussian blue. There was some brandy left in the glasses when I examined them, and I managed to detect the poison in one of them. To my horror I realized that Nils Gustaf had been murdered."

"But you didn't say anything to Brahe!"

"No, for a long time I thought that he was the one who did it. Only after a great deal of painstaking consideration did the pieces fall into place. Let us return to that evening in the cottage. Before Nils Gustaf could develop the glass plate you bade a hasty farewell and left with your pockets full of his money. Nils Gustaf locked the door for the night, as was his wont. Suspecting nothing, he drank from his glass and immediately began to feel unwell and lay down on his bed to rest. The following day he was found dead in his cottage, which was locked from the inside. Death was assumed to be from natural causes. And you, Michelsson, thought that you had committed the perfect crime."

I watched the constable's face blanch, his skull outlined like a pale death mask. And then the veins swelled, the skin darkened, a surge of blood welled up from inside him and took control, and with a low, gurgling growl he bent over me. I was horrified by his transformation. The human was forced out by something else, a being from another world, sulfurous and incandescent. I sensed shadows circling against the church roof with tails lashing and jaws agape, I heard Beelzebub's war cry from a thousand throats. As Michelsson closed his claw-like fingers around my neck, I fought with all my strength. He squeezed, his mouth was open, his teeth bared, juices dribbling from his maw. I twisted my hips and tried to wriggle away. But he pushed all his weight onto me and all his strength into the thumbs digging into my throat. All the time I sought his gaze, but it was utterly empty. Like a pike's. Coal-black water surrounded by the flames of hell. And I looked at him as the women must have done before he extinguished their gaze. He was too strong. I couldn't get away. But despite the unbearable pressure, I still resisted. Here was one thing that distinguished me from the women. My white, well-sewn clerical collar. It ran all the way round my neck, and it was sufficiently broad and stiff to afford me a breath of air.

My hand grasped the narrow metal shaft of the object in my pocket and with my thumb I managed to open the blade. I swung it sharply up toward his arm. The edge was razor-sharp and the blade of my pocketknife went straight into the flesh between the two bones of his forearm. He froze, not understanding at first what had happened. Then his grip slackened and I felt the weight of his body keeling over to the side. With a frantic heave I pushed him over. I kicked hard—my legs, albeit short, were resilient from miles of wandering—and I tried like a wildcat to strike his stomach. He rolled backward toward the altar rail, looking around for a weapon. On the altar stood the heavy wooden cross. He grabbed it and swung it violently toward me. At the last moment I backed away and felt the cold rush of air across my face as it hurtled past. Next to me was the baptismal font. A silver bowl sat in the wooden pedestal. Desperately, I took hold of the edge and managed to prize the bowl loose. I raised it as a shield against the next blow and Michelsson's cross hit it with the clang of a bell.

"Jeeesus!" I screamed. "JEEEESUSSS . . ."

Over and over again. My voice was strong, a voice crying in the wilderness. It forced its way to the church door, down across the parvis, out over the meadows, and up to the foundry, to all the crofters and the maids. Could no one hear me? Michelsson hit out once more, but I parried with the bowl. In my other hand I was still holding the pocketknife.

"JEEEEESSSUUUSSSS . . ."

Michelsson's arm was dripping blood. With a neat kick he hit the baptismal bowl, which clattered away into the darkness, and I fell backward. He took a run at me for his next kick, this time aiming for the side of my head. I tried to crawl away to save myself, but I couldn't move my legs. He rushed toward me, raised his boot, and kicked with all his might. I twisted away but was far too slow, and I desperately held up my arms, shut my eyes, and waited for the heavens to fall.

There was a dull thud, like the sound of someone chopping wood. Michelsson's flailing body sprawled on top of me and he rolled sideways before the next thump was heard. In the air above us hovered the heavy altar crucifix bearing the mild gaze of Jesus, and for a moment the afternoon sun shone through the window straight onto our Savior's face, and the cross gleamed as if it were made of gold, before hammering down for the third time on the constable's body. He howled with pain, and maybe with fear too. Like a devil in dark clothes he jumped to his feet and limped away between the pews.

Jesus was picked off the floor once again and turned his face to me. I could see that the crossbeam had come off. But Jesus was still holding his arms wide, as if he wanted to fly, float up to heaven. With a sweep he took up his position back on the altar. Only then did I see that a woman had been holding him. It was Milla Clementsdotter. She was small and thin and wearing a threadbare tunic. Her breathing was fast, and she watched me as I lay groaning in my delirium.

"Milla, you saved me. . . . My beloved Milla."

Her lips parted but there were no words. She raised her arm and made the sign of the cross to symbolize the Holy Trinity. Then she turned and padded away in her soft-soled curled-toe shoes. Everything was so strangely quiet. I heard no footsteps, as if she were a dream.

I struggled to my feet, limbs aching, and dizzy with pain. A piece of wood was still on the floor. It was the crucifix's lost crossbeam, which I laid on the altar, thinking that it might be possible to glue it back on. I limped across the church to the door, holding on to the pews for support.

69.

THE VERDICT AGAINST JUSSI SIEPPINEN WAS ANNOUNCED ONE bleak and rainy morning. The defendant was found guilty of the murder of Hilda Fredriksdotter, the attempted rape and subsequent murder of Jolina Eliasdotter, the attempted assault on a farm maid, and the theft of Nils Gustaf's money. The prosecutor's evidence and the defendant's signed confession were considered sufficient in the case. The sentence was death by beheading.

I received the news at home, where I lay bedridden on the truckle bed. Under me I had something hairy and warm with an aroma of anthill and bark. It was the newly tanned skin of the she-bear. When the farmers who killed her found out I was ill, they gave it to me as a tithe.

"It has healing powers," they said. "He who lies on a bearskin can never die."

After hearing about Jussi's death sentence, I lay there numb. Brita Kajsa sat down by my sickbed and stroked my forehead gently. I tried to lie completely still, my body aching after all the blows and kicks. By some miracle no bones were broken, but my front teeth felt loose. I could wiggle them in my gums and suspected they would never be firm again.

"Beheading," I said in despair.

"You did the best you could, dear priest."

"I couldn't save Jussi. He could have been our son, Brita Kajsa!"

"You fought as bravely as a lion."

"Give me some paper. I need to appeal. Fetch the inkpot!"

She pressed her palm against my chest when I attempted to sit up.

"Later," she said firmly.

Her light hand massaged my sore ribs.

"Was it really Michelsson who beat you so badly?"

"He and no other."

"Was he the one who attacked the women too?"

"I'd suspected him for a while. But the murderer was left-handed and I noticed Michelsson used his right hand when he wrote. For a long time, I couldn't understand how it could all tie together. But then I remembered something Juhani Raattamaa told us."

"What was that?"

"During his visit in the summer Raattamaa said that he forced his left-handed pupils to write with their right hand. And Raattamaa had been Michelsson's teacher. That was why Michelsson wrote in such a strange way, with his left hand clenched behind his back."

Brita Kajsa nodded grimly.

"We have to report him."

"To whom? I don't trust Sheriff Brahe."

"You gave Michelsson a knife wound in the arm."

"Should I have turned the other cheek?"

"I mean it's proof that you were attacked."

"Michelsson can claim I attacked him first. That he was simply exercising his right to defend himself. His word against mine."

"But are you going to let the monster walk away? Michelsson is like the killer bear, a beast who's had the taste of women's flesh."

"Michelsson is afraid of me now. In all likelihood he'll soon leave our region."

"Then he'll just carry on his evil deeds elsewhere!"

Of course my clever wife was right. But what could I do? Now that Jussi had been sentenced, Michelsson could no longer be prosecuted for the crimes put to the court.

"I heard he visited Maria yesterday," Brita Kajsa said.

"They plan to go away together. I think it was Maria who told Michelsson where Nils Gustaf hid his money. And then the idea of murder came to him."

"He must be the devil," Brita Kajsa said.

"I've thought so too."

"He tried to kill you!"

"But he could never have killed the revival. Even if I had passed away there at the altar, it would have lived on. They will never touch the revival movement."

Brita Kajsa quietly squeezed my hand.

"I don't think we've seen the final battle," she said after a while.

"What's on your mind?"

"I think it will get worse. I have a foreboding of something dreadful."

"It won't be so bad."

"I dreamed of blood. Of blood and burning buildings. And you were there. You saw it all happen but couldn't stop them."

"Who?"

"They were like ordinary people, but they called themselves angels. They were ashen-faced, as if they'd been consumed by lightning bolts in heaven."

"Do you mean Kauto—" I began.

Abruptly she put a finger over my sore lips and held it there anxiously as she looked over her shoulder. But there was no one there.

IMMEDIATELY AFTER THE JUDGMENT was passed, the convict Jussi Sieppinen was taken in chains to the prison convoy that would transport him to the crown prison in Umeå. I never managed to say goodbye. He left behind the Bible I had lent him. I would rather he had kept it, so that in his death cell he could have leafed through and found the word of God in the pages where I had so often sought comfort.

I lay in my sickbed looking gloomily through Jussi's Bible for something to give me strength in this hour of need. Ecclesiastes: "All is vanity and vexation of spirit." Undeniably true, but not what I needed to hear just now.

While I was searching through the thin pages my fingers could feel that the margin was strangely rough. I stopped and ran my fingers over it. I could feel tiny wrinkles and dents as if the paper had been creased by someone browsing carelessly. Perhaps they might disappear if I pressed the book under some heavy weights? A few pages on I discovered a similar roughness. My irritation grew. I always looked after my books; who could have been so remiss? From the beginning I had taught Jussi to turn the pages carefully, one of my conditions if he wanted to come anywhere near my library. Maybe it was the clumsy fingers of the prison guards who creased the Bible during their inspections? I was about to carry on browsing but I stopped short. I sat as if paralyzed, just staring.

"Selma! Fetch a pencil!" I shouted.

My youngest daughter came in carrying the inkpot.

"No, a soft lead pencil," I explained. "Bring the one that's on my desk."

She returned at once. I looked at the page in the Bible and hesitated; it went against the grain to sully God's words. But I placed the lead against the paper and started solemnly shading the rough surface. With light movements I observed the grooves being transformed into small white symbols.

When I peered through my magnifying glass I could see that they were letters, and they were forming words. For safety's sake they were written in Sami. Jussi had remembered the trick I had shown him and he must have used something sharp to scratch with, maybe a nail.

That whole evening, I sat in my bed, deciphering the text. I had scarcely time to eat the evening meal and when Brita Kajsa tried to speak to me, I was in another world. Jussi had written about his life. About his childhood, about the darkness he lived in before I found him. About his sister Anne Maaret, who was called the runt, with her sore bottom. How she stayed behind when he left.

I lowered the magnifying glass and rubbed my tired eyes. I had never read anything like it. It was the introduction to a book. A depiction of reality as it looked here in the north, far from all the lecture theaters and auditoriums.

When an ordinary, simple Sami boy could achieve this, others would follow. Farmers and reindeer herders, hunters and fishermen, maids and lumberjacks. One day they would be able to tell the story of their lives themselves. Instead of spending money on brandy, they would buy books, gather in the evening to talk to one another about the light of heaven, about the plants of the forests and meadows, about what it meant to be a human being.

My wife was sleeping deeply when I crept under the quilt. Outside it was dark, except for the points of a few sharp stars poking through the ceiling of the sky. They would never kill Jussi, I thought as I lay there. Somehow I would save him.

70.

Winter was at the door. Violent northern winds brought thick banks of clouds and constant rain across the land of the north. Despite the aches and pains in my body, I forced myself out into the dreadful weather and along the slippery wet marsh path to Pajala. I approached the large villa where the sheriff had his lodging and office, knocked on the door, and entered.

Constable Michelsson was sitting at the desk, writing. He stiffened at the sight of me and lifted the metal nib from the paper. His lips tightened over his teeth; he dried the ink with the blotting paper and gave me a cold stare.

"I'm looking for the sheriff," I said.

"He's traveling."

A blazing stove spread a fierce heat throughout the room. I pulled out my portfolio, unfolded the rain-soaked cloth I had wrapped round it for protection, and opened it.

"I have our writ here. Jussi Sieppinen hereby appeals to the Upper Norrland Court of Appeal against his judgment. I would prefer to see Sheriff Brahe receive our application for onward submission."

"In the sheriff's absence it is I who takes care of the formalities."

Michelsson's voice was restrained and rather hoarse. His pale blue eyes showed no emotion when he saw my injuries. My battered lips had started to heal, the bruises on my neck were turning yellow.

"In that case, I'll have a written receipt."

I placed the piece of paper on the desk. Out of one of the drawers he took a pad and filled in the receipt with his right hand, holding his left hand behind his back as Raattamaa had once taught him. His fingers were long and slender and the pen nib made a rasping scratch, his handwriting as always very neat and elegant. Much more graceful than my own. He quickly laid the blotting paper on top and ran a roller over it, before handing me the receipt. I made a move as if to take it, but instead I swiftly grabbed his wrist and twisted it. He shrieked, tried to wrest his arm away, and at the same time swung at my hand with the other arm.

"Oh, is Michelsson in pain? Maybe your arm's been hurt?"

He stood up and made as if to hit me again. I let go and he pulled his arm back.

"I don't know what the pastor's talking about!"

"Maybe about our . . . shall we call it a discussion about a glass plate? In Kengis Church, if my memory serves me."

"The pastor is mistaken."

His tone was proper and polite. And furthermore, he was the constable. In a courthouse he would appear very convincing.

"My wife Brita Kajsa obviously knows about your attack. She is prepared to testify against you."

"I really don't understand what the pastor is talking about. The perpetrator of the summer's brutal attacks has already been arrested and sentenced. Soon he'll lose his head as well. And if the pastor slanders me he can expect to be reported for false allegations."

Was there a little smile? A sardonic little smirk?

"You want to kill again," I said. "You've had the taste of it."

"I request that the pastor leave me and my future wife in peace."

"Wife? Do you mean Maria?"

Michelsson nodded stiffly.

"We don't consider the pastor an appropriate wedding officiant, so we mean to settle in a different place very soon."

"With the money you stole from Nils Gustaf."

"Would the pastor please leave now? I have a great deal of work to do."

He gestured awkwardly toward the door.

"You're bleeding," I said.

I must have opened up the knife wound on his arm. A dark patch had appeared on his shirt and a blood-red drip landed on the desk.

"Not at all," he said.

In a practiced movement he reached for the blotting paper and pressed it onto the desk. The drop of blood was soaked up and disappeared. With a flick he tossed the blotting paper into the stove and watched the flames consume it, while I slowly buttoned up my coat. In silence I went out into the teeming autumn rain.

FROZEN AND SOAKED, I returned to the parsonage and entered the warmth. Brita Kajsa met me at the door and said in a low voice:

"The pastor has a visitor."

Something in her voice made me chary. I went inside to give my usual God's peace greeting. On a stool sat a very young, thin Sami woman. She didn't answer, but she raised her eyes toward me and I stopped abruptly. Milla, was my only thought. Milla Clementsdotter . . .

But then I saw that it wasn't her. I had only just met this woman, somewhere considerably closer than Åsele.

"I found her out in the cowshed," Brita Kajsa whispered in my ear. "She was hiding in the straw, but I noticed the animals were disturbed."

"In the cowshed?"

"I think she's been milking the cows, to drink. She seems to have been there for several days. I've asked her, but she refuses to answer. I haven't got a word out of her."

I approached the woman cautiously. Her tunic was very worn and seemed to be sewn together from old rags. When I took her hand it was icy cold.

"God's peace," I said again, this time in Sami.

She didn't seem to have heard. But then she squeezed my hand with unexpected strength, her fingers pressing so hard that the cartilage clicked. I wanted to pull away, but it felt as though she had hooked herself on. The fixed expression on her face was frightening, the small nose like a little snout, the arch of the eyebrows, there was so much in her that reminded me of an animal.

"I thought at first you were Milla from Åsele," I said, as kindly as I could.

She quickly shook her head.

"But now I recognize you. You were the one who defended me in the church, you saved my life."

I gently held her, like a block of ice, in my arms, warmed her in my embrace. With a mouse-like whimper she relaxed and I felt her body come to life and breathe more deeply.

"*Mun lea . . . lea . . .* I am . . . I am . . ." she stuttered in Sami.

Her voice was surprisingly harsh, as if it had suffered injury, broken by screaming.

"I know who you are," I whispered. "Your name is Anne Maaret. You're Jussi's sister."

The woman smelled strongly of marshland and sweat, after presumably walking for mile after mile.

"She didn't want any food," Brita Kajsa said, almost reprovingly.

"But now she does. Don't you, Anne Maaret? Now you'd like something to eat, wouldn't you?"

I led her to the kitchen table and Brita Kajsa brought a bowl of porridge and a spoon. I sat down on a chair next to her and watched the woman lean forward and sniff at it like a fox would. Unaccustomed to a metal spoon, she held it up between her thumb and forefinger and studied her distorted reflection on its shiny surface. With slow, inexpert movements, she divided up the porridge with the edge of the spoon and shoveled the pieces into her mouth from the rim of the bowl. It was like watching a toddler try to eat. Maybe her hands were too cold.

I turned to my wife, who seemed uneasy. She could see me rubbing my painful knuckles after the woman's strong grip.

"It's Jussi's sister," I said. "Her name is Anne Maaret."

Brita Kajsa saw the porridge being ravenously devoured.

"Would you like more?" she asked. "More to eat?"

Anne Maaret did want more. While I filled up the bowl from the pot, Brita Kajsa began to make a bed for her on the floor. She would have the same place Jussi had had.

When I rose the next morning, Anne Maaret was not in her bed. Wondering where she could be, I went into my study, and there she was, sitting on the floor in front of the bookcase. She had opened a book and her lips were moving silently. None of the household would have dared to enter my study like this. No one except Jussi.

She looked up when I sat down in my chair, almost as if it were her room I had strayed into. The book she had picked was one I knew very well, it was Bishop Sundell's autobiography—no great literary masterpiece, in my opinion.

"So Anne Maaret can read?"

She nodded.

"Was it Juhani Raattamaa who taught you? Or one of my catechists?"

"My brother taught me."

I was caught by surprise.

"Jussi? When did he have time for that?"

"When he came on his visits."

It made me think of the long periods when Jussi had simply disappeared. He had been away for several weeks, sometimes a few
months, only to return just as unexpectedly.

"How did he teach you?" I asked.

"He drew it in the earth."

"Did he write the letters? And did he then make the sounds?"

She gave a quick nod. I could see it all before me, a boy and a girl
going down to the mountain brook and there, by the rippling
water, is a spot with a narrow clay bank. Jussi takes a stick and draws
some zigzag-shaped letters.

"A," he says. "Aaaaaa . . ."

"Aaa," she echoes.

"Aannnnee . . ." He sounds the letters, pointing with his stick to
the strange curlicues.

"Aaannne . . . Anne!"

"Jussi would have made a good catechist," I said, half to myself.

"Mm."

"What did Anne Maaret do up there?"

"Looked after our mother and father."

"But Jussi never talked about them. I thought he was an orphan."

"Mother and Father are dead now. They died in the summer."

"My condolences."

"They were drunkards."

She said it in a thin voice, almost airless. I felt such tenderness for
her and wanted to take her my arms.

Even though I had written about it in *The Voice of One Crying in the Wilderness*, I found it difficult to speak about. Father's drunken yells when some domestic trifle aroused his anger. Mother, who had to manage for months on her own while he was away on business down by the coast. Petrus and me, who heard the blows when he returned; that was the worst of all, when he hit Mother and we couldn't help her, when we took cover under the kitchen table like frightened puppies.

"Has Anne Maaret maybe come to tell him of their death?"

"He already knows." She shut her eyes for a moment. "I came to fetch him."

"But Jussi is . . . Maybe you haven't heard? Jussi has been convicted of having used force against women."

"He's innocent."

"I know," I said quickly. "I was Jussi's advocate during the trial, but regrettably the court didn't listen to me."

"Where's my brother now?"

"He was . . . Jussi has been taken to Umeå in a prison convoy. We've appealed against the judgment. There's a chance he might be pardoned."

"Pardoned?"

"Didn't Anne Maaret know? Jussi was sentenced to death by beheading. I am sorry."

The girl looked at me, her eyes empty.

"He didn't do it," she repeated. "It must have been someone else."

"Yes," I agreed weakly.

"The man who hit you in the church. It's him."

Her pupils were like black buttons. Something distended crawled out of her neck band, a fat cattle louse.

"But how can we touch him? How do we catch a constable?"

"He's the one who should be beheaded, not my brother."

"Perhaps Anne Maaret would like to wash up?" I interrupted, glancing at Brita Kajsa. "I'll ask the farm maid to heat the sauna."

The girl's odor was sharp and very noticeable and it filled the study. Wet bogs, rancid animal fat. A smell preferably not experienced indoors.

"There are clean clothes as well. We'll have your own clothes washed and get rid of the lice on the hot sauna stones."

She groped for my hand and tried to squeeze my hand again. But this time I squeezed hers first.

"Lice are like sins," I explained. "We're all afflicted by them from time to time."

THAT NIGHT I DREAMED about Milla Clementsdotter in Åsele. She was standing outside the church, it was winter, and a large crowd of people were there waiting, parishioners who wanted to attend the service. I stepped up to the church door with a bunch of keys and put one of them in the lock. But it was too small. I tried another. It was too big. Increasingly nervous, I put one key after another into the lock. I tried every one in my large bunch, but none of them fit. Now the people were beginning to show their irritation, accusing me of being a fraud, of tricking them into coming. They showed me that the building was in poor condition, and now I could see they were right. The walls were starting to rot, the roof was threatening to fall in, several of the windows were broken. Terrified, I backed away and asked the congregation to move to safety. But no one listened to me, they pushed forward and grabbed weapons to intimidate me, logs, stones, someone drew a knife. When I feared it was all over for me, I suddenly heard a clear and penetrating voice. It drowned out the mob, and I noticed everyone turn round. It was Milla. She had climbed onto a pew that someone had put there, and now she was speaking to them all. I stood next to her on the pew and discovered that she was taller than me, and while she spoke she grew even taller and turned into a giant woman. She gave a sermon, she cried out until the building shook, she displayed a holy wrath I had never encountered before. And the congregation before her were spellbound by her words. I saw men and women clench their fists and howl like wolves, but instead of attacking her, they showed that they all stood by her side. Ordinary, poor people, who started to grow in stature like her, changed into giants. Only I stayed my normal size, and soon the pastor was the smallest person in the congregation. Then I heard a crash like a roll of thunder, and when I turned I saw the whole building sway in its foundations and with a protracted rumble come crashing to the ground.

71.

BY THE NEXT MORNING ANNE MAARET WAS GONE. I WAS informed that she had been seen leaving the sauna in her freshly washed clothes, and after that she disappeared.

"She doesn't seem to have spent the night in here," Brita Kajsa said. Her bed was untouched.

I felt anxiety mounting, but was unsure what to do. Brita Kajsa handed me a piece of boiled fish from the previous day. The flesh was white and flaked away as I pinched it off the bones with my fingers.

"What was the pastor dreaming about?"

"Dreaming?"

"You made the whole bed rock with your twisting and turning. And you were talking as well."

"Talking?"

"'Milla,' you said several times. 'Milla, Milla.'"

"I was dreaming about the revival. I felt the force in the crowd of people. How it built up, how the anger of these poor people sought an outlet."

"And what happened?"

"I don't remember."

"Yes, you do."

As so often, she seemed to see right through me. I tried to laugh but it sounded more like a cough.

"The church collapsed," I muttered.

"Was it destroyed?"

"It was already rotten. And then it fell."

I licked the fish grease from my fingers and took a deep breath.

"Do you think, dear wife, that the revival touches women more deeply than men?"

"It often seems that way to me."

"But why? Is it maybe that women are closer to God?"

"Men have more to lose."

"And why is the spread of the revival stronger among the poor than among the rich?"

"The rich have more to lose."

"Men and the rich have just as much to gain as anyone else," I protested. "Do we not all seek eternal life?"

"Is this another day of doubt?" she said, feigning sternness.

"I was just thinking—what if the oppressed start to stand up and raise their voice, will the world really be a better place?"

"Do you mean that women in the congregation no longer have to be silent? Maybe the pastor should train a female preacher."

"Would men listen to a woman?"

"The pastor listened to Milla in Åsele. It was her speech that inspired the revival, as we've said before!"

"Yes."

"A woman's words."

"I only mean . . . that mankind appears to be facing perilous times. That lurking there, deep down in its cave, is a wakened monster."

"Surely the pastor doesn't believe in dragons?"

"Brandy dragons, thieving dragons, vain dragons. What times will the coming generations face, our poor grandchildren and great-grandchildren?"

"A time called the 1900s."

"Nineteen is a strange number. Made up of a one and a nine. The lowest and the highest."

"Like life."

"And war."

She didn't reply, and I could see from her face I had unsettled her. She had already finished eating and I had barely started. I wanted to qualify what I had just said, explain I had slept badly, but she had already risen from the table and was by the cupboard, getting on with her morning tasks. I could feel my unsteady hand and taste the bitter acid rising in my throat.

72.

THE WET WALLS OF THE UMEÅ TOWN PRISON ROSE IN THE autumn gloom. Inside, Thorstensson the prison warden sat in his office going through the correspondence, which concerned among other things the winter requisitions. Grain, footwear, prison garb lined against the winter cold. And a letter from a lecturer who had heard that a young Sami man was going to be beheaded and who was very eager to keep the skull. He enclosed an addressed transport box filled with salt for this purpose.

One of the prison guards came in with his nose dripping. He was called Holmlund, a country boy from Sävar who was always scared of making a mistake. He stood shuffling his boots, unwilling to speak before he was addressed, whipped off his cap, and pressed it to his chest.

"Well?" Thorstensson muttered.

"She's here again. The sister of the condemned man."

"The Lapp girl?"

"She's brought food for the prisoner."

"What sort of food?"

"Bread and butter."

Thorstensson looked out of a window equipped with iron bars, just like the prison cells.

"How has the prisoner behaved?"

"Without reproach," Holmlund answered.

"And you've made sure he's been kept separate from the other prisoners?"

"As Thorstensson wished."

"Well, let them see each other. Go through the food in case there's something hidden in it."

"Of course, Warden."

"Does she come every day?"

"Every day. But she . . . alas, I fear she steals the food in the town."

"Is Holmlund certain?"

"She's so poorly dressed. How could a Lapp beggar afford to buy butter?"

"Good. It's good that Holmlund is vigilant. Go!"

Holmlund saluted and returned to the guardhouse by the interior wall. The Lapp girl was there with her bundle, wearing her ragged tunic. Her face was dirty and from her clothes came the sour smell of smoke. With a stern expression, Holmlund turned the bread out onto the inspection table and systematically broke it into crumbs. He hesitated at the lump of butter, but then seized it in his hand and pressed so hard that the golden fat squashed between his fingers. No unauthorized objects to be found in there. He quickly scraped together the sorry mess into her dirty cloth and licked his own fingers.

"The warden permits a visit."

"Thank you," she whispered, and curtsied.

He escorted the sister to the cell of the condemned man Jussi Sieppinen and unlocked the door. The prisoner was hunched on the bench with his legs drawn up under him, as thin as she was, both of them a head shorter than the lanky Holmlund.

"Handcuffs!"

Jussi held out his emaciated arm and looked pleadingly at Holmlund.

"Not so tight," he said. "Please, Holmlund, not so tight."

Meanwhile, Anne Maaret had kneaded together a large ball from the bread crumbs, spread it with a good knob of butter, and offered it to Holmlund, who picked up the clattering chain, fastened one end to the cell wall, and screwed the fetter round Jussi's wrist, not very tightly at all. Full of anticipation, he accepted the ball of bread and took up his position on guard outside the cell door. Almost reverentially he munched on the farmer's bread and the smooth, freshly churned butter. Inside he could hear the brother and sister speaking in Lappish, that animal language that made every Christian shudder. He could hear the chains rattle as the prisoner began to eat. Some might think the sister's gifts were pointless. The poor lad was soon going to lose his head anyway.

Inside the cell, out of sight of the guard, Anne Maaret took hold of her brother's arm and deftly spread the butter round his bony wrist on both sides of the handcuff, making his skin oily and slippery with the grease.

When Holmlund unlocked the cell door and announced the end of the visit, the Lapp girl was sobbing inconsolably, her face hidden in her hands. The youth was leaning forward on the bench, apparently praying to higher powers. His face was contorted, saliva running from the corners of his mouth, his hair hanging in front of his face. Holmlund decided to leave the prisoner chained up until he had calmed down. He slammed the door, turned the key twice, tried the handle for safety's sake, and established that the door was locked. Then he escorted the sobbing Lapp girl along the stone corridors through the interior and from there to the outer door. She just shook her head helplessly when he tried to speak to her, and it was with some relief that he watched her squelch away in her wet curled-toe shoes along the cobbled street. But the butter had really tasted good, even if it had probably been stolen. Authentic Västerbotten farmers' butter.

73.

ONE MORNING AT THE END OF OCTOBER, THE CROFTER'S WIFE Elina Mukka was walking along the uneven village path from Kengis to Pajala. The recent night frosts had made the ground slippery and her smooth-soled boots skidded into the holes several times. She decided it might be easier to walk to the side of the wheel ruts, a short distance into the trees. That was how she discovered the body, lying almost hidden from sight in the undergrowth. The right arm was stretched out as if wanting to embrace the earth, the left bent behind its back. The fingers splayed out in the frostbitten grass had a bluish pallor. But what horrified Elina most was the head. It lay some distance away, completely separated from the body. The truncated windpipe gaped like a mouth in the congealed blood, the cap had come off, the hair on the scalp was thinning, almost bald, and at the back of the head was a crater of splintered bone and tissue.

"*Jumalan auta* . . . Lord help us . . ." she wailed, the hem of her apron pressed to her mouth. She recognized the man; his eyes were half open and the irises seemed to be covered by a thin, glassy film.

It was the village constable who lay there. Constable Michelsson.

I RECEIVED NOTIFICATION OF THE death from one of the crofter boys. Despite winter's imminent arrival, the boy ran barefoot, quick as a weasel, and as soon as he had delivered the message, he scampered off to the next farm. I hurriedly put on my boots and coat and made my way to the site of the discovery. A dozen of the closest neighbors were already assembled, doffing their caps, bowing and curtsying. I pushed through the crowd and looked at the dead man. They had moved the body, arranged him on his back, and done their best to clasp his rigid fingers over his chest. They had placed the head where it used to sit, the face covered by the deceased's own cap. I lifted it up and noted that a number of blows had been needed to cut through the neck and that in addition there was a deep wound to the back of the head. The act of violence had been carried out with some sort of ax. The blow to the back of the head had presumably occurred while the unsuspecting victim had been walking along. The angle indicated that the perpetrator had been shorter than the victim.

"Have you summoned Sheriff Brahe?"

"He's on his way."

In spite of all the trampling feet, I could follow the trail of blood where the body had been dragged from the village path into the bushes. The beheading had taken place in here, judging by the amount of blood. It took me only a moment to detect that the perpetrator had been waiting behind some fir trees. The moss was flattened and on the left side of one of the tree trunks I found the long, narrow indentation of something pressing on the ground. From the shape I guessed it was an ax-head.

The perpetrator had carried the ax in his left hand and leaned it against the tree while he waited for his victim. The footprints were from smooth-soled curled-toe shoes. They were small, and I felt my stomach tighten.

I swiftly went through Michelsson's pockets. There was a dirty handkerchief, some coins, a pocket watch with its brass chain attached. The murderer could hardly have been after valuables. In his coat I found a pencil and some folded pieces of paper, on which, when I opened them, I saw his elegant, neat handwriting. They were short verses of some kind, he had clearly written poems. When I read them, the scent of a predator made my blood run cold. The poems were about his victims.

I straightened my back and looked around at the assembled people.

"There's nothing more we can do," I said grimly.

With bowed head I prepared to leave.

"But . . . isn't the pastor going to pray for the dead man?"

"Yes . . ." I mumbled, "of course I am."

I carried out my priestly duties and then hurried home before Sheriff Brahe could arrive. The parsonage was silent, the waterfall roaring, and none of the servants were to be seen. I walked over to the woodshed, where I hesitated, before finally going in. The ax was standing in its usual place, leaning against the block. When I examined the finely forged ax-head bearing my initials, I could see brown spots. At first glance they appeared to be rust, but when I looked more closely, I saw short strands of hair sticking to them. I stood there for some time, breathing deeply. Then I carried the ax to the sauna and scrubbed it with a brush until every speck was gone.

CONSTABLE MICHELSSON'S FUNERAL SERVICE was held at Kengis Church, with me presiding. His mother came from Pello, a tall thin woman, her face gray with sorrow. It was she who had insisted that the region's famous parson should hold the service.

"My son spoke well of the reverend. He often talked about becoming a priest himself."

"Is his betrothed coming from Pello?" I remembered to ask.

"No, he was never betrothed," his mother said. "He was always so shy of women, the reverend understands. Such a fine and sensitive boy."

Her voice broke and she bent forward in desperate, dry-eyed weeping. My funeral address was about the absolute arbiter we would all meet one day. He who would scrutinize our every deed when we stood before him as transparent as glass, our dark sides all revealed. And then I dropped three scoops of earth and sent him off to hell where he belonged. Sheriff Brahe gave an impassioned tribute to his fallen colleague, speaking of the difficulties of a profession in which it was easy to make enemies. A policeman's courage and sense of duty, however, would never waver. It was loyal and dedicated officers like Constable Michelsson whom we had to thank for the fact that the violent criminal of the summer was now imprisoned in Umeå. And Michelsson's murderer would soon be arrested too, that Brahe could promise, in a voice charged with emotion.

Then the coffin was carried to the churchyard and lowered into the cold autumn earth. I should have taken his skull, I thought, boiled it clean, sent it to a museum in Stockholm.

Back at home after the burial, I washed my hands fastidiously. They felt sticky after all the handshakes with the sheriff and the innkeepers.

74.

O N THE MORNING OF THE EIGHTH OF NOVEMBER 1852, A LARGE
group of Sami arrive in the north Norwegian town of
Kautokeino. The mood is wild and militant. The Sami profess to
belong to the revivalist movement the pastor started, and with
Christian battle cries they unharness the reindeer from their sledges.
From a nearby fence they break off stakes for weapons and head toward the house of the merchant Carl Johan Ruth. Shouting at the
top of their voices, they storm into the courtyard, where they find
Ruth with Sheriff Lars Johan Bucht. Their leader, Aslak Haetta,
lunges at the sheriff, screaming.

"Repent!"

Without waiting for a response, he attacks the sheriff with his
cudgel. Bucht tries desperately to defend himself and a violent
struggle ensues. Haetta comes close enough to sink his teeth into
the sheriff's nose, and bites so hard that the nose comes off. Bucht
tries to draw his knife, but Haetta gets hold of it and stabs the blade
deep under the sheriff's arm. Several of the Sami rush forward,
among them Ellen Skum, they assail the sheriff with blows until he
collapses to the ground. He manages to get up and staggers across to
the servants' quarters, but there Aslak Haetta catches up with him.
They hold the sheriff while Haetta sticks his knife into his back,
right underneath the shoulder blade.

Meanwhile, the merchant Ruth attempts to help Bucht. He grabs
a stake from one of the women, but he is overpowered and so badly
beaten that he too collapses. Several of the women, Ellen and

Kirsten Spein, Berit Gaup, and Marit Sara, continue battering the fallen man with cudgels until they have crushed his skull, cleaved his neck, and rammed splinters of bone into his brain matter. Finally, Thomas Eira sticks a knife into the merchant's chest and with Ole Somby's help forces it into his heart.

In this time, Sheriff Bucht, despite his severe injuries, manages to escape into the house. He staggers up the stairs and locks himself into the guest room on the first floor, where, exhausted, he lies down on the bed. Mons Somby follows him and manages to break down the door with his ax. The violence continues mercilessly.

"He's still moving his eyes," he screams down to the others.

Both men and women charge upstairs to strike the by-this-time-defenseless body. Aslak Haetta stabs a knife into the sheriff's chest but the blade gets stuck in the sternum. His brother Lars hammers it in up to the hilt with a log and blood pours out of the wound as the last spark of life is extinguished.

While Ruth is being attacked, his wife escapes to the parsonage with the youngest child in her arms. She enters screaming.

"They're killing Ruth!"

The priest Fredrik Waldemar Hvoslef rushes there in an attempt to help him. He finds the lifeless merchant in the courtyard, surrounded by creatures dressed in pelts, more like wild animals than people, beating the fallen man's body with stakes. They soon realize Hvoslef is there and overpower him with blows as he hurriedly tries to take off his spectacles to protect his eyes from the broken glass. The priest is beaten by men and women and even children, who spit in his face and rip up his linen shirt. Aslak Rist stands in front of him as this goes on, shouting.

"Make amends, you child of the devil, you murderer of souls!"

With violence and imprecations, they try to drive the devil out of Hvoslef. Finally, they take him to the parsonage, where the occupants have barricaded themselves in. The attackers break the windows to crawl inside, and violent floggings begin. For several hours a number of those who took cover there are bound and dragged around the floor amid loud cursing. While Aslak Rist keeps watch, the women carry out the violence. They set upon their victims, lashing at their heads and faces most of all, until they swell up and are covered in wounds, and many of the victims lose consciousness. The pastor prays the whole time in a loud voice, aware that the attackers appear to calm down somewhat when they hear the name of Jesus often enough.

After a while a bright light is seen on the kitchen wall, coming from outside, and Aslak Rist takes Hvoslef out onto the front steps. Merchant Ruth's house is in flames and Aslak points to it.

"There, now you can see the unrepentant burning in hell."

Some of the assailants hastily make their way to the shop, to carry off any valuables as loot before the whole lot is ablaze. This occasions a temporary pause in the floggings and Hvoslef tries to talk calmly to the afflicted. He is impressed by Ruth's wife, who is standing there holding her little girl in her arms, maintaining her composure, even though she has just seen her husband killed. But the attackers are soon back and the violence recommences.

It is almost four in the afternoon before the counterattack comes. A small group of nearby Sami have gathered in defense, among them Ole Thuri, and Johannes and Isak Haetta. Now they organize a concerted attack on the assailants. A full-scale battle with stakes ensues, in which the rebels Ole Somby and Marit Spein are so badly injured that they later die, and the other assailants are beaten unconscious.

The Kautokeino uprising is finally over.

———

IN TOTAL, THIRTY-THREE PEOPLE are tried for murder, arson, assault, intimidation, and theft. Aslak Haetta and Mons Somby are sentenced to death and the execution is carried out by beheading. Others are given long prison sentences. Many believe that one person bears particular blame for this senseless bloodbath and should also be condemned, namely the one who started the revival movement that inspired the perpetrators of this outrage. The parish priest in Kengis.

The revival is facing its downfall.

75.

At dawn, the condemned man Jussi Sieppinen was woken in his cell in the Umeå town prison and offered a cup of coffee and a slice of bread. He refused to eat anything and appeared to be very apprehensive about what lay ahead. The barber cut off the back of his long hair so that the neck was bare for what was to come. Two prison guards led him in chains to the inner yard. In the grainy early morning light, a handful of men stood next to the block, their expressions taut and impersonal. The prison warden Thorstensson fumbled to get his metal-rimmed spectacles out of their mother-of-pearl case and placed them at the end of his nose. In a morose voice he read out the adjudged verdict of the district court and the letter dismissing the appeal to His Majesty the King.

The prison chaplain took a step forward. In a detached voice he recited the "Our Father" and preached severely about God's greatness and the opportunities for the forgiveness of sins. Even the most heinous of sinners who humbled themselves could enter the Good Father's embrace. Thus there was one last possibility for him to open his heart before those gathered here, and meet his Creator with a cleansed mind. Was there, therefore, anything Jussi Sieppinen wanted to say before the procedure commenced?

The Lapp youth squinted at them from under his long fringe.

"I'm a woman," he said in his broken Swedish.

The men looked at each other, uncertain how to react. Despite the shackles, the condemned man managed to grab his prison trousers and pull them down slightly. A cursory glance established that the penis appeared to be missing.

Thorstensson stood for a moment as if paralyzed. Then he cleared his throat and ordered the prison doctor to inspect the prisoner's body. In uncomfortable silence the doctor crouched down and after some time was able inform the prison warden that the prisoner lacked male genitals. On the other hand, the upper body bore small, tightly bandaged female breasts.

"What the devil!" Thorstensson exclaimed.

An indignant murmuring broke out among the men. The solemn atmosphere they had tried to maintain was gone. The executioner, who had hitherto concealed himself in the adjacent doorway, peeped out to see what was afoot. Thorstensson turned awkwardly to the prisoner and asked point-blank who he was.

"I am someone else," came the reply.

"So you're not Jussi Sieppinen?"

"Not anymore."

"What do you mean?"

"I have transformed. I've made myself someone else."

"That's not possible!"

"Yes, it is. For a *noaidi*."

One of the prison guards, the farmer's son Holmlund from Sävar, had misunderstood the situation and now resolutely went into action. He brought out a blindfold and tied it around the prisoner's eyes, as previously instructed. The executioner took this as the go-ahead and came out of the doorway with his heavy, sharpened ax. The prison guards rendered assistance by positioning the prisoner's neck over the slit in the chopping block. With distracted gestures, Thorstensson indicated that the executioner should wait. He frantically waved the chaplain, the doctor, and the black-clad witnesses toward him. In low voices they started discussing what could have gone wrong. Was it possible that the wrong prisoner had been brought out? But the prison guards were adamant that there had been no mistake. This person was the one who had been sitting in the death cell, and there was currently no one else in the prison condemned to death. They all gazed upon the tiny prisoner without being sure what they saw. The hair was long and lank and there was no facial hair to speak of, but that was often the case with Lapps. Their men and women were strikingly alike to outsiders. It would look bad for the prison officers if this came out, not least in view of the recent Lapp uprising in Kautokeino. How would it look if a Sami murderer were seen to outwit the judiciary? Perhaps they should simply . . . let the executioner get on with it?

Guttural sounds could suddenly be heard from the kneeling prisoner. Eerie hooting and humming rose up as if from the underworld. It sounded so ungodly that it made the hairs stand up on the necks of the assembled gathering, it sounded like an animal's curse, a prolonged and threatening magic spell.

"*Oooh-ooh-aaah-oooh-ooh . . .*"

The prison chaplain began to pray in a clear, loud voice to drown out the heathen chanting. The prison guards put their fingers in their ears while the executioner took up his position and raised the terrifying ax. With clenched teeth, Thorstensson turned to the doctor, who glanced nervously at the chaplain.

What should they do?

Yes, what the hell should they do with the Lapps?

76.

THE SNOW FALLS SLOWLY. WE LEAVE WET, BLACK FOOTPRINTS along the paths. Every day we walk as far as we can. If we are lucky we find a hay barn. Otherwise we curl up together under a dense fir tree, so close we manage to survive in each other's warmth.

I will go wherever you want.

And that is what has happened.

The night before we left, we went to the parsonage. We stood in silence for a long time while the pastor held our hands.

"How does Jussi regard the child?" he asked.

"We're going to take care of it," I answered.

"Even though it's not yours?"

"It's mine now."

The pastor turned to Maria, with her stomach bulging in her milking clothes. She had not had time to put on anything better.

"Hadn't you intended to become Michelsson's wife?"

Maria looked down.

"It was the demons. But now I've stopped listening to them." She looked the pastor in the eye. "It's Jussi I want."

The pastor moistened his lips.

"I will remind you that, as far as we know, Jussi Sieppinen is still in prison in Umeå. The man at your side, consequently, must be someone else."

He looked at me, inviting a response.

"The pastor can write 'Josef,'" I said.

"Josef Sieppinen?"

"No, just Josef. That's enough. It goes well with Maria."

The pastor leaned forward and changed the name.

"Do you take each other as husband and wife?"

"Yes," Maria whispered. "Yes, we do."

Gravely he dipped the pen into the ink and registered us in the book of marriages. Right next to each other.

"And where are you planning to go?" he asked in an unsteady voice.

"North," I answered. "To the coast of the Arctic Ocean."

"'Family reported to have moved to Norway,'" he wrote down.

With a deep sigh the pastor laid down his pen. He took hold of my arm and examined the sleeve.

"You've washed it."

"Yes," I admitted.

"The left sleeve is clean, but not the right?"

I couldn't answer. He put his nose to the cloth and took a deep sniff.

"Bear," he muttered. "It smells of killer bear."

I wriggled out of his grasp, embarrassed. He took a Bible from the table and handed it to me, the same one he had lent to me in prison. I leafed through it and saw that he had managed to find my hidden writings.

"Keep writing," he said.

"Thank you," I whispered. "Thank you, dear pastor, I shall."

He threw his arms around me; it felt as though he wanted to say more and his chin quivered against my shoulder. Then he turned away and wiped his hands on his trousers as if they were wet. As if he had just washed them.

"We'll meet again, won't we?" I said uncertainly.

He met my eye, his gray cheek glistening with tears.

"It will hardly be in this world."

"But thank you. Thank you for writing me into the book. Without that, I wouldn't have existed, Father. . . ."

That was the last word he heard me say. Master. Pastor. The man who became my father. I knew I would never see him again.

We crept silently out into the night. When I closed the parsonage door I felt Maria huddle closer to me. We stood quietly in the cold air. She, called a whore by the villagers. And I, the murderer.

Maria's stomach was big and I could see the tightness of her kirtle. I carefully embraced the woman who was now my wife. From her pocket I heard the jingling of coins, and I murmured, "Sorry," my hand in front of my damaged mouth.

"It was Nils Gustaf's money," she whispered. "But now it's mine."

Cautiously, she pulled my hand away from my lips and looked straight into my ugliness. Then she snuggled closer, so sweet that my heart was racing. And then she kissed me. My beloved wife. Whom I would walk beside for the rest of my life. The soft skin of her neck, the tip of my tongue against hers, a love so strong it reached through the darkness of this northern land.

WE KNOW THEY WILL come after us, that they will never stop searching. Every day we wander farther north. We face the cold, the wind, and the deepening darkness. We disappear like animals into the silence of winter. The snow covers all our tracks.

EPILOGUE

THE PASTOR LARS LEVI LAESTADIUS HAD HIS PORTRAIT PAINTED a number of times during his lifetime. An oil painting by François-Auguste Biard portrays him instructing Sami people amid towering ice hummocks in fanciful Arctic surroundings and dressed in wolfskin and a top hat. The painting was exhibited in the Salon de 1841 in Paris. Better known is the charcoal drawing by the French artist François Giraud, which exists in various reproductions. On Laestadius's chest hangs the medal of the Legion of Honor, awarded to him by the French for his contribution to their expeditions. The painting started in this story, however, has never been found.

Since no one knew of a photograph of the pastor, it was a great surprise when in the summer of 2016, during restoration work on the parsonage in Pajala, a photographic glass plate was discovered hidden between joists in the roof. After so many years the image on the plate is remarkably well preserved. The figure of a man in dark clothes can be seen staring at us, sitting outside the church building in Kengis, now long since demolished.

A life story entitled *Mu eallin* (*My Life*) was published in northern Norway around 1890 and is one of the earliest known Sami documents, written from within Sami culture. It has in large part inspired this novel. The author's name is unknown.

The registers in which the pastor entered all the parish births and marriages were kept for many years in Pajala. But on February 21, 1940, the war unexpectedly struck. Soviet planes flew over Swedish territory when the navigators mistook Pajala for the Finnish town of Rovaniemi. Forty-eight high-explosive bombs and hundreds of incendiaries rained down on the village. One of these exploded in the churchyard, only a few meters from the grave of the pastor and Brita Kajsa. Others made craters just outside the church and damaged several more buildings. By some miracle nobody was hit, the only casualty being one of the village horses. The parish registers fortunately survived intact, but the event aroused great concern. In order to afford the important documents greater protection, the archive was moved north to the village of Muodoslompolo. But only one year later, on November 24, 1941, an accidental fire destroyed the parsonage in Muodoslompolo. The registers in which Laestadius had written the parishioners' names were lost forever in the flames.

The author of this book grew up a stone's throw from the old parsonage in Pajala, where Lars Levi Laestadius lived with his family until the day he died in February 1861, age sixty-one. According to reports he was lying on a bearskin.

AFTERWORD

ALL SAINTS' DAY NOVEMBER 2017, AND I'M WALKING TO PAJALA Cemetery to light candles on my parents' graves. Winter has arrived and the paths are covered with a thin layer of snow. In the darkness thousands of lanterns twinkle with fairy-tale magic, as if all the stars in the firmament have descended among us. Here and there in the dark I make out shadows bending by gravestones and I see the flicker of flashlights.

I carry on to the older part of the churchyard and soon find my way to the famous tombstone where Lars Levi Laestadius and his wife Brita Kajsa lie. Lars Levi—who started the revivalist movement that bore his name and still today has tens of thousands of followers in Sweden, Finland, Norway, and the United States. And yet the old couple's grave is in darkness. I take my last lantern, sweep the snow aside, and place it on their stone.

OVER TIME, MANY PEOPLE have shown an interest in the charismatic pastor. Märta Edquist, Per Boreman, and Bengt Larsson have all written very noteworthy biographies. The pastor's collected sermons have been translated into several languages and are still in use within the movement. Laestadius was a frequent essayist in the fields of botany, philosophy, theology, and Sami mythology, and many of his letters and articles have been preserved, including his autobiography in the magazine *Ens ropandes röst i öknen* (*The Voice of One Crying in the Wilderness*). Thus, for those so inclined, there is a wealth of material to delve into. Over the years he has been portrayed fictionally in novels and plays. Sometimes as the fire-and-brimstone preacher; other times as an exalted mystic or leader of a social revolt. The pastor's personality was full of contradictions, not always to his advantage. Perhaps it is precisely these many facets that appeal to us. He was aware of his own shortcomings and throughout his life he battled with the "devil of ambition" tempting him with worldly success. Who wouldn't want to have a newly discovered plant named after him and be immortalized in botanical registers? Election to the Royal Swedish Academy of Sciences was within reach, but perhaps he was deemed too difficult to handle. The pastor's favorite hymn was "Wretched Worm and Wanderer That I Am," and despite his celebrity he made a point of dressing as simply as the Sami and settlers he preached to. His fiery temperament probably came from his father, who is said to have distinguished himself with "good cheer, practical jokes and flashes of wit,"* but who could also be violent under the influence of alcohol. It is clear that this upset his sensitive son. Throughout his life the pastor had difficulty with male authority, and his abhorrence of brandy presumably had its roots in his childhood.

On the other hand, he had great respect for his mother, whom he saw as devout and loving. It is no coincidence that it was a simple, poor Sami woman who inspired him to start the revivalist movement. The woman sought him out while he was holding a service in Åsele. Their conversation gave him "a foretaste of heaven's joy," as he writes in his autobiography, and he continues: "I shall remember penniless Maria for as long as I live and hope to meet her in a happier world." After their encounter his sermons took on "a more elevated tone" and soon the revival movement was in full swing.

---

* *Ens ropandes röst i öknen* (*The Voice of One Crying in the Wilderness*).

Maria, or Milla Andersson Clementsdotter, as she was actually called, can be found in the parish registers. Her life was hard; as a child she was placed with a foster family while her parents kept moving with the reindeer herd. She was reviled and beaten and she attempted to flee back to her parents dressed only in her underclothes, but was forced to return to the foster family. As an adult she married, had a daughter, and probably moved to Norway. But there the trail ends and no one has managed to trace her thereafter.

The Sami boy Jussi in the novel similarly runs away from difficult conditions at home and becomes a wanderer, *matkamies* in Finnish. The word appears in hymns and in many Finnish ballads as well. A *matkamies* is alone in the world and is often burdened by great sorrow, by the pain of living. He leaves his everyday life behind and is lost in his solitude, carrying the little he needs in his knapsack. He has no goal, the wandering is his purpose. The English equivalent is a tramp, a vagabond. When Jussi meets the pastor a different wandering begins, into education, into reading and writing. Over the last hundred and fifty years all we Tornedalians and Sami have made such a journey.

The pastor championed people's education and progress, but at the same time he felt a grave apprehension about the future. He gave prophetic warnings: "Firstly, we will have a war in the whole of Europe on our hands. Secondly, there are major revolutions to come."

Elsewhere he writes: "If old governments fall, there will always be some ambitious blackguard who will rise to power through popular appeal. And thus there will be no scarcity of tyrants. . . ."

Perhaps it was the vibrations of the impending twentieth century he could feel. Trenches, tanks, Hitler and Stalin, and two devastating world wars.

During the pastor's lifetime scientific racism began to rise, something that would lead to genocide and the death camps. No one yet knew anything of this, but it does seem strange that the pastor took part in the hunt for skulls himself. In his ministry he committed the deceased to their final resting place, but that didn't stop him, on two occasions, from assisting while graves in the abandoned churchyards in Enontekiö and Markkina were plundered. What the researchers wanted access to were "Lapp crania," which were much sought after at this time. Those who are interested can read more in Olle Franzén's excellent book *Naturalhistorikern Lars Levi Laestadius* (*Lars Levi Laestadius, Natural Historian*).

The pastor was buried in Kengis in 1861. Some years later his body was dug up and moved to the newly created churchyard in Pajala. Not even there was he allowed to lie in total peace. As mentioned in the epilogue, a Soviet bomb detonated next to the pastor's grave in 1940. As it happens, this occurred on February 21, exactly seventy-five years to the day after his death.

AND NOW I AM standing by Lars Levi and Brita Kajsa's tombstone. With frozen fingers I strike a match and light the candle wick, watch the little flame grow and spread its light. I think, Thank you for the inspiration. Thank you for being there.

MIKAEL NIEMI
Pajala, May 2018